LYNN MARIE HULSMAN

I'm a writer. My mother's death brought an epiphany. "Life is short," said my inner voice. "Thanks, I.V.," I replied. "I know what I have to do." In short order, I got an agent, co-wrote two books, ghost-wrote another, published an article, and sold a novel.

Kentucky-born, tall tales and hyperbole are in my bones. I love story. My real jobs? Equity actor. Ad copy writer for casinos, ("Loose slots!") Stand-up comic. Pharma editor. Cheese cube passer-outer (admitted low point). I'm an Ideation Agent (sounds fake, right?) and run an improv company in NYC. My favorite, favorite thing to do is write Romantic Comedy.

I live with my family in Hell's Kitchen, and am seen around town auctioneering for charity, hosting gay men's fashion shows, and calling bingo games.

You can follow me on Twitter @LynnMarieSays.

Summer at Castle Stone

LYNN MARIE HULSMAN

Harper*Impulse* an imprint of
HarperCollins*Publishers* Ltd
77–85 Fulham Palace Road
Hammersmith, London W6 8JB

www.harpercollins.co.uk

A Paperback Original 2014

First published in Great Britain in ebook format by Harper*Impulse* 2014

Copyright © Lynn Marie Hulsman 2014

Cover images © Shutterstock.com

Lynn Marie Hulsman asserts the moral right to
be identified as the author of this work

A catalogue record for this book
is available from the British Library

ISBN: 978-0-00-810638-6

This novel is entirely a work of fiction.
The names, characters and incidents portrayed in it are
the work of the author's imagination. Any resemblance to
actual persons, living or dead, events or localities is
entirely coincidental.

Automatically produced by Atomik ePublisher from Easypress

For my children, Rose and Wolf.
You are my everything.

Chapter One

Who keeps his tongue, keeps his friends.

"I'm sorry, there's no table for Shayla Sheridan." I couldn't read the tall hostess's expression behind the ebony curtain of hair obscuring her face, but I can tell you this: she didn't sound sorry.

Soaked from a surprise downpour, I stood dripping on the polished wood floor in the vestibule of *Le Relais*, a restaurant situated roughly 40 blocks hipper than I was used to. I peeled off my soggy Adirondack jacket and folded it over my arm, hoping to raise my profile a little. I so didn't want to be there.

Before Maggie called, my Friday night plan was to grab a burrito from La Paloma and get my dark roots touched up and my hair straightened at the little walk-in hair salon around the corner from my apartment. Instead, I stood in the driving rain to catch a 20-dollar cab from midtown to Soho for the privilege of being ignored. I cleared my throat.

The hostess shot me a glance, annoyed that I was still standing there. Dragging her eyes down the length of me, she huffed out a small noise of disapproval. Understand this: I'm a native New Yorker. I know better than to show up at a place like this wearing a twinset and flats. But I'd come straight from the office and really, if I had stopped home to change, what did I have in my closet that was much of an upgrade? Even if I liked shopping, I don't have the time. I work a 50-hour week at Haversmith, Peebles, and Chin Publishers, not to mention ghostwriting how-to books, and working on my own book.

My own book. My stomach plummeted. Brenda Sackler, my terrifying bulldog of an agent, had red-lighted it this very afternoon. Boom. She didn't even invite me into the agency to talk about it. Just a no-go over the phone. Access denied. Dream dead on arrival. I wanted a vodka and soda more than I wanted to breathe air, and this clothes hanger on stilts was standing between me and sweet relief. Squaring my shoulders, I mustered a shred of strength from the depths of myself, ready to engage in battle. Who did she think she was, anyway? As if looking like an upmarket shampoo ad qualified her to be the gatekeeper of those precious bottles of Skyy lined up behind the bar.

I caught an unfortunate glimpse of myself in the side of a towering metallic vase, filled with sharp, pointy birds of paradise. Even handicapping for the fun-house distortion of the mirrored curve, I could see clearly what I looked like and it wasn't good. Dark circles under my eyes, frizzy two-toned hair, and a gray cardigan. The top pearl button had fallen off at lunch, and I'd stuck it back on with a safety pin. By New York standards, I wasn't even a 5. Disgusted, I shook my head at myself in my reflection. Why would I even think like that, ranking myself? Fucking Soho. So much for all those Women's Studies classes I'd taken at Sarah Lawrence. I felt so exposed in the open-plan restaurant, with the vaulted ceilings. I just wanted to blend in and get my body behind a table. And, for the love of God, to have a drink.

I didn't like to do it, but I had no choice. Leaning in, I whispered, "Can you try Shayla de Winter?"

"Mmm-mm, sorry" the hostess said automatically, shaking her head no. "Wait!" Her body went stiff. She flipped her hair over to one shoulder and squinted at me. "You mean, like, Hank de Winter?"

"Yes, he's my father," I mumbled.

"Bruno!" she shouted, still gazing at my face. An almond-eyed man-boy in a crisp white shirt appeared at her side. "Take Miss de Winter's coat." The stunning and obedient Bruno bowed his head and gently urged the formerly offensive canvas garment from me as if it were a Russian sable, disappearing as quickly as he'd shown up.

"Right this way," she said, flashing her dazzling white teeth in a smile she now decided I deserved. In a fluid motion, she whisked menus from a discreet cubby in the hostess stand, turned sharply on her heel and Olympic-walked down a wide aisle, hips keeping time like a military metronome. She landed at a "good" table. Not too near the kitchen or powder rooms, and sufficiently in the middle of the room to facilitate seeing and being seen. I would have preferred something along a wall.

But the attention made me feel dirty. Of course, I'd grown up gliding along on Dad's notoriety, but that hadn't been my choice. Known equally for his investigative journalism and his novels of manners featuring thinly veiled members of high society and politics, he walked straight past velvet ropes and never paid a parking fine.

I began using my mother's maiden name the summer before college, the summer I got a job to support myself by working at Austen and Friends Booksellers. To be fair, Dad did pay my tuition. Sarah Lawrence is only the most expensive liberal arts school in the country. But I paid for the rest, except maybe some books here and there and the summer abroad in Amsterdam. Since then, though, I haven't taken a thing from him other than letting him pick up the checks at restaurants when we see each other, which is rare. And that's because he always chooses stupid expensive places like this one.

Finally seated, with my shoes semi-hidden under the long, white tablecloth, I relaxed a little. There was a vodka and soda in my hand. Things were looking up. I checked my phone for the time.

Maggie was 15 minutes late. Another 15 and I could walk out and claim that I figured she wasn't coming. "C'mon, 15 minutes!" I silently willed, fantasizing about warm pajamas.

I plucked a fat green olive out of a dish of herb-infused oil and popped it in my mouth. Rolling the pit on my tongue, I scanned the table for a polite place to deposit it. The napkins were cloth, of course. I couldn't just spit in on the table under the watchful eyes of the countless waiters and bussers. I tried to catch Bruno's eye. I had an ally in Bruno. He'd bring me a demure pit dish. Or let me spit it discreetly into his waiting palm. The saliva was getting to me. I picked up my purse, and like a horse with a feedbag, rid myself of the offending seed. No more olives for me. I made a mental note to ask for some bread instead.

Surveying the bar off to my right, my gaze landed on a guy sitting alone. A neat whiskey sat at his elbow. He was wearing dark-wash jeans, polished lace-up shoes, and a dress shirt. He wore glasses. Like his outfit, there was nothing ironic about his demeanor.

"I'm so sorry I'm late!" Maggie came barreling into the vestibule and down the wide aisle in geisha-like steps. Even in her towering heels, she managed to overtake the hostess. Smoothing her long, curve-hugging skirt, she lowered herself into the chair opposite me, and gave a satisfied sigh. "There!"

"You look amazing," I told her. And she did. Maggie may have grown up in the middle-class beach town of Spring Lake, New Jersey, AKA "The Irish Riviera," but she'd adapted to Manhattan flawlessly. Her chic Bumble and Bumble haircut (done by a student stylist during her lunch break — I covered her desk at work) was none the worse for wear from the rain, and she had on the exact right shade of MAC lipstick ("buy drugstore mascara and powder, Shay, but drop real money on your lips").

In the beginning, I represented something to Maggie. You could say that my parents belonged to the intelligentsia, but that word makes me uncomfortable. Money or no money, they traveled in circles with innovators, movers, and shakers. Maggie's parents, and their parents before, worked with their hands and functioned in the practicality of the here and now. Whereas Maggie had lived in a dormer bungalow situated in a neighborhood filled with people who only drove into the city for the Rockefeller Center Christmas show or to consult with medical specialists, I'd grown up in a high-rise surrounded by writers, editors, and those who had the money to see that magazines, newspapers, and books got printed. Even my grandparents had been schoolteachers, professors, and artists. Maggie absorbed every story about being sent to camp at the artsy Usdan Center, and the noted personalities at the cocktail parties thrown at our Upper West Side apartment when I was a kid. Rough around the edges, Maggie tried to blend in with this kind of society. So it didn't take long before she realized I'd been trying to blend in my whole life. We kept each other's secrets. How much we needed each other went unspoken. Maggie was reared to be tough and hard, and I was reared to keep my failures under my hat. I loved her, temper and all, and she protected me.

"Thanks," she said to the waiter as he handed her a linen napkin. She signaled to the waiter and whispered something in his ear. "Now then, I want to hear everything about your book deal. Start from the beginning, and don't leave anything out." She reached across the table and squeezed my hand. "Twins in success!"

"What?" I asked.

"You go! Then, I'll tell you my news." She beamed at me, eyes wide open.

"Right, about that. Well, Brenda said no." I drained my glass, and held it out to a busser.

"What?" She spat, biting off the end of the word. "Are you telling me that she didn't pick up *The New Adult's Guide to Making it in the Big City*? That's ridiculous!" Did she see your two articles in the Observer? *How to Be an Adult at Work* and *How to Be an Adult at Weddings*? Pure genius! Did you tell her that they're thinking of making *How to Be an Adult* a regular column?" Her eyes blazed.

"Never mind," I said. "You win some, you lose some." I didn't want to ruin our night out together with a pity party. Changing the subject would do me good.

"Anyway, how was your day, Mags?"

"It was, you know…" she tapered off and her eyes got really big. She was looking over my shoulder, shaking her head "no" in small, twitchy movements. I turned around in my chair, and caught the back of a waiter carrying champagne in a silver bucket, heading in the opposite direction.

"What was that?"

She shrugged.

"So what about your blog, Shay? The writing is solid and witty, and your timing couldn't be more on the money. It's so current."

"To be honest, my blog hasn't gotten much traction."

"It still might. You've proven yourself with the book contracts Brenda's given you. And for almost no money! After all those Dumbass Guides you've ghostwritten for her? *The Dumbass Guide to Picking a College*, *The Dumbass Guide to Getting Him to Propose*…You could write *The Dumbass Guide to Writing a Dumbass Guide*! Did you offer her the alternate title? *Adulting*? That's so fresh! I can see the short-haired girls starring in the HBO series now! Why would she think twice about putting your name on a cover as sole author?"

"Well, the phone call didn't last long…

"And after you swooped in, cleaned up that mess of a green smoothie book that that idiot personal trainer slash diet guru, slash cable TV personality couldn't write? OK, tell me this: Are you getting your name on the book as co-writer or not?" She took a greedy gulp of water. I shook my head. I hated giving Maggie the disappointing news.

"Wait, what? Brenda, your agent, told you no on the phone? She didn't give you the courtesy of delivering the news face-to-face?"

"Well, you know how busy she is," I said, my face heating up. "To be fair, it was a quick conversation. I shouldn't have called on a Friday."

"She's your agent! Evan would never treat me like that. You're allowed to call her." Maggie shook her head. "I've been saying for a year that you need to let me talk to Evan about you. He's a big fan of Hank's. I think that's why he signed me, because I dropped both your names. He'd snap you up in a heartbeat."

I shifted in my chair. The waistband of my skirt was bunching up from the dampness. "You know, Brenda's been pretty good to me. Like she said, tons of writers would kill to do this ghosting."

"Bullshit. How many people out there write as well as you? This should have just been done and dusted. Your proposal is brilliant. I bet she didn't even read it. Does she know who your father is?"

"Probably, but we've never talked about it. I want to get a deal on my own merit. You know it wouldn't count in Hank's eyes if I got it through him."

"That's on you, not your father. He never said that. Look, first thing Monday, you need to just show up there and insist that Brenda pay attention to you."

I snorted. "I can't just barge in."

"Yes, you can. Even if I have to drag you in by the hair, you are going to see Brenda Sackler on Monday. And she'd better give you the kind of book deal you deserve!"

Maggie finished the rest of her water and her shoulders relaxed. Thank God. I just wanted to move on and stop talking about books. *Le Relais* wasn't where I wanted to be tonight, but it was wonderful to spend time with Maggie. Ever since we met on Day One as slave-assistants for HPC Publishing, we'd clung to each other. I found her in the copy room, cursing out a notoriously volatile senior editor who cut the line in front of her. She had her fist raised to punch him. The words "you're fired" sat on his lips when I intervened to usher him out to the hallway. I "explained" that she'd just had a scare with an ovarian biopsy. The mention of gynecology and cancer will cow any man. Maggie appreciated that I'd risked my job for hers. That kind of loyalty meant something, and from that day forward, she had my back. It was just a matter of time before she forced out her dippy, model-wannabe room-mate, and moved me in to our tiny, illegal sublet Hell's Kitchen.

A busser appeared and set a basket of assorted artisanal breads before me. He must have read my mind. I was starving. "Can I get another vodka and soda, and can she have a dirty martini, up, three onions?" He nodded and glided toward the bar. I sighed with pleasure. My blood had begun to warm. The first drink did me a world of good, and another was on the way. Being out on a Friday wasn't so bad after all. In fact, I was starting to enjoy myself.

"You never answered me. How was your day?" I asked, dragging a slice of dark, grainy bread through the modernist ramekin of herbed oil the olives were lounging in.

"My day? Hey, did you notice the cute guy at the bar checking you out?"

"What guy?" I sat up poker-straight and a fish flipped in my chest cavity. It had been ages since I'd gone out with a guy, and longer still since I went out with a guy I actually lusted after. "Is he wearing dark-wash jeans and a blue shirt?"

"Uh-huh." she whispered. "Don't look!"

I was already looking. He was smiling toward our table. I smiled back. He quickly looked down at his drink. I shouldn't have busted him. "Anyway, enough about me already. Are you ever going to tell me about your day?"

"Well," Maggie said fiddling with her cutlery, "It was really, really good. There's something I want to tell you, but for right now, I just want tonight to be about us. We never go out together anymore. I'm always sleeping over at Eric's, and you're always staying late at the office. And we've both been pounding away on our own books."

Our waiter floated up to the table and set a pretty pink cocktail with a strawberry on the rim in front of me. "From the gentleman at the bar."

"Well, well, well," Maggie said, eyes twinkling. "Looks like your day's about to get brighter."

"Oh my God, what do I do?" I leaned toward her, whispering. "Do I accept it?" I locked eyes with Maggie, willing myself not to look over at the guy. "If I do, what does that mean? Do I have to go eat dinner with him, then?" I panicked. What if he turned out to be boring, or a creep? Plus, I was here with Maggie. It was a girls' night. "Should I clink glasses with the air, but in his direction? Like they do in the movies?"

Just then, the waiter reappeared. "My apologies, ladies." He picked up the glass, moved it to Maggie's side of the table, and bowed, sliding backwards from our table, and down the aisle toward the kitchen. Maggie looked down into her lap and sighed.

"It's OK, Mags. Seriously." I tried to laugh. "Did you think I thought that was for me? Pfft! I was joking! This is good. I mean, this is great! Now I don't have to eat dinner with him. Oh no, do you? Have to go eat with him? You can, if you want to…"

"Shh!" Maggie raised her eyebrows at glasses guy. She held up her left hand and pointed to her engagement ring. She toasted him with her glass and mouthed "thank you." He turned his broad back to us and faced the bar.

"His butt's flat. He's not that cute," she said, wrinkling her nose. I took a last look at his broad shoulders and shiny black hair. He kind of was that cute.

"You can do much better," Maggie told me. I doubted it.

"Anyway, you have a date tomorrow with whatshisname, that hot guy from Ray Diablo's book launch."

"I know, right? So hot," I said. I concentrated on forgetting about my ex-future husband at the bar and tried to recall what the guy I'd met at the launch actually looked like. And his name.

Hundreds of people had come and gone last night as I sat working the door at the launch. From outside, I listened to all the fun happening inside the ballroom at the Puck Building. Ray Diablo's brand was the flavor of the moment, and there was a parade of A-listers from the food world, and plenty of television people to boot. Hundreds of people came and went, carrying plates of fancy nibbles. A trash can sat next to my station. I watched as dainty talk-show hosts and botoxed second wives took only a demure bite of their spectacular canapés and trashed the remains. The smell of food dizzied me. I had half a mind to dive in after some of the less-sampled morsels.

I was told not to eat on duty, and by the end of the night the two white wine spritzers I'd sneaked had gone straight to my head. When Jaden (Bradyn? Devon?) laid his card down and said, "54 Below, Saturday, 9 p.m.," it had felt more like a summons than an invitation. But maybe that was sexy, what did I know? "Really, really hot."

"Come on, let's order," Maggie said, summoning a waiter, and we did. After the starters came and were eaten, I felt a lot better. By the end of the meal, I had forgotten my troubles and had moved on to enjoying myself. The restaurant was, after all, a feast for the eyes, and every bite I put to my lips was sublime. I can't cook, but I adore fancy food. Besides, I was getting to spend hours gossiping and chattering with my best friend.

"Hey, it's getting late and you never told me your big news! We talked a little bit about Eric's new job, and then I talked the rest of the time about how Ray had that hissy fit, and fired his co-writer in the middle of the launch party."

"Ray Diablo is a giant dick," Maggie said. "I'm tired of seeing his smug face all over the Food Channel. I hope that poor writer got a ton of money for her trouble."

"From what I hear, she did. And her name on the cover. She's one of Brenda's clients, but way up the totem pole from me."

"Phht! You write better than she does."

"Maybe, but she's making country-house money writing for famous chefs and I'm not. More to the point, no one knows my name." Over Maggie's shoulder, I saw a crowd gathering at the hostess stand. The hostess pointed to our table. A gorgeous girl in a gold dress and matching silver wig and false eyelashes, and holding a bouquet of gold and silver balloons was being led down the aisle toward our table.

"Margaret Doyle?" the shiny girl asked in a loud voice. Maggie nodded.

"These are for you, from your father, Mr. Patrick Doyle: Congratulations on selling your novel!" She tied the balloons onto the back of Maggie's chair, as the tables near us broke into light applause and a mixed chorus of "congratulations," "well done," and "awww!"

Just as the back-patting and well-wishing died down, Maggie's phone rang. She dove sideways to fish in her bag.

"Your novel sold!" A quick stab of jealousy lit up my ribcage and it embarrassed me. "Why didn't you tell me?" I felt dazed. "I mean, that's amazing, Mags."

She held up a finger, mouthing, "Sorry, one sec."

"No, it's fine. Take the call," I said, forcing my face into what I could just tell was a twisted grin. It was just as well she wasn't looking at me.

"Yes, Daddy, they just arrived, this very minute. Thank you!" Maggie gestured helplessly, pointing at the phone with a knitted brow. I waved her off. "It's fine!" I whispered. I sipped my drink and pretended not to be there in order to give her the feeling of privacy. I looked away and caught sight of Mr. Gorgeous from the bar descending from his stool and walking out.

"Well, I'm hardly a little girl! Yes, I'll always be *your* little girl… I'm happy you're proud, but Eric was naughty for spilling the beans…"

"Hey, Shayla. I didn't mean to make a huge thing out of my book deal. It's just…I thought we'd be celebrating together, shoulder to shoulder."

"No, it's fine!" I insisted. "You didn't know. I kind of set you up, I guess. I should never have said Brenda was excited about my book. I got carried away. 'Don't count your chickens till they're hatched,' Hank always tells me." A lump rose in my throat. Maggie's dad always told her things like, 'You can do anything you want to do in this world,' and 'Go get 'em, Tiger!'

"This is your time," I said. "I'm happy for you! Seriously. With the engagement, you know, and the book, and everything." I reached across the table and squeezed her hand.

"Thanks for being so great." She squeezed back. "You're my best friend." She was fizzing with nervousness and smiling like a maniac. "Let's get out of here. I'll get the check. Dinner's on me." We looked up to find a waiter, but one was already swooping in for a landing. In his hands was an exquisite, sculptural cake topped with sizzling sparklers. "Here you are, ladies. Enjoy!"

On the top of the cake, in swirling script, it said "Wonder Twins."

I held my hand up to shush my friend. "Don't."

We ate the cake in silence.

Chapter Two

Never love anybody who treats you like you're ordinary.

Stretching my leg out as far as I could, given the narrow skirt Maggie had lent me, I launched my body across the slushy pool at the curb on the corner of 45th and 9th. Good thing she also outfitted me in her waterproof suede La Canadienne boots. I'd planned to wear wool pants and my Timberlands, but Mags put the kibosh on that, pronto. "Shayla, this isn't Alaska, it's the capital of the world. Men expect you to show up for a date dressed like a woman."

"I do dress like a woman. A comfortable woman!"

The next thing I know, I was outfitted in a pair of thigh-slimming Spanx and this skirt so slim my knees touched.

The weather in the city this winter had been the worst since I'd been born. You'd think by mid-March Mother Nature would cut it out with the freezing temperatures and wintry mixes.

When I'd agreed to go out with Jordan (that's his name – Jordan Silver, I checked his card), I hadn't realized that this Saturday was St. Patrick's Day. I make it a policy not to leave my apartment on it or New Year's Eve. In Manhattan, those nights are strictly for amateurs. My oversight meant that now, on top of patches of black ice on the sidewalk, I had to dodge pools of green vomit and steer clear of gangs of college boys singing Danny Boy. I wrapped my scarf a little more tightly around my neck, headed uptown, pushing into the wind that was trying to blow me backwards.

My mind flashed back to the early morning, when I'd had every intention of canceling. Maggie caught me red-handed on the sofa with his card and my cell phone in hand. I was perfectly happy in my fuzzy robe and slippers, my overgrown hair up in a couple of chopsticks, a pile of manuscripts at the ready on the coffee table. I planned to laze around and drink coffee all morning, then get a jump on my day job by reading slush-pile submissions that I was behind on from working Ray's book launch. There was no choice but to dig in and get on with it. "Editorial assistants who make excuses never become editors," Hank had told me more than once. He'd either heard it from his own editor, or from some editor he dated, I couldn't remember. It didn't matter; I instinctively knew it was true. Come nightfall, I'd order Chinese from Foo King, and put the finishing touches on *The Dumbass Guide to Motorcycle Repair* so I could hand it in before Brenda's deadline. That way, if I ever did bring up my book again, I'd be on her good side.

Before I could punch in the number, Maggie came stalking out of her room, wearing the hand-painted silk kimono Eric had brought her from a business trip to Japan, and snatched the card from my hand.

"No."

"C'mon, Mags. I'm not up to it. I've got brunch tomorrow at Hank's and I went out with you last night. Isn't that enough for one weekend?"

"Not when you live in the city that never sleeps."

"Well, I sleep. That's where the city and I differ."

"Yeah, well, you sleep alone. Why don't you change that tonight?"

"Like I'm going to have sex with this guy whose name I can't remember. I'm not sure I can pick him out of a crowd."

"You don't need to know much to strip off and slide under

14

the covers."

I shot her a look. Maggie knows I'm not impulsive like that.

"Have it your way. What do you know about him?"

"Nuh-thing! I have no idea why he asked me out. We weren't even talking."

"How about because he liked what he saw? C'mon Shay, give yourself some credit. Any guy would want you. But a lack of confidence is a turn-off. Time to prepare! You have to plan about what you're going to say, and planning how you'll shift the conversation if it gets boring."

"I'm not going to do homework for a date! This is dumb. I'm canceling." I picked up the phone and started to punch in numbers.

"You can't cancel the day of. He'll think you're a bitch."

"So?" She snatched the phone from my hand. "So? So he's in publishing, right? New York is a small town for being a big city. For all you know, he could be your stepping stone to getting a new agent. Or he could be the assistant to an editor who'll hire you and give you a promotion. You have to play the game."

"I don't want to play the game."

"Too bad. How do you think your father got to be where he is today? He played the game."

"He's a man."

"Then act like a man! That's what I do. You don't see me crying in a corner when an editor throws a coffee cup at my head. You don't see me being seen and not heard when I'm around VIPs at The Frankfurt Book Fair or at famous people's book launch parties. I do what I have to do to get ahead. That's why I'm not a housewife in a one-horse town in Jersey. That's why I have a novel coming out!"

"Well, I guess you're better than I am, then," I mumbled.

"Hey, I didn't mean it like that."

I looked away.

"Shayla! I'm on your side. Don't curl up into a ball. Fight! I'm not tooting my own horn, I'm just underlining the fact that you can have everything I have, and more if you want it. There's a reason you're my best friend. My time is limited; I don't waste it on losers. You're funny, bright, talented, and you've always been an amazing problem-solver. You're just in a slump. Pull yourself up by your bootstraps. You have it in you. And the best part is, you don't have to do it alone. I'm here for you, Shay."

I tried to shake off the sting of hearing the truth. "I know."

"You're just tired."

"I'm always tired. Maybe being a Jersey housewife wouldn't be so bad."

"Sorry to have to kick your ass, but now's not the time to rest, now's the time to push."

I knew she was right, deep down. "I don't like pushing. Everything shouldn't be this hard."

She sighed. "Well, it is. I don't know what to tell you. This is the way it works, Shay." She walked over to the fridge, swung open the door and got the milk. Then she grabbed the coffee pot off of the burner. Topping up my cup, she said, "you're going to drink that, then we're going to my room to pick out an outfit for your date tonight. Something sleek and sexy. Then we're going to pick out an out an outfit for when you go see Brenda on Monday. Something professional and powerful."

"I don't really want to go on the date, and I don't really want to confront Brenda."

"Fine." She set her jaw. "Your choice. It's that or lie down and give up. Might as well pack your bags and move to Kansas, Dorothy." She planted her hands on her hips and stared at me.

I couldn't help laughing. If someone as dynamic as Maggie believed in me, who was I to argue?

"If I'm Dorothy, who are you? The Wizard of Oz?"

"I'm about to be the bad witch if you don't do what I say," she said, shaking her finger at me. "And believe me, those flying monkeys fall into line or suffer for it."

I took a slug of my coffee, then stood up. "OK, you win."

"I always do," she said. "So it's pointless to sass me when I tell you to sit still while I blow-dry your hair and pluck your eyebrows. And you're going to shave your legs if I have to stand outside the shower and watch you. My way or the highway!"

I gave her a quick squeeze. "Hey, Mags… you're better than a sister. Just, thanks."

"Come on, Sappy," she said, shaking it off and bounding toward her bedroom. "Let's get you into costume."

Heading out of the wind and down the icy steps to the supper club, I was grateful that Maggie had let me off the hook and allowed me to wear her wedge-heeled boots instead of the ones with the skinny heels. The place was all leather and wood, and scarlet tapestry. I was glad the club was warm and not one of those sterile chrome-and-glass affairs.

I pulled off my hat and tried to fluff my crushed, damp hair. Scanning the bar for Jordan, I panicked, realizing I didn't know what he looked like. There was a blonde guy walking out of the restroom. I raised my eyebrows and smiled. He put his arm around a thin brunette in a leather jacket and gave me a stern look. This was a stupid idea. I pulled my hat back on, ready to leave.

I felt a pair of hands on my shoulders, and I spun around, ready to snap. I recognized the green-eyed man as Jordan. Wow. He was actually a man. I didn't remember him as being so filled out.

"Hi, Shayla? Are you all right? You look, uh, upset."

"No! Not at all. Hey…you!" Brimming with nervous energy, I went in to kiss his cheek, to seem like a smooth player. When I lunged in, I caught my toe on his heavy boot. I fell forward, and he grabbed me hard by both elbows. Whipping his head around to keep his balance, he cracked me in the bridge of the nose with his jawbone.

"Motherfuh… uh…uh…oh, *man*," I stopped myself from swearing even though I saw stars. The pain was so sharp, I didn't even worry that blood was dripping onto my (Maggie's) silk turtleneck. At least it was black.

"Hang on," I heard Jordan say. I couldn't see him with my eyes squenched shut. In a flash he was back, shoving a handful of bar naps into my hand. I pressed them to my bleeding nose and managed to open my eyes. His eyes crinkled at the corners, and on his lips sat the threat of a smile. "Why don't we sit down?"

"OK," I said through my napkins, "but not at the bar."

Taking my arm, Jordan led me to a cozy leather banquette. "Two Maker's Mark Manhattans," he said to a passing waitress. I wanted a vodka and soda with lemon, but I let it go. "Why not at the bar?"

"I swore off perching on bar stools on my 21st birthday. Friends took me out to celebrate and I woke up so sore the next day I felt like I needed traction. I like to be comfortable."

"Are you comfortable now?" He asked, smiling. "Because I am. It's nice to relax with a gorgeous woman."

My hand flew to my nose to make sure it was clean. "Ha ha, yes, this place is great. Small warm rooms feel kind of like a hug."

He cocked his head and smiled. "I just have a thing about… I don't know… not being cold. I positively will not go into a cold Lucite and metal bar. At least not in winter. It's one of my rules."

"You have a lot of rules."

"No I don't," I said automatically. "They're not rules, *per se*. Just ways that make sense to live.

"Umm hmm. You were saying you haven't sat at the bar since age 21. How many years ago was that?"

I hesitated. He was asking my age.

"Five. Why?" I examined his face. What was he getting at? "How old are you?" I countered. I didn't like being on my guard.

"Twenty-three, but a very mature twenty-three. Graduated Yale at twenty-one, because I skipped a year of high school. I interned at a couple of small newspapers while I was there — did some beat reporting — and got hired by Cooper-Prentiss when I graduated. As an associate editor. I skipped doing the whole assistant thang."

"I'm doing the assistant 'thang' now." I watched in horror as my hands made air quotes. "But not for long, you know." I took a big slug out of my drink. The whiskey burned the back of my throat but my mouth was full. I coughed through my nose, sending tiny droplets of blood onto his pant leg. Struggling to stifle my sputtering, I barked out "I…am…so sorry."

"Not a problem." He picked out some of the cleaner napkins from the table, and dabbed at his knee. Embarrassed, I swept the rest of the bloodied pile into my bag.

"Sorry," I said.

"You apologize a lot."

That shut my mouth. He was right. I didn't feel sorry about anything. But I had gotten sucked in by his image, and I was playing a game falling all over myself trying to impress him. Sure, he was some kind of publishing wunderkind. Sure, he had a real tan, earned on an adventure trip to someplace like Costa Rica or maybe Australia. But like Maggie pointed out, I wasn't so bad myself. Relax, Shayla, I coached myself. Just be yourself. It's good enough. Attractive as Jordan was, I wasn't dying to touch him or kiss him, though. That was kind of weird. But it was also good. Realizing that gave me back some of my power.

"Shayla?"

"Anyway," I snapped back to the conversation, "I was telling you that I'm a writer." I said this with confidence. "So, I won't be doing the assistant, uh, I won't be an assistant for long."

He looked at me with interest. "Really? I feel like I should know that, Shayla Sheridan."

The way he said my name uncurled something inside me. His voice was strong and clear, hinting more at a man's than a boy's. As a little test, I smiled. He smiled too, and draped his arm over the back of the banquette, looking like he had all the time in the world. Hmm, perhaps there's more to him than I thought. I did like it when a man pulled off being smooth. Maybe I could have a one-night stand. I hadn't done that in ages, since well before Noah, and before Noah, I'd gone out with Josh for a long time.

It's not fair to compare Josh, though. With Josh, we'd been more like best friends than the last of the red-hot lovers.

"Tell, me, Shayla, what have you written?"

I hated this question. It's the American way to define people by their jobs and to make them prove that they're contenders. The next questions were invariably A) What have you written that I've heard of? And B) So you're following in your father's footsteps?

After suffering scrutiny at countless weddings and cocktail parties, I'd gone back to calling myself an administrative assistant. That always cut the conversation off at the knees. Maggie didn't like that tactic. She told me to stick with saying writer. 'Dress for the job you want, Shay, not the job you have,' she always says. Tonight, I could see her point. Jordan was making me feel competitive. Rather than concede, I parried.

I took another substantial slug of my drink. "At this point, I've collaborated on some non-fiction, and have solely written some works for which I didn't negotiate cover credit." What was I doing? God, I sounded like an ass. Jordan is an associate editor. He could tell when someone in the business was putting lipstick on a pig.

"Nice," he said.

"The Observer is picking up my column, *How to Be an Adult*." Oh my God. Stop talking, I told myself. "Anyway, I'm pitching my real book to my agent on Monday," I ploughed on. "Brenda Sackler?" I name-dropped without shame.

He shrugged.

"Global-Lion Literary?" I tried. Nothing. I drained my glass.

"The work is sort of a manifesto for post-teens meets new adult non-fiction-y girl's guide to the city mash-up. You know. That kind of thing." Dear God, did I just call my book, 'The Work?'

"Cool." Jordan's eyes browsed the room. A leggy cocktail waitress with a severe blonde bun and sheer blouse buttoned to the neck smiled. "Hi…I didn't get your name."

Her smile broadened. "Sabina."

"Sabina," he pronounced. "I'm a private club member." He

handed her a card, which she read and handed back. "I think we'll have two more of these and then move into the lounge."

"Excellent, Mr. Silver." She did a yoga squat to table level, hovered knee-to-knee with Jordan and loaded our glasses onto a tray. Through sheer force of abs, she pulled herself to standing and purred, "If I can do anything to make your evening more enjoyable, don't hesitate to ask."

"Can I get a vodka and soda with lemon instead? I'm not so much a brown liquor kinda girl. You know what Thomas Jefferson always said, 'Whiskey claims to itself alone the exclusive office of sot-making.'" I laughed but they didn't join in. "Big fan of the former president."

Jordan and Chiara looked at me, waiting maybe, I gleaned, for further explanation. "So, no whiskey for me thanks. Just, you know," I explained, "trying not to be a sot."

"Thank you, Sabina," Jordan released the waitress, and she drifted away.

"So, are you into heading for the lounge? All the Broadway people swing in here before and after shows to do a set or sing a tune."

"Yeah, no."

"No?"

"I don't like listening to cabaret singers. When I'm up close, I feel like I have to gaze into their eyes and be all like, 'Yes, that's great! Keep going!' It's exhausting." I could feel the whiskey warming my toes and loosening my jaw. "Like I'm responsible for making them feel good about themselves, you know? No one's sitting around going, 'Yay, Shayla, that paragraph was awesome! Keep writing!' I wish I had some cheerleaders."

Jordan was looking at me with knitted brows.

"Never mind. Forget I said that. Cabaret singers are great. It's not their fault. I was just thinking, like, how it would be great to have some applause. Just for me. 'Go, Shayla.'" I waved imaginary pom-poms. My face was growing hotter. "Not from you, of course." I could feel Jordan waiting patiently. In a Barry White voice, I said, "You must think Shayla wants some immediate grat-i-fi-ca-shuuun."

"What did you say?"

"Nothing," I mumbled. "Never mind."

"I just…couldn't really understand what you said. Your voice got strange."

"Ffft…forget it. Just the flu."

He looked alarmed. "Not the flu. I'm not contagious. Just a cold," I said, waving it off.

Sabina had appeared and was setting two Manhattans in front of us. Not a vodka and soda in sight. "Your table is ready in the lounge when you are, Mr. Silver."

"Thanks Sabina, let me just settle this." As he was signing the check, Sabina looked straight at me and shook her head slowly back and forth, slitting her eyes. When Jordan handed back her pen, her eyes widened and she smiled. "Hope to see you again soon, Mr. Silver." She gathered the check. "The bar area closes at three tonight. That's when I get off." She smiled one more time before walking very slowly away.

"Listen," I said, pulling on my hat. "Thanks for the drink. But like I said," I coughed a few times, "I have a cold." I pretended to sniffle and tasted blood. I forced myself to swallow and took a drink of the whiskey to wash it down. I stood up. "I'd better just get going."

"Wait!" he cried. "You can't go yet." He took my arm down to a sitting position. "We haven't finished talking. Ten more minutes." He looked into my eyes, his face softening.

"Please." He flashed me a smile, this time with lots of teeth. They were, of course, very white. I relaxed onto the leather seat. Why did I say I had a cold? No one wants to have sex with someone who has a cold. "OK, just a little while longer."

I imagined his chest underneath the tight-fitting black western shirt with the surprisingly masculine turquoise embroidery. It snapped up the front instead of buttoning. It would be so easy to undo. I reached for my drink.

"Great. I was having such a nice time. I didn't want it to end", he said. Sabina passed by, walking closer to our table than I felt was strictly necessary. Jordan's eyes were on her as he said, "So tell me, what makes Shayla de Winter tick?"

"Excuse me?"

His focus landed back on me. I could see him back-pedaling, trying to figure out why I was snapping at him. "Uh…"

"Did you just call me Shayla de Winter?"

For a brief moment, he appeared rattled. I watched him pull himself together, face relaxing, opening his legs a little wider to take up more space on the bench. "Yeah, I did," he owned it. "I mean, you are after all."

"Why did you ask me out?"

Without missing a beat, he said, "Because you looked so cute sitting there in front of the name badges. I had my eye on you all night. Didn't you feel it?"

I wavered. If he thought I was cute, maybe I'd get to feel his smooth skin under the palms of my hands. On the other hand, if he was using me to get to my father, I had an appointment with the shower head. Hat still on my head, I challenged him.

"I'll give you two more minutes. What question do you want to ask me more than anything?"

His face contorted in frustration. He was struggling to come up with the right answer. I stood up. "Wait!" he said. "Hang on."

"Clock's ticking," I said, faking confidence.

"All right, all right! I guess… can you get me a meeting with your father?"

Son of a bitch! I grabbed my coat. It bumped across the table, upsetting my full drink. Now the hem was doused in whiskey, and it dripped down the back of my tights as I pushed my arms into it, heading for the door.

"Shayla, wait!" he called.

The question couldn't have been, 'What do you love about your book?' or 'If you could live anywhere other than New York, where would it be?' or even, 'Do you drink coffee or tea in the morning?' could it?

"Shayla!"

I blew past Sabina and she deftly protected her tray of full drinks. "Loser," I thought I heard her whisper, but it was hard to hear with my hat on.

I took the stairs two at a time, pushed open the heavy, upholstered door, and hurled myself out onto the slippery New York street. Veering in toward the wall of the building to avoid a crowd of St. Patrick's Day revelers, walking three abreast, and caterwauling Irish drinking songs. I bumped into a pale young man decked out in green from head to toe, wearing a leprechaun hat. "Sorry," I said.

He whipped around and looked me bleary-eyed in the face. "No, lady. I'm sorry," he slurred.

"Why?" I asked. I looked down. He was peeing on my boot.

Chapter Three

As the big hound is, so will the pup be.

Coffee in hand, I padded to the door of the apartment. A flashback of last night's date debacle threatened to play in my head. "No!" I said out loud. Living through the humiliation once was bad enough, I didn't have to play it on a loop. Why did every guy in this city have to be a jerk?

I undid the chain, the lock, and the deadbolt, and bent over to pick up my New York Times from the mat. The Times was the best thing about a Sunday morning. Scratch that, The Times was the best thing about living in New York, period. This morning was especially sweet because Maggie had stayed over at Eric's and I had the place to myself. I love Maggie, but our apartment is tight, and we're always on top of each other. I wish we had a terrace, or a little backyard like the brownstones in Brooklyn, but publishing assistants couldn't afford outdoor spaces in Manhattan. I wondered what the advance money was for Maggie's book. If she got rich, would she leave me and get her own place? I shook my head hard. If she did, she deserved to enjoy it. Maggie worked hard, and I was proud of her success. My stomach dropped. I was ashamed that I hadn't asked her about her book deal since Friday night. I would, though, and with a smile on my face.

25

Later, I took the L train up to Hank's, stopping in at Zabar's to pick up a pound of Nova lox to bring with me. I knew it was kind of silly. He always hired caterers to do the food for his brunches. Gourmet fish wasn't within my budget, either, but it was my father's favorite and I wanted to make him happy.

Hurrying up the block on West End Avenue, I spotted the weekend doorman, smoking out by the curb, semi-crouched behind a parked van. Noticing me, he rushed to throw down his cigarette, and rushed back under the pre-war canvas awning that ran the length of the carpeted walkway that lead to the glass-paned double doors at the apartment building's entrance. It was painted with the words *The Witherspoon*. The font seemed old-fashioned to me when I was growing up there, but had now taken on a retro-hip quality. I shuddered to think what new tenants, without rent-controlled leases, paid for the three-bedroom apartments complete with maid's rooms, formal dining rooms, and high ceilings today. Not that Hank couldn't afford it.

"Miss Shayla! How nice to see you. You never come around anymore."

"I'm pretty busy, Dmitry. Got bills to pay and all," I was rushing in, worried I'd be late.

"Well, your dad misses you."

I stopped. "Did he say that?"

"No, he didn't say that in those words," Dmitry answered, popping a mint, "but he's your dad! He must. Right?"

I headed in. "Right. By the way," I called over my shoulder, "Don't toss away a cigarettes on my account. I'll never rat you out."

"You are a beautiful girl, Miss Shayla!" I heard him call as the elevator doors closed. Yes, that's me, I thought, beautiful. Wowing the over-60 crowd. It would be nice to hear that from a man who wasn't paid to say it.

I knocked on the door, even though I have a key. I'd walked in on more than one half-dressed woman in the last decade, and I didn't need a shock on top of my bad-date hangover. The door swung open, and Hank said, "Oh, Shayla. It's you. There are Bloody Marys in the kitchen." He headed over to the docking station and fiddled with the music. Soon, Django Reinhardt was twanging out of the surround-sound speakers.

"I brought you some lox," I said. He didn't answer. To be fair, his hearing wasn't what it used to be. "I'll just put it on a platter." I swung through the heavy wooden door to the kitchen, and came face-to-face with Brenda Sackler. She was pouring extra vodka into one of the pre-made drinks on the sideboard.

"Oh! What a surprise. Hello, Brenda."

"Shayla!" she barked. I don't think she's capable of whispering. "Imagine seeing you here." Was that a command? A pleasantry? She leaned over and slurped the top of her too-full drink. "Huh!" She plunged a long stalk of celery into it and swung out the door, leaving me hanging.

While I was plating the fish and making myself a virgin cocktail, I heard the bell ring a few times and the murmur of voices growing louder as the number of guests grew. Hank told me it was going to be a small party. I didn't feel very social. I wished it were just him and me eating bagels in front of the TV, like it used to be when I was young. Him in that flannel bathrobe, me in my jams. I made myself push out into the dining room to mingle.

About a dozen people stood or sat in pairs and trios. Looking around, I took in the faces. Aside from Brenda, there was no one there whom I knew personally, though I recognized a couple of people. Hank always drew an eclectic crowd. There was that hot young Canadian actor/producer/director, and that columnist from The Atlantic, and a guy I was pretty sure was Hank's bookie. I put both halves of an everything bagel on a plate, and dressed it up with scallion cream cheese, capers, and my lox. Then, I piled on sliced red onion. What the hell. I had no one to kiss.

"I admire that you're a feminist," a young woman said, pointing at my brunch. I looked at my bagel, then looked at her. "What?"

"Eating whatever you want. I think it's great!" I scanned her face, sussing out whether she was joking.

"Carbs!" she stage-whispered.

Involuntarily, I checked her plate. On it sat baby carrots and pepper strips from the crudité platter, and a brown lump that resembled nothing on the table. She saw me looking.

"Oh, this. I pack my own food. You know."

"No, I don't."

"Gluten," she stage-whispered. Who did she think was going to hear us?

"Excuse me," I said, heading for the kitchen, this time for a full-octane Bloody Mary. The situation screamed out for 'hair of the dog.'

"Wait! Are you Shayla Sheridan?"

"Yes." I braced myself for the inevitable question: 'You're Hank de Winter's daughter, right.' Instead, she said, "You work at Haversmith, Peebles, and Chin, right?"

"Yes! I do."

"That's so cool. I truly admire Lizbeth Black. She's my dream editor."

"She's my boss. Are you a novelist?"

"I hope to be," she said, blushing. "I'm the features editor at The Frisky. You know? The online sex and dating magazine?"

"I know it."

"Sorry. I'm just so used to having to explain myself. Guys and old people never know what I'm talking about. It must be fun working in a publishing house."

"It can be." My stomach growled. I never ate dinner last night. My stomach had been sour after skipping out on Jordan. I eyeballed my bagel, wishing I could take a big bite. "There's a lot of drudgery."

"Really? It seems so glamorous."

"Not at all," I told her. "For instance, one of my jobs is to go through the slush pile. You know, the unsolicited manuscripts that 'come in over the transom,' as we say."

"I know what a slush pile is."

"Sorry," I said. "I'm just so used to having to explain myself." We both laughed. She was all right, I decreed. I took a huge bite out of my bagel, dropping capers and pieces of onion onto the plate I held beneath my chin. I was so hungry, I talked while I chewed, but I didn't think she'd mind. She seemed pretty into me.

"So, the best part of the job is discovering a diamond in the rough, you know? I'll sift through 30 manuscripts, one worse than the next, and then I'll hit on something that sings."

"That must be an amazing feeling," she said, eyes shining.

"You know, it is," I went on, encouraged. "The idea I can make or break a career!" I knew I was puffing things up, but she seemed genuinely interested in my work, so I didn't think taking a little license was so bad. I bit off another huge hunk of bagel. The oily piece of fish slid off the top in a sheet and slapped me in the chin. "Excuse me," I said, mouth full, swiping at my chin with a napkin.

"It's fine, eat."

"Anyway," I said, putting down my plate and picking up my disappointing non-alcoholic drink, "I don't like to brag, but you know that novel about the girl from the Pakistani fishing village who builds a reed boat and finds asylum on a PETA schooner?" I paused for effect. "Me."

"No way!"

"Way. I found it in the trash on Lizbeth's desktop. I fished it out, and the rest is history." I smiled what I hoped was a humble smile. "I'm going into the kitchen to get a cocktail. Wanna come?" She nodded, following.

"But there are two sides to the coin, you know." I pushed through the door to the empty kitchen. The tray of pre-made drinks was empty, so I mixed one. "Bloody Mary?" I asked. She shook her head no.

"Alcohol," she stage-whispered. I threw in an extra splash of vodka.

"So, like I was saying, I have to read through mountains of crap to find the needle in the haystack. I was merrily plowing through manuscripts the other day and I come across a 'romantic suspense' book. Wrong editor! Rookie mistake from a newbie author. So the story is this: There's this girl alone in a cabin in the woods and for whatever reason she's wearing an evening gown and heels. With little or no fanfare, Bigfoot breaks through the door and… they have sex!"

My new friend wrinkled her nose in disgust.

"Right?" I said, tasting my drink. "I didn't sign up for that." I stirred in more horseradish. "I thought I was going to have to wash out my eyes with bleach."

"But doesn't Lizbeth handle only literary fiction?" she asked.

"Exactly! That was my point." I said. It felt good to connect with a kindred spirit. "Do your research, people. Worse yet, there's the awful, terrible, abysmal writer who should never put a word on the page but *thinks* his work is full of gravitas and import, like he's the next John Steinbeck or Margaret Atwood.

"Ugh, those people," she agreed.

"I cracked one open last week that was so pretentious, with such bad grammar, I excerpted it and sent it around the office. I'm pretty sure it wound up being posted on Miss Snarky's blog." I smiled and raised my eyebrows. "You know, the one run by the anonymous editor?"

"Sure, I know it. What was wrong with the book?" She whispered, smiling back.

"To start, the protagonist's name was…hang on, heh heh, heh. Oh!" I dabbed at my eyes. "The protagonist's name was Keanu!"

Her smile faded. I was losing her.

"Because who on the planet has ever been named Keanu other than Keanu Reeves?" I tried.

"Was his girlfriend named Suri?" she demanded.

Oh. My. God. "How did you know? Um, wait, what did you say your name was?"

She turned on her heel and pushed through the swinging door. Now I knew her name. I'd last seen it right below the line

"Frenemies: A Love Story" on the title page of the worst novel I'd ever read. Hanging my head, I took a deep breath and pushed the door open a crack. I spied her with her coat on, kissing my father's cheek at the front entrance. And then she was gone.

I could see Brenda in the corner, watching the whole goodbye transaction with an eagle eye. The minute my father was standing alone, Brenda was at his elbow. Oh. My God. She was hitting on him! She wasn't a bad-looking woman. I suppose they're roughly the same age, but Hank hadn't dated a woman roughly the same age as himself since Mom.

My phone rang in my pocket, startling me. Feeling guilty, I shut the door and fetched my drink. "Hello?"

"Shay, do you want to come over to Eric's parents and watch the game?"

"The game? Since when do I watch games? No!"

"Please? I have to be here and it's so boring. But there's sushi, and weirdly, hot sake."

"I'm at Hank's brunch, remember? And guess what. Brenda's flirting with my dad. I didn't know they even knew each other."

"You are *kidding* me. That's great!"

"Euw. Why is that great?"

"Use it! Put the phone down right now, walk up to her and demand to be seen tomorrow! I mean it. I'm only 12 blocks from Hank's. If you don't call me in 15 minutes and tell me you did it, I'm coming over there."

"You just want an excuse to get out of there."

"Shayla!"

"OK, I'll call you later."

"Fifteen minutes. I mean it."

I refilled my drink for Dutch courage, choosing to ignore that I was drinking a lot these days, and strode into the living room. Brenda was holding on to Hank's arm, pushing her hair behind her ear girlishly. I concentrated on not making a face.

"There she is!" Hank bellowed. "Oh ho ho, you have done it

this time, my girl."

"Done what?"

"That little number who writes for The Nooky or the The Spanky, or whatever-the-hell, is not a fan. Ho ho, not at all a fan."

"Yeah, I know." I said trying to end the conversation quickly. I didn't want to bring up the concept of rejecting books in front of Brenda, lest she get any ideas.

"You screwed the pooch! Do your homework, kiddo. She's going to work for the New York Times Review of Books starting next week. You know what they say, don't shit where you eat."

My stomach plummeted. "I don't think that phrase applies here, Hank."

"Wait a minute. Shayla, you are his daughter, right?"

"Yes," I admitted, making space for the elephant that has always been in any room in which Brenda and I dwelled.

"What's with the 'Hank' business?"

"It just…makes more sense that way." I didn't want to talk about it. I didn't want to admit that she knew we were related, and I didn't want to explain that I'd started calling Hank 'Hank' from a very early age, long before I wanted to be a writer.

"I'm not really the 'Daddy' type," he chuckled. I nodded and laughed along, but hearing him say it was like a punch in the gut.

In my pocket, my phone rang again. Maggie. I reached in and silenced it. "Hey Brenda," I forced myself to say, "Can you fit me in around lunchtime tomorrow?"

"I don't have my planner with me," she said, airily.

"It'll be quick. I'll just swing by for a few minutes."

"Mondays are tight for me," she said, glancing at Hank's face. I pressed on, knowing she was uncomfortable. It was to my advantage, but I'd never been the barracuda type. As much as I didn't like being pushy, career networking was better than discussing Hank's fathering skills.

"So I'll stop in around 1?"

"Hank and I just made a plan for a working lunch on Monday."

"So you'll do Tuesday," I bossed. Extreme discomfort was making me reckless. I wanted to get in and get out. "Hank's pretty flexible. Right, Hank? Good. I'll see you Monday at 1, Brenda. You're welcome for the lox, Hank." I walked past the buffet table and dropped my half-empty glass. I'd hung my coat and bag on the rack by the door, the one at a child's eye-level that no one but me ever used. I swooped them up, exited, and shut the door behind me. If I headed home now, I could still spend the better part of Sunday in my pajamas, reading the Times.

Button on the elevator pushed, I pulled out my phone and dialed Maggie. "Mission accomplished," I said. The doors opened, and there stood Jordan Silver. Ignoring him, I left the party just as he was arriving.

Chapter Four

I was at the HPC office and seated at my desk by 7:30 on Monday morning. On super-early mornings, I liked to buy myself a rare treat: breakfast to go from Sarah's Bread around the corner from my apartment. If I had to be out of bed at six, headed in for a day of abuse at the hands of Lizbeth Black, the editor wears Prada, walking into the warm shop redolent with the smell of dark coffee and baking loaves was a balm for my tortured soul. They offer a special morning menu with lovely combinations. The Manhattan Breakfast consists of yeast bread twists, cream cheese, jam, and an American coffee. The Parisian Breakfast comes with two slices of baguette, butter, jam and a café au lait. This morning, I was having the Dublin Breakfast, featuring two wholemeal and raisin Irish Soda bread rolls, butter, jam and an Irish breakfast tea. It cost an arm and a leg, like anything decent in New York. I'd had coffee at home, tea would suit me better. I didn't want to be a shaky wreck when I saw Brenda.

Nate, the cute guy from publicity who always wore belted cardigans (which I found irresistible) got off the elevator. I tried to swallow the bite of bread I was eating before he walked by. I'd made up my mind that the next chance I had, I was going to ask him to go down to the Truffaut retrospective at the Film Forum. He was walking fast.

"Hey, Nate," I enunciated, spraying crumbs all over my desk blotter.

"Hey, Pal," he said, flashing me a smile and punching me in the upper arm. I watched him head toward his office. Along the way, he fell into step with Padma, from the legal team. From the way he put his hand on the small of her back, I guessed he didn't call her 'Pal.'

If I was going to sneak out to Brenda's at lunch, I had to cross my T's and dot my I's. By 8:15, I had checked off half the items on my to-do list and was blasting through a stack of Lizbeth's snail mail that required answering. Between tasks, I was contentedly buttering bites of soda bread and taking sips of my strong, milky tea.

"Dear Lord, you eat like a farm hand," Matty Dentino said, sneering and perching on the side of my desk. Matty, all five foot three of him, had started here a week before I did. He worked for a less prestigious editor, and it was no secret that he thought he was better suited to work for Lizbeth than I was. "Ever hear of Greek yogurt?" He smoothed down the front of his crisp, checked shirt, and re-centered his skinny knit tie. "If you eat all that, you won't be able to fit into the suit."

He wanted me to ask him what suit he meant, but I wouldn't give him the satisfaction. "Go away, I'm working."

He snorted. "Barely. Well, you'd better get it all done by 1:30. We're due at the Javits Center at 2 for set-up, so they're sending a van."

The Publishing Expo. I pounded on the keyboard to call up my iCal, hoping against hope Matty had gotten the dates wrong. Of course he hadn't. Shit. Maggie said she'd cover my desk today, but she couldn't help me with this. My hands trembled. I closed my eyes and tried to form a plan. OK, Brenda's office was nine blocks away. If I left here at 12:30, I could maybe be there by quarter to one, or one at the latest. Maybe she'd see me early. If I talked fast and stuck to my agenda, I could be back on the sidewalk by 1:30

if not sooner. I could feel myself calming down.

"You should cut out the coffee," Matty said, pulling a white handkerchief out to clean his glasses.

I grabbed a tote bag that advertised one of the books we'd published, *Microwave Meals for Fast Family Suppers,* and stuffed in all of the supplies I'd need for the Book Expo. "You should look into tissues, Brooklynite Poser. What man under the age of 75 uses handkerchiefs. Who are you, my grandfather?"

"Who are you, Woody Allen? You are so neurotic. And not in an entertaining way. You really should see someone about going on Paxil or Lexapro. Or at the very least some Xanax. Here, let me give you an Ativan."

"No! I don't need medication." I threw duct tape into my bag for the Javits Center, along with a stapler, some breath mints, and some sticky notes.

"Agree to disagree," he said, sweeping the last half of my breakfast into the trash can. "At the very least, you need to get laid."

"What I need is for you to take your Ativan, your non-prescription vanity glasses, and your stupid Confederate soldier beard away from my desk."

"Fine, but don't come crying to me the next time you need someone to run down to FedEx or get Lizbeth a table for lunch somewhere that matters." He half-hopped down off my desk and headed toward his end of the giant room of cubicles.

"Wait!" I hated myself for what I was about to ask. "What suit?"

"Oh, you'll see," he said, still walking. "And when you do," he called over his shoulder, "you'd better not ask me for an Ativan, because the answer's no."

Huffing from the run over, I pushed through the glass doors of Global-Lion Literary's inner office without stopping at reception.

"Hey," I heard from the girl at the desk, as I took in the view of my agent's tweed-covered back from across the room. Squaring my shoulders, I strode purposefully toward her, determined to leave with what I came for.

"Brenda!" I shouted. "Thanks for fitting me in. I wanted to ask you about…"

"Tsst!" my agent hissed, pointing her coral-colored talon at my chest. Then she brought it to her lips, shushing me with a scowl.

I recovered from my tunnel vision to notice Ray Diablo sitting in the wing chair next to her desk. He was wearing one of his trademark bowling shirts, this one embroidered with bright-orange flames. I don't know how I could have missed him.

"Naw, it's OK Brenda," Ray said, standing up. "I'm on my way out. You can take your next meeting." He gave me a smooth smile. "I didn't catch your name."

"I'm Shayla Sheridan," I said. "I'm a big fan of your cookbooks," I lied, shaking his hand. "I heard you lost your co-writer," I blurted. I hoped I'd phrased that with diplomacy. Everyone in the Puck Building had heard he "lost" his co-writer the night he fired her in a screaming fit at his book party. "I just co-wrote *Smoothie Skinny* for Tilly Auslander, and I've written several Dumbass Guides…"

"Ray, she's early," Brenda cut me off, and shot me a warning look. "Sit."

"I have a lunch with the people from Channel E.A.T. I'd better head out anyway," he said, still holding onto my hand. "Do you have a card or something?"

"No, she doesn't," Brenda said. "If you need her, I know where to find her."

"All right then," he chuckled. He took a card out of the back pocket of his jeans and handed it to me. "Here's where you can find me. You know, if you need me." He looked me straight in the eyes, and paused there for a second. "Later, Brenda," he said, and walked out the glass doors. The phone on the desk rang.

"Brenda Sackler," she proclaimed. She waved me toward the empty rolling chair at the desk beside hers. No wing chair for me. Obediently, I sat down.

I was pumped with adrenaline from making speeches in my

head to plead my case, and my interaction with Ray had only thrown fuel on the fire. I could feel the fight rising up in me. Keep a cool head, I thought to myself. Don't do anything rash. Act like a grown-up, and this will be your time.

I knew I had a winner of a concept, I just knew it. But we needed to strike while the iron was hot, and I was so sick of waiting for my turn to be noticed. Right now, the phrase "New Adult" was being splashed around the pages of the New York Times like vinegar and oil over ladies' lunches. Every book aimed at females aged 13 to 30 was being billed as the next New Adult hit. The funny thing was, no one even knew what New Adult *was* yet. If I got in the door now, I'd be one of the definers.

I'd get booked on public radio shows to expound on what the phrase New Adult meant in publishing, maybe sit on panels with that bookish darling of Tin House Magazine, the Hotchkiss dropout who wrote that thousand-page novel. Maybe I'd wind up hosting a show on MTV called New Adult featuring all the former child stars who now did art films in order to be taken seriously. The time was mine to become a writer whose name people knew. My name, not my father's.

What I banked on was this: I had a million-dollar idea. A true "high concept." No one had yet thought to leverage the concept for non-fiction, and I was the perfect candidate to capitalize on the trend, even though I knew deep in my gut that I was neither cutting edge nor particularly adult in my dealings. But I could write. And I could research.

Not to mention I grew up in New York City, Mecca for all proper New Adults. It's no accident the *Manhattan Girls* series of novels starring 18- to 22-year-olds takes place here. I went to high school here, I went to Sarah Lawrence, and I interned here. I was tossed head first into the selection-or-cut interview process with my first private preschool on the Upper East Side when I was four. The fact that I didn't always mesh with my cohort was beside the point. I had a pedigree.

Brenda was silent with the phone smashed to her ear, tapping a pencil against a cup of the blackest, thickest coffee seen this side of hell. I scanned her desk for my proposal.

It was freezing in the climate-controlled skyscraper. Yeah, so it was close to the end of March, but when it's still spitting snow, people need the heat on. The chair leather froze my legs through my thin tights. Stupid work dress. Temporarily distracted by the cold, I eyeballed the cozy-looking deep-red pashmina draped on the coat rack next to Brenda's desk. That's precisely the kind of thing a stylish, professional New York woman keeps on hand. Luxe, upscale, useful. One could drape it around one's shoulders during a business meeting and still look modern. Or, when called to a sudden business dinner at a fancy restaurant, one could pair it with a matching MAC lipstick, and seamlessly take one's outfit from day to evening. I wanted that pashmina more than any physical object I'd ever laid eyes on.

Why was I never prepared? You know those girls who have band-aids, a sewing kit, a compact umbrella, and a light cardigan sweater tucked into their chic shoulder bags? I'm not one of them. I'd left the office for this meeting carrying a brown suede Le Sac purse from my last year of high school, containing exactly my phone and my wallet (no hairbrush), and a plastic grocery sack in which I carried an overdue library book and a pair of shoes that needed heel taps. I'd grabbed the sack without thinking and now I was stuck with it.

"No," Brenda said. "No, no way." She opened a file on her desk and scrolled through the pages like she was in a race. "No!"

I tried to catch her eye to let her know I'd be right back. There was a Starbucks in the swanky marble lobby downstairs, and I figured if I just popped down to grab a giant extra-hot latte, I might survive. Plus, I knew I'd need the caffeine jolt if I was going to make it through an afternoon at Book Expo America. I could feel Brenda not looking at me. Like a waiter with too many tables, she had thrown up an invisible wall to deflect my raised eyebrows and head jerks.

"No!" she barked at some poor schmoh on the other end of the line.

Resigned, I told myself it couldn't be longer than a few more minutes. I'd use the time to psych myself up.

I mean, she had to love my idea, right? I'd researched like a maniac, edited and re-edited it. I even paid that grad student ten bucks an hour, which I cannot afford, to proofread it. How could Brenda not shop it around to every editor in town?

I could just picture it. There would be a bidding war, I'd get a huge advance, and finally *finally* I'd have my name on the cover of a book. That would show Hank I was a real writer. And Jordan Silver. And that snivelly little Matty from my office.

I glanced at the clock on the wall. If she didn't get off the phone soon, there'd be no time for Starbucks. Panting with nerves, I grabbed a rubber-band ball and rolled it around Monica's desk. Monica Bigelow is Brenda's partner, and like Brenda, she represents the books of a stable of well-known chefs including that sexy vegan woman with the dreads and the guy who all but invented gastro-science.

"What part of 'Monica's not reachable in Nepal' don't you understand? I'm the decider." Brenda snapped. "It's her daughter's wedding, and she hasn't taken a day off in five years. I told you I'm handling her contracts until she's back, and I say no. We're not using that drunk hack to write Tom O'Grady's book. Tom's a goddamn celebrity chef! He and his fiancé were Europe's Kathy Lee and Regis." She paused. "Whatever, Europe's Beyoncé and Jay-Z then. It doesn't matter, they were goddamn household names!" She listened for a second or two. "I know the show's not on the air anymore. I know London's not New York. I don't care, "Health and Happiness Matters" was big news as a lifestyle show. People won't forget it any time soon. Rumor has it that it's going back on the air, and there's talk of it coming to America. The point is, Tom agreed to a cookbook deal based on having first refusal on the writer, and your washed-up lush couldn't meet a deadline if it shook his hand and asked him to dance!"

The sticky ball I was rolling around caught on the corner of a manila file folder. TOM O'GRADY, the tab said. I glanced at Brenda before easing it open. It held magazine clips, menus, press photos, and a bio sheet. 'Personal and Confidential,' the top of the sheet read.

Brenda swung her chair around toward me. I snapped the folder shut.

"Well, my 1 o'clock is sitting here, so this conversation is over," she said into the phone. Finally, I thought, it's my turn. I flashed her my most grateful smile. "What's my final answer?" she asked, incredulous, holding the receiver about a foot from her face, and glaring at it. "No!" She stabbed a button on the phone and threw it onto her desk.

"So Brenda," I began.

"I'm going to pee," she said, standing up. "Hang tight."

I watched her stride through the glass door into the outer office where the interns sat. An idea lit up my brain, and it was like seeing God. I could be the one to write Tom O'Grady's book! Before I could think, I slid the folder into my grocery bag. I noticed the outline of it through the plastic, I realized. I needed to mask it. In one quick motion, I grabbed the pashmina off Brenda's rack and shoved it in on top of the folder, tucking it around the corners.

Oh, man, I thought, prickling under my arms despite the arctic temperature. I'm going to get arrested, and then I'll never make it back in time to catch the van to the Javits Center. The time! I sneaked a look at my phone for the time. 1:10. I turned off my ringer in case snotty little Matty tried to track me down. I had to get this show on the road. Luck was on my side. Brenda was barreling towards her seat. She must pee as fast as she talks. I pushed my grocery bag under my chair with my foot.

Landing heavily in her chair, Brenda shook her head at me. "I read your proposal about the New Adult guide…"

"Did you?" I asked. "Did you read it?"

She ignored me. "My final answer is no." She turned back to her computer, turning sideways to me.

My heart sunk. "Why not?" I tried not to whine. "It's smart, it's on-trend, and you cannot say my sample chapter isn't well written."

She sighed a curt sigh. "If I start sending it around to editors, the first thing they'll ask is what kind of traffic you have on your blog…"

"I can start a blog!"

"Even so, Shayla, these kinds of books get their sales through promo junkets and press tours." She continued to scroll through her email. "I'm not saying the idea isn't good, but look at you. You're not right to be the face of it. Do you really see yourself on camera, charming the pants off Matt Lauer on a morning show at 6 a.m.?"

"It's MY idea. I have written a good chunk of this particular book."

"What I'm saying is, I can't see you as a guest on some pre-Oscars show giving fashion and dating advice on the red carpet. Look at the state of you. You're about as polished as a grad student from Bennington College. You write well, but why would anyone follow your advice if they don't dream of being you? It's aspirational. If you really want to do this, get a makeover, spend a year clubbing and getting your picture in the Post, try to go out with someone with name recognition, and maybe publish sexy, edgy articles like, I don't know, like the ones in The Frisky."

"That's bullshit! It's about the book. It's a great idea and great writing."

"I have a better idea, but you're not going to like it," Brenda said.

I braced myself. "Go on."

"Why don't we give this book to some hot celeb's daughter? Like an *au courant* reality TV star or actress from an acting dynasty family? Or a poor little rich girl who grew up in high society, who needs to ditch the dog in her purse and prove to the world that she has substance?"

"How does that help me?"

"You would write it!"

"I don't want to co-write my own book."

"Not co-write, ghost-write. It would never work with your name on the cover."

"No, it's my idea, it's my book, and it's going to get my career started. It has to."

"Well, I can't represent it. Editors will want to know why they haven't heard your name."

"They haven't heard my name because I don't have a book out yet! That's what a debut author is…new."

"It's a chicken-egg thing. Maybe in a year, if you build up a following.

I knew talking to Brenda about my book was hopeless. I had five minutes before I had to tear out of here and get back to meet the work van. I girded my loins, ready to make a bold proposition. "All right, then, let me co-write Ray's next cookbook."

"You know I can't let you write for Ray Diablo. He's big, big money and you don't have a track record." She stopped tying for a second and looked at me. "Do *not* call him behind my back."

"I wouldn't!" I said, sure that my face read as guilty. This whole meeting had been a disaster. I was about to leave with less than I'd come with. How could I possibly tell Maggie that Brenda suggested I ghost-write my own book? I had one more card to play before I folded.

"If you can't let me write Ray's book, let me write Tom O'Grady's."

She turned her chair to face me. "How do you know Tom O'Grady?"

"I've been a big fan of his since that show, uh, "Happiness… and To Your Health." I trained my eye on Brenda to see if she was buying this. "Watched it all the time during my vaca…um, summer abroad in London. Besides, I love his recipes for like,

Beef Wellington," I said, naming the first dish that popped into my head, "and Turkey Tetrazzini," I fumbled along, wondering if I'd gotten the name of that dish right.

She sat very still for a moment, wheels turning, then sighed. "He wants to break the contract and not do the book. He feels he lost control of the last book deal. The writer and editor didn't know how to handle him. They let him think he was in charge." Brenda hacked twice then. I think she was laughing. "Anyway, I pushed everyone on this new deal and it's hanging by a thread. We're already balls-deep in pre-production. The pitbull of an editor over at Parson Turner Publishing is counting on this book for her upscale, gourmet list. Tom O'Grady just needs to see it's in his best interest to let the book people do our job and spin this into a package. He's a chef, not an author. And what should he care, if it's lining his pockets?"

"Maybe he wants to make sure his stamp is on it." My mind whirred, trying to take in the whole story from every angle.

"It's going to take more than Turkey Tetrazzini to please that bitch-on-wheels editor. The cover-brief buzzwords are 'upscale,' 'nouveau,' and 'deconstructed.' They've hired a photographer with a huge price tag, put it on the calendar, everything. I'm not going to look good if he drops out."

"So, let me write it!"

"He's been very difficult. After the book he hated pubbed, and some other stuff happened in London, the scuttlebutt is that he mistrusts slick, big-city types."

"You just finished telling me I'm the opposite of a slick, big-city type."

"You're from New York. That's a black mark. He didn't get along with the last two writers we put forward to save this project. He wasn't getting them recipes, he wasn't keeping Skype appointments…"

I checked the wall clock. If I left in one minute, there might be a chance I'd make the van. "If I can get him on board, do I get my name on the cover as co-writer?"

She sighed. "Don't get too excited. Even if you write the book, it has to be approved by Parson Turner. We don't know how it'll fly in the States; it's mostly for the UK and Irish market."

I knew a delicate moment had arrived. I smelled that she was going to say yes, if I just didn't blow it. "But if I can get this written, you'll give me cover credit?" I took a breath and pressed on. "And a 50/50 deal on advances and royalties?"

She looked resigned. "I can only try, but I think this one may be dead in the water."

Yes!

"And if I deliver this book, and the editor loves it, which I know she will, will you consider giving me a crack at Ray Diablo's next one?"

"Shayla, Ray Diablo is big potatoes..."

"I said 'consider.'"

"Sure," she said, with an eye roll. "I'll consider it." Time was ticking. I really had to get back to the office.

"So, about *How to Be an Adult...*"

"Don't push it," she cut me off. "Your dad's cute but not that cute."

I jumped to my feet, realizing it was better to quit while I was ahead. "Thank you so much for this chance, Brenda."

"Tom still has to agree."

"I'll hunt him down and pin him to the ground if I have to." I smiled, sharing the joke.

She didn't smile back. "Just get it done." She swiveled her chair back to face her screen. I waited for a beat, but apparently the meeting was over. I gathered my purse and bag, and hurried out, not bothering to say goodbye.

Rounding the last corner to the HPC building, I surveyed the street for the van as I ran. None. I didn't dare slow down to pull out my phone and check the time, instead I hurtled my body through the revolving door and into the lobby. Flashing my ID badge at the desk, I pushed through the turnstile and yelled, "Hold it!" at the bank of elevators. Safely inside, I pressed my back to the wall, shut my eyes, and tried to breathe.

I hustled to my desk, looking around to make sure Matty or any other gossipy assistants weren't hovering around. God, I hated it here. I'd been spanked for working on outside projects before. If I made this call to Ireland quickly and discreetly, I could have this deal sealed before I left for BEA. I didn't need international calls on my phone bill. Money was tight enough as it was.

I pulled out my stolen folder. All I knew about Tom O'Grady's was what I'd just overheard in Brenda's office. I had my work cut out for me, I figured, to craft a best-selling cookbook featuring nothing but a bunch of beef stew and boiled potato recipes. And if he was the other side of the pond's answer to Regis Philbin, the elfin, 80-year-old talk-show host, the food was going to have to be the focus.

I looked at the time on the desk phone. 2:05pm. All that rush was for nothing. I should have figured they'd be late. I could just see my boss's back end through the crack in her open door. She was rooting around in a box of books on the floor. As soon as I made this call, I'd check in and let her know I was back from lunch. I'd offer to call the van service to see if they were *en route*.

Opening my folder, I saw a fact sheet on Tom O'Grady, clearly prepared by a publicist. Born in County Wexford, Ireland, attended hospitality school with an emphasis on culinary arts, then did a course at Ballymaloe Cookery School when he was only 17. A stint as a sous chef at La Gavroche in London, worked a year under Alice Waters in San Francisco. Impressive. Back to London, where he had his own place for a while in Soho, called Wild. Currently head chef at Grange Hall, the Michelin-rated restaurant on the grounds of Castle Stone, situated in the same village where he was born.

I punched in the number of the restaurant. I'd leave my name and number, then the ball would be in his court. I flipped through the folder as I listened to the tinny connection and the unfamiliar abrupt buzzing rings.

Date of birth…whoa, wait. He's only 33? I shuffled the papers, looking for more facts.

"The Grange Hall. Can I help?"

"Oh, uh hi!" I said, focusing. "I'd like to speak to Tom O'Grady. This is Shayla Sheridan, calling from Brenda Sackler's office."

"Would you mind holding for a minute, then? Thanks very much." A pleasant traditional Irish tune featuring a fiddle and a flute played while I waited.

Underneath the printed fact sheets lay some tear sheets from a magazine. There he was: Tom O'Grady. Twinkling aquamarine eyes squinting against the wind, thick and wavy dirty-blonde curls tousled and pushed back from his forehead. He had his arm draped around the neck of an enormous black and white cow, who posed solemnly for the photo. The green of the rolling field of grass and the blue of the sky blinded me. I examined the page more closely, trying to see if it was all a trick of retouching.

"Tom O'Grady here." What? I never expected to get him on the phone.

"Hello, Mr. O'Grady," I heard myself say. It sounded ridiculous and formal. The young man in the picture wearing a bone-colored Henley stretched tight across his shoulders and chest didn't seem like a mister. He looked fresh and guileless. I'd just let him know how things were going to play out. Most "authors" who got books based on their brand appreciate that from their writers down in the trenches. This would all be wrapped up in a flash.

"Tom," I amended, "I'm Shayla Sheridan, calling on behalf of Brenda Sackler in New York. I'll be your new co-writer on the cookbook."

"Will ya, now?"

"Um, yes, I will." Out of the corner of my eye, I saw movement in Lizbeth's office. I needed to put this to bed and get back to my day job. "I'm available to start immediately. I think we should pencil in a Skype session to discuss chapter headings and recipe ideas immediately."

"What did you say your name was?" I could hear the clinking of crockery and a drone of voices in the background."

"Shayla Sheridan."

"Well, Miss Sheridan, if you'd bothered yourself to look at my contract, you'd have seen that it says I have final say over who the writer is. Full stop. I didn't choose you. I'm doing dinner service at the moment. Tell Brenda she'll hear from me soon enough."

"Wait! Tom!"

"Mr. O'Grady," he said.

"Mr. O'Grady, please," I begged. "I'm perfect for the job."

"Oh? Why's that, then?"

Because I wanted it so badly? Because it was the only shot I had? My brain bounced off the walls of my skull, trying to think of an acceptable answer. "I can send you a bio right now. I can literally have it to you in one minute."

I fiddled nervously with the pile of papers from the folder. I found more photos: a beauty shot of a crown roast, complete with paper panties, a photo of world leaders from the G8 conference standing around a table laid with fine china and silver, a trio of lemon desserts plated so artistically you'd be ashamed to stick a fork in it.

"Your details will convince me that you're the one for me, so?"

I knew the answer was no. Nervous, I flipped through more photos and came face to face with a tight headshot from the cover of *Sustainable Gardens* magazine. Tom O'Grady's expression seemed wiser in this photo; there was a hint of old soul in the set of his jaw behind his closely trimmed beard. I noticed how his eyes were slightly lidded. Bedroom eyes, my mother would have called them. But with a steely resolve. For whatever reason, the word "revolutionary" flashed through my brain.

"My bio probably won't convince you, even though I am more than qualified. But maybe my idea will." I was winging it big time, but I forged on. "What if…" I struggled, thinking on my feet, "What if your cookbook…in addition to showcasing your skills as a gourmet chef…included, say, things you cook for your mom?"

Without warning, a lump grew in my throat as I flashed back to carrying a steaming bowl of chicken soup on a tray to my own mother. It was her favorite food and one of the few things she ever taught me to cook start to finish.

"That's…" he began. There was a pause. "That sounds interesting, Miss Sheridan. I like it better than anything I've heard before, to be honest with you. But I'm sorry, since the last time I spoke to Brenda, I've decided to put a stop to the deal."

A woman with dark hair and a shape similar to Lizbeth's, but who was not Lizbeth, walked out of her office. Maybe someone from legal? It didn't matter, if Lizbeth wasn't in her office, where was she? A whoosh of adrenaline shot through my limbs, leaving my fingertips numb.

"Oh no, Tom…Mr. O'Grady…you can't do that. You see, I…" My mind was racing. Everyone must already be at the Javits Center. I pulled my cell phone out of my pocket. I had 15 missed calls and texts coming in every 30 seconds to the tune of "where the hell are you?"

"You see, I just know I'm the one to write your book." I hadn't known this when I picked up the phone, but in the course of five minutes, this book had become *my* book. I had inklings of pages in my head. I didn't have it yet, but I imagined a large pot of chicken and vegetable soup. Home.

"Sorry to disappoint, Miss Sheridan, but my mind is made up." He paused for a moment. I sat stock-still, straining to hear something in his breathing that would give me hope.

"Nah," he finally said. "It just won't work. Good luck to you."

I couldn't even speak.

"Goodbye then, I suppose," he said and put down the phone.

I shoved 12 dollars I couldn't afford to spend into the cab driver's hand and flew across the wide sidewalk to the myriad glass doors of the Javits Center. People everywhere carried tote bags and wheeled little carts stacked with displays or swag collected from the booths at the Book Expo.

I had no idea where I was supposed to be, but I was running all the same. I detoured by the information desk, trying to grab a map off the stack as I went.

A Chanel-suited grand dame in giant black sunglasses slammed her cocktail-ring-encrusted claw down on top of mine.

"Ow!" My hand flew to my mouth and I sucked on my knuckle. I tasted blood. "What the hell, lady?"

"I was here first," she said, snatching the top map off the stack.

"No you weren't! And even if you were, would it kill you to say 'excuse me?' There are rules to living in society."

"Don't you lecture me, you…" she gave me the once-over, "you…riff raff!"

"Who says riff raff?" A crowd was gathering.

"Don't you shout at me! According to the law, that's assault!" A pair of NYPD cops ambled over from the opposite corner of the outer hallway.

"You assaulted me!" I hissed. "Look, I'm bleeding. Listen," I said to the information guy, "don't call the police, they're right there. Here's my card."

I shot a look at the indignant Dowager of Manhattan. "If the police want to file a report, tell them to come back and talk to my bleeding finger." I blew past the old lady, who was literally shaking her fist at me.

I ran past miles of booths, some offering snacks, some blasting music, and some with long lines of fans clutching books to be signed by their favorite authors. I spied Matty from a mile away. I could have seen him from space. He was wearing one of those Ralph Lauren Olympic cardigans, and handing out ski caps emblazoned with the title of an inspirational biography we'd published by a double-amputee downhill skier. Next to him, another assistant, one of the office hotties, was wearing a leather dress and handing out ping pong paddles printed with the title of a kinky sex book for housewives. I tried to blend in and swim through the bodies to the back while Lizbeth was busy yelling at an intern.

"There you are," Matty hollered. "Lizbeth! Shayla's here!" He hopped up and down, trying to catch my boss's attention over the heads of the crowd. Lizbeth turned away from the pie-eyed intern midsentence and cut a straight line through all the bodies to get to me. "You're late! Don't apologize, I don't care. Give me some packing tape, now," she held out her open palm.

Frantically, I patted my purse. My supply bag! It was sitting under my desk. "I'll run to the drugstore and get some. I can be back in 10 minutes."

"Useless," she muttered. "No! I'll send an intern. Get dressed and get into your spot."

"Yes, Lizbeth," I said walking away, but in no particular direction. I'd missed last week's staff meeting after cracking a filling on a stale bagel I'd found on a leftover platter from a client meet-and-greet. I did not know the plan. I had no choice but to ask Matty what was what. He was wearing a red carpet-worthy smile and schmoozing one of our authors and her handler when I approached. The second the author shook his hand and walked away. Matty's smile disappeared. "What?" he snapped.

"Where am I supposed to be?"

"Somewhere in middle America, running the obituaries column for the local newspaper." He flashed a smile at a passerby and pressed a hat and a press kit into her hand.

"Come on, Matty," I pleaded.

He exhaled an elaborate sigh. "Go between the booths and put on your outfit. Look at the chart back there and go stand at your post."

I shoved through the crowd and wedged myself into the narrow space that we used as an office-slash-staging area. There was a mirror on the wall, a plot of our booths, some folders with papers in them, and enough space for three or four people to gather behind a makeshift curtain. I hung my garment bag on one of the hooks and unzipped it. Inside was a gingham pinafore, a bonnet, and a plush, stuffed shepherd's crook. Oh, no, no, no.

I snatched an agenda out of a hanging folder and read:

Shayla, first shift: Handing out press kits and hand puppets for Little HPC's 25th Anniversary Re-release of *Cuddle the Lamb: A Bedtime Story*, **southeast corner of Booth Number 3, side aisle**

Shayla, second shift: Straightening pamphlets and literature on the table/coffee run.

I scanned down the page to see what jobs other assistants and interns had been assigned during my missed meeting. Matty was, of course, on the main aisle in front of booth 1, wearing his designer sweater. His second shift was meeting the breakout novelist of the year at a swanky hotel and escorting him here for his book signing and acting as his handler onsite. Maggie had been crossed off the list and someone had penciled in "office coverage." This was seriously the worst day ever. I wouldn't even have her here for moral support. I scanned down the list:

Carly, first shift: Handing out HPC bookmarks / Greeting guests in front of booth 2, main aisle

Carly, second shift: Handler for Theodore Reichel / book signing Booth 1, 4 p.m.

No way. Carly was an intern who hadn't been in the office more than a couple of months. I worked 50-plus hours a week, and had for over three years. I was in line for an associate editor position. Fucking broken filling. Fucking Matty.

I peeked out the curtain and saw Carly standing by a small table off to the side, filling a shoulder bag with bookmarks. I made a beeline straight for her.

"Carly, change of plans," I said, snatching the bag and turning her by the shoulders toward the staging area. "You're me and I'm you," I declared. "Lizbeth said," I lied. "*Cuddle the Lamb* by booth 3, then you're doing coffee. I can already tell you I want the biggest latte you can get me. Full caf." I gave her a little shove. "Go."

I took my position on the main aisle, pasted on a smile, and greeted passersby.

"Hi, have you read the latest from Haversmith, Peebles, and Chin? Thanks, have a good day. Complementary bookmark? Come back at 4 to meet author Theodore Reichel, in a rare public book signing. Here you go, something to mark your page. Join us at 4 for a book signing from famously reclusive novelist Theodore Reichel," I hawked, shoving bookmarks into people's hands. Out of the corner of my eye, I saw Matty down the aisle. He looked furious. I turned my back to him. "Book signing at 4! Care for a bookmark?"

Plunging my hand repeatedly into the sack of bookmarks, opened the cut on my hand from the old crazy lady's ring. I knew I shouldn't leave my post and draw attention to myself, but I got skeeved out at the thought of infection. That ring could have germs residing between its prongs dating back to the Titanic. I looked around for Lizbeth and didn't see her. Making my move, I stayed off the main aisle and came around the back of the staging area.

"...but she was assigned the lamb puppets and the bonnet. And she was an hour late," I heard Matty say behind the curtain.

"My hands are tied. What would you have me do, fire her?" Lizbeth answered.

"Why not? Louise is about to go on maternity leave, so she won't miss me. Carly is excellent for an intern. She could cover Louise for the last few weeks, and I could just move to Shayla's desk and work for you. Problem solved."

"I wish, but I can't do it. You know who her father is. Besides, things are shifting. In three months, I'm planning to put you into an associate editor spot."

I sucked on my finger. She was skipping me to promote Matty, that sneaky little medicated bastard! I should pull back the curtain and quit right here and now. Wouldn't Hank make a meal out of that? "Well, Shayla," he'd say, "can't say I didn't see this coming. Not everyone is cut out for publishing. Takes a thick skin. You've always been sensitive, like your mother. Never should have moved her out of Rhinebeck. Dutchess County was more her speed than Manhattan."

I hated that it was due to Hank's reputation that I was even hanging on by a thread. It was so unfair! I hated riding on his coattails, but bailing on my job without something better on the horizon would just confirm what he already predicted: I wasn't born to be a big dog.

I went back to my post, half-heartedly distributing the contents of my bag of bookmarks. At one point, Matty stomped up behind me, and spat, "You're supposed to be on *Cuddle the Lamb*." I stared straight ahead, pretending he wasn't there. Game on, Matty, I thought to myself. You're going to need all the Valium and Klonopin you can lay your hands on. I hated being petty, but I couldn't just stand by and watch him take my promotion. I sensed I couldn't fully trust him, but I always think the best of people. I hadn't realized he was a true snake.

I pulled my phone out of my pocket and checked the time. 3:55. I had no idea where I was supposed to pick up Theodore Reichel, and really, there was no one I could ask. I'd have to be shrewd. At the side of booth 1 there was a small, makeshift dais with a table, a stack of his books, and a handful of pens. OK, that's where I'd take him once I found him. Check! Maybe he was being dropped out front by a car service.

Still dressed in her pinafore and bonnet, Carly whooshed up behind the chair and unrolled a screen-style floor display featuring Theodore Reichel's face looking serious about the blown-up jacket of his book, and snapped it neatly into place. Shit, shit, shit! I was supposed to be doing that.

To my horror, I saw Lizbeth coming up the aisle, leading Mr. Reichel. That was supposed to be my job, and now my boss was doing it herself.

"Mr. Reichel," I said, rushing up to them. "I'm Shayla, and I'll be here to help you with anything you need." I wedged myself between him and Lizbeth and took him by the arm. "If you'll step this way, your chair is all set up for you." Lizbeth looked irritated, but allowed me to guide the elderly gentleman to his seat. She could hardly make a scene. Okay, hurdle one jumped, I thought to myself. If I just keep doing one right thing after another, she'll forget about my being late. "Can I bring you some water?" He nodded and grunted what I assumed to be assent.

"Back in just a sec," I said, racing for the staging area. There was a plastic tub of bottled waters floating in what was probably once ice, but was now slightly unclean water. I took out a bottle and wiped it on my dress. "Psst, Carly!" I called. I needed to get her and her Little Bo Peep get-up out of sight. She was a walking reminder that I wasn't doing the job I'd been assigned. "Lizbeth told me to send you on a coffee run," I lied. "A cup of tea for Mr. Reichel, and don't forget my latte. Bring Matty an Americano with an espresso shot." She looked at me funny. I shrugged, "That's what he asked for," I told her with wide eyes. Matty only drank decaf.

I could not believe what was coming out of my mouth. I never lied. To me, it was always more trouble than it was worth. Besides, it felt slimy. Who was I? Oh well, in for a penny, in for a pound, I thought. "No, Carly! Go the back way, it's faster."

"All right. Tell Lizbeth I'll be right back," she called over her shoulder.

"Will do!" I called, giving a huge wave, like I was sending someone out to sea.

I slipped around the curtain and saw that a line was forming at the table. The crowd thickened.

"Ladies and gentlemen," I shouted about the hustle and bustle of the expo. "If you'd like to purchase a book, step to the left. If you have a book to be signed and would like to meet Mr. Reichel, please step to the right." Pleased with myself, I stepped up onto the dais and positioned myself behind and to the right of the author. I felt cool, like a royal guard or a secret service agent.

I heard her before I saw her. It's hard to believe the click-clack of those Chanel pumps as worn by a 90-pound woman could be loud enough to carry, but it did. Hurtling toward the HPC area was the crazy lady from the lobby, flanked by the two uniformed NYPD officers. "Step right up, please," I told the first woman in line. "If you could all have your books open to the title page, that would be a great help to Mr. Reichel," I advised, stepping down off the dais to cut off the officers at the pass. I'd simply ask them not to disturb my author, and let them know I'd find them to make a statement after the signing. As I stepped down, the be-Chaneled gnome in the giant bug glasses tried to step up. The officers appeared at her side in a flash, lifting her like a dancer from a 1960s Broadway musical onto the level with the renowned media-dodger and hermit, Theodore Reichel.

"Ma'am!" I said sharply from the ground. "This is a private event. You cannot be up there." She ignored me, walked over and took Reichel's hand.

"Ma'am!" I said sternly.

"This is my wife," the author said. The old lady whispered something in his ear.

"One moment, ladies and gentlemen," I shouted to the crowd. "Please continue to open your books to the title page to assist Mr. Reichel. Officers," I whispered, beckoning them near, "I can explain. You see, *she* attacked *me*." I leaned in, "She's very confused. I won't press charges, I have a soft spot for the elderly." I smiled humbly as they stared at me. Maybe I wasn't exactly a hero, but I was impressed with my own maturity. They must be grateful for my making their job just that much easier. I flashed them a winning smile.

I stepped up and put my hand on Reichel's shoulder just as Lizbeth was easing the old woman off the other side of the dais. Matty rushed forward to grab a wizened, silk-covered arm. "I am so sorry about that, Mr. Reichel." I glanced sideways to see Lizbeth bent double, the Park Avenue Madame whispering into her ear.

Sick with dread, I made myself look at Lizbeth.

"You're fired," she mouthed.

Chapter Five

There is nothing so bad that it couldn't be worse.

Maggie opened the door to the apartment like she was entering a hospital room.

"Hello?" she said, softly knocking on the half-open door, even though she lives here.

"No point tap-dancing around it; I got fired." I was sitting at the kitchen table in my pajamas and bathrobe, my hair pulled back into the scrunchie I used when I washed my face. I had the stolen cashmere pashmina from my agent's office wrapped around my shoulders like a shawl. Spread out in front of me was an open bottle of sauvignon blanc, a glass, and Tom O'Grady's bio materials.

"I know. I heard."

"At least you didn't have to see it." I'd had to leave the Javits Center and report to HPC security in order to clear out my desk. It was just like the movies. Two armed guards gave me an empty cardboard box with a lid and escorted me to my desk, watching carefully to make sure I didn't make off with any staplers or hand sanitizer. Like a prisoner leaving the penitentiary, I was led to the front door and launched out onto the world without a roadmap for the future. I wanted to take a cab, but I lugged my box to the bus stop instead. The unemployed didn't take cabs.

"Want a glass?"

"Yes, please," she said taking off her coat, and setting her computer bag aside. I grabbed a glass from the cabinet and poured in what was left of the bottle. It was a scant half inch. "Oops."

She went to the fridge and pulled out another. "You've been drinking a lot lately, Shayla."

"I just got fired!" I defended myself. She had a point, though. Historically speaking, I was not a big lush or partier.

"Right, and tonight's understandable. But it's not like you to go overboard so many nights in any given week." She kicked off her shoes and poured herself a drink. "Is something wrong?"

"Everything's wrong right now," I said. I felt guilty. I didn't want to put Maggie on the spot for being happy. She deserved her boyfriend and her book deal, and even her shitty job at HPC, where she'd be promoted in no time flat, if she didn't quit to be a full-time writer. "Hey, don't worry about me. I just need a night to process all of this. Tomorrow, I'll see the bright side." I wasn't sure that was strictly true, but I didn't want to be a complete downer.

"I know you're putting on a brave face, but there is always a bright side. If you really feel like everything's wrong, you have to make a radical change. When I was in college, I got dumped and I moped around the dorm with dirty hair, playing Duncan Sheik albums for a month. Finally, my hall monitor sat me down and said, "Look, you have to do *something*. It doesn't matter what it is, but do something. You're annoying.""

"Are you saying I'm annoying?"

"Not yet, but you will be soon enough if you don't take action. Annoying and an alcoholic."

"I'm not an alcoholic! I'm just drinking to take the edge off. Matty said everyone in New York is on anti-anxiety meds and tranquilizers."

"If your nerves are strung that tight, then maybe you need to move to Arizona and join a sweat lodge, or a go to a Buddhist monastery or something. I mean it, Shay, sometimes a really radical change is called for. Look at Oprah. She wakes up one day and decides to stop doing Jerry Springer-like TV and be uplifting instead. Next thing you know, she's queen of the world." Maggie pulled a photo out of my pile of papers and spun it around to face her. "Hell-o! Who's this hottie?"

"That's right! I haven't seen you all day. He's the guy whose book I don't get to write."

She held up one of him in formal chef's whites and a tall hat. "Nice," she declared. She held up another of him posing stiffly in a tux, in mid-handshake with the president. "Handsome," she declared. Pulling an action shot of him shearing a sheep while wearing a waffled thermal shirt pulled tight across his chest, and a pair of torn cords, she yelled, "Yes, please!"

"I know, right?"

She rifled through more photos and tear sheets. "He looks good dressed up, and all, but the sweet spot for me is that farm-boy thing. Sweaty and dirty with muscles rippling. Mm-mm-mm! Hey look, this restaurant is just a town or two over from Wicklow, where Gran's sister and the rest of that side of the family live over in Ireland. Did Brenda give you this stuff? And by the way, is that a new pashmina?"

I ignored the pashmina question and gave Maggie the blow-by-blow beginning with breakfast with Matty, to my meeting with Brenda, to getting shot down trans-Atlantically by Tom O'Grady, to my near-arrest and, finally, my firing.

I finished my tale of woe and she sat silent for a minute. Then she poured herself another glass and declared, "You have to go there."

"Where?"

"To Ireland, of course."

"You're out of your mind. For what?"

"To write his book."

"He said no."

"So. Go over there and make him say yes. *Do* something."

Images flashed through my head: Me, stepping off the plane

and into a waiting limo to be whisked to Tom O'Grady's world-class restaurant, where we'd drink champagne while he told his life story into a recorder; Me, yawning awake in silk pajamas between high-thread-count sheets in one of Castle Stone's master bedroom-range guest rooms; Me, posing for photos at The Guild of Food Writer's Awards, Hank in the front row, clapping with satisfaction.

Maybe it was the wine, but it dawned on me that this idea was the best and only possible answer. "Yeah, that's something I could do. It's better than sitting around being annoying, right?"

There was a light in Maggie's eyes and I could see her wheels turning. "Get me my laptop," she ordered. "And open another bottle of wine."

While I uncorked our last bottle, she got to work pricing airfares, and emailing and Facebooking relatives. "Give me your credit card," she demanded.

"Are you booking a flight? Right now?" Curling my legs under myself, I realized I felt gun-shy. "I just got fired. I'm still paying off my student loans and that credit card debt from right after college."

"Good point." She leaped up and fetched her purse. "I'll put it on mine." Before I could protest, she held up a warning hand. "Stop. You'll pay me when Brenda cuts you that advance check."

Weakly, I told her, "There's no promise of an advance. I don't even have a contract."

"No matter," she said. "You're going to get that book written and then she'll have to pay you. The money will come later rather than sooner. You have a verbal agreement and if she punks on it I'll have Eric send letters from the firm. If we need to lawyer up, we'll lawyer up." I was alarmed. It must have shown on my face.

"It won't come to that," she assured me, typing in her credit card numbers. "Brenda needs that book done, she assigned it to you, and you are going to deliver."

Warmth rose up in my chest. I stared at my friend, who was efficiently setting my life's wheels in motion. How lucky was I to have someone so firmly in my corner. The way Maggie treated me was so different from the way Hank treated me.

"You really believe in me, don't you Mags?"

"Damn straight, I do. And I'm never wrong."

I couldn't argue with that. Maggie has always bet on the right horse and come out a winner.

She continued, "Oh, look! My cousin Des is answering my PM. It's late there…he usually works nights. Must be his day off. He's typing…he says 'Ah sure, I'll pick her up at the airport' and asks 'Is she a ride?'" Maggie laughed. "He's disgusting," she said, typing back. "He says tomorrow morning he'll ask my Auntie Fiona if you can stay with them. I'm sure she'll say yes. She's the one who helped me apply to that summer literature seminar at Trinity College. Then I stayed at her house in Wicklow. It's close to where you need to be. Castle Stone is in Ballykelty. It's a little village in County Wexford. The beach there is where they filmed Saving Private Ryan, but you'd never know it. There's not a sign in sight. The locals don't like to draw attention to themselves. You're going to love it, Shay!"

Hearing Maggie rattle off the names of the foreign people, buildings, towns, and counties made me dizzy. Or maybe it was the wine. I'd forgotten to eat dinner again. "Starting tomorrow," I vowed, "I'll take better care of myself. I'll start the day with herbal tea and eat balanced meals. I'll start sending out resumés and get a lucrative day job somewhere where they'll treat me with respect."

I heard my phone ping. I glanced at it and struggled to focus. It was an e-ticket confirmation from Aer Lingus.

"Uh, Maggie. When is my flight?" I held the phone back from my face, trying to read the tiny, blurry words.

"Tomorrow morning." She slammed her laptop shut. "The car service is coming at 4:30, so we'd better start packing. You're welcome."

Chapter Six

*The future is not set, there is no fate but what we make for
ourselves.*

I was counting the seconds until the plane hit a comfortable
cruising altitude. My hands shook. I had barely gotten three hours
of sleep and I was pretty sure I was still drunk. I needed a coffee
just to keep me upright. Sitting in the window seat almost at the
back of the plane, I held hope that the middle seat in my row of
three would stay empty. Just as the crew swung the cabin door
closed, a cheerful red-faced guy pushed in, banging every person
on the left-hand aisle in the head with his briefcase, apologizing
to each. Of course, he wedged in next to me, where his hammy
forearm was now hogging the armrest. I was freezing, but I didn't
dare push the call button for a blanket lest I draw attention to
myself and give him a reason to speak to me.

What had Maggie been thinking, sending me to the ends of
the earth to chase down a crabby chef who wanted no part of
me? As I walked through the temporary hallway-on-wheels, I
told myself to simply turn around and go home. I didn't have
the guts to defy Maggie, though. So here I sat, trapped next to
Sunny McSausagefingers, being forced to inhale his fresh and
grassy aftershave.

Contorting my body in the tiny space, I fished between my legs to root around for my (Brenda's) pashmina. I felt a hard, rectangular something wrapped in crinkly paper. I wedged it out of my bag and into my lap. It was a present, with a card on the front.

Dear Shay — I was saving this for your birthday, but I want you to have it now to keep you company on this trip. I know you must be scared, but I have a feeling you're going to get everything you ever wanted. Love, Mags. P.S. If you have the chance to leap into bed with a sexy aul Irishman (anyone but my cousin Des!) do it. What happens in Ireland, stays in Ireland.

What did Maggie know about being scared? She was a luck magnet and her future was being paved for her in gold, brick by brick. I knew Maggie loved me and that her goal was to reach down and pull me up with her. I knew how lucky I was to have her pushing me. And yet… and yet… why everyone else and not me? My guilt at thinking this about my best friend made my muscles tight. Was there any feeling worse than covetousness? I had to talk myself down off a ledge. As they say, "compare and despair." I reminded myself that Maggie wasn't born with a silver spoon in her mouth, and shifted my focus to the positive. After all, she'd set the wheels in motion to help me fix my life and she'd packed me a gift to boot.

I slid my present out of the wrapping paper. It was a beautiful journal, covered in nubby, sage green, handmade paper with yellow dried flowers pressed into it. It looked like a spring field. It was almost too pretty to write in. There was even a pen to go with it — just the kind I liked, with a clicker on top, a clip for attaching, and a nice heavy weight. It was a retro sunny yellow color. The words *Kate's Paperie* appeared in demure typeface on the inside of the back cover of my new journal Maggie knew that was one of my favorite stores in all New York. I turned the book over in my hands. I admired it. Maggie intended to make me happy with this gift, pure and simple. I noticed a little sheet sticking out. It read,

This present is not for saving, it's for using. Signed, Margaret Doyle, Queen of Everything.

I lay my head back against the seat, smiling about my new gift. Packing a neck pillow would have been a good idea. I was tired, but so tense at the same time. My shoulders were in knots. "I'll just close my eyes for a minute, just until the beverage cart come by with some coffee," I thought. I tried to rest, but my mind wouldn't quiet.

Tracing my fingers lightly over the relief of the flowers on my new journal, I remembered the daffodils that pushed up at my grandparent's house upstate, sometimes before it was really even warm outside. My mom grew up in that house, situated on the east bank of the Hudson River. I toured colleges up that way: Vassar, Bard, Concordia. Hank pushed for Columbia or NYU so I wouldn't have to leave the city.

"New York is the capital of the world," he told me. "It's the place to grab life by the balls." At the time, the idea of grabbing anyone or anything by the balls seemed out of my wheelhouse. I needed to proceed at a slower pace; to test the waters. We compromised on Sarah Lawrence. "Good for writers; close to urban life," so Hank said. The scholarly and artistic atmosphere suited me. That, and the culture of accepting hairy legs and a wardrobe of sweat suits. My seminars required prep time. I didn't have the time or energy to doll up for classes.

When I was a little kid, mom and I had spent summers with my grandparents in Rhinebeck. I could almost smell the tomatoes she grew; she loved them so much, sometimes we'd eat them straight from the vine, still warm from the sun. And Grandma had her wonderful black and white Border Collie, Pip. I was so sad when he had died. Poor old Pip. When his time came, he was so weak Grandma fed him baby formula from a dropper to keep his mouth moist. His breathing became more and more rattled with each hour. That last night, we curled up next to his fuzzy donut bed by the fireplace and laid our hands on him as his body shook in one last violent spasm before he lay quiet. She and I spooned together and cried. We didn't bury his body till the next morning.

I pushed away my thoughts and lay my head back, trying to blank my mind.

"Focus on one breath in, one breath out, breathing in a circle," the yoga teacher from the one class I'd ever taken tried to teach me. I didn't want to think about Pip, or Grandma, or how scared I was to be going halfway around the world alone. I pictured the tension in my shoulders liquefying, draining away. My body craved sleep. Breathing in, breathing out. The buzz of the aircraft and the vibration of the seat lulled me. The voices of the other travelers, popping of the soda cans, the thump of tray tables all faded away.

I emerged from the nothingness walking the hallway of Hank's Upper West Side apartment, or at least it seemed like Hank's place. Vines adorned the ceilings. They crawled with hissing cockroaches and tiny birds that shrieked occasional high-pitched complaints. I didn't want to walk underneath these creatures.

It was very cold and dimly lit. I was only in my nightgown, wrapped in a red duvet, but when the elevator door opened, I got on anyway. Lizbeth and Jordan Silver were on, too. I stayed still so they wouldn't see me. On the ground floor, I hugged Dmitry and told him I'd miss him, and that he'd been like a father to me. He tried to hide the cigarette in his hand. The smoke choked me but I said, "No, please smoke. You have every right to make yourself happy." And I meant it with all my heart. He waved, smiling, as I walked out the door. Instead of exiting onto West End Avenue, I walked onto Grandma's lawn.

The grass was cool on my feet, but the sun was warm on my face and shoulders, so I threw off my duvet. Pip was barking, and frisking; he beckoned me to follow. Seeing him made me so happy, it felt like my heart was filled with helium. I screamed, "Good boy! Good boy!" But it only came out as a wheeze. I chased after him, and he led me to a big double bed covered in soft pillows and pastel quilts. Mom was tucked in and she stretched her arms out to me. I climbed in and snuggled into a hug. Pip sprung aboard, turned around several times, and curled into a nose-to-tail circle. "I love you, my girl," Mom said. Tears of joy flooded from my eyes. I could hardly make out Mom's face through the water, but I could see that she was smiling.

As I wriggled around to get comfortable, the sheets started to feel scratchy. The sprawling bed was now a tight hospital cot and my spine scraped against the metal bedrail. Mom's skin felt cold against my hand, so I smoothed back her hair. It came out in a clump. I couldn't shake it off my hand. Her skin felt waxy. I pressed her shoulder to wake her up, but she wouldn't rouse. I sobbed. Pip stood up, pinning my leg with his front paws, and barked. "Yip! Yip! Yip!"

"Miss…Miss. Miss!"

I opened my eyes to see my seatmate holding out a package of tissues and a concerned flight attendant holding out a steaming paper cup.

"There, there, love. Wipe your eyes." The heater had been aimed in my direction and I was covered in an Aer Lingus blanket. "You were shivering, so I took the liberty of covering you up. Hope you don't mind. The air hostess here has a cup of strong tea for you, with lots of sugar. Sure, it helps the shock. Drink up." The flight attendant was looking at me with such warm concern, I immediately felt better..

I dabbed at my eyes with a tissue. I sipped the hot, sweet tea. The fragrance and the taste seeped into me, the warmth soothed the back of my throat, and lit a path down through my chest to my gut. It was so good. I finished the cup in greedy gulps. It was like that cup of tea was what I'd been waiting for all my life.

"Better now?" asked the pretty girl in the crisp, white blouse and green scarf.

I nodded.

"You wouldn't have an aul snack for the girl in the back there, wouldja?" my seatmate asked. "It's only that dinner's not on, and she's under the weather."

"Gotcha. Back in two shakes," she said.

On what planet are people this nice? I wondered. Certainly not planet New York City. Back in the office, I'd dragged myself in with the flu for a mandatory staff meeting on the coldest day of the winter. Not only did Matty refuse to get me a cup of tea citing "very real SARS concerns," Lizbeth tagged me to run down to Pick-A-Bagel to check on the breakfast order. And I'd grown up with Hank. From an early age I'd learned to rely on myself or do without. Apart from Maggie, I hadn't experienced people falling all over themselves to help me out of sheer kindness in forever. Since Mom. Since Grandma.

"Brian Lynch," the man said, holding his huge hand out for me to shake. I blushed, thinking of the mean things I'd said in my head about him. I had a wild moment thinking he could read my mind, but judging from his genuine smile, I could see that he expected the best from me.

"Shayla Sheridan," I replied.

"Good to know you, Sheila. I have a daughter near your age, and two married ones, a bit older. Pretty girls, all, just like you. Now, don't let me trouble you. Go and get your rest."

"No," I said. "I just had a rough morning. And," I paused. He was looking at me with really kind eyes. I dropped my defenses and sighed a cleansing sigh, "I had a bad dream. I'm good now." I rolled my head around on my shoulders. The tightness had subsided. I took a moment to check in with myself. Was I OK? I really was.

"Then tell me, Sheila, what brings you to Ireland?"

Maybe it was that loneliness that comes along with flying far above the oceans that spurred me on, but I broke my own rule about never talking to strangers on a plane, and told Brian Lynch the whole story. An excellent listener, he interjected with "Say it's not so!" and "You're joking!" and "Too right!" at all the appropriate intervals. In mid-story, Moira — that's the flight attendant — brought me two scones, a tiny jar of jam, and a pot of clotted cream. "Put that inside you, it'll do you a world of good" she said. "And here's something to wash it down with." More tea. I didn't object.

I tried to imagine any young, hip girl in New York insisting that I eat a dense sugary bread roll spread with the creamiest, fattiest, sweetest ambrosia anyone's ever tasted on this earth. For those of you who've never had clotted cream, I can only tell you that it must be mother's milk from an angel. When I'd dug out all I could from the little foil cup using my plastic airline knife, I couldn't stop myself from licking it clean.

"Good girl," was Brian's response.

My tray was cleared and I came to the end of my story. I took out the folder to show him Tom O'Grady's photo.

"Ah, sure I know Tom O'Grady. He was in the papers not long ago, shaking hands with your president, and the prime minister, and all the rest. The missus and I stayed in Castle Stone on our silver wedding anniversary, back before they refurbished the place. Lovely then, of course, with the horses trotting the paths, and the manicured gardens, and the old chapel for mass, but I've heard it's splendid now."

"Care for some dinner?" Moira interrupted. "Would you like the pasta, the chicken, or the beef? Pasta, chicken or beef?" The cart had made it down to our row. Brian took the beef, so I figured, "when in Rome." We arranged our trays and tore the tops and wrappers off of all our little packages. The second the smell of the gravy hit my nose, I was ravenous. It was like the scones never happened. I was thrilled to see chunks of carrot and potato nestled in with the cubes of roast.

"Care for something to drink? Sparkling water, beer, wine, a cocktail?"

"Orange juice for me, please," Brian said. "Car's parked at the airport. I don't live far, only on the north side of Dublin, but I never risk it."

I almost ordered a vodka and soda with lemon, just out of habit, but I really didn't want a drink. I liked chatting with Brian, and I was feeling sharp. I felt better than I had in weeks. "Orange juice for me, too, please."

"Full of vitamin C," Brian declared. "Won't do you a bit of harm." I liked the way he said 'vit-amin,' rhyming 'vit' with 'bit'. We ate our meals companionably.

"I understand your man Tom gave up the high life in London to go home and help out the old Lord."

"He's not my man!" I corrected, shocked. "I've never even met him."

"Turn of phrase," Brian explained. "Anthony Stone, Earl of Wexford's the name. I read something in one of my girls' tabloids about the place falling to ruin, the family not being able to keep up with the taxes or what have you. You see that kind of thing more and more these days. The titled losing vast tracts of land that's been with them for centuries."

"So what does that have to do with Tom? Tom O'Grady, I mean."

"That part I can't tell you. The magazine was one of them girly jobs. Only paper I had with me on the train one day, so I read it cover to cover. It talked more about him splitting with that girl he had the television show with. Something about her demanding a yellow diamond for an engagement ring, and him leaving London heartbroken, barely able to lift his head. Said he took to the drink. To tell the truth, I'm embarrassed to know all this. Those papers are pure gossip and lies, all. I shouldn't be repeating what they say."

I finished every scrap of my dinner, including the little Bakewell tart in a cup, topped with custard. Brian and I chatted comfortably while the meal was cleared. We took turns excusing ourselves to go to the lavatory, and stretched our legs by standing in the galley with Moira for a while. He showed me pictures of his wife and daughters and I told him what it was like to grow up with a famous father. "But don't tell anyone, please," I entreated.

"Your secret's safe with me, pet." When I thought about it, it kind of was. Brian though my name was Sheila. He hunkered down in his seat, and in that way old men have, dropped off to sleep almost immediately, snoring softly. This time I didn't mind his arm on my armrest.

Careful not to awaken him, I took out my journal and cracked the stiff spine open to the first creamy blank page.

Dear Mags, I watched my hand write. Strange. I'd kept journals over the years, but I'd never written "to" anyone. I'd never even used the salutation "Dear Diary." Oh well, I was writing in ink, so I decided to go with it. *"I owe you an apology. I've been thinking vile thoughts about you all day, and I'm so sorry. All during the ride to the airport, I convinced myself that you'd cooked up this scheme to get rid of me. In my head, you'd jettison me to another country, go into HPC and laugh about me over cocktails at my desk with Matty, and move in a new roommate who is more fun and who actually has a job, like maybe Carly the Intern. I'm so bad! If you hated me, would you have stayed up all night straightening my hair so I could look like a modern, urban writer? All you did was try to dig me out of a hole, lend me money, and throw in the most perfect gift I've ever received in to boot. On second thought, you really are trying to show me up, aren't you? Kidding! Thanks for wishing me sex, too, though that prospect is highly unlikely. If what I hear about Ireland's climate is true, even Colin Farrell would have to cut me out of my long underwear using scissors! Anyway, my parts must be frozen from lack of use. Whatevs! Totally unimportant because I'm going to be in and out of there like a cat burglar. I plan to find O'Grady, get him to tell me a few colorful stories about leprechauns or shillelaghs or potato famines, or whatever, and get this book written. I will not be long in the land of flat caps and frizzy hair. Boom! Brenda will kvetch and kvell, I'll be her hero, and there will still be plenty of time to call Ray Diablo on his personal number before he hires another writer. Uh oh! They're calling for seatbacks and tray tables. I'll call T O'G (how do they do initials with apostrophes??!) in the morning from your aunt's house. Today's the 20th and you have me coming home on the 24th. I know your aunt offered to keep me the whole time, but I think after I nail this, I might treat myself to a hostel in Dublin and do a little sightseeing. I'd tell you to wish me luck, but you already have. Love, Shay."*

I patted myself on the back for not having checked luggage. In reality, I had Maggie to thank for that. She'd edited a book about packing and organization, and she'd internalized all the flight attendant's tips. Besides, I'd only be here a few days. She brutally cut out all but the essentials, but tucked every manner of jewel and accessory one could imagine into the toes of shoes, the inner circle of rolled up belts, and between layers of flat, folded clothing.

When Brian and I parted at customs, I felt sadder than I expected to.

"You look after yourself, Sheila," he said. "I don't like the thought of you being on your own. If you need anything, anything at all, you ring me." He gave me his card. "Brian Lynch, GlobeCo, Director of Sales and Distribution, Ireland-UK-US."

"Anything at all, hear? I couldn't bear the thought of one of my own daughters wanting for anything in a strange country. I'm as near as the telephone."

I gave him a hug, not the sort of thing I usually do, but I really didn't want to let him go. His kindness had shone a spotlight on my loneliness. He patted my back in a fatherly way.

"Thank you," was all I could manage. I smiled and walked away quickly. I didn't like goodbyes in general and this one hurt more than it should. I waved without turning around, and heard him call, "Keep outta trouble, Sheila!"

As I stood in line, waiting to go through customs, I realized I'd left my winter coat in the overhead compartment. Shit. Should I try to reboard? There was nothing in the pocket except my gloves; I'd either get it back or I wouldn't.

With only my carry on, and my small rolling suitcase I felt small and underprepared. The longer I stood waiting, the more dread I felt. On the plane, where I was being fed and watched over, everything seemed fine. Now dread poked me in the ribcage. Closer to the front, I could just make out the conversations of some other travelers, reminding me that the more you reveal at customs, the more questions they ask you. I'd keep it simple.

"Welcome to Ireland," the kind-faced agent said. "Are you here for business or pleasure?"

"Pleasure," I declared firmly, looking her straight in the eye.

Chapter Seven

Need teaches a plan.

As I exited the building and breathed in my first fresh air in nearly a day, I was surprised at how warm it was. As promised, Maggie's cousin Des met me right on time outside the terminal. I must have looked lost, because he spotted me right away, and jumped out of the car.

"Shayla?" I nodded. He swooped in and loaded my suitcase into the back. "Hiya! I'm Des." He was tall and had a sexy, sporty look to him. "Ready for an almost two-hour trip? Lovely night for it." It was a lovely night. Ireland was downright balmy compared with New York. The air was moist and fresh.

Two hours. Now I'd owe him big-time. Running people from midtown to LaGuardia was a pain, but this was above and beyond. He didn't even know me.

"I didn't realize it was so far. I should have taken a bus or something," I said, opening the car door and sliding in. "You have to let me pay you," I offered, my stomach squeezing because I had no idea what a fair price might be. Probably more than I had.

"Not at all," he brushed off my concern.

"Well, I want to give you something."

"It all works out in the end, doesn't it?" He stood looking at me. "Are you driving?"

Startled, I looked around and saw that I was sitting in front of the steering wheel. "Oh!" I scrambled out, and got in the other side. I'd travelled to Italy, Spain, Mexico, and The Netherlands, but I had found traveling to London by far the hardest transition. In the other, very foreign, places, I expected up to be down, and black to be white. In England, however, everyone spoke English, and we shared a lot of common culture — the United States having been a colony of theirs and all — so I got a false sense of security. Then, I'd get in a phone booth and be all thumbs or I'd have to take a freezing shower because I couldn't figure out the buttons and knobs. It unsettled me. I suspected I'd feel similarly off-balance in Ireland.

"Buckle up," he commanded. "Safety first. I drive a hotel limo, that's why I work nights. I could do this drive in my sleep. It's not often I have such a pretty passenger, though."

I remembered Maggie's warnings about her cousin being a ladies' man, but he didn't seem so bad to me. As he chattered on about his job, and how he liked to play football (the kind where you use your feet, I was schooled), I stole a sideways glance at him. Red hair, high cheekbones, full lips. He reminded me a bit of the ginger one from the Harry Potter films, all grown up. Not bad at all. My mind wandered to what he'd look like with his shirt off. And maybe his jeans. He looked to be the long and lean type, with a torso like a runner. And working down from there…Wow! I hadn't had those thoughts in a while. Maybe it was the saltiness in the air, blowing in from the sea.

Shut it down, I told myself. His mother graciously offered you a bed to sleep in, she didn't offer to fill it. There was no doubt that he was a piece of eye-candy, but one-night stands weren't me, typically. I wasn't above them, far from it. It's just that it had been so long since I'd been with a man, you could call me a reborn virgin. There was a part of me that wanted my next time to be special. Or at least a great story.

"Would you mind if I just closed my eyes?" I asked. If I took a little nap, there'd be nothing to worry about. No point stirring the pot, I wouldn't even be here long enough to start trouble.

"Not at all," he replied amiably. "You must be knackered from the journey."

I closed my eyes, and before I knew it, the car pulled into a short, paved drive alongside a neat little modern suburban house. Maggie's Auntie Fiona immediately appeared at the front door. She must have been listening for the car.

"Get her bags inside, Des, and show her where to wash her hands. I've a smoked cod pie warm in the oven for your tea."

"You didn't have to cook for me," I protested. I realized, too late, that I hadn't packed a hostess gift. Maggie had shoved me out of the country with practically only the clothes on my back. I was utterly unprepared.

"Nonsense! It's not a bit of trouble. Come through, Shayla, you're very welcome."

I could smell the sea. We had to be close. The high-pitched, plaintive, womanly cries of the gulls confirmed it. The salt air and the light chill snapped me awake, and my appetite along with me. I was ravenous. I'd never had smoked cod pie, but I was willing to give it a try.

With clean hands and brushed hair, I stood by the table. Normally, I would have touched up my makeup and changed into something unrumpled, but it didn't seem called for. "There she is! Fresh as a daisy," Des waved me toward a chair next to him at a tidy little kitchen table. "Doesn't she look gorgeous, Mam?"

"Sure Des is a keen one for the ladies, Shayla," Auntie Fiona (as she instructed me to call her) said, pulling a box of tea down from the pantry. "'Course she's gorgeous, but don't embarrass the poor girl. She's only just arrived, she can do without your charms, I'd say. Go on, darlin', sit down and make yourself comfortable."

"Seat's open here," Des said. He checked to see that his mother's back was turned and patted his lap. I sat on the chair next to him, surprised to feel a smile creeping onto my lips. I didn't dare look him in the face. I could feel him smiling at me. That made me smile harder.

"Tuck in," Maggie's aunt said setting a plate bearing a giant slab of savory pie in front of me, then scooped a steaming, crispy pile of thick-cut French fries alongside it.

"I never have pie without chips," she said.

From that moment on, I hoped I never would, either. The potatoes were golden-brown and crispy on the outside, and steaming and fluffy on the inside. Des pushed a bottle of malt vinegar toward me. Why not? I thought. The combination of the saltiness and the tang made my taste buds sing. I took my first tentative bite of the pie. I'd had some sketchy smoked mackerel in the past, and the fishy, oily memory was lodged in my brain. This pie was the farthest thing from it. The flaky chunks of white fish had just enough smokiness to make it interesting, but the wholesome flavor of the ocean was the star taste. The truth is, I'll eat about anything you put in a flaky piecrust and surround with creamy white sauce, onions, and peas, but the fish was a standout.

Maggie's aunt excused herself to go hang the laundry. On a clothesline? I wondered. I made a mental note to take a look at that later. Even Grandma had used a giant tumble dryer, and in Manhattan the closest thing we had to clotheslines were the metal fire escapes on tenement buildings.

Des and I chatted about this and that, but the real conversation took place beneath our words. A glance from beneath the lashes here, a lick of the lips there. This was more like a date than my date with Jordan in 54 Below had been. I wondered if my chances of scoring would be higher. Realizing this line of thinking was reckless, I willed myself to sit up straight and to stop speaking from below my waist.

Des told me about ten times that he'd have to eat quickly and rush off. He said this between charged stares and brushed of his knee against my thigh. I encouraged him to go, pointing out the time. The longer he stayed, the more I wanted him to. I couldn't believe myself. I usually went for the nerdy intellectuals, the ones whose flaws you had to overlook to get to the good stuff. The ones you had to fix and coax. No subtlety slowed down the slam of my attraction to Des. Sex sat right on the surface of our every interaction.

"I wish I hadn't promised the fellas I'd meet up, so," Des told me over his second cup of tea. "I'd rather pass the night here." Late-shift work turned his sleep schedule upside-down, he explained, and he'd made a plan ages ago to meet his mates in an after-hours club tonight. He'd never live it down if he bagged on them. It was just as well because I didn't trust myself. I'd think of him lying awake down the hall while I was trying to sleep.

I couldn't remember the last time I'd just had sex for sex's sake. Probably the break-up sex with my last boyfriend Noah. By the time we broke up, I hated him so much that he was like a stranger. It had been like role-playing; me taking all of my anger and aggression on him in bed. Too bad the only hot sex happened the last time I ever saw him. And before that, it was Josh. Sweet, reliable Josh. Our sex together had all the heat of a firm handshake. I'm not sure which of us liked it less, but neither of us ever mentioned the embarrassing fact that zero sex was had the last three months of our time together.

I thought of Maggie constantly telling me that I just needed to get laid. For the first time, it dawned on me that she was right. And I wasn't even drunk! Out of my comfort zone, away from my New York structure, I was seeing everything in a new light. Even a stranger like Jordan told me I needed to break my own rules.

I stole a sneaky look at Des's long, jean-clad thighs. His legs splayed open in a deep triangle as he reclined on his kitchen chair, luring my eye up to the bulge under his zipper. Bad girl, Shayla. Even though Maggie told me to get laid, she'd strictly forbidden doing it with her cousin because of his reputation. The thought made it even hotter.

Des finally peeled himself away from the table. From the door to the kitchen, he said, "I'm going for a bath." I could swear the next words he whispered were, "Come along if you're dirty" but it was hard to hear with Auntie Fiona bellowing "On the Rocky Road to Dublin", as she carried her wicker basket through the hall.

Sitting down with her own cup of tea, Fiona asked me about where I was born and where I grew up, and how I passed my time. I complimented her house and was told it was technically a bungalow and less than a kilometer from the water. It had been passed down, she explained, and they were lucky to have it. Property prices had skyrocketed in recent years, she explained. She asked about my family, and did I follow sports or politics or pop stars. Not once did she ask me where I went to university, or what I did for a living. When I mentioned I was a writer she said that was grand, and asked if I didn't come to interview that young chef from Castle Stone and left it at that.

Bringing a fresh pot to the table, Auntie Fiona asked, "Is the tea all right with ya, or would you care for something stronger?"

The scalding hot, milky tea was exactly what the doctor ordered. And something stronger might impair my judgment in the Des department. No, tea aired with the simple, filling pie and potatoes was fine. It left me with the effect of being wrapped in a soft quilt. "The tea is good. Everything is good." With Des out of the picture, I relaxed in the unhurried atmosphere. Everything was nice and simple. Until my brain shot out signal flares. Tom O'Grady. I remembered why I was here in the first place. I had to get a win. If I didn't, what else did I have?

"How far away is Castle Stone from here? Does the train or bus go there directly? Do you have wifi? Would you mind if I jumped on it?"

"Easy now. Tomorrow's another day. Have yourself a bath, why don't you?"

Was Des gone? I wondered. A flash of my lowering my naked self onto his body in the tub sizzled through my brain.

"Help yourself to anything you fancy in there," she said.

Oh dear God.

"We've all sorts of lotions and potions," she continued. I let out my breath. "Now that our eldest has moved out, we let that room here and there during the high season. Make yourself at home. Sure, you've flown over the Atlantic, for heaven's sake! You deserve a long lie-down."

I hesitated.

"Work'll keep," she insisted.

I pushed past my normal tendencies and took her advice. I gathered my pajamas and toothbrush from my case. The house sat quiet. Des must have left. I felt a twinge of regret in my nether parts, but told myself that it was for the best. One less thing to think about.

Upstairs in the bathroom I filled the tub with steaming water and threw in a liberal handful of seaweed bath salts. I lay all the way back, submerging my head so that only my mouth and nose protruded from the water. It sounded the way a large conch shell does when you press your ear to its side. We used to call it, "listening to the ocean." It sounded like a woman's voice, and as if I just listened that little bit harder, I might be able to make out what she was saying. The tone was beckoning, I just couldn't make out the message. I lay there trying until the water went cold, then pulled myself back out into the world. Back in my room, I was asleep before my head hit the pillow.

I awakened at 5:30 a.m. and the house was still. There was no danger of Des getting up soon, and surely Auntie Fiona slept past dawn. I padded quietly into the kitchen and looked for a coffee maker. No luck. I couldn't remember a day since I was fifteen that I hadn't started my morning with a cup of coffee. There was, however, an electric tea kettle. I'd always considered these a waste of space. Funny how everyone in Ireland has one and no one in America does. Who couldn't heat water on the stove?

Why bother with a kettle? When the water boiled before I could even put a teabag in a mug, I had my answer. I went for the milk in the fridge, even though I never drank milk in tea at home. It was like I was on autopilot, being called by the song of the lost souls of the Irish people who'd always put milk in their tea. It felt weird, but I had to admit that the tiny pint-sized plastic jug, and the unapologetic way it called whole milk "full fat" charmed me.

Not only did I not start my day with my usual cup of coffee, I couldn't check my phone or email because I wasn't set up for that yet. It dawned on me that I had no idea what to do about phone service. If I just tried to use my phone, each call might cost a mint, and I couldn't afford to throw money around. I'd left so fast and without a thought about practical matters. Worse yet, my brilliant brain couldn't figure things out because it wasn't my playing field. I was not the master of my universe. But then, had I ever been?

It wasn't quite six o'clock and I had nothing to do. I was itching to call Tom O'Grady, but I didn't know how to use the phone. I felt vulnerable; like if there was a disaster, I wouldn't know the drill. "No, Shayla!" I told myself, nipping it in the bud. Go out and get some fresh air and this idea will seem better when the sun comes up. I crept up the stairs, still in my pajamas, and quietly brushed my teeth. I heard the front door open and some jingling keys being put on a hook. I heard Des clear his throat and I slipped through the bathroom door, intending to race back to my room before he saw me. Which would have been the best possible thing. Obviously. Instead, what happened was this: With Des's high energy and long stride, he was up the staircase, and standing in front of me before I could think. His blue eyes lit up the dark like a couple of headlights and I was frozen. I couldn't look away.

Before I could take a breath, his mouth was on mine, and my arms were wrapped around his neck, me standing on tippy-toe, gasping for air. His lips were firm and insistent. I tried to whisper "no," but the thought of waking Auntie Fiona quieted my voice. I signaled with my body that we should stop, that it was too risky, we'd get caught. He met every bend of my neck and every jolt of my hips like a tango master. Every touch, every push and grind made me forget why I wanted to stop.

He tasted like fresh beer and spearmint gum; it was the taste of being wild with a boy at a club. I was only wearing a thin t-shirt and no bra. His hand kneaded my breast and I leaned into it. He picked me up at the waist, me straddling his long frame sloppily, and he dragged me into his room, the closest one to the bathroom.

"Oh," he moaned, "Shayla, I am going to give it to you like you have never had it before." Just like that. No discussion. No request for permission. My mind was sizzling and my body melted. No man had ever talked to me like that before. All my other lovers had gone out of their way to be chivalrous, real 21st-century men, determined to prove how sensitive they were. It was clear that Des planned to take what he wanted. His attitude electrified me and I was right behind him. I couldn't stop now if I wanted to. I wasn't leaving this tangle till my tension got relieved.

He lay me back on the bed and peeled my shirt up. He scraped the stubble of his beard up my belly and covered my nipple with his mouth, circling his tongue and humming with pleasure. It lit me on fire. Then, pulling his head up and panting into his mouth, I reached down to undo the snap on his jeans. I popped it open and tugged at the zipper, all the while wrapping my legs around his pelvis, trying to grind into his hardness.

He untangled my greedy fingers from his hair and pulled my shirt up over my head, only stopping our hungry kiss long enough to pull the collar past our mouths. With the skill of a magician, he used one of his hands and his knee to strip off my jogging pants and panties while keeping me drunk with kisses and teasing my aching breasts. I didn't recognize myself, I was so out of control. When he shifted to wriggle his jeans past his slim hips, I actually pouted and humphed. A second was too long to wait for contact. I was long past having manners. What we had here was a matter of need, not want. Slowing down would be like trying to turn a cruise ship around.

The feeling of his hot skin pressed against me from my ankles to my cheek set off something primal. I grabbed the length of him with my whole hand and stroked it to the tip. Uncircumsized. The newness of it drove me wild.

"Now," I demanded, forgetting to whisper.

"Oh, God, Shayla, yes, yes," he chanted again and again as he ripped open a condom packet with his teeth and reached down to roll it on. I swung up on top of him, balancing myself by digging the heels of my hands into his pubic bone like it was the horn of a saddle. I loved that part of a man. Especially a tall, skinny one like Des.

I lowered myself down, taking him in all at once, not bothering to tease. By the way he used his fingers, I could tell Des had been around the block a time or two, and with women, not just girls. I slid up and down, taking full advantage of the fact that I'd claimed the top position, and ground into that bone, taking him deeper and deeper. "Oh dear fuck, Shayla," he whispered. "That is delicious."

At that point, I closed my eyes, and went into a kind of trance, nearly forgetting that Des was there. Up to this point in my life, I had never, never taken what I wanted so aggressively. I was Super Woman, capable of anything. From that point forward, it was all hands, and mouth, and pounding. I worked hard and got what I came for. I changed my movement to near stillness, and was rewarded by electric pulsing from where I was sitting.

"Shayla," he moaned.

"Shh!" I warned him. "Ah-ah-ah-ah!" I cried out, forgetting utterly about keeping this secret from Auntie Fiona. I couldn't have stayed quiet if I'd tried.

Oh. My. God. I felt so loose, so calm. I flopped over onto his chest, and listened to my own heartbeat for a few seconds. He didn't say a thing. Like I said, he was good at this. Way better at it than I would have given him credit for. I rewarded him with a firm kiss on the mouth. He was still inside me, "Lie back," I told him, "here comes yours."

I left Des sleeping, washed up, and quietly pulled on some clothes. There was no hairdryer to be found, let alone a curling iron or a pair of straightening tongs. God, I hated dealing with all this hair. What happened to the days of wash-and-wear? Deep down, I knew Maggie was right about how a 20-something's coiffure was supposed to look in the city, but I didn't have the time nor the patience to maintain an amazing style that was meant to look effortless. I ran a comb through it, but it was not interested in being tamed. The clock said 7 a.m. I threw my wallet and new journal and pen into a tote. There were keys on the hooks by the door. I had to lock the door behind myself. I found the right one on the third try and set out walking in the pre-dawn glow, hoping that this was a safe neighborhood. I could smell salt water, so I tried to use my lizard brain to find the seafront. Auntie Fiona had said it was about a kilometer away. "About a mile," I thought. Then I questioned myself. The half-assed attempts to teach us the metric system in school hadn't really stuck. I walked blindly on, hoping I'd get where I wanted to go sooner or later.

I sat down on a flat rock and gazed out at the horizon. Breathtaking was the only fitting word for it. I pulled out my journal and wrote:

Dear Mags, It's hard to believe I'm in Ireland sitting on a seawall, watching the sun rise. The blazing orange and pink of the sun is illuminating everything, but leaving the edges soft. I wish I could show it to you. Sunrises, like dreams and falling in love, mean so much to the person they're happening to, and always pale in the description. There are plumes of smoke rising from the chimneys of the clean-lined houses, scenting the air. It doesn't smell like the smoke from houses upstate. It's earthier than woodsmoke, and mixed with the sea breeze, it calls to mind both dried blood and babies being born. It's not unpleasant, though. The only word I can think of to describe it is organic.

I think the air here is giving me superpowers. With each breath I take, I feel like I'm connecting. To the rock I'm sitting on, to the calling birds, to the tall grasses waving in the breeze. It all looks so foreign and unfamiliar. The rugged landscape, the quirky rusted red and brown tug moving along next to the wooden fishing boats. I wonder if this actually is the prettiest view I've ever experienced, or if it's simply the post-coital buzz talking. Oh, right. I suppose I have to tell you: I had sex with Des. I know, I know! It just happened. I'm glad, though. I wouldn't have wanted to break my dry spell with someone real, if you know what I mean. I got it out of my system. There. Done. Weeeeeelll, maybe it's not quite out of my system. Don't get me wrong. I'm not in love with him or anything, but you know that expression, "A taste of honey's worse than none at all?" I have to admit, it was pretty good for a desperate quickie. And look, I know Des didn't go to college or write a book, or cure polio, but that's OK. Am I a snob for saying he's not husband material? On the other hand, maybe marriage could be pretty sweet if you got a dose of that every night. Whatever, he's pretty cute and it was super-fun for what it was. I'd die of embarrassment if your aunt found out, but if I had the chance to do it again, I feel like I might. The truth is, I don't feel like myself. But in a good way. Have you ever sat quietly, and said your name over and over, and asked yourself, who am I, really? What does it mean to be me? Well, you probably haven't. You're so much more grounded than I am. When I was a little girl, I felt ethereal and unformed, like I hadn't landed in my body yet. I thought that when I grew up, it would click into place and I'd feel whole. I'm still waiting, I guess. But today, I don't know…I feel more like I'm in here, you know? I think I'm getting a glimpse of what it would be like to land in…well…me

All right, the sun's completely up now, and I see what looks to be a touristy coffee shop by the waterfront. I don't even have any Irish currency yet. Cross your fingers that they take plastic, because

I think a cappuccino is in order before I pick up the phone to call Tom O'Grady. I'll let you know how it goes! Love, Shay.

Walking back to Auntie Fiona's with my large takeaway latte, I unzipped my fleece a few inches so I could soak up the maximum amount of sun. After the early morning sex and the caffeine boost, the only thing that could make me feel better would be sealing the deal with Tom O'Grady. I walked up the drive and turned the key in the lock as quietly as I could. As I was fiddling with it, the door swung open and I stood face-to-face with a girl with shiny dark hair, pulled into a high ponytail. She had on a full face of evening makeup.

"Hiya," she said. "Come through."

I peered behind her to make sure I was in the right house. I saw the back of Auntie Fiona's head at the kitchen table, where she was sipping tea. I combed back through the stories Maggie had told me. Her uncle had passed away at a young age, and I thought Fiona only had the two boys, Des, and Michael, who was married and out of the house.

"Is that Shayla?" Auntie Fiona called. "C'mere till I tell ya! Ashleigh here has a friend, Mary, who works in the stables over by your man Tom O'Grady at Castle Stone."

"She only started in the stables doing work experience, but that can turn into a position if you prove yourself. Mary's done just about every job on the grounds, there. In less than five years, she's worked her way up to the position of 'Director of Volunteer Learning' and she oversees the whole program. Not a day goes by that she doesn't swear she owes her whole career to my brother Timmy, who arranged to wipe her juvenile arrest records clean, and get a few business owners to claim she'd worked for them." Ashleigh positively beamed with pride. I was speechless.

She poured herself another cup of tea and looked at me. "Why are you faffing about? Sit down, will ya?" She fetched another mug, and poured me a cup of tea, to which she added milk without asking. Maybe I had the story of Maggie's family wrong. Was this Des's sister? Was there a brother named Timmy?

"Does work experience mean an internship?" I asked blandly, hoping that how this girl fit into the puzzle would be revealed through conversation

"Internship? What's that when it's at home?" Ashleigh cackled. "You know, work experience, like when they hire you for no wage. Sometimes they feed you and keep you. I did that after cosmetology school and the spa kept me on. I can't strictly say I passed the written exam," she said, winking, "but Timmy found a way around it. Who asks you what your scores are when you're slathering their face with Dead Sea Mud, anyway? Now, I'm a fully licensed aesthetician," she said, puffed up with pride again. "In fact," she said, examining my hair critically, "If you're stopping here for a while, I could do something about your color. No offense, but you've got roots to Jaysus and that shade of blonde is washing you out like a ghost."

"I'm sorry, I'm Shayla," I said, reaching to shake her hand. "I'm Fiona's niece Maggie's best friend."

"Sure I knew that. Des told me you came last night.

"He told you what?" I said, panic rising.

"He told me he gave you a ride."

"Well, he, um," I couldn't think of what to say. "Who are you, exactly?"

I'm Ashleigh, Des's fiancée."

"Wow," was all I could manage to say. "That's…wow. I did not know that."

Des came skidding down the hall like Tom Cruise in Risky Business, all socks and underpants. He looked panicked. "Shayla! Ashleigh! I thought you wouldn't be here until lunchtime."

"Finally, the dead arose and appeared to many," Auntie Fiona quipped into her cup of tea. "Have you forgotten the two of you are due in at Father Flanagan's at 11 a.m.?

"And put your trousers on, for feck's sake! There's a lady at the table. I apologize for him, Shayla. He behaves like a savage."

"Tell me something I don't know," I thought, slowly adding spoonful of sugar to my tea like I was performing brain surgery. Maybe if I didn't talk, they'd all go away.

"He acts like an eejit. Feel free to give him a right schkelp, if you like."

I looked at Des for guidance. Had I, already?

"I'm having a bath. Could someone bring me a cuppa tea in there?" and he disappeared off down the hall.

"Not me!" I called, involuntarily. "Of course not, because…it's not my house, is it?"

All the tension I'd shaken off down by the water was back, mixed in with a healthy dose of panic. Well, that'll teach me to be impulsive. Maybe having a rigid set of rules wasn't such a bad idea.

Ashleigh laughed heartily. "Shayla, you're gas! Are you married?"

"Nooo. Not married. At all." I glanced involuntarily down the hall toward the bathroom where Des was, presumably, naked. Snapping my eyes back to Ashleigh's face, I picked up my cup of tea and finished it in one glug. Auntie Fiona immediately poured me another cup. At this rate, I could just float to Castle Stone.

"I also don't have a boyfriend, or any dates, or a lover." Eeuuww. Lover. Why would I say that? Nervous, I ladled sugar into my tea. "In fact, I'm a lesbian."

Whaaat? Why would I say *that*? Ireland isn't Manhattan. Probably even lesbians didn't go around blurting out that they were lesbians. Good thing I wouldn't be here long. Auntie Fiona stirred her tea. "Well, to each their own, as they say. Erm, you and Maggie aren't…?"

"No, God no, Maggie's with Eric." I turned to Ashleigh and said, "Eric is a man."

"Ha!" she barked. "I should hope so! Imagine the sight of a girl called Eric. Brutal! Anyway, your secret's safe with me.

"It's not a secret," I said, defensively. I didn't think gay people should hide in the shadows. But then again, I wasn't gay. I was just digging myself in deeper every time I opened my mouth. "I mean, if I were in a relationship, it wouldn't be a secret."

"Well, we won't tell Father Flanagan, at least," she said, with a big wink. "Des and I are going for pre-marriage classes. It's where the priest tells you what it means to be a married Catholic, and you swear to obey the commandments and raise your kids right, and what have you."

"Again, wow. Just, many happy returns to the both of you. And now, Auntie Fiona, if you wouldn't mind helping, I have to get my phone and computer set up so I can call Castle Stone."

Ashleigh carried on, blind to my discomfort and attempts to get out of the massive grave I'd dug myself.

"Mary's told me a few things about Tom O'Grady, the first being that he's dead sexy. She said there's not a girl who works there that hasn't made a fool of herself trying to turn his head, especially the one at the front desk. Can't think of her name, Catherine? I can't remember. But you'll spot her. She's a right wagon. 'Course, you'll be immune to his charms, you liking the girls and all.

Recalling the photo of Tom in his workshirt, I doubted it.

"Next, she told me he's mean as a snake. She was there well before he came back to fancy the place up. In the end she was glad he did, mind you, because it was falling to ruin. She thought she'd be made redundant if it was run into the ground. Now, there are more guests than they have rooms for most times of the year, and the wedding trade is booming even with the top-shelf prices they charge. No chance we could afford it. It's kegs of beer in the church basement for us, but it'll be a laugh, won't it Fiona?"

Auntie Fiona replied, "We'll make sure it's a grand wedding, don't you worry."

My mind was still back on Tom O'Grady. "That chef, at the castle…did Mary say in what way he's mean? Does he, like, throw things at his employees?"

"No," she laughed, "nothing of the sort. It's more that he's short with his answers, and quiet-like. She said he's not one to joke, and you never know where you stand with him. Every time she's asked him for a pay rise, he's given it, but she has to work up her nerve for days to walk into his office because he's so cold.

There's a certain type of girl that's drawn to that type, though. The dark ones they can't get their hands on. Waste of time, to my mind. Grab a thick one like, Des, and you know where you stand. Some say it's to do with that girl from his TV show…what's her name? Ah, doesn't matter. She treated him badly or some such, and blackened his heart. To my mind, though, how scary can the fecker be? He's a chef, for cryin' out loud, not a boxer or a bouncer at a club." I suspected Ashleigh and I had different definitions of what constituted scary. Still, her story made me want to call him even less than before.

I rose reluctantly from my chair. "If you'll excuse me, I need to figure out how to get my computer online so maybe I can Skype him."

"Ring him from here, pet! Won't cost us a thing extra with our phone plan. No point worrying about connecting all your gadgets and doo dahs when we have a perfectly good telephone just waiting to be used. There's an extension in your room.

"Thank you," I said, setting my mug in the sink. "I'm hoping I won't be on long. Hopefully I'll be heading to Castle Stone to interview him today."

"Stay as long as you like," Auntie Fiona said. "The company will do Des good. Now Ashleigh, where are those wedding magazines you promised?"

On my way to my room, I heard Des sigh in the bath. Unfortunately, it was now a sound my muscles remembered, and they yearned for him without the permission of my brain. I vowed to stop thinking of him, and went into my room away from home, to look at the folder with Tom O'Grady's details.

I sat cross-legged on the bed and took a deep breath, and punched in the number.

"The Grange Hall. Can I help?"

"May I speak to Tom O'Grady? I'm calling from Brenda Sackler's office, in New York."

""Would you mind holding for a just a moment, please?" The same traditional Irish music as last time trilled on in the background while I held.

"I'm very sorry but Chef O'Grady is busy at the moment. Can I take your details and let him know you rang?"

"Is he there?"

The girl hesitated, so I pounced.

"It's urgent. Will you please help me? I'll hold for an hour if I need to."

"Chef asked me to tell you…"

"So he is there!"

I could feel her caving. I went in for the kill. "Listen, if I don't speak to him, I'll lose my job. You can understand that, can't you?"

"Ah, sure. We all know what that's like."

"So you understand. I promise I won't get you into trouble. In five minutes, will you try again? Don't tell him my name. Just say it's his agent from New York. Please?"

"I'll leave you on hold, then. No telling how long it'll take, or if he'll come to the phone."

"Thank you! I'll hold forever!"

Her voice was again replaced by the jaunty tune. I leafed through the photos and fact sheets again, even though I'd done it a dozen times. The door to my room opened and Des slipped inside, wearing only a towel.

"What are you doing?" I whispered, panicked. "Your girlfriend, no, your fiancée, is out there with your *mother*. You cannot be naked in my room."

"I just popped in to say thanks." The nerve of him!

"Thanks? Really?"

"Yeah, really. It was incredible. I enjoyed that, I did."

"Get out of here! Now!"

"Who's that fella, then?" Des asked, looking upside down at the photos of Tom O'Grady. He walked over and picked up a headshot.

The hold music stopped abruptly. "Hello, this is Tom O'Grady."

"Is that your boyfriend?" Des asked.

I covered the mouthpiece with my hand. "Get out!" I whispered.

"What was that?" Tom asked.

"Yes, hello. Mr. O'Grady," I began. "*Get out!*" I hissed at Des. I frantically waved my arms toward the door.

"Dessie?" I heard Ashleigh call from the kitchen.

"Hello? Who's ringing?" Tom O'Grady asked.

"Good morning, Mr. O'Grady, it's me, Shayla Sheridan from Brenda Sackler's office in New York." Des sat down and rooted through the stack of photos. I shoved him by the hip, pushing him away from the bed. "I'd like to talk to you about your book." The clasp of my bracelet snagged on Des's towel, leaving him naked.

"We've been over this, Miss Sheridan, there is no 'my' book." Des bent over and nibbled my neck.

"Get dressed," I hissed, slapping him away.

"What's that?" Tom O'Grady asked. I was distracted by the growing evidence of Des's affections toward me, and had trouble focusing. He had moved on to massaging my shoulders.

"I was just saying, Mr. O'Grady, *get off,* that I have a list of reasons why seeing this book to completion will be to your benefit." This time I was actually prepared. I'd jotted notes on a sheet of paper during the flight, but where were they?

"Just one second, please." I scattered some papers around haphazardly, looking. I knew it was to do with appealing to high-end cuisine magazines, or something, but my brain wouldn't work with Des sucking on my neck. I saw the list stuck to Des's thigh, which was still damp from the bath.

"Des?" Ashleigh called. I could hear footsteps coming down the hallway.

"Point One," I read off the damp page with the now-bleeding ink, "Since the last time we spoke, I've researched the most elabo-rate menu offerings of every restaurant for which you've ever worked." I stood up and used my shoulder to body-check Des off the bed. I heard a hand on the doorknob.

"And?" Tom O'Grady prompted.

Des just managed to scoop up his towel, wrap it around his waist, and cover his lap with a pillow in order to mask his now full erection. "Des? Ashleigh asked, eyebrows raised.

"And, um, Point Two," I said into the phone. I couldn't read what I'd written since the ink was dripping. Again, I was left to winging it.

"Shh! She's on the line." Des crossed his legs and pointed at me, in case Ashleigh was confused about whom he was speaking.

"Point Two: Emphasize your skills in presentation, to interest magazines in doing features on you, thus furthering your brand."

"We have to meet the priest. What are you playing at?" Ashleigh asked in full voice.

"Shh! I begged. "I'm so sorry, Mr. O'Grady. Just one second."

"It's not what you think," Des said to Ashleigh, whispering. He must have felt sufficiently chastened at this point, because he managed to stand up. "Nothing happened."

"Mr. O'Grady? Are you still there?" I asked.

"Yeah, I'm here. I'm thinking."

"Course nothing happened," Ashleigh bellowed. "Shayla's a lesbian, you could waggle it in her gob and she wouldn't give it the time of day. Now get on with ya. We'll be late. Ashleigh pushed Des into the hall and followed, closing the door.

"Mr. O'Grady?" I couldn't tell if he'd hung up.

"It just isn't going to work. You sound bright enough, but this whole thing just isn't me."

"Please, Tom!" Oops. I waited for him to bristle at the familiarity, but he didn't. "Just give me a chance."

"My answer is no. I don't want to elaborate. If I ever reconsider, I'll try to remember your name." With that he put down the phone. I fell onto the bed in a heap, defeated. I didn't have the book. I didn't have a job. I was in a foreign country. I'd just had sex with a guy who's engaged. Everything was so overwhelming, I just switched off. I shut down my brain and drifted into a tortured sleep in which I never got comfortable because I was rolling around on top of my folder of headshots and press clips. My unsettling dreams featured disparate scenes woven together from the Book Expo's Bo Peep outfit, the screams of the gulls at the waterfront, and being caught rolling naked with Des by a looming, faceless Tom O'Grady.

Auntie Fiona woke me at half past six, saying she was worried about me. I'd been asleep all day. I was still as tired as if I'd never closed my eyes. She told me to sit in the bath awhile, then join her in the kitchen for a bite. I listened hard, but couldn't hear any sign of Des. I figured it was safe to take off my clothes. I filled the bath to the rim with warm water and simply allowed myself to float. I tried to empty my head, but Tom O'Grady's voice kept echoing through it.

After pulling on some yoga pants and a hoodie, I took out my journal.

"Dear Maggie, I've just made the most expensive phone call in history. If you factor in the last-minute plane ticket, and the change fee for coming home early, my curt rejection from Tom O'Grady cost me thousands. When will I learn? Wild luck and Hollywood endings are for girls who can walk for miles in pointy-heeled boots and whose lip gloss stays inside the lines. He told me no via phone when I was safely on U.S. soil. What made me fly here to get the same answer on a different phone? I know I've been jealous of you, Mags, for getting good things. But I'm still happy for you and I know you work so hard for them. Maybe Carly the intern and Padma the Exotic and that crafty waitress from 54 Below also work hard and I just don't see it. There's my answer: I just have to work harder. But Mags, I'm tired. It seems I work and work and I'm still standing at the starting line. Oh, well, it is what it is. In a few days, I'll be back in New

When I showed up at the kitchen table, Auntie Fiona put a cup of tea in front of me. I was dying for a java hit. I considered walking down to the coffee place on the water, but I doubted I had the energy. I still hadn't connected my phone or my computer. The apocalypse could have come and I wouldn't have known it.

"Ah, you poor lamb. Everything will seem brighter after you've had your tea. It's not much to speak of. I've cooked bacon and cabbage, and a bit of white sauce. There's onion and some carrot and mashed turnip to go with it. Ah, I've forgotten to toss a few potatoes into the pot. Could you face chips again?"

"Yes, I really could. That sounds delicious." How many nights had I hunkered over the coffee table, editing manuscripts for Lizbeth while eating Doritos and salsa for dinner? I only knew how to cook a few things and my whole adult life I'd been too busy to learn more. "I just realized, I haven't eaten today."

"Bless! That won't do at all. I'll give you some cheese and a bite or two of bread to go with that cuppa. Des and Ashleigh should be back soon enough, but no use in your suffering." Before long, she set a plate before me with two large slabs of cheese, a few slices of apple and some slices of soda bread. I spread a bit of the blue cheese on a corner of the bread and took a bite. It was fragrant and had a wonderful granular texture. It managed to be sharp and creamy at the same time. Washed down with the hot, milky tea Auntie Fiona had just topped up, it was like a meal unto itself. Next I tried the blander looking of the two and found out looks could be deceiving. It had the weight of cheddar in my mouth, but in addition to cheddar's sharpness, it featured the bite of a good Parmesan, along with a nutty, Swiss-like flavor. With my mouth still full, I asked, "What are these?"

"That one's Dubliner, and that one there's Cashel blue."

"Are you a fine cheese *aficionado?*"

"Not a bit. That's just what I pick up down in the market."

"Your everyday cheeses live on a different planet from ours." I didn't even want to admit that I had plastic-wrapped cheese food singles in my fridge.

Just then, Des and Ashleigh came through the front door fighting. "Ah, sure, it's not worth a shite," Ashleigh said, hanging her jacket on a peg. "'lo, Shayla," she said. "Did you get everything sorted with goin' up to Ballykelty to see your chef?"

"Not gonna happen." I popped another slice of Dubliner into my mouth to soothe myself.

"Say it isn't so! Tell us everything." She took an apron off its hook and tied it on. "Fiona, you sit, I'll finish the tea." Auntie Fiona and Des took chairs. I couldn't even be bothered to notice how close Des's body was to mine. I told the short, sweet story of how I got shot down.

"There must be a way around this," Auntie Fiona said. "Shayla, when is your flight back booked for?"

I honestly didn't know. I hadn't paid attention to my flight details, since Maggie had taken everything in hand. At some point over wine at the kitchen table, we'd discussed my staying four days. So, maybe March 23rd? 24th? "I have to check my ticket," I told her, getting up from the table.

"I've a naughty idea," Ashleigh said, cutting potatoes into strips.

"Not in front of my mam," Des mumbled into his teacup.

"Shut your cakehole! I mean about that one needing to be at

Castle Stone." Ashleigh had a chef's knife in her hand, and so far, to me, she seemed like the kind of girl who knew how to use it. If I were Des, I'd watch my step.

I rooted out the printouts from my plane ticket and my boarding passes, but they only reflected the date of my outgoing trip. I scrolled through the emails on my phone, even though I didn't have service. Something might have come through before I'd taken off. There! An email from Maggie spelling out my itinerary and an alert from Aer Lingus. From Mags:

Hey Shay, the cheapest last-minute round-trip I could find has you coming back Saturday the 24th. It would cost a mint to change the ticket, so if you get everything taken care of before then, I know a cheap hotel in Dublin called The Harcourt where you can kill time until your return flight. The airport coach is easy to catch from there...

She went on to suggest places to visit, and to spell out directions for trains and coaches. Little did she know, I was going to have days and days to kill. It was only Wednesday morning and my flight wasn't until late Saturday night. Maggie and I thought that Tom O'Grady might arrange for me to stay free at Castle Stone's cottages or in the hotel. We'd even had a giddy conversation about my being put in one of the Castle Heritage or Master Bedrooms, the ones with the period furnishings. One thing was for sure, I couldn't stay here another night, given the fact that I'd taken Auntie Fiona up on her invitation to "help myself to anything I fancied" in the form of her engaged son. Phone in hand, I took off down the hall, scrolling as I walked. From Aer Lingus:

Dear Ms. Sheridan,
We know you have the choice of many carriers, and we'd like to thank you for choosing Aer Lingus...blah, blah, etc.
I scrolled down.

I stopped walking. Rereading the entire email carefully, "Oh my God and fuck!" I swore.

"Did you need me, Shayla?" Des called into the hallway, half rising from his seat.

I walked in and plonked myself down in a kitchen chair. "I need something," I said, staring into the middle distance. I felt my current need reach out and grab hands with my last unmet need, then the one before that, and so on. A ticket back, an interview, a cover credit, a job, a boyfriend, notoriety, love, a dad. The feeling of emptiness was primal.

Without my consent, two hot fat tears pooled in my eyes until they were giant, then plopped on the cheery yellow tablecloth when I blinked. I willed myself not to give in to more. I didn't speak, knowing if I did, a sloppy sob would escape. Auntie Fiona put her hand over mine; an act of kindness that lured the sob up toward the surface.

Ashleigh set a glass before me. All business, she said, "We've no whiskey, but get that down you, and fast." I took a long pull from the glass of warming Rioja. My first breath came out as a staccato gasp for air, but at least I wasn't crying.

"Good girl," she said. Like a dealer at a blackjack table, she shuffled plates out before us, and one for herself. Taking her place at the table, she gave me a straight look and said, "I've a plan. Fill your belly while I tell you what you're going to do."

Chapter Eight

The truth is rarely pure, and never simple.

For the first chunk of the car trip, Des chatted mindlessly about football scores and what bands would be doing concerts in Ireland during the coming summer. I was so nervous about what would happen once we reached Castle Stone, I kept ignoring the elephant in the car, as it were. If he wasn't going to bring it up, neither was I. We drove along the quay on the way out of town. I was charmed that the road signs were in both English and Irish. I turned off my mind and let the beauty of the landscape wash over me.

"Oh look!" I cried, breaking my silence. "Seals!" I couldn't believe I was seeing sleek, dog-like creatures thumping along on the rocks and diving into the sea outside of a zoo.

"We've got loads of them 'round here. If you wait long enough, sometimes you'll see a whale. Pretty amazing, if you ask me." He looked at me sideways, keeping one eye on the road. "You're pretty amazing yourself."

The lower part of my belly turned to warm liquid as memories of our time in bed flashed through my brain. A hand here, lips there, his breath on my cheek. "Look Des, I didn't know you had a fiancée."

"And I didn't know you were a lesbian," he countered.

"I'm not!" I protested.

He laughed softly. "I gathered that. I'm only taking the mickey. It was smart thinking, though. You've fixed it so we can meet up and no one will think twice."

"That's not why I said it." I thought back. "I'm not a liar, in general. Maybe it was the jet lag or the panic."

"Maybe you weren't a liar up to this point, but you'd better get used to the idea, Sheila Doyle," he teased, chuckling and shaking his head. "You've got to hand it to my Ashleigh and her brother Timmy. If they can't go through a thing, they always find a way to go around it."

My stomach fell. I couldn't believe I'd agreed to this plan. Like a meteor hurtling toward the surface of the earth, I had momentum. There was no way to stop now, and I'd soon crash and burn.

I gripped the car door handle, tense. "I don't think I can do this."

"Ah, you seem a brave one to me. You got on a plane at the drop of a hat. I'd call that downright impulsive. And then, you seduced me. I'd say that was reckless."

"You're the one who grabbed when I was in my pajamas, still wet."

"Mmm…say 'wet' again." He put his hand on my knee.

"Stop it, stop it, stop it," I said pushing his hand away several times in a row. "Stop." I waited, guard up. When I was satisfied that he had his mind back on driving, I explained.

"Fair enough," he said, feigning aloofness. "I was hoping to get you out of them black clothes. For self-preservation purposes. It's depressing to look at in the middle of the day."

"What's wrong with my clothes?" I had on a long-sleeved, scoop-necked black tee, a pair of black wool Anne Taylor sailor trousers, a black silk cardigan, and a pair of black patent boots. One of my work outfits. "I think I look fine."

"For a Portuguese widow. You looked prettier in your pajamas. Better still in your birthday suit."

"OK, time to get this straight. It's not like me to jump into bed with guys I don't know. I never would have done it if I knew you were engaged."

"Engaged isn't married."

"I'll bet Ashleigh would have a different view."

"There's no call to involve Ashleigh in our affairs. When I'm married, I'll behave."

"I doubt that." I thought back to the year my parents had separated. Mom and I had moved upstate with Grandma and Poppy. I'd gone to school there for 5th grade. When my parents reconciled, I asked if I could just stay in Rhinebeck. I was so angry. Even though no one spelled it out, I got the sense that Hank had cheated on her. I just knew. Looking back, I'm glad Mom said no. It would have meant losing precious time with her. "Anyway, I have a rule: I don't sleep with married men."

"I'm not married yet. We have until the autumn if you fancy another go."

"No thanks." The truth was, I did fancy it. Apart from the fact that it was just wrong, Ashleigh had gone to a lot of trouble to help me. It could never happen again.

"Suit yourself, but the door's open until I'm legally wed."

"Oh, look! There's a Costa," I said, changing the subject. "I'll buy you a cup of coffee if you'll stop."

"Can't have you getting the shakes now, can we? Tea's more my speed, but I'm happy to oblige if it'll bring you pleasure."

We didn't speak of what happened between us again. He turned up the radio, and bopped happily along to classic rock as we sped around the sharp turns and roundabouts that dotted our drive. My mind drifted off to Maggie. The very second I got to Castle Stone, I had to call her, even if I did it collect from a pay phone. This scheme Ashleigh had cooked up may have sounded practical around Auntie Fiona's table when we were all sipping Rioja and possibly even early this morning among complete strangers while I was filling my face with sausages and fried potatoes, but now I saw it for what it was: insane. I couldn't stay here till September.

I had bills to pay, rent on an apartment. I'd talk to this Tom O'Grady, and if he said no, I'd just head to Dublin and call the whole thing off. I pushed all thoughts of how I was going to come up with two grand for a flight out of my head. With my lingering jet lag and only half a cup of coffee in me, I could only tackle one problem at a time.

Before I knew it, we were off the highway and driving through the main road of a picturesque village. There were stone walls along one side, covered in ivy and flanked by an impossibly narrow sidewalk. The houses and shops were humble and squat, none more than three stories tall, and some were topped with sloping triangular roofs and even spires.

"It's gorgeous," I breathed. There were flower boxes lined up on the other side of the road, with tender daffodils and crocuses poking through the soil, and the shuttered windows featured window boxes filled with the same, plus green shoots, yet to reveal their natures. "Flowers!"

"Mam says the early blooms signal a hot summer ahead. I don't mind the heat, but the sun doesn't agree with me. I went to Ibiza with some mates last year and came home looking like a boiled lobster.

There she is. If you look ahead, you can see the castle just there, at the top of the hill."

And there it was, to me like something from a film. All stone walls, pointed rooftops and chimneys, one side covered in lush green moss. There simply are no buildings in America that look like this. It was, in a word, ancient.

"This is going to sound stupid, but I thought castles were supposed to be bigger."

"Maybe so, but it's still quite a pile."

"Totally! I didn't mean that it's not spectacular. I guess I was picturing Cinderella's castle from Disney World, or the one from Rob Roy.

"Some might call Castle Stone a manor house. We were taught

in school that the old castles were on the smaller side in order for the inhabitants to be able to see enemies approaching from all sides, so they could defend themselves. When we get to the top of the hill, you'll see the other buildings on the estate. The place is huge. Something like 1000 acres if I remember right. Can you fathom it? That huge tract of land and everything on it is owned by one man! The Earl of Wexford himself. Born to it. Luck of the draw, and you're the man! He's a bit of a crank, the old Earl. I heard he went to a wedding in the village wearing only his pajamas and a top hat."

"You can't be serious."

"Ah, who knows what the truth is? When you're rich, you can do what you like, can't you?"

We turned off the town road and onto the private drive leading to the castle and I drank in the view. A thrill went through my body. There were green lawns as far as the eye could see, really green lawns. The manor house was at the center, and extending from one side there was a long, roofed walkway made from the same stone, with arched window after arched window. At the end was a taller structure with a glass roof.

We drove through heavy, wrought-iron gates, surrounded by a tall, irregular stone wall. As we continued along the main drive, I could see myriad paved service roads leading to other, smaller houses, a circular cul-de-sac of cottages, and even a chapel. There were no fewer than five or six horses in my sightline, some trotting along dirt paths, one galloping at top speed right across the green grass toward a lake.

Des drove slowly, as the signs warned guests not to spook the horses. There were gardeners clipping at shrubbery and digging in the peaty dirt. We passed a group of ladies, all of a certain age, walking leisurely alongside the drive. I assumed they were guests of the hotel. A golf cart with four men of mixed ages, all dressed for the game came into view in the near distance. "There's a golf course?"

"Sure, there is. You can golf, fish, row in the boats, ride a horse, whatever you fancy. The guests can, I should say. You, Sheila Doyle, are here for work experience."

I felt sick. "Stop calling me that."

"You'd better get used to it. I'll make you a bargain, though. If you'd care to join me in my bed again, I'll happily call out your real name. But here at Castle Stone, you're Sheila now."

Chapter Nine

A closed mouth, a wise head.

My hand refused to pull the door handle. I sat in the hot car, watching guests and workers enter and exit the main doors to the huge, old building. It would be so easy to have Des start the car again and drop me off where the airport bus could pick me up to take me back to Dublin. In less than a day, I could be curled up in my own bed back in New York. I turned to Des and said, "I've been thinking it over. There's something else I need from you."

He unbuckled his seat belt and straddled me before I could see it coming. His open mouth covered mine and his hand was on the bare skin of my belly, inching upwards.

I wrenched my head sideways and screamed, "Des, get off of me." As I pushed him back with both arms, I caught a silver-haired matron in sturdy walking shoes out of the corner of my eye. She looked directly at me and tsk-tsked. Yanking my shirt down, I elbowed Des in the jaw. "Everyone and his mother can see us! These windows are made of glass, you know."

"Hey!" he cried, covering his head with his hands and retreating to the driver's seat. "I figured doing it in public turned you on. You told me you wanted to!"

"No," I smoothed down my hair and checked my lips in the

rearview to see if they were all puffy and pink. "I said I needed a favor."

"My bad." He shifted in his seat, panting, and rearranged the fabric of his jeans. "What can I do for you?"

"Never mind." Des really was a sweet guy. "Thanks for the ride."

"Call me anytime you want another one."

I laughed despite myself and forced myself to pull the door handle. After Des dropped me at the door of Castle Stone, luggage and all, I was determined to find Mary so I could explain that I wouldn't be staying. After clarifying to the girl at reception that I wasn't a guest, she said, "Ah, you're American. Are you Sheila who's doing work experience in the restaurants?"

I didn't say yes. "I just need to see Mary, please. Is she available?"

"Let me just get someone to show you the way." He led me to Mary, where she was seated at one of the many desks, behind a half-screen.

"Welcome to Castle Stone, Sheila," she said standing to shake my hand. Her hair was cropped close and she wore a forest-green polo with the Castle Stone logo emblazoned on the front, tucked into a pair of chinos, belted at her thick waist. There wasn't a trace of makeup on her wind-chapped face.

"Cheers, I'll take it from here," she said to the uniformed young man, who nodded and left. "So, have a seat, have a seat," she said to me. "Perfect timing," she said, "there's no one around at the moment. Any friend of Timmy's is a friend of mine, so I'm glad to help."

I didn't mention that I'd never met Timmy, or that I'd just slept with his sister's fiancé. "I've been thinking about this whole thing, Mary. I'm really grateful, but…"

"Not at all. Between Ashleigh and me, we figured it all out. I have to keep a file on everyone here on the grounds, so I'll need to copy your passport and all that in case we're audited by immigration. Apart from that, no one but me needs to see the particulars. I'll take care of you." She looked me up and down.

"Make no mistake about that."

She sat back in her chair and smiled. "I'll just misfile the thing, as it were, once I've filed your status with the government. After that, they don't care a whit if we call you Shayla or Sheila or Uncle Sam."

"I'm not really comfortable playing fast and loose with border patrol, so Mary…"

"That's the beauty of it! You'll never earn a penny since you're on work experience. It's not as if the Earl will be breathing down our necks. He's just as happy not to be involved in the day-to-day admin, plus he trusts me. You're grand. The fact of the matter is, I don't have to file with any tax departments or what have you. And," she said winking, "if we do get into hot water at any point, Timmy knows a fella down at the embassy or the green card department — one of them places — who can iron over any wrinkles. Best not to ask too many questions."

"Can I have a word, Mary?" I heard a firm, rich voice behind me say. Infused with authority, the question was more of a statement. I knew without looking it was Tom O'Grady. My breathing sped up.

"Of course, Chef," she said, rising from her chair.

"No, keep your seat. I just wanted to let you know Callum won't be continuing in the kitchen. I'll send him in shortly so you can let him go." I resisted the urge to crane my neck around to get a look at Tom O'Grady.

"Oh, I'm sorry to hear that. I'll take care of it. Chef, if you don't mind, I'd like you to meet Sheila Doyle." I swallowed hard, preparing myself to tell him the truth about who I was and make one last-ditch effort to convince him to let me write his book. If only I had a pitch; I needed some hook to convince him why. I stood up, turned around and extended my hand.

"Oh," I breathed. I'm pretty tall, for a woman, but Tom O'Grady is easily a head taller. He sported a blinding white chef's coat that buttoned diagonally up the shoulder, accentuating the broadness of his chest. Instead of the traditional tall, white chef's hat, his unruly dirty-blonde curls were tied back in a black bandana-style head wrap. "Ninja angel," I thought. "Karate pirate." These phrases sat on my tongue, and I didn't dare speak lest they pop out. He grasped my hand firmly and shook it.

Before I could explain who I was, Mary stepped in with, "This is Sheila Doyle, she's training on kitchen duty."

"How soon can I have you?" he asked. I examined his strong jaw. His hair was dirty blonde, but the beginnings of his beard were red-gold.

"What?"

"Mary!" A young boy with a skinny neck protruding from his work polo, and an unfortunately pimply complexion, poked his head around the office door. "The Qatari Princess and her ladies just arrived, and the Earl's sitting in the lounge in his dressing gown watching videos! I haven't read the protocol sheet but I'm fairly certain that won't do."

"If you'll excuse me for just a quick second," Mary said, rushing out the door.

"I asked how soon I can have you." I searched his face. As I waited for him to elaborate, my heart flopped around my ribcage. "It's only that I just let go of that useless what's-his-name and I could use a body. Have you experience?" he wiped his hands on the kitchen towel he carried.

"Not…uh, some." I didn't know how to answer. My breathing had grown shallower. I couldn't get enough air through my nose. My lips parted involuntarily and I was embarrassed to hear myself panting. "I wish I had more."

He narrowed his sleepy eyes and his full mouth pulled up at the corner. Little crinkles appeared at the corners of his eyes. Still, he seemed irritated. "You're from America, I take it." He looked past my face and deep into my eyes. My leg was going numb from being wedged against my chair in the tight space. I could smell him from where I was standing; a combination of heady musk and sharp, tart apple. If I took a step forward, I'd be chest-to-chest with him.

"Yes." I sensed I shouldn't elaborate.

"You're not going to tell me you're from New York City?"

"I'm not." He stood still, waiting. I'm not going to tell you, anyway. Might as well add this to the growing list of lies. "I'm from Rhinebeck, New York State. Way upstate. Nowhere near the city. The city!" I shuddered. "No. Not this girl."

"More the country type, then." He draped his kitchen towel over his shoulder and crossed his arms. He stood there like he had all the time in the world.

"You could say that." I wouldn't, of course, I shifted uncomfortably. My leg was now fully numb. I tried to shuffle sideways from between the desk and chair, dragging it along with me like it was made of wood. Putting weight on it was a mistake. I pitched forward. With lightning reflexes, he caught me by the wrists.

"Easy," he commanded. That voice. It was deep and smooth enough to lull me, but even with that one word, I caught a whiff of condescension that brought me to my senses. Sorry, farmerman. You're not better than I am. Let's see who can write a book and who goes to bed at night smelling of bacon fat. I could feel the Manhattan sass in me rising up. New Yorkers didn't have a reputation for being aggressive for no reason. I inhaled slowly. Baring my teeth wouldn't get me what I needed.

"Don't you have to get back to the restaurant?" I pushed myself back as far against the desk as I could, trying to leave an inch of daylight between us.

He stayed exactly where he was. "I don't have to do a thing that I don't want to do." I could tell by the way he said it that it was true and it flattened me. He didn't want to do this book and he especially didn't want to do it with me. "A few years back, I learned that the key to happiness is pleasing myself."

"Well, that's just unrealistic for most of us," I huffed. Smug, selfish bastard. "Some people have to pay their dues and suffer, and work really hard." I thought back to my awful assistant job at HPC.

"I never claimed not to work hard."

I felt pinned to the wall. "Well, not everyone just gets to do exactly what they want when they want." My skin was hot and prickly. No one handed me a book deal. Manna wasn't dropping out of heaven and into my lap. "Sometimes you have to toe the line."

"Mark my words, Sheila. There's more than one way to skin a cat. I learned that the hard way."

He stared at me and I stared right back.

"Apologies, all. Just had to suggest to the Earl that he might be more comfortable up in his rooms until he was ready to dress for dinner." Mary let out a heavy sigh and plopped down into her chair.

"Mary, you never said new girl was American."

"That she is, Chef," Mary enthused. "But never mind! She's excellent references and she'll fit right in. If it's all the same to you, she'll start in the morning. She's only just stepped in the door, and we've paperwork to sort. Could I possibly pull one of the bar staff to help you in the kitchen, just for today?"

"Fair enough," he said to Mary, still looking at me. "You didn't say, have you been in Ireland before?"

"Never."

"London?" He didn't look away from my face.

"For a week, a long time ago."

"I had a restaurant there," he said, searching. "Maybe that's it."

"Maybe that's what?"

He crossed his arms. "People here call me Chef, you know. And what I was saying was, I can't shake the feeling I know you."

"Well, you don't."

His face darkened.

I knew I sounded rude, but the stakes had been raised. He couldn't find out who I was. In the last two minutes, getting this book done had become the most important thing in the world, and I could tell from the way he was acting that he would never cooperate.

"Thank you for stopping in, Chef," Mary cut in quickly, rising from her chair and literally pushing Tom O'Grady to the office door. "We'll see to Sheila, teach her the rules, make sure she's sorted."

"As long as I can have her for breakfast," he said, walking out.

Once his footsteps faded, Mary turned to me and said, "He must like you."

"Why do you say that?"

"The last girl who talked to him like that was made redundant before she unpacked her bag."

Chapter Ten

A cabin with plenty of food is better than a hungry castle.

Mary opened the door and I peered into the tiny, dorm-style room. On one side was a narrow, single bed, with a locker at the foot. In that corner, there was a school-sized desk, with a single ladder-back chair. The walls were made of cinderblock. The only feature that kept it from looking like a jail cell was the mirror that hung at chair-level.

Across from the bed was a door that I prayed led to a bathroom. That was it. Not a picture on the wall or a shelf to rest a knick-knack on. The only feature that kept it from looking like a jail cell was the mirror that hung at chair-level.

"You'll see that they built the dormitories here, behind the big barns, and the stables. With the mews houses and the self-catering cottages, the guests have to go out of their way to see them. Keeping them simple didn't ruin the views, you see."

Simple was one word for it.

"Now, I don't kip in here myself, I've a room over in the main building. But if there's ever anything you want, or need, I'm but a few steps away." She smoothed back her hair and popped the collar of her polo shirt.

"Thanks, Mary," I said. "Really."

Mary explained that this was the women's section and that bathrooms were shared and down the hall. She told me to leave my bag, so we could continue on the tour of the estate. It took the whole afternoon to cover the sprawling grounds, but Mary told me she was happy to hit every mark because it kept her out of the office. "Having a stretch of the legs on such a fine sunny day'll keep a person fit. I miss working in the stables and tending the gardens with Danny's team."

No wonder Mary was in charge of the program. She was capable of doing nearly every job on the grounds. Turns out, she's a fine horsewoman, having grown up around them herself. She showed me the stables and introduced me to the grooms and student learners. Guests could take lessons, do trail riding, or even check out a horse like a library book, provided they could prove themselves capable.

I couldn't resist taking photos as she walked me around to the greenhouses, which she referred to as "glasshouses" and the "orangerie." There were flowers and vegetables growing in the little tropical oases, and even, Mary explained, hydroponic gardens that didn't require soil. More workers buzzed about repotting this or harvesting that. As hard as I tried, I could not keep up with their names.

Along the way, we met Danny, the head gardener, who looked like he was born to the job. Tiny, elfin, and quiet, he seemed to blend in with the shrubs and wildflowers around him. He didn't seem to say much, but everyone working for him treated him with great respect. "Danny has the original green thumb. Chef brought him in shortly before the restaurants got a face-lift. Not only has he changed all this from overgrown fields to manicured plots and that Japanese water garden there, he's put Castle Stone on the map as far as weddings go."

I couldn't imagine the unassuming little man putting anything on the map. "How did he do that?"

"He does the flowers for the wedding parties, the hall, and

even the chapel. We call him the 'Mother-of-the-Bride-Whisperer.' They'll come in asking for poinsettias in May or a church full of orchids on a beer budget. They walk out every time with exactly what he tells them to get, thinking it's their idea."

"He's the gardener and the florist?"

"Too right, and he works night and day. He's a genius with budgets. I listen at his knee, hoping to learn it all someday. He orders what's in season, repurposes what's at the wedding breakfast for the Mass, and when he likes a family, he'll go out of his way to match the flowers we always have in the hotel to the colors of the wedding. Chef gives him the run of the place, and rightly so."

Mary walked me down to the largest lake, pointing out that there were smaller ones and ponds everywhere. Along the way, we walked across part of the golf course, which was swarming with players due to the fair weather. A gunshot rang out. I ran to the nearest tree and ducked behind it. Mary laughed and laughed. "That's just the clay pigeon shooting. Glenn runs it. He's a safety officer and he's certified by An Garda Siochana to carry out gun competency training lessons. No one's been shot yet. Well, not in the past couple decades, anyhow."

I couldn't believe the array of activities and experiences available on the estate. There was falconry, row-boating and kayaking, dances and live music events in the Main Ballroom, beekeeping lessons, the upscale restaurant and the pub, and a world-class spa.

"Maybe I could treat you to a massage one of these days. If you like that sort of thing."

"Well, who doesn't?

Mary smiled and opened the frosted-glass doors to reveal the spa. I swooned from the earthy, spicy fragrances of the lotions and treatment oils. I longed to sink down into one of the warm tubs with bubbling jets, only to emerge to receive a full-body massage and a calming facial. I had to admit, I was tired. We'd done a lot of walking and the jet lag was catching up with me.

"You look a bit done for," Mary remarked. "I won't walk you

out to the cottage mews or the self-catering cottages today. You can see them just there, over the bluff. It's another 15 minutes along that path." She led me in the other direction, heading back toward the Castle.

"I might as well tell you, I don't know what either of those things mean."

She laughed good-naturedly. "Looks like I'm going to have to show you the ropes," she said with a sly tease. "So, the mews houses were built in the Victorian period. They're set inside an interior courtyard, back out of the way. Lots of privacy. Inside, they're fully modern, of course. Self-catering means you bring your own food and do your own cooking. You can avail yourself of maid service or not, as you like. Big families like to stay there for reunions or what have you. Oh, the O'Grady house, and there's Mrs. O'Grady out the back."

Mrs. O'Grady! Brenda said fiancée, not wife. Maybe I'd gotten the story wrong. Since he'd left his restaurant in London to come back here, the media trail had gone cold as far as his personal life was concerned. I had shots of him posing with local growers, and dignitaries who came to dine at The Grange Hall, but it was all about the food, and only about the food.

I craned my neck to see her, anxious that she'd look like Kate Middleton but curvier, with fresh country roses in her cheeks. Knock it off, Shayla, I chided myself. You came here to get a story. Maybe it'll be easier if you can get the wife on your side. Still, I had to admit that some wind had escaped my sails at the thought of it. I walked a little further around the corner and Mary followed.

The cottage was built of great slabs of stone, severe in their angles and pristinely whitewashed. There was a low stone fence with a gate, and the low windows featured green wooden shutters that matched the front door. Finally, I saw a white sheet billowing in the breeze and a pair of hands taming it into submission onto a clothesline. "How long has Tom, uh, Chef…really, Chef?" Mary nodded soberly. "How long has *Chef* been married?"

"He isn't."

From around the waving bedclothes walked a woman. I broke into a smile. How fabulously, wonderfully beautiful! Tall and sturdy, with a low center of gravity, she wore a vee-necked sweater over a crisp white blouse, and a pleated wool skirt of a sensible length. Her steel-gray curls were cut close enough to her head to keep from being a worry, but not close enough to rob her of her femininity. His mother, I thought. She shielded her eyes from the sun with both hands, examining us, then waved us over. "Good afternoon, Mary!" she called. "And who've we here?" She stood in front of a large wicker basket, folding towels.

We crossed through the gate and into her garden. Everything was tidy and trim and tiny buds of color were raising their heads out of postage-stamp-sized plots and pots. I tried to peer in the window to get a sense of the place. Did Tom grow up here? Calling him Tom in my head made me blush. He'd made it clear that he was Mr. O'Grady, or Chef, to me. Feeling caught out, I looked right and left to make sure no one noticed.

Along one side of the stone wall, a black and white Border Collie patrolled tirelessly from one end to the other and back again, keeping his eyes on the sky. He looked like Pip, my grandmother's dog. I liked him instantly.

"Don't mind that daft beast," she said affectionately. "We call that hunting for angels. No idea why he does it. Nap, when you find one, bring her in for a cuppa tea. We can use all the guardians we can get."

"Mrs. O'Grady, this is Sheila Doyle. She'll be with us doing work experience in the kitchen." She put down a handful of wooden clothespins and took my hand in both of hers. They were warm and pliant, like bread dough.

"You'll be working alongside my son, then," she said, offering a warm smile along with an appraising eye. "Surely you're not local, are you?" I wished desperately that I were wearing something other than my Manhattan street uniform.

"I'm not, Mrs. O'Grady. I'm from America."

"Pretty little thing, isn't she Mary?"

"I'd say so, Mrs. O'Grady."

"Lots of ours went over to the States back in the day. Your name's Doyle, you say?" she squinted at me hard, not needing to look at her towels in order to fold them like a precision machine. The sun felt hot on the back of my neck and I wished I were wearing fewer layers.

"It is," Mary jumped in, "Sheila's all ready to start work in the morning. She's only just arrived, so I'm showing her the lay of the land."

"Have you had a bite to eat?" Mrs. O'Grady asked. "Will you girls come through? I've bacon and some lovely wheaten rolls, and a bit of jam and some nice cheese."

My stomach was rumbling. Something about the air in Ireland left me starving, desperate to get everything I saw inside me. Plus, I could start taking notes for the book, here and now. My senses told me that the secrets to softening Tom O'Grady toward this project blew on the winds around here.

"I was just going to take Sheila to the workers' canteen, Mrs. O'Grady. There's also a workers' pub," she whispered to me.

"I won't have it!" Mrs. O'Grady insisted. She set her basket down on a rough-hewn wooden table and shooed us toward the heavy wooden door. "Come along, girls." It was split in half, from top to bottom, and the top half was wide open to let in fresh air. The lock was huge and rusted on the outside. I could tell it wouldn't accept a shiny modern key cut at a local hardware store. Only a skeleton key would work. I was dying to ask to see it.

The door opened into a very small, cozy sitting room furnished with a small wooden table with a cheery robin's-egg blue oilskin cloth and four wooden captain's chairs. There was a chintz sofa, its back lined with delicate crocheted doilies, and its arms piled with an abundance of embroidered cushions of various colors, shapes and sizes. The fireplace hosted a very small fire. There was no blaze, just a red glow and ambient warmth. Mrs. O'Grady saw me investigating.

"Tom put an efficient woodstove in upstairs. It runs on sustainable wood pellets and he tells me it's more efficient. This fireplace was built with the house, back in the 17th century. When himself and I first married, this is where I made the bread." She gestured to a photo of a solemn man with kind eyes that hung above the sofa. "I only just got a cooker when Tom was toddling about. I still burn peat down here. The smell makes it feel like home, and we rely on a constant fire to keep the roof timbers and the thatch dry. Some say when it burns out, the soul goes out of the people of the house."

My eye was drawn to the crucifix above the mantelpiece with a small red lamp burning beneath it. The lamp looked like it was made from Bakelite. The cord was retro; maybe it was from the '50s. I itched to take out a notepad and to snap some shots with my phone.

"How can I help you, Mrs. O'Grady?" Mary asked.

"If you girls will just boil the kettle, I'll be right down. You'll find butter and jam in the pantry. If you need anything else, you've my permission to root about in the press. I'll do the bacon in a jiffy. I'm just going to pop to the toilet."

Mary walked through and began setting out lunch like a trained waitress, which, to be fair, she was. She'd worked in every aspect of the hotel and she wasn't a bit shy. I admired her. She was one of those women, like Mrs. O'Grady I suspected, who just spotted a need and got the job done. And she was so young. It reminded me what a mess I'd made of my own career back in New York. Nothing I had done built on anything I'd done previously. Mary seemed like a real adult. I certainly didn't feel like one.

On the far wall stood an open cabinet stocked with china. It was a Chinese-looking pattern of birds and trees in brilliant blue against a creamy white background. The centerpiece was a jug and washbasin. It was surrounded by gravy boats, soup tureens, thin china cups, bowls, plates and tiny dishes; it seemed to be a lifetime's collection. I picked up one of the cups and turned it over. Delft.

Mary opened the door to what looked to me like an antique dresser. It was taller than I, made of reddish-brown wood, and had an elaborate chalice carved into the front of it, made up of interlocking knots. She swung open the door and I gasped.

"All right?" she asked, reaching inside and pulling out an earthenware butter dish and a jar of jam.

"It's just…that looks so old. I thought it would break." Furniture like this in my grandmother's house was kept in the 'good' dining room. As a child, I never went in there or the 'good' living room except on Christmas or Thanksgiving. It reminded me how young a country America is in the grand scheme of things and how ancient Ireland is.

"The pantry? No. It's fine. Look." She invited me over for an inspection. I put my hand on the marble shelf.

"It's freezing!"

"'Course it is," she said, looking at me funny. "It's a pantry. How else are you going to keep things cold?"

Before Mrs. O'Grady even returned, Mary had meat sizzling in a pan. It smelled like heaven, honeyed and salty all at once. I peered in at the small, sizzling slices of ham. "I thought she said we were having bacon," I whispered.

"That is bacon, you barmy cow," she said, laughing. In my book bacon came in long strips and had stripes. She seemed pretty sure of herself, though. I didn't argue with her.

"Sheila, perhaps you'd like a chance to wash up?" I was delighted our hostess pointed the way to the bathroom. Making my way down the narrow hallway, I took a chance to inspect the rest of the house. To my left was their formal sitting room. There was a small spinet piano at one end, over which hung a photo of John F. Kennedy, circa 1960. At the other was a wooden podium and a very large crucifix. Arranged around the walls were a number of satin-and-velvet-covered chairs and some end tables.

Instinctively, I ducked my head at the low entrance to the stair-well. I didn't need to, but a tall man might. The wood on the stairs and the bannister was gorgeous. Rich and deep, and polished to a shine. At the top of the stairs, I found the bathroom, used the toilet and washed up. The toilet had a pull flush and the sink taps were separately hot and cold. There was a rubber stopper on a chain dangling in the sink. I set it back beside the bar of French-milled violet soap because it seemed the right thing to do. I dried my hands and left quickly, patting myself on the back for resisting the urge to go through the medicine cabinet.

The landing creaked when I stepped out of the bathroom, so I stood still and listened for a second. I could hear cups clinking and the two women sharing stories. Gingerly, I tiptoed around the door of one of the bedrooms. A quick peek told me it was Mrs. O'Grady's. The simple wrought-iron double bed was covered in a white crewel-work bedspread. On the wall was a wedding photo, which I presumed to be the O'Grady's, and small crucifix, this one chunky and three-dimensional, with a tuft of folded dried palm tucked behind it.

Easing myself around the other side of the landing, I pushed open another door. Tom's room. I told myself I was doing research for the book, but in my heart I knew I was snooping. For the book, I needed to look in his kitchen, not his bedroom.

Photographs of him, mostly in chronological order, took up nearly every inch of space. Children lined up in school uniforms with their smiling teachers in class pictures, graduation photos, Tom standing with various young girls in semi-formal dresses with corsages pinned to their blossoming bosoms, pictures of Tom in chef's whites from various restaurants. Near the door were a whole array of photos of Tom with Tabitha. I recognized her from the promo pictures. Tabitha with Tom on the set of the show, smiling and getting their mic packs attached. Tabitha with Tom, laughing against a backdrop of bleached-out white buildings and Aegean blue sky of Greece. Tabitha with Tom at a family wedding, the bride beaming between the two of them, pulling them closer for a hug. Finally, Tabitha with Tom, head dipped demurely, smiling up through her lashes and holding out her engagement ring. I was dizzy with homesickness. I wanted to be back with Maggie.

"Sheila! Did you fall in?" Mary cackled, and Mrs. O'Grady laughed along good-naturedly.

I scurried down, and around the corner.

"Jaysus, you put the heart crossways in me," Maeve exclaimed in a high-pitched voice, clutching her heart. "Sit yourself down. A pot of tea's hot and waiting on the table."

The two women sat me down and filled me to my toes. Mrs. O'Grady must have asked me a dozen times if I'd like my tea warmed up. She asked if I'd like honey instead of jam, did I prefer soft cheese to the cheddar, and had I gotten enough to eat? I'd like to say I minded my manners and ate like a bird, but the truth of the matter is that I took her up on every offer and didn't leave a crumb on my dish. Everything was just so good. I may have skipped a few meals the week before I left, and maybe I drank my dinner one too many times, but it was as though I'd been on rations up to this point. I thought back. Since I'd stepped foot on the plane, I'd eaten every scrap of what was put before me. It was like I'd been starving to death. I couldn't say why. Of course in New York, eating — or rather, not eating — for women had the status of a competitive sport. Who could order the smallest salad with the least dressing at lunch? Who wanted to eat when the constant stress hovered at fight-or-flight level daily? Even if people wanted to eat, when was there ever time?

To make some gesture of manners, I did manage to mumble, "Oh no, you shouldn't wait on me hand and foot," at some point between butter-slathered bites of bread. I was so relaxed. Maybe it was all of the bready, heavy food talking but it was as though time had stopped. As I thought about it, I realized most of my eating was done at my desk or over the kitchen sink. And when I sat down for a restaurant meal with Hank, I was always on my toes.

"Did you bake this bread?" I asked. The two women burst out laughing.

"'Course I baked it. What do you think?"

I didn't know. At home, it came in plastic bags from Food Emporium, or else I splurged on pricey loaves over at Sarah's Bread. I'd never made bread in my life.

"Can I have the recipe?" I asked. I'd take what I could to get the book rolling, but I wished it were for a more intricate dish.

"You can, sure. And I'll just go slice another loaf. You'll starve while you're sittin' there."

"Please, keep your seat."

"Because I'm an aul lady?" she asked. I was mortified. Before I could sputter an apology, she and Mary laughed. "I'm teasing you. Don't mind it. It's our way. But grant me the pleasure of feeding you two gorgeous girls. It does me good to see you enjoying food at my table. It's true, I am an old lady but I'm fit as a fiddle, and expect to be till the day I join Eoin in the family grave, God rest his soul."

"I'm sorry for your loss," I said. The word loss made me think of my mother, and I felt my eyes sheen over.

"All right, pet?" Her voice softened with such gentle concern, it brought the lump that had been threatening to rise up to my throat. I nodded. I coughed and then managed to say, "Just tired, thanks." When she looked away, I dabbed my eyes with my linen napkin from lunch.

"You know, Tom still doesn't like talking about his Da. He sets flowers on the grave out in the churchyard on Eoin's birthday and whatnot, but keeps his thoughts to himself. As for me, the hurting has dulled and turned to joyful memories over the years. I lost my dear husband 21 years ago this April."

"And have you dated much since then?" I asked taking a sip of tea.

Mary and Mrs. O'Grady looked at each other with raised eyebrows and burst out laughing.

"What's so funny?" I asked.

"It's just, well…" Mrs. O'Grady knit her brow. "I wouldn't know how to explain it."

Mary stepped in. "You see, Sheila, it wouldn't be common for a widow to start keeping company after her husband passed. Not a respectable one, anyhow."

"But why not?" I pressed. "If a Catholic woman is faithful, and her husband dies, then shouldn't she have another chance at happiness?"

Mary's lips struggled to form words. "It's hard to explain, it's perhaps a custom or tradition. I don't even know if it's to do with being Catholic. Maybe it's to do with being from a small village, or with being Irish."

"Does it have to do with widows being past childbearing age?" I asked. I was framing the situation through my New York, feminist, Sarah Lawrence College-lens. Why wouldn't a woman have a right to physical intimacy, regardless of her age? If she remarried, it wasn't adultery.

"It would just be weird to us," Mary blurted. "This isn't New York after all. We don't go around talking about our personal lives. Now, do you need a top-up on that tea?" She poured, not waiting for me to answer.

"It's just our way," Mrs. O'Grady said. "I had my married life with Eoin and if there's any justice, he's with the Lord right now, looking down on this gathering, proud that I've done right by his name." Although the sentiment was nice, I felt a little squirmy. Hank is a vocal atheist. My grandparents were holiday Catholics. They only graced the doors of the church on Easter and Christmas. And to be fair, for the occasional funeral or wedding. My mother and I had accompanied them to church on occasion, but I didn't grow up imagining guardian angels or lost loved ones watching over me. I hoped no one mentioned ghosts. I'm kind of a chicken when it comes to the supernatural, even if the otherworldly beings are supposed to be on my side.

"It's awful to think Chef lost his Da so early." Mary said. "He's a fine man in his own right, despite it. That's all down to you, Mrs. O'Grady." She raised her teacup in a toast.

I raised mine in reply. I saw a flash of black and white beside me, and turned to see Nap the dog balancing precariously on four spindly legs atop a birdbath outside the window. "Go on, shoo, you disloyal creature!" Mrs. O'Grady shouted. The dog jumped down and skulked away.

"Since the very day Tom brought me that beast, no bigger than your fist he was, he's been sneakin' off like a thief to beg scraps and cuddles off Lord Wexford, the very Earl himself. Disrespectful pup! Swanning right up to the Lord of the Manor, no doubt looking for a cozy spot in his antique bed that sits three feet off the ground!"

"Ooh, that sounds gorgeous. Who could blame Nap for wanting to curl up there? When did you see his bed?"

Mrs. O'Grady blushed slightly, and said, "I didn't see *his* bed, strictly speaking. I'm remembering his room from when his departed wife was still with us. The point is, the dog was meant to keep me company. Tom felt I was too lonely. Pish! You did me no good, though, did ya, ya mangy mutt? One scratch behind your raggedy ear from the Earl when you were a pup and you worship him," she hollered after the dog. "I like to give him a hard time," she confided, "but I can't blame him for being fond of the man. Tom wouldn't be a patch on the man he is today if the Earl hadn't stepped in. After Eoin passed, he could have turned us out of this house and no one would have thought a thing of it. My Eoin was a stone mason," she said, turning to me. "He mended the walls, the roads, the stable mews buildings, you name it. He built a fair number of new structures as they were needed as well."

"I heard tell he was a jack of all trades," Mary prompted.

Mrs. O'Grady buttered a piece of roll, beaming with pride. "He stepped in wherever a pair of hands was needed, just as you do, Mary. Capable and hard-working, like yourself. He cared for the cows, looked after the horses, dug ditches when the ponds were overflowing. For his trouble, he got to stay in this cottage, where his father and his father before him lived, and draw a salary."

"The Earl did the right thing, letting you stay," I said.

"Not only did he let us stay, he pays me the same as he did Eoin. Always has!"

"And it's a bargain for him," Mary said emphatically. "Who else would have taken charge of the henhouse when it needed someone stepping in? To say nothing of the fine breads and pies you do for the restaurants. Besides, you're the eyes and ears of Castle Stone. The Earl can't be bothered to oversee all the goings-on around here. And all that's to say nothing of how you cared for his wife during her illness. I only arrived at the end, but I witnessed it with my own eyes. Lady Helen couldn't have known a tenderer nurse if she'd had children of her own to look after her. He's got a friend in you!"

"Ah," she said, her eyes shining, "He has. There's no denying that." She stared into the distance for a minute. "Sheila, tell us about yourself. Mary and I have been gabbing, and you've hardly said two words together. Are you married?"

"No."

"No, she's definitely, definitely not," Mary said, winking at me sideways. Great. Ashleigh told her I'm a lesbian. I made a mental note to straighten that out as soon as possible. Here, in front of Mrs. O'Grady and a representation of Jesus, didn't seem the time nor place.

"That's a shame," she looked at me with kind eyes. "I've a feeling that you're the sort who would make a man a good wife." Under her scrutiny, I felt like a failure. I wasn't sure what made a good wife, but I doubted I had it. I always saw myself more as a pal than someone a man wanted to marry. Or at most, someone a guy would date for six months, and break up with in order to find himself, only to be engaged three months later because he'd "found his soul mate, and wasn't I so happy for him?" "At any rate, I'm sure you'll be a help around the estate. There's nowt so valuable as an able pair of hands, and there's plenty of work to be done 'round here. Our Tom'll be overjoyed to have you in the kitchen."

"Thank you for the lovely meal, Mrs. O'Grady," I said, folding my napkin. "But shouldn't we be getting back, Mary?"

"Ah, sure, you must be wrecked."

"Mrs. O'Grady, you've spent your whole day taking care of me. I'm sure you have better things to do." I wanted out of there before we could start discussing how well I could tat, or what kind of experience I had curing meats. Lying to a rotation of front desk clerks and undergardeners was one thing, but I didn't relish the idea of duping this kind woman. I'd have to make it my business to stay as far from her as possible during my period of treachery. Maybe if I dug in seamlessly, got the story I needed to get for the book, and got out quick, they'd all forget about me as quickly as they'd known me.

Every plan I had for a speedy getaway was foiled as Mrs. O'Grady pushed clean cloths filled with fresh rolls, brown paper envelopes containing the luscious creamy butter she'd served us, and jars of jam on us. She sat at the table and hand-copied her soda bread recipe onto a note card, then did one for the blackcurrant jam while she was at it. She wanted to fry me some more bacon. I practically had to break into a run to get away from her hospitality.

"Just bring back the towels and the jars when it suits you," she called, waving. "When you come, we'll sit down for another good aul chin wag!"

There was no getting around it. I'd have to go back and visit.

Dear Mags, I wish I could just call you right now, but I haven't had a minute to look into a phone plan. Maybe Mary, Ashleigh's friend and the intern coordinator, can help me out tomorrow. I'm not blaming you, but there's a mistake on the plane ticket. You have me coming home September 24th, not August 24th. Can you imagine if I stayed that long? I'll bet it's going to cost Fort Knox to change the flight, but once I pin down this book, there'll be the promise of money coming in, so I can pay you back. So, you know how we imagined me soaking in an ancient claw-foot tub with cucumber slices over my eyes, catered to by hot and cold running servants? It seems the luxurious, historical rooms in the castle that we saw on the internet are occupied by exotic foreign royalty, and the eccentric old lord who owns the joint. As I write, I'm lying on a cot that St. Francis of Assisi would have complained about. It's a step up from summer camp, but a step down from a college dorm. I can tough it out for a day or two, or even a week, if that's what it takes.

It's not all doom and gloom, though. Walking around the grounds is like being in a Merchant Ivory film, but in Wizard of Oz technicolor. You wouldn't believe how green the grass is or how blue the sky is if I told you. Mary has been very nice. After our tour, insisted on swinging me by the worker's pub, a little room off the back of Uncle Jack's — that's the uber-luxe pub for the guests. I told her I was only up for one drink, and I asked for a vodka and soda with lemon. Mary told the barman, who was also a stable mucker (apparently we rotate shifts there?), to ignore me and give me a large Guinness. That stuff is an iron fist in a velvet glove! I met a lot of the other estate workers and interns, but because of the Guinness and the jet lag, it was kind of a blur. Just as I was about to call it a night, Tom O'Grady came in, wearing a dark wool pea coat with the collar flipped up, and his hands jammed in the pockets. He walked straight up to the bar and stood next to my stool. When I asked if I could buy him a drink, everyone in the whole place sucked in his or her breath and went still. "No," he kind of yelled at me. "I'm just in here to hand over the key." He finally tacked on a "thank you," but it seemed to take considerable effort on his part to force it out. After he left, Mary leaned over with big eyes, laughing at me. She told me that Chef never drinks with the gang. A handful of the guys offered to "stand me a pint" and clapped me on the back, saying "Good on ya, Sheila," and "Nice one." I left pretty soon after. Mary offered to walk me, but the moon was out. Reflected off of the lake, it lit up the whole estate. I stuck to the paths, but I still got a little turned around heading back to my cell. I wound up around the back side of the castle. T O'G was sitting on a stone bench, with his hands clasped and his elbows on his knees. I could feel him pretend not to see me, the way you do when you wind up on a subway car with someone you kind of know from the office. Still, when I walked away from him on that path, I know he was watching me. It kept me from being scared alone out there in all that open space. I'm so tired, Mags, and I have to be up at the crack of dawn. I'd better sign off and go to bed. I wonder where T O'G sleeps. I mean for the book, of course. So I can write it into the headnotes or whatever.

'Night, Mags. I like writing to you in this journal. It makes it feel like you're not so far away. Love, Shay

Chapter Eleven

There is no luck except where there is discipline.

Turns out my cellblock is right behind the chicken coop. I don't believe in Satan, but if I did, I'd swear he'd taken the form of the rooster who woke me up before dawn. What originally erupted as a textbook "Cock-a-doodle-doo" morphed into a scream and ended with a repetitive barking laugh. The feathery bastard obviously enjoys his job. I wonder if the hens have ever gotten together to form a plan to peck him to death in a Dionysian fury.

Mary told me I could take the late morning shift and join the crew at 6:30. She winked and told me not to spread it around that she was giving me special treatment. 6:30 is special treatment? I had half a Guinness in me at the time of this announcement, so I didn't have the stomach to ask when the early morning shift began.

I'd gotten up extra early to type notes about the meeting with Mrs. O'Grady into my laptop. It felt shifty using the information, as she'd invited me as a guest into her home. Still, it was all in the interest of the book. And in the end, that was all for her son's good, right? I pushed away any guilt and put down every detail she'd shared about his childhood, and every aspect of the house and her lifestyle that I'd observed.

Realizing I needed to hurry in case I got lost, I ducked quickly through the no-frills shower. I didn't have time to put on makeup. It was a good thing the uniform I'd been given came with skullcap. The dark stripe of my roots was descending by the hour, and without my electrical appliances, my shoulder-length long bob was looking very 1970s free love. I wondered if I could pop out this afternoon for a touch-up. For the time being, I twisted it into a bun and popped on my little scarlet hat. I pulled on my white trousers, which I have to say were baggy in all the wrong places and didn't do me any favors, and buttoned up my black and white striped chef's coat with Castle Stone embroidered near the shoulder. I looked in the mirror. I didn't recognize myself. I resembled me, but that was about the extent of it. I looked like I could be my younger cousin. I looked closer. My skin looked really good. It was clear and dewy, and there was color in my cheeks. I remembered the reflection of myself in the potted plant the night I'd met Maggie at *Le Relais* down in Soho. That girl looked sallow and oily. The girl I examined now looked rested and healthy. Must be a combo of the hat color and the lighting, I thought, heading for the door.

When I walked through the front entrance of the main castle, I was swiftly intercepted by a natural blonde wearing a pastel twinset and conservative pumps. She seemed about my age, but had the bearing of a matron. "Catherine Daly, Manager" her shining gold name badge read.

"Help doesn't come through the front," she said walking out the front door and around the flagstone porch toward the side. No pleasant Irish "How ya?" or "What might your name be?"

"Kitchen entrance is through the screen door, over near that car park." With that, she turned on her heel, and clacked back to the door, slipping noiselessly inside. The morning was cool and dewy. I could smell warm, yeasty bread well before I pulled open the heavy-framed, wooden screen door. It had a squeaky telescoping mechanism that slammed it shut automatically. Tom O'Grady's strong back was to me and his shoulders undulated rhythmically as he kneaded a large ball of dough. I looked around and smiled, expecting someone to usher me in. No one so much as looked up from his work.

"You're late," Chef O'Grady said without turning around. I glanced at the giant, plain-faced industrial-white clock on the wall. 6:32. "The shift starts at 6:30." I stood there silently, for longer than was comfortable. Finally a short, stout, sweaty man in a tall toque and a neckerchief approached.

"Name's Bill. I'm the Sous."

I offered him my hand in reply.

"Don't shake my hand," he said shortly. "I'll only have to wash it." Feeling a flush rise, I put my hands behind my back. I was embarrassed that Tom O'Grady had heard the exchange. "Take that station," Bill said pointing. "You can make scones." My heart sped up. I'd never made a scone in my life. Take a deep breath, Shayla, I told myself. There was a recipe fixed in a clear plastic holder, and an array of bowls and spoons next to a mixer. OK, one step at a time. I stood reading the sheet of paper, but fear was scrambling my synapses. I read the ingredients. Self-raising flour, never heard of it. Caster sugar, nope. Sultanas, oh my God. I stood frozen to the spot, aware that time was ticking and no scones were forthcoming.

"Bill," a very young girl with a beaky nose and some funky necklaces worn over her chef's coat piped up, "I've been here longer than the new girl." I felt acid rise in my throat. The jig was about to be up. She was going to sell me up the river. "It's only fair I get to make the scones and she has to peel the potatoes." Behind Bill's back, she gave me a quick wink, and nodded her head toward the giant pile of potatoes in the deep stainless-steel sink.

"I don't like your sass, Brigid, but there're two heads on me this mornin' after watchin' the footy with the lads last night and drinking for Ireland. I swear, startin' today, I'm givin' up my pints. So, shut your mouths and do what you like, just make sure it all gets done."

131

"Pay no attention to Bill," she whispered, "he's never even said a kind word to his own mother." Wordlessly, she flipped a potato around in her hand, showing me the most efficient way to peel it, and how to dig out the eyes using a paring knife. I methodically went through the pile, all the while watching her produce perfect little dotted rounds of dough that she lined up in regiments on baking tray after baking tray. Under her breath, and during the whirring of blenders and mixers, she narrated what she was doing.

"See here?" she'd say. "Not too wet." Or she'd grab my attention with, "Look at this. You have to sieve the flour first." When I finally got a batch right, she exclaimed, "Ah, that's ace. See? You're not useless!"

It was when she brought me a hot cup of tea that I began to believe in guardian angels. I understood that this was all a construct. I didn't need this job the way Brigid and Bill did. I could simply walk away. Still, it felt like I'd landed in a prison camp, and she was the veteran who'd show me the ropes to ensure my survival. My hands were cramping, and my lower back was screaming out for relief but I kept on, assuming if I fell to the ground, Brigid would drag me out and bury my bones.

The very second I had washed, peeled and cut the eyes out of the very last dirty potato, Bill pointed to a sack of onions the size of a large child and grunted, "Get them peeled and chopped. Not minced, mind you, chopped." Upright, the bag stood nearly half my height. Moving it was awkward. Every time I got a grip on it, the onions inside shifted like marbles in a bag, and it tilted and toppled above my head. I'd be lucky if I made it through a day in this kitchen without being hospitalized. Nearly dislocating my shoulder, I managed to heave the onions onto my workspace, and Bill immediately shouted at me for contaminating the area. I pulled the sack back down, and Bill yelled at me again for bruising the produce. He barked that I needed to sterilize the counter top, and replace my knives, which had been knocked off onto the floor, nearly severing off a few toes on the trip. Not to point out the obvious, but kitchens are dangerous places with heavy stock on high shelves, and all the ultra-sharp knives laying on counters, stuck to walls, and flying around in people's hands. I'm surprised more horror films aren't set in kitchens.

I fumbled around with the heavy paper of the sack. It seemed to have some kind of string netting inside it that I couldn't tear. Brigid pulled a pair of kitchen shears out of a handy holster on her belt and handed them to me. I sliced open the top of the bag, and its contents shifted, sending a wave of rolling onions fanning out across the floor.

"Sheila!" Bill bellowed, red-faced. Chef O'Grady turned around from his work and shook his head. I skittered around the room, gathering onions in my arms, dropping them as fast as I could capture them. Brigid handed me a giant mixing bowl.

Onions contained, I got down to business. Through a series of grunts and pantomimes, my protector sent me down the right path. After the senseless massacre of a couple of the innocent bulbs, I learned to peel them without losing half the flesh, and to chop them into relatively uniform pieces using an impressively large French knife. After the first five, the fumes got to me. Tears pooled in my eyes, and I had to contort my neck sideways to keep them from dropping in the food. I went to wipe my eyes with the back of my hand, forgetting I was holding a giant knife. The point caught my skullcap, and pulled it right off of my head, just nicking the side of my scalp. I put the knife down and clamped my hand to my skull. Was I bleeding? Barely, thank God.

"Sheila! Get your cap on," Bill shouted. "That's a health and safety violation!"

I re-hatted myself and went back to the monotonous chopping. This fresh batch of tears wasn't coming from the onions. I chopped through the blur, offloading my tears to the side until there seemed to be no more moisture left in my body. Every now and again, I felt Chef O'Grady checking me out. I didn't dare look at him. I could only imagine he was filled with derision and scorn. The morning had not been the success I'd visualized at all.

The longer I stood in the close kitchen, though, the more I internalized its rhythm. In a short time, I learned a lot through trial by fire. I now knew to stand frozen when someone yelled, "Hot behind!" meaning a scalding hot pan or pot of boiling water was being whisked within an inch of my body. Although I hadn't yet learned how to dance, I noticed the choreographed moves of the waiters, bussers, and "dish dogs," as they called the young men carrying huge bus pans and racks of clean glasses, as they wove in and out of each other's personal space.

And all the while, I checked in on Tom. I'd decided to start calling him that, in my own head, anyhow. Screw decorum. If anyone heard my thoughts, so be it. I'd been bruised and shed buckets of tears. I felt like I'd earned the privilege. I wasn't some publishing assistant calling from a climate-controlled office in midtown, who could jump up and get a Starbucks or waste a sneaky hour surfing on Huff Po or Buzzfeed. I'd lost blood on the front lines, and I stood on a hard kitchen floor peeling my way to carpal tunnel syndrome while rivulets of perspiration snaked down my butt crack.

Now that things in my corner were running more smoothly, I was fairly sure Tom O'Grady had forgotten that I was in his kitchen. I'd tracked his every movement since I'd walked in, but I'd hardly seen his face. I'd heard his resonant voice steadily commanding everyone around him. I'd glanced at his back so many times, I could probably draw a fairly good rendering of the black tails of his head wrap grazed against the thick, dark-blonde curls tucked into the high collar of his white chef's coat. And the shape of his body. My original goal was to watch what he did in the kitchen, to try to get a feel of who he was as a chef so I could write reflective essays in his voice. But I kept drifting off topic. Tall and solid, his body resembled an upside-down triangle. Broad shoulders, tapering down to a thinner waist and ending at a tight high rear, carelessly accented by the thin draping jersey and elastic waist of his chef's trousers.

At some point, Brigid approached me with concern. "You're allowed the occasional bio break, you know. Don't be scared of Bill. He's a gobshite."

"Bio break?"

"You know. Human needs. Tea. Food. The toilet. Come with me."

For the first time in hours, I crossed through the kitchen. Tom, who was doing some kind of elaborate slicing and wrapping of a long, thin strip of meat dotted with bones, looked up from his work. I'd have to get the recipe for whatever that was. I looked around his station, hoping to see it displayed in one of those see-through holders.

Tom lasered his blue eyes right into mine with a knowing look. He's getting ready to fire me. He's going to let me work here all morning then he's going to have me thrown off the grounds with nothing but the uniform on my back. I'd have to walk to Dublin in shame, fraudulently dressed as a productive member of society. I couldn't look away. I'm sure guilt was written all over my face. He looked at me hard, just before his countenance softened and I caught the slightest hint of a crinkle at the corners of his sleepy, bedroom eyes. Then Brigid pulled me by the sleeve.

"Toilet's through there. When you're finished, come to the break room."

I used the toilet and splashed my face with water. Aside from going swimming or to the gym, I hadn't been out of the house with zero makeup since I was maybe 15. I hurried back to the break room, trying to avoid making contact with anyone else. Keep it simple, Shayla. I told myself. You are an international spy. James Bond didn't go around making friends with people and going home with soda bread wrapped in their tea towels. You are here to do a job. I threw my shoulders back and tried to walk like a chef. I'd gotten better, hadn't I? By the end, I was pretty sure I was doing more good than harm.

Brigid was sitting at a table bathed in a thick slice of sunshine.

"There's a bacon and egg bap for you, with loads of butter on, and I fetched you a cup of coffee from the guest area, figuring you might like that, being American and all. Hurry, though, we've only a few minutes."

My heart wanted to reach out of my chest and give her heart a hug. This morning had been so hard. I'd only been on the job for mere hours and I was exhausted to the bone. I bit into my sandwich like a starving person. Being around the delicious smells of baking sweets and roasting meats had set my animal brain on high alert. I had been hungry, and there was food all around. I washed down the sandwich with a huge glug of coffee. I could feel it joining with my blood, filling me with warmth and energy. Maybe I wasn't getting fired after all. She wouldn't feed me to keep me alive if I were, right? She'd leave me to die like the runt of a litter and invest her resources elsewhere.

"Thank you, Brigid," I said, filled with warmth for her. This tiny slip of a girl was my hero. She could have sold me up the river and had me bounced out on my ass five minutes after I walked in.

"Not at all," she said, waving me off. "It can be fierce intimidating around here when you're new. You'll find your feet soon enough."

"Hey, I'd love to get my hair colored today. Do you think you can show me how to get to town when we're through with work?"

"The shops'll all be long closed by then."

I was confused. Maybe they closed for a siesta in the middle of the afternoon, like in Spain?

"OK, then maybe after?"

"You're on a twelve today," she said. I blinked.

"That means you work twelve hours."

No. Way.

"Apart from the odd corner shop, businesses will be locked up by the time you're off duty. I know how you feel. I did a course in Dublin – art – and after, it was hard getting used to the early hours again." My mouth fell open, with a large hunk of unchewed bap resting inside. It wasn't just that I had to live with my hairdo, it was that I had to keep this up until 6:30 tonight. Already my knees felt creaky and my neck ached from bending sideways. "You'll need to find your way into Ballykelty before long, though. Those shoes aren't doing you any favors. She pointed to my black ballet flats, with the gold double-C Chanel logo on the toe. They were a birthday present from Hank — chosen, purchased, and wrapped by Maggie. They were damp, greyed out by a fine dusting of flour. "You'll need a pair of clogs before you slip on the grease and crack your head, or irritate your sciatic nerve by standing all day on the slate floor."

"And you're telling me that stores aren't open at 6:30 p.m.?"

She shook her head. "Most close at 5 and a few stay open till 6."

What was this, 1930? I never left my desk before 7.

"Wow, village folk sure know how to kick back and take it easy!"

A tall shadow fell across our little table. "Certainly looks as though some do," Tom O'Grady said. Brigid picked up her plate and cup, and was on her feet before I registered what was happening. I found my bearings, and gathered up the remnants of my snack.

"One minute, Sheila, if you don't mind."

This was it. I flinched. He was going to fire me. I'd just gotten fired from HPC. Even though I was faking doing a job under a fake name, I didn't think I could live through it again.

"So um, Chef…" The title sounded so odd coming out of my mouth. I checked in to see if it had fallen wrong on his ears, too. He was waiting, watching me. I tried to think of something, anything, to say that would fix what had happened. Words failed me. Some writer I was. I looked at the floor. "I guess I'm fired, then," I took the last gulp of coffee from my mug, set it on the table, and slumped over. Nothing left to fear. At least now I could breathe out.

"Will you follow me, please?"

Oh, come *on*. Here I was for the second time in a week, being escorted out of a place of business. He led me out of the side door of the restaurant, out to the service side, next to the car park. Why not just do it next to the dumpster?

"So?" My desperation brought out my belligerence. "If I'm fired, fire me." I crossed my arms. *"Chef."*

"I didn't say that." He gave me a serious look. "Do you need this position?" It was warm in the direct sunlight. He loosened the buttons on his chef's coat nearest his collarbone.

How could I answer? And why would he care? Yes, I needed this position, but not for the reasons he might think. I hated digging in deeper and deeper with the lies. I chose my words carefully. "My situation is complicated." I kicked at some pebbles at the edge of the grass.

"We've all been down that road, haven't we?" He pulled off his head wrap, freeing his waves and curls. He raked his fingers back through his hair. "Listen, could be that there's something I need from you."

"Oh, anything! I'll do whatever you ask. I-" A fresh sprig of hope uncoiled in my ribcage. He held up his hand to stop me from talking.

"I haven't quite worked out a plan. And I'll not ask you to give your word about something before you have the facts. For the time being, let's say you'll keep working here and we'll take it hour by hour." He looked pained. "I'll think of something to tell Bill."

"Aren't you the chef? Now my high school French isn't very good, but the last time I checked, that meant chief." He gave me a thunderous look. It scared me. "I'm sorry," I said immediately. "I thought we were playing."

"Well, we aren't." His face closed off. He tied his headwrap back on. "I have a restaurant to run," he said, looking at his sleek black rubber waterproof watch, "Now, get in there and make 40 portions of Sticky Toffee Pudding for the dinner service."

My breath caught in my throat. "But, I don't know how to make Sticky...that."

"Of course you don't." He buttoned up the side of his jacket. His eyes softened into genuine, undisputed crinkles this time. His lips spread into a smile. "*That* was playing."

I laughed. "Hey, I'm sorry I'm a disappointment. I wish I were better at this."

"Ah," he said looking into my eyes. "I wouldn't call you a disappointment." His gaze hung on me for a second or two. I crossed my arms and looked down at my feet.

"Thank you," I whispered.

"New plan altogether," he said, clapping his hands together. Wash salad for now, stay out of Bill's path, and try not to do any harm to yourself or others. At half-past two, meet me in my mother's kitchen." He tied his head wrap back on over his wild curls. "I'm going to teach you a lesson."

"Hello? Mrs. O'Grady?" I called from the path in front of the neat whitewashed cottage. I opened the gate and approached the door. Nap bounced wildly along with me, tangling himself in my feet as I walked the path. I peeked in the window. Tom sat at the kitchen table, reading a newspaper and sipping a cup of tea. He wore a heather blue vee-necked t-shirt that, if I remembered right, matched his eyes exactly. He looked softer out of his chef's coat.

I knocked. He didn't answer. I knocked again. After waiting for a minute or two, I eased the door open, calling "Hello?" I surprised myself at how quietly I said it. I could see through to the kitchen, where Tom still sat, calm in his private moment. His shoulders were relaxed and his face at rest fell into what was almost a serene smile. In the kitchen, his expression alternated between determined and guarded.

"I'm here," I said. I tried again. He still wasn't aware of me. "I'm here," I declared. Tom looked up and raised his eyebrows.

"So you are." He put down his mug and the paper.

"Do I have the time right?" I asked. As I neared the table, I saw that my memory had been correct. His eyes did match his shirt. I felt a little tickle right below my stomach. "Where's your mother?"

"She has a Ladies' Altar Society meeting this time every week."

He put his mug in the sink. "Let's get started."

I felt shy knowing we were alone. I followed him into the little kitchen and saw an array of knives and measuring cups laid out in neat rows on the countertop.

"Right, measure a teaspoon of flour into that bowl there."

I examined the measuring spoons for writing. There was none. I took a guess and picked one up. I glanced at Tom, who nodded. Confident, I scooped out a measure of flour and poured it into the bowl. I waited for my praise.

"Wrong."

My heart sank.

"You don't know what kind of teaspoon. Level, heaping…it makes a difference. Try again." For half an hour, Tom made me ladle sugar, oil, butter, and flour into bowls using everything from teaspoons to half-cup measures to the palm of my hand. It was fiddly work, and the likelihood of missing the mark felt high-stakes. I told myself that mastering this was important because the book required that I keep my kitchen position. I pushed aside the truth that I wanted Tom to approve of me.

"Can't I just riff? You know, put my own spin on it?" I liked rules, but this level of rigor was like being in prison. I thought about how great I'd been on the debate team and at taking essay tests. In those realms you win by emphasizing what you know and taking the spotlight off of what you don't.

"Sure, you can improvise if you never want to be a baker. Baking is pure science. There's delicate chemistry involved and there are universal laws of physics at play. But if you like your bread rolls to sink in water, then by all means wing it. Once you know how much salt fits in your palm, you have freedom. You won't be tied to utensils," he coached. "It becomes intuitive. Don't be in such a hurry to master this. It takes time and practice. Try again."

I filled a measuring cup with softened butter and leveled the top using a butter knife the way he'd shown me. I tipped it toward him and he nodded. I carefully ran the knife around the edges to get every dab and transferred it to a bowl.

"That's right," he said, with the trace of a smile. "Was that so hard?"

"It's just that when you said 'wrong,' it reminded me of my father. Nothing I ever do with him is good enough, if you know what I mean." I wiped my greasy hands on a tea towel, and wondered why I was telling Tom this.

He leaned against the counter. "I can see why your Da would have high expectations. There's a spark about you, like any minute you're going to do something remarkable." He stood up and started whipping the ingredients I'd measured into a dough. "I mean to say, it's clear that you're a bright woman. Let's move on to knives."

For the next hour, I memorized the names of every knife in the kitchen, and their uses. French, chef, paring, serrated, fish…and on and on. We sliced tomatoes, onions, potatoes, bread, mushrooms, and blocks of cheese.

"I wish I had some Kalamata olives for you to try. Slicing around the stone is tricky. I picked up some pointers from a chef in Greece."

"I saw that picture of you there."

"What picture?" He took his hands out of the dough he was working and waited for an answer.

I had no choice but to answer truthfully. "The one in your bedroom. With…a woman."

"You mean my old bedroom," he said. He washed his hands. "Funny you were in there." I used an old trick of Hank's. I stayed silent. It worked, and eventually Tom went back to the lecture. "You choose your knife based on the texture of the food. Some foods require sawing, some pressing. The sharper the knife, the better, especially for something with multiple textures, say, like a tomato."

"Sharp knives scare me," I said.

"You're less likely to get cut on a sharp one than a dull one." He glanced at me. "But I'm not sure that rule applies to you, Sheila Doyle. I'd better use caution."

Embarrassed, I needed something to do with my hands. Taking

initiative, I started chopping the lettuce leaves we'd set aside, before he stopped me. Gently, this time. He took the knife from my hand and explained about the living cells in fruits and vegetables. Tearing lettuce, or using plastic knives designed for the purpose discouraged bruising and oxidation. "Now, use your hands to shred the rest of that head into small pieces, while I pop this into the oven." He paused. "Please."

I couldn't get the hang of mincing garlic. No matter how hard I tried, I wound up spraying large chunks of garlic, all of varying shapes, off of the cutting board and onto the floor. A judgmental look flashed over Tom's face. I saw him consciously calm his expression.

"Here, let me help." He sprinkled a little salt on a few whole cloves. "This helps keep the garlic from sticking to the knife." He slid behind me, and put his hand over mine on the tang of the chef's knife. "Make sure the tip stays in contact with the board, like so," he said, moving my hand in rhythmic motions. "Let the weight do the work."

As I leaned in to relax my shoulder so I could chop, my hip pressed into the space between his legs, and his zipper was flat against my waist. My body flicked and Tom lost control of the knife. "Careful, you'll get us both hurt."

We stood there together, turning cloves into slices, slices into sticks, and sticks into mince. "Work from root to tip, using a rocking motion. There, that's the way." After we'd gone through two heads, I began wondering how much garlic two people could need.

"There," he said, separating his hand from mine and stepping away. My palm tingled from where he's applied pressure. He poured tea into a mug and handed it to me. "Why don't you step out into the garden for a few minutes? I'll call you when it's ready?"

The tea tasted good. I needed it. After such an early rise, and the effort of riding the learning curve, I felt I could take a nap right there in the warm sunshine. Nap the dog cemented himself to my calf and sat panting contentedly. The pressure was like a hug.

I had just begun to wonder why Tom invited me over when he knew his mom would be out when his voice through the window called out, "Sheila!"

Nap pressed through the door with me when I opened it, and I tried not to call attention to the fact. Having him there calmed me. If Tom noticed, he didn't let on. "Have a seat," he said.

I'd only been outside a few minutes, but he'd laid out a feast. There was a basket of freshly baked soda bread, a large green salad, and two steaming vegetable omelets flanked by a pile of fried potatoes.

"This is unbelievable!" I said, taking my seat. Nap hid himself, curled under the table by my feet and put his head in my lap. Clever dog. "How did you make this so fast?"

"I made the bread while you were chopping," he said, slathering butter onto a slice, "and you prepped everything else. That's why a *chef de cuisine* has a *sous*, a station chef, a *commis* and so on. The final execution and plating is simple if you know what you're doing. I'm like the doctor who steps in at the last minute and takes credit for delivering the baby after the support team and the mother have toiled over the labor for 18 hours."

I savored the freshness of the summer-ripe tomatoes and the creamy eggs. "I'll happily give you credit. I'll give you anything you want if you keep putting this kind of food in front of me." He tilted his head at me. Luckily he was chewing. "I mean, any kind of credit," I said quickly, before he could answer.

We ate companionably. He asked me about what kinds of foods I did or didn't like, I asked him about the grounds. Our words were small talk, really. All of my understanding about Tom came from a gesture here, a frown there. Our increasing ease around one another developed during the pauses. I could feel that he was starting to understand things about me. That pressed against the walls of my comfort zone, but I pushed myself to tolerate it. I sensed there would be a payoff. From time to time, I slipped morsels of food to Nap. We didn't get personal.

When the meal was over, and no more tea could possibly be drunk, Tom said, "I'd never have pegged you for a softie."

"What do you mean?"

"That dog. Mam'll have both of our hides if she finds that animal in the house eating off her china."

"Oh," I said, standing. "Come on, Nap. Out you go. Shoo." He went promptly and obediently. It was clear that he'd enjoyed the time-out from the rules, and he knew not to push it. My hand on the doorknob, I took in the picture of Tom leaning back, relaxed in his chair, legs splayed, arms open. I followed Nap's example.

"Thank you for the lesson and for the meal. I really need to go and organize my room."

He didn't move. He looked up at me from under the heavy lids of his eyes and said, "Sounds like the right thing to do." My heart raced as I closed the door to the cottage behind me. "Well, you did have two pots of tea," I told myself. I saw Mrs. O'Grady in the distance, coming from the direction of the church. I walked leisurely back toward my dorm, half-glad and half-sorry that I'd chosen the right thing to do.

Chapter Twelve

As I cut through the lobby, I felt like a million bucks. The sun was out, and I'd carefully chosen a bright outfit to wear to reflect the cheer of the spring-like weather. Granted, by bright I mean khaki trousers, a taupe blouse, and a navy jacket, but at least it wasn't black. Brigid had lent me a statement necklace that she'd made herself, strung together from large, pale-pink stones, so I felt I was making strides toward fitting in. My hair, however two-toned, was bouncing with joy at not being confined in my skullcap. Being freshly showered and wearing street clothes with a swipe of lipstick was such a treat. I almost felt like me.

After nearly a week of long shifts in the kitchen, I had a half-day off. My hands were nicked in several places, I had a long burn along my forearm where I'd backed into a line cook holding a hot pan (my fault), and every muscle in my body ached from standing, hauling and bending. Still, today I felt light and strong. Better even than when I used to go to the gym. Plus, now I knew how to make soda bread, wash spinach (the real kind that's gritty with sand, not the pristine bagged baby leaves), chop any salad vegetable you could name into the most appetizing shape for its genre, and even make gazpacho. Bill still hollered at me and gave me all the worst jobs, and Tom — I simply cannot call him Chef unless I'm backed into a corner and there's no choice: even then, I squirm — would never defend or protect me. The hierarchy of a kitchen is like a dog pack. I could not be farther from alpha, but as I've said, my eye is on the prize, so I'll suck it up. It couldn't be clearer that Bill thinks I should be fired, and he's trying to figure out why I haven't been. So am I, to tell the truth, but I'm thanking my lucky stars. Meanwhile, I'm trying to make every minute I have here count. Shoes have been known to drop in my life without warning. Making hay while the sun shines only makes sense.

Tom O'Grady, decked out in freshly starched chef's whites pushed in the front door, eyes to the ground, cutting a swathe through the guests milling about the lobby. He didn't have his head wrap on and his wavy blonde hair seemed to have carried in the sunlight. He clipped my elbow and looked up apologetically. "Sheila?"

"Tom? Chef! Hello."

He looked me over. He looked like he was about to say something important, but thought better of it. I watched him shake it off.

"What?" I asked bluntly.

"Nothing," he retorted. "What do you mean what?"

"I don't know," I said, balling up my fists. "You were looking at me as though you were about to say something."

"I wasn't staring at you," he said with a raised voice.

This was escalating quickly, but now I was so hot under the collar I couldn't keep my mouth shut. "I didn't say staring. You said staring!" He was officially ruining my day.

"Pardon me, Chef?" a short middle-aged lady in a powder-blue pantsuit inquired.

"What?" he snapped. "That is to say, how can I help?"

"I just wanted to let you know my husband and I ate in The Grange Hall last night and I can honestly say I've never had a better meal." She hooked her arm in his and steered him toward the ballroom. "The smoked salmon and capers, together with the dulse oatcakes were a triumph…" she continued talking as they drifted farther away. He threw me one last scowl over his shoulder before he disappeared.

"Sheila," Catherine, the receptionist, beckoned from behind the desk. She was wearing a lavender suit jacket, and had a navy and white scarf tied high around her throat. It looked perfect, the way scarves always do on flight attendants. I've never worn a scarf out the door. I always tie them on, filled with confidence and purpose, and wind up stuffing them in my bag before I make it past the hallway. "You have a telephone call."

Could it be Des? I wondered. He hadn't crossed my mind since he groped me in full view of everyone in the hotel parking lot the day he dropped me here. Don't tell me he somehow found out it was my day off so he could invite himself into my bed? My one stab at being a "bad girl," and it was going to haunt me forever. Couldn't his fiancée keep him on a shorter leash? I could see the phone's light blinking on the phone by Catherine's computer.

"At least, I think the call is for you. The girl down the phone kept saying 'Shay-la, but I suppose that's her American accent. And she asked for 'Shay-la' Sheridan. Sounds like a solicitation call, though why they'd bother to track you down across the sea is beyond me."

My heart soared — Maggie! I went to pick up the receiver and Catherine laid her hand on top of mine.

"Sheila?" she said, with the air of a hospital nurse informing a family member of bad news, "While it's not strictly forbidden for you to be in the lobby with the guests, it's discouraged."

"Poppycock!" erupted the Earl, who was sitting in an ornamental chair next to a tall plant stand.

"Good morning, Your Lordship," Catherine trilled, temporarily losing her composure. "I didn't see you sitting there."

If she didn't, it was certainly understandable. He was wearing a brocade dressing gown that rivaled Joseph's biblical Technicolor Dreamcoat, and an embroidered silk cravat to top it off. It was hard to tell where the chair ended and he began.

"Treat the estate as a home, and the guests will feel welcome, I always say." Then he muttered under his breath, "When the lads and lasses running the place have it their way, even I don't feel welcome."

I watched the hold light blinking, worrying about how much this phone call must be costing Maggie.

"That's a lovely sentiment, Your Lordship, and one worth remembering. I was simply following the guidelines handed down from the managers via Mary." She offered him a serene smile.

"When I'm toe-up in the ground and the builders change the name out front to Castle Manager, you can turn all of the lively youngsters out of the main house, but until then stuff the guidelines. You there," he called to me, "I'm spitting cotton. Order tea for two and join me at the table by the front window. We'll look at people's clothes and wager on what country they're from."

"I'm just about to connect her to an overseas call, Your Lordship." She spoke to him the way solicitous ladies speak to the elderly.

"No need to shout. I'm old, I'm not deaf. So you order the tea! You," he called to me, "first do your chatting, then come and have a sit-down."

I reached for the receiver, but Catherine's hand was quicker. I pulled my own hand back, and waited. "One moment for your call," she said, brightly. She handed me the receiver and pushed the button with the flashing light. She made no signs of stepping aside to give me my privacy, so I turned my back on her, whispering, "Mags?"

"What the hell?" Maggie exclaimed. "I've been on hold half my life listening to those jigs and shanties. I think I just earned an honorary degree in Irish folk music."

"Hi! I'm so happy to hear your voice," I cradled the receiver between my shoulder and chin, and cupped my hand around it to muffle my conversation. Catherine set to work cleaning the computer keyboard with a tiny brush and a can of compressed air. Turning my back further, I said, "I'm sorry I haven't called. I haven't had time to set up a phone plan. The days just keep getting away from me."

"Never mind that, spill, and it better be good. I honestly thought you'd been abducted to Brunei and added to an international harem."

I whispered the condensed version of how I wound up as Sheila Doyle, kitchen assistant, all the while aware of Catherine's commitment to a spotless front desk. Maggie punctuated my stories with various exclamations, including but not limited to, "You gave it to my cousin, you dirty bird!" and "I told you to stay away from him…being engaged doesn't mean he'll keep it in his pants!" and "I didn't say engaged? Oh, that's on me, then" and "If your name's Doyle now, then you're my real sister and not just my sister from another mister!" and "I can see you as a lesbian, you've certainly got the shoes for it."

After catching me up on some office gossip (Nate is definitely doing Padma from legal, and Matty is still a dick) she dropped a bombshell.

"I really hate to tell you this over the phone, Shay, but you need to know sooner rather than later. Eric asked me to move in with him, and I said yes."

"Congratulations, Maggie, that's great," I said, trying to sound cheerful despite the shock. Of course that made sense. I just didn't see it coming this soon, especially while I was out of the country. Even though the wind had been knocked out of me, I put a smile on my face, so the goodwill would shine in my voice. Maggie deserved my support. "I'm happy for you. Really." I heard my friend let out a heavy sigh.

"I'm so relieved to hear you say that. He asked me before you even left, but I didn't want to stress you out. It makes sense since we're saving for the wedding and all. Our old place is obviously paid up through this month. I found someone to take my room.

Someone Eric's friend from work used to date. I don't think you'll mind living with her at all."

"Sounds great," I lied.

"When are you coming back, anyway?"

I told her about the dates on the plane ticket, and before I could even finish, she jumped in with a plan. Maggie always saw the big picture. Before I knew it, she had the girl's sister — who was moving to New York for a summer internship and was also looking for a place — sleeping in my bed. On the one hand, it meant saving rent money; on the other hand, what if I wrapped this up and came home early?

"You'll stay with Eric and me for the rest of the summer!" she declared. "Oh, this is great. I'm strapped with all the wedding deposits and my agent said my royalty check won't be coming in for ages. You know what they say, 'Nothing happens fast in publishing.'"

I knew she wanted that to be the final answer so she wouldn't have to feel guilty. As for me, I didn't relish the idea of being a third wheel. And Eric was a good guy and all, but I preferred him in small doses. I'd cross that bridge when I came to it.

The Earl was waving at me, miming that the tea had arrived and was getting cold. He pretended to drink from a cup with his pinky extended, and then wrapped his arms around himself in an elaborate reenactment of shivering.

"Maggie, we're going to have to talk later. I'm being called away from the phone."

"I hope it's Chef Bedroom Eyes O'Fills-Out-His-Jeans. You should totally have sex with him! Now that you've tasted Irish, you'll never go back, they say."

"Who says that? What? No." I stammered. "There's nothing sexual between me and Tom O'Grady. He's my boss. And, he hates me."

The dust near the phone I was on needed urgent attention. So much so that Catherine ignored a bellman who needed a signature at the other end of the desk in order to clean it.

"Boss? You're the boss, Missy. Don't let the author steer the ship. It's a road to disaster. You're the writer. You have to get a book on paper. You need to ride him like a show pony."

"I'm not going to simply hop on and ride him," I insisted. "I've been gently coaxing for a week now. I can't just go in there and take what I want." Catherine's pretty pout turned downward for a quick second, before she resumed pretending not to listen to my conversation. Out of the corner of my eye, I saw the Earl pantomiming his own death from dehydration, complete with pretend vultures pecking out his eyes.

"I'm sorry, I really have to go. I'll find a way to call you soon." Before I could deposit the receiver back into its cradle, Catherine intercepted it. She made a big show of spritzing it with cleaning spray and wiping it clean.

"Ta, my job to see that everything stays clean here at The Castle," she chirped.

The Earl whistled.

"Young lady, are you prepared to take responsibility for ending the line of the family Stone? If you force me to observe good manners, bringing about my untimely demise, then I along with the preceding eleven dead and decaying Earls of Wexford shall haunt you for the rest of your days on earth."

"That was dramatic," I said, sliding into the heavy oak chair across from him. He burst into a rollicking, joyful laughter. Catherine flicked us an annoyed look.

"That's calling a spade a spade! I like you," he said, shoving a fragile bone china teacup across the table at me. It wobbled in its saucer before settling to a halt.

"Tell me your name."

"It's Sheila."

"Right, Sheila, I'm called Tony. I'll be mother while you tell me about yourself, Miss America." He poured tea for both of us, while I talked. After I served myself a scone, he heaped mounds of sandwiches and small cakes onto his plate. If you ignored the crumbs down his front, he really was quite elegant for a man his age. His dancing green eyes were deeply set and his face featured fine bones under his weathered skin. I imagined his face reflected a life of riding horses, rowing crew, playing tennis, and whatever else rich men that weren't required to work did to pass the hours. In contrast to his otherwise noble bearing was his hair. It amply covered his scalp, with a heavy part down the side, but each strand was fine, giving it a downy quality. Individual hairs reached out from his skull like the tentacles of a sea creature, and the sun falling in through the high window lit them up, lending a halo effect.

I realized that if I was going to make it in to the village to find a beauty salon, I needed to get going, but this was a golden opportunity. In addition to the pleasure I got from watching Catherine's agitated glances from behind the desk, this tete-a-tete allowed me to ask all about Tom O'Grady's history on the estate. I felt a little guilty, but Tony — he told me to call him that — delighted in regaling me with tales of Tom's successes. I made a mental note to ask more questions about his culinary training. I wanted to be able to cite awards and achievements for the book. As Tony said himself, he couldn't be prouder of the boy if he were born of his own loins. He chuckled in appreciation when I suggested that might be more graphic a phrase than was needed.

"That lad saved my bacon. He could still be living like a king in London town, but he gave it all up to come back here and drive away the bean counters."

"Didn't he have lady troubles?" I asked, crumbling up a tiny raspberry tart with the tines of my fork. "I was told that's why he came back to Castle Stone." I felt sleazy, like an undercover reporter for a pulp magazine.

"Bah, don't breathe that woman's name in my presence. When he first landed back here after she'd had her way with him, he was like the walking dead. Whatever the reason, I bless the day he came home. I'm the first to admit, I've no head for business.

My dear wife was the brains behind this organization. After she passed, things turned swiftly downhill. I put my trust in a pair who promised to run the estate. I feel a fool about it now. Swindlers and embezzlers, and I never saw it for the scales over my eyes. It took Maeve O'Grady to sit me down and show me the light of day. After the lawyers examined the books and proved her right, she ran the two off the land with a pitchfork." He closed his eyes, picturing it. "Spunky lady, our Maeve."

The Earl signaled to a bellman who was crossing the lobby, "You there, lad! Would you be so kind as to ask the kitchen if my companion and I could have a touch more hot water?"

"Certainly, Your Lordship." The boy beelined in the other direction, eager to please.

"Nice lad, that one. He likes the fellas." I raised my eyebrows in surprise at his candor. "Don't mention it to Father Walsh, over in the chapel. He's high-strung enough as it is."

"Er, I won't then."

"I must say that this happy accident nearly makes up for my missing my stories on the telly. 'Wouldn't you be more comfortable watching your videos up in your rooms, Lord Wexford?'" He mimicked in a high voice. "I certainly would not! I'm lonely enough as it is without having to watch telly on my own like a pensioner in a home. Feck the taxes! If running the castle as a resort means I have to sit alone at night or 'wear suitable clothing in public areas,' then sell the whole lot and set me up in a semi-detached number with housemates to share my crisps with. Where's the fun in *Strictly Come Dancing* if one's shouting by oneself?"

I guided the conversation back to the topic at hand. "From the way they tell it," I said, crossing my fingers under the table, "they owe their lives to you. You allowed Mrs. O'Grady her house and a job, and you sent her son to culinary school and bought him a restaurant." It made me uncomfortable to fish this way. I took extreme liberty with Mrs. O'Grady's actual words, and I knew it. I pushed on, though, thinking that this might be the hook for the book I'd been flailing to find.

"They owe me nothing. What have I done? Let Maeve live in that ancient cottage that she's preserved and kept neat? Tossed her a few coins for doing the work of a true farm wife? And as for Tom, he earned plenty of attention in the youth competitions for hospitality workers when he was still wet behind the ears. I didn't gain him entry into those fancy schools and programs, he got those on his own merit. I paid a few fees here and there to speed things along. And as for backing his restaurant in London, well, I got my money back and more when he sold it, didn't I?"

A waitress in a crisp white top and long, emerald-green apron appeared and refreshed our tea. Catherine came out from behind the desk and made a big show of replenishing the stack of brochures on the console near our table. She glanced at me, my bag, and my plate, searching no doubt for a clue as to why I was sitting with the Earl of Wexford having tea, while she was running credit cards and answering the phones.

Using silver tongs, the waitress added tarts, scones, and tiny cakes to the plate. She used a crumber to neaten the table, and lay down fresh linen napkins on top of smears and stains on the tablecloth (embarrassingly, all on my side of the table). With a wordless smile and a nod, she disappeared.

"In the end, there's no way I could ever repay Maeve." He took a contemplative sip from his cup. "When Helen was ill, it was she who saw us through. It must have been nine months that she stopped living her own life and devoted herself to Helen's care. At first, supporting her through physiotherapy, then dealing with the nausea and pain. For those last months, I don't know if Maeve saw daylight. What I do know is that the last thing Helen saw was Maeve's kind face smiling above her bed. If there was a discomfort she could be spared, Maeve made sure to spare her of it."

My lip trembled, remembering a similar time. I bit it, took a deep breath and asked, "How did she die?"

"Ovarian cancer."

Without warning, my eyes filled up. The Earl pulled a clean handkerchief from his breast pocket and handed it across the table.

"Your mother?" he guessed. I nodded.

"Beastly thing, cancer."

We sat in silence for a few minutes. My tears eventually subsided. He asked me a few questions about my mom; I asked him a few questions about his wife. It was good to talk nitty gritty details with someone who understood, and to have a laugh or two about some of the dark parts without being judged. Hank had shut the door on the conversation shortly after the funeral.

"I'm sure your mother is looking down on you with great pride. I know I'd be proud to have a fine daughter like you." He looked out the window, quiet for a moment. Several horses were being walked along the trail, led by grooms and students. I wondered where my mother was. I liked the idea of her looking down on me, but I just didn't feel it.

"Thank you," I said simply.

"Helen and I were never blessed with children. We'll never know if it was something related to the illness, but it doesn't matter now. In the end, she was enough for me. But her passing has left me very, very alone." Outside, a bird called. Three high chirps and a lower trill.

"Now then, I've kept you quite long enough."

"To be honest, I have to get into Ballykelty before the shops close. Is it far?"

"Not at all, just a stretch of the legs and you're there. It's a fine day to walk in the village. Go mingle with the young folk. Spring is in the air, as they say. Before you're off, however," he pulled several small disposable plastic containers from various pockets in his dressing gown, "Pack away some of these goodies. They'll only be binned and I'll bet around midnight tonight you'll be walking the floors looking for some of Tom's sweet treats. Oh, speak of the devil himself!"

I looked up to see a tall, youthful man wearing dark-wash jeans, hiking boots and a black knit turtleneck sweater. He was hunched over, looking at the floor with his hands in his front pockets. I would not have recognized him as Tom O'Grady.

"Tom!" The Earl called, beckoning. "Headed into the village, are you?"

It was with clear reluctance that Tom approached our table. Angling his body slightly toward his benefactor, he asked, "Can I run an errand for you? I'm off to meet with a few vendors at the green market."

"I've everything I need and more," the Earl said. "But Miss America here could use a guide. As a favor to me, will you show her the way?" My heart thudded. This was exactly the chance I'd been waiting for. I just wished I didn't feel like a schoolgirl whose best friend's older brother had been forced to ask her to the dance.

"Sure," Tom said, hooking his thumbs into the back pockets of his jeans and filling his chest with air, then releasing it in an elaborate sigh. "As a favor to you."

Chapter Thirteen

Better good manners than good looks.

New Yorkers are known to be fast walkers, but the combination of Tom's long stride and determined pace left me jogging alongside him by the main drive leading to the walls of the estate. The few breathless stabs at conversation I'd made had been met with not much more than a terse yes here and a no there. About halfway to the main road, it hit me. "You're embarrassed to be seen with me, aren't you?"

"Embarrassed? No."

"Is it my hair?"

He turned and looked at me for the first time. "Your hair? What about your hair?"

Now I was embarrassed. "You know, just that I have to get it done. The color's grown out and it needs a trim."

"I hadn't noticed," he said, eyes back on the road. That stung. Had he looked at me, ever? Feeling hurt put me in a prickly mood.

"What else didn't you notice?"

Eyes straight ahead, he said, "I didn't notice that you've enough glop on your lips to power an oil slick. And I suppose I didn't notice that you've lined your eyes like a raccoon."

"For your information, *Chef*, this is the fashion!" I was speaking on borrowed authority from Maggie, and hoped I was getting it right, but anyway, what did he know?

"I've no doubt it is."

"Then what's your problem?"

"I've no problem."

Jogging a few steps forward so I could be shoulder to shoulder with him, I asked, "Then why did you bring it up?"

"I didn't. You did."

"You just told me I looked ugly!"

"I never did." He pulled a roll of mints from his pocket, peeled back the paper, and offered me one. I shook my head no and waved him off. "I merely pointed out what I observed. You're wearing a lot of makeup."

"Oh, and you don't like that?"

"No, I don't." He popped a mint in his mouth. "I prefer things natural."

"Oh, you mean like Tabitha What's-Her-Name?" The minute I said it, I knew I'd blown it. Any anger or irritation that had shown on his countenance dissipated; his face was a mask of placid nothing. He walked on like I wasn't there.

Fuming, I stomped along next to him, enjoying the mild pain in my heels from smacking my shoes on the paved road. It gave me some release, kept me from needing to shout at him. It kept me from beating myself up the way Hank would if he saw how I let my emotions overtake me. "I become who I have to be to get the story," he always preached. "You can't be a big girl about it."

I had my fish on the line and I'd let him off. How stupid was I to worry what Tom O'Grady thought or didn't think of me. This was going all wrong. I intended to ask him about his philosophies of food, and to tease out stories about his life growing up here at Castle Stone, not alienate him. If he noticed my stomping, he did a good job ignoring it. We continued on without uttering another word. We turned along a busy road and walked single file along the side until we reached a crossroads at the top of a hill. Cars were buzzing past, so he held out an arm to block me from walking into the road.

"Careful," he growled, like he was in charge of me. He looked both ways, then put an arm around my shoulders, manhandling me across the street. Warmth and scent rose from his armpit, the pleasant musk with a sharp tang I remembered from the first time we'd met. Without thinking it through, I leaned in and inhaled deeply. The manly smell stirred something slumbering in my lower belly. "It's dangerous here if you don't know what you're doing."

Once we were safely across, he jammed his hands back in his pockets. "Here's the Ballykelty high street," he said, walking a few steps ahead of me.

We headed down the old, narrow road and eventually made our way onto a thin strip of sidewalk. To my American eyes, each shop was more atmospheric than the next. There was a butcher's shop with high glass cases featuring legs of what I assumed were lamb, and whole hogs' heads. The butcher himself stood dapper behind the counter in a full suit, complete with vest, and a wool hat on his head. There was a knit shop with a wooden sign touting "Aran Jumpers" in which an old woman actually sat in an armchair in the corner, knitting. Even the candy store was intriguing. Through the window, I saw boxes of bar candy with labels I'd never seen, and jars of pink lozenges, gummies shaped like babies, and some rectangles that looked like yellow sponges.

As we approached a side street, Tom stopped and announced, "This is where I'll leave you."

"Oh, all right." The abruptness of it threw me for a loop. I guess I hadn't expected to spend the day with him, but then again, what had I expected? The thought of separating from him made me lonely. "It's not him, Shayla, it's being alone in a foreign country," I advised myself. Plus, I hadn't been anywhere other than my cell, the worker's canteen and pub, and the kitchen for as long as I could remember. Being in the open space and seeing strange faces was making me feel vulnerable. Big girl's blouse, now. Tell him goodbye.

"Well good bye."

"Cheers," he said, hesitating for a moment before turning and walking away. I was bothered that he didn't look back.

I peered down the direction he was walking, and saw stalls and stalls of fresh vegetables, fruits, and an array of colorful flowers. Still others showcased jam jars of different sizes, open burlap sacks of grains with giant scoops in them, and even slabs of handmade soap. It was a place I'd want to browse later, but if I was going to get my errands done, I had to get moving.

I hurried to the only bank in town and withdrew some money. Up to now, I hadn't really spent much. My tab at the canteen and pub was on my card. Cash in hand, I sought out the uniform shop Brigid had told me about and bought myself a pair of clogs for the kitchen. I asked a lady on the street where I could find a drugstore, and she laughed and cooed over my accent. "The chemist is just past the tea shop, lamb. Good luck." She was so sweet and motherly, I wanted to follow her home. Back in New York, a woman on the street was more likely to ignore me, or worse yet, spit in my face, than take the time to stop and make friends with me. I pictured her feeding me soup and then tucking me in for the night. Was Ireland filled with such women?

On my way back to the candy store, I stumbled upon a hair salon that was open. Wary, I pushed open the door to the dubiously named, "Hair Ya?" It had an old-fashioned bell that tinkled up by the transom, and I liked that, so I decided to stay.

"Can I help?" A middle-aged woman drying a comb on a small towel stepped out from behind a screen, past the two other stylists who engaged in conversation with their be-robed clients as they snipped and curled. Her smock was stitched with her name: Grainne. "Do you have an appointment?"

"No, sorry, do you take walk-ins?"

She checked her watch. "We do, but it's getting late in the day. What were you looking for?"

"Foil highlights on my roots and a trim?"

"Sorry, love, a color correction and highlights would take too long."

I frowned. Who said anything about color correction? "Well, is there anything you can do to clean me up? I won't have a day off again for a while."

She sat me in the chair and fastened a shell-pink cape around my neck. She picked through my hair like an ape grooming its mate. Finally, she offered, "I can do a single-process to match your natural color. See the roots? You're a light golden brown."

It was one thing to be told my name was Sheila Doyle, but to be told I wasn't a blonde was another thing altogether. "No, I'm a dark blonde with platinum highlights."

"You might well have been back in the day when you started bleaching your hair, but you've aged since then." Insult to injury. And I prefer the delicate moniker "highlights" to "bleach," if you please. But what choice did I have? I couldn't go around looking like a zebra.

As my stylist mixed the color and painted it on my hair, she asked where I was from, and why I was in Ireland. She, like every other woman in Ballykelty she told me, was keenly aware of who Chef Tom O'Grady was.

"Wasn't long after that Tabitha flew off to Martha's Vineyard with that filthy American hedge fund fella, beg your pardon, and left your man Tom holding the bag a week before their wedding, lots of the girls around here thought they might be the one to salve his wounds. If a man'll commit to marriage once, he'll do it again, was the thinking." She kneaded the brownish-maroon paste into my hair with her gloved fingers. It felt so good to be touched. Ever since Des, I'd been craving any kind of contact. Before that, it had been so long. Now that my body remembered the feeling, it wanted more. I closed my eyes and relaxed into the massage.

"So, tell me, Grainne…"

My stylist laughed. "It's not pronounced 'Grainy,' it's pronounced 'Grawn-ya.'"

"Oh, sorry." I should have known better than to try to sound out any word with Gaelic roots. "Anyway, tell me," I asked in what I hoped was a casual way, "Did they? Salve his wounds, I mean?"

"Not long after he came back and opened the restaurant up there — glad to have him do it, too, we were. The whole town's economy would've come crashing down if Castle Stone failed. My own son works as a porter on the estate — that witch came to Ballykelty. And didn't she bring the circus with her! There were them paparazzi hiding in every corner, trying to get photos of her and poor Tom O'Grady. There were guards everywhere at the top of the road by the castle. I forgot to lock my car in the street one morning, and one of 'em was hunkered down in my back seat. Turns out he heard Her Majesty, Tabitha the Terrible, was getting her hair done by us. I swatted him up the street with my morning papers. Come along, love, let's get you rinsed."

"So, you never answered. Did any women around here actually salve his wounds?" I had a graphic image of a creamy-skinned Irish beauty rubbing lotion into Tom's muscled flesh.

"Whoops! Sorry, love." She'd let the hose slip. A puddle of soapy water sat on my eyelid. Tamping my eyes with a towel, she said, "I've ruined your mascara. If we have time, I'll do you a make-up application, free of charge."

She led me back to her station. With a dry mouth, I forced myself to ask yet again, "Do you know if any local women licked Tom O'Grady's wounds for him? You never said."

"People say he swore off women, so none that I heard of. But not for lack of trying. On the occasion that he came into Ballykelty, he moped about like a shadow. Course that's catnip for some. Girls want to be the one to change a man. I say it can't be done. A man's got to come to it on his own. End of. But there's no denying a dark and broody one can tempt you to try."

I shifted my eyes and got a good look at myself in the mirror. "Ah, look at the sight of you," she breathed. "Lovely."

I took the image in. I looked softer and less obvious. In a way,

I blended in with my surroundings more than I had before. But one thing was different: my eyes. On forms, when pressed to fill in the box for eye color, I'd always written "hazel." The color had always read as neither here nor there. Now, my eyes shone green, without question. I squinted and looked more closely in the mirror. They were still rimmed in gold, but the green was what popped.

"See what finding harmony with what you were born with can do for you?"

I nodded.

"The reddish tones in your natural hair color contrast with the green of your eyes. If you don't mind my sayin', that tan top isn't helping the cause at all. A young girl like you should think about wearing some color. Did you notice how the pink of the cape makes you look more lively? Now, about your cut. You've an inch of fuzz at the bottom. Would you trust me to cut it shorter? Say to around your jawline?"

I'm in this deep, I thought. Why not? Grainne obviously knew more than I. Again, I nodded.

I closed my eyes and drifted while she combed, snipped, and razored. For a moment, I imagined I was sitting in the chair at the salon around the corner from my apartment in New York. I imagined having to go to work at HPC tomorrow and then it hit me afresh that I didn't work there anymore. I shifted in my chair. Before long, I'd need to find a job. I didn't relish the thought of tapping my father's well, but the publishing world was a small one. Once it got around that I'd been fired, I wondered who'd have me. Even if anyone did, I'd be bottom assistant and certain recipient of weekend projects and coffee cups thrown at my head. Or, I could just get a job in retail and scrape along on my crumbs from writing Dumbass Guides.

A long piece of hair fell from above and brushed my cheek on its way to my lap, pulling me back to the present. Uh oh. This was not a trim. I didn't open my eyes; I wanted to save the shock for one big blow. I took a big breath and banished all thoughts of New York. For now, I was in Ireland, the land of slowness. My workdays were physical, but at least I didn't have the weight of the world on my shoulders. I'd deal with all the rest when I had to. For now, it was just nice to rest in the cushy chair and feel the warm blow dryer on my neck.

"And Bob's your uncle," the stylist said. "There. Open your eyes."

I stared. I looked like a completely different person. My brows were knit and I had a very serious look on my face. Judgmental.

"Go on, then, nobody died! It's just hair," Grainne laughed. "It grows every day."

Her humor was infectious and I burst into a laugh. I watched my mouth spread into a broad smile and my eyes lighten from clouded to bright. The more I looked at myself, the more I liked what I saw. Grainne was watching me look at myself. Two bright spots appeared high on my cheeks when I caught myself thinking, "Hey, you look pretty."

"Now, I'll stay after so we can re-do that makeup of yours."

"Is my makeup that bad?" I asked, already knowing the answer was bad.

"Not at all," she insisted, way too heartily. "It's just that I smudged it, so. It's my fault entirely that the spray got away from me."

I checked the time. I really wanted to see more of the village before everything closed.

"No thanks. Could I just get some makeup remover and splash some water on my face?"

"Yes! Let's just do that, then," she said eagerly wiping the cosmetics I'd applied. "So much better. Sure, you're gorgeous now."

When I left the shop, the sun was still strong but on the wane. It was a warm afternoon, with enough breeze to whisk away the stillness. I didn't have a plan, but found my feet carrying me up the high street and down the side street to the greenmarket. The colors and smells everywhere awakened my appetite. I bought an apple and crunched into it as I walked.

A sketch artist, working in pencils and charcoals, sat among samples of his work. Gulls on the waterfront, rolling hills studded with sheep, and an array of portraits. The faces varied in type from bubbling toddlers, chins soft with baby fat to wind-cured old men, some with pipes, some in caps. He waved me over and beckoned me to sit. I told him I didn't have the time nor the money to spend. I'd never had my portrait drawn, but I didn't enjoy having my photograph taken, so I doubted I'd like this.

"This one's with me," the shaggy-haired young man said. "Sure, you'll be doing me a favor, saving me from death by boredom and maybe bringing in some trade." I hesitated. "It won't take a minute, I swear."

Reluctant, I sat down and watched him go to work. The breeze felt soft on my face, and I liked the feeling of my legs being in the shade, while my face was in the sun. For the first few minutes, I couldn't imagine being able to stay still for the amount of time it would take. Gradually, my muscles grew used to just resting. After a while, I enjoyed doing nothing. As promised, he was done in a fairly short amount of time. When he showed me the picture, I was moved. It didn't quite register as me, at first. The dark hair, curling slightly under at my jaw threw me. Once I adjusted to that, I focused on my expression. It was softer and more serene than usual; nothing like the girl in the mirror in my apartment on 43rd Street. I could see the shadow of my mother's face in the lines of my own. I liked it.

"You're a really fine artist. I have to pay you something." I rooted in my bag for my wallet.

"Not at all, the pleasure was mine. A bargain's a bargain. Good luck with it."

I meandered around and stopped at the soap vendors, where I sniffed every bottle and bar. The fragrances of lavender, rose, vanilla bean, sandalwood, and lemon flooded my senses. I bought a small bottle of cinnamon conditioning oil to match my new hair.

I browsed bushel baskets of cabbages of hues ranging from

greenish-white to deepest purple, jewel-pink rhubarb, and carrots with the jaunty green tops still on. Next stop, a stall boasting giant barrels filled with every pickled item you could dream of. Round red peppers, cucumbers of every size from midget to jumbo, and something I didn't examine too closely that looked worryingly like eels.

At the herb and greens stand, I couldn't resist burying my face in every bundle and inhaling the scents. There was spicy arugula, tingly mint, savory oregano, and my favorite: tangy lemon verbena. I closed my eyes and took a deep sniff. That's when I heard his voice. "Sure, he sounded keen, but he's not signed the paperwork yet."

Tom O'Grady was standing on the inside of the stall, talking to the farmer who ran it. I shifted over slightly, to be hidden behind the back of a flatbed truck.

"It makes all the sense in the world," the farmer said. "We've been certified organic 100%. Do you know how much effort that took?"

"Aye, I do," Tom replied. "And I want to see it pay off just as you do."

"Did you tell him about how healthy rapeseed oil is? Did you make him understand that as a rotating crop it's perfect for the land in Galway?"

"We've been over all that. Course I did. If it were up to me, we'd be bottling it and labeling it with my logo tomorrow. But it's not up to me. We could lose our shirts without a distribution partner. Don't you think I'm eager? If we get the rapeseed oil going from your farm, my next step is jam and chutney with the Castle Stone brand. If it took off the way my business plan outlines it, it could get the estate out of debt in a matter of five years.

"When do you see him again?"

"Not for a few weeks yet," Tom said, running his fingers back through his hair. "But I've got to work something out."

"Then do it, man! What a boon it would be for me, after all these years of struggling. And you'd do the same for the fruit and veg farms with your other scheme."

"I'll give it my best effort," Tom said, shaking hands with the man.

I ducked further back behind the truck and watched him walk on to the next stall. He picked up a head of cabbage and turned it over in his hands. Bin by bin, he dwelled on various types of potatoes, spending more time with each than I could have thought possible. For the first time since I'd laid eyes on him he appeared relaxed. His brow wasn't knit and his shoulders were down.

Blending in, I followed him. The gait with which he ambled from vendor to vendor was unhurried and even light. His face was open. He smiled at people. They say there are things in life that deplete a person and things that recharge. Walking among the spoils of the land and chatting with the growers who coaxed them from the earth and hauled them here infused Tom with vitality in an obvious way. I couldn't look away from it.

I continued to follow, standing behind this pole or that stack of empty baskets. I couldn't help but draw closer and closer, upping my risk of being caught. At a stall run by goat farmers, Tom stood perusing the wheels and pots of cheese. A weathered woman proudly handed over a generous slice and Tom popped it in his mouth. He closed his eyes and savored the morsel. I was near enough to hear the deep purr in the back of his throat as he moaned "ummm." Drawn to his pleasure, I inched closer. His face was the picture of surrender. When he opened his eyes, I was caught.

The expressions on his face shuffled from ecstasy to surprise to guardedness. He searched my face, quizzical. I watched him register who I was, and his face melted into a liquid smile. Helium filled my heart.

"Well, hello there," he said.

I couldn't think of an answer.

"I might not have known you." His eyes ran over my hair, my eyes, and then down my body. I felt exposed. "It suits," his voice warm and deep. His eyes continued to rove. I looked down to check if my blouse was undone. His expression changed back to cool. "Anyhow, I'm just off home," he said, and he veered up the side street.

"Wait!" I called urgently. He stopped and turned around. "I was going to go look for a coffee. Will you join me?"

"No, I won't," he said. The bottom dropped out of me.

"Oh, OK…"

He smiled. "But I'll have a cup of tea."

Tom escorted me to one of the few places in town that served coffee that wasn't made by stirring powdered crystals into boiling water. He didn't drink coffee himself, but as a chef he understood my desire for the real version of the thing. The peace I'd witnessed in him at the market had vanished on our short walk down the side street, and the rest of the way down the cul-de-sac where the patisserie sat. He'd resumed his round-shouldered posture, hurrying along with his head down and his hands in his pockets.

His demeanor changed again once we were seated. He seemed calmed by the fact that the cozy little place was nearly empty, and the counter person who brought our hot drinks took no particular interest in us. He drank his tea with obvious relish.

"Are you hungry?" he asked. It seemed that the answer to that since I'd been in Ireland was always yes. I nodded.

"Let me just go get us both a treat." He returned to the table with two massive slices of fruit cake, each decorated with a white ball toasted brown on the top.

"Simnel cake," he explained. "You only find it around Eastertime. There are eleven of the marzipan balls on top. One for each apostle, minus Judas. That's what you get for betrayal, I suppose. Cast out and forgotten." He laughed a light, mirthless laugh.

I wondered if he was referring to Tabitha, but I chose not to dig deeper. The tinge I felt around my own dishonesty closed my mouth. I comforted myself with the fact that my lies were different and only meant to help Tom in the end. It felt sour in my belly.

I stuffed it all down with a huge bite of the sugary almond paste.

"I make one for my own mam every year, o' course, and she always fusses over the decorations. I know, though, that she's happier with something simple. I could give her the choice of a box of diamonds or a box of my shortbread, and she'd take the shortbread." He smiled, thinking of her.

"She must love eating in The Grange Hall."

"Truth to tell, she could take it or leave it. When I re-opened the place under my name, I intended a casual atmosphere. People still tend to dress smart, so Mam feels she must, too, when she comes in."

"But does she like the food?"

"She does, yeah. But she prefers simpler fare, like what I make her at home. I try not to overwork the food, even in The Grange Hall. I like to let the individual flavors stand for themselves. But high-end guests want a bit of pizzazz. A spun-sugar cage over a pudding here, a tri-colored terrine there. Mam only comes in if there's an occasion. If she eats out of the house at all, it's in Uncle Jack's Pub. The secret there is the menu is fairly well the same but the dishes are plated more casually and have homelier names."

"Speaking of your mom, do you live with her?" I asked, putting a great deal of effort into taking normal bites of my cake. I hoped I'd slipped that question in skillfully. I didn't want to seem too interested.

"I don't, no. I lived in her house as a boy, and she keeps my room there for me." Tom stared past me, thinking. "I owned a flat in London for a while. Thought I'd settle there but things didn't go according to plan."

"Where do you live?"

"If pressed, I'd have to say The Castle. I sleep in what's called The Triangle Room, in the front, right corner. Tony told me to take what I liked but I couldn't see any sense in taking one of the better rooms that could be rented, seeing as how it's just me. It's temporary. I'm just here to get the restaurant up and running and

169

the finances back on track."

"Temporary? How long have you been back?"

He laughed. "Years." He rubbed his eyes hard with the heels of his hands, then shook his head. "Ah, I don't know what I'm doing." I let that sit there, waiting. He didn't speak again.

"So, what do you cook when you're left to your own devices?" We were having such a nice conversation, I felt arch for steering it toward my goals. He'd opened up to me, finally, and here I was doing an undercover interview. Maybe he was right to be suspicious of New York types.

"Meat and veg, to be honest. I like to do a roast joint on a Sunday, with a bit of salad if it's in season. That or a nice colcannon or maybe some mashed potato. In the spring, nothing beats a shepherd's pie. I've worked hard to buy as much local meat as possible. We're close to 85 percent, and I'm still at it. Same goes for fish. We're surrounded by water. What's the point in flying in seafood?"

It felt wonderful to be having such an amiable chat. It sure beat chafing off of each other all the time.

"Surely you've tasted how sweet and fresh it all is at The Castle. No doubt you've seen the fishmongers come with the trucks now you're up before dawn to peel the spuds?" A teasing smile overtook his face, and I couldn't stop myself from smiling back. "How long do you reckon it'll take you to learn to boil water?"

"Well, if someone would actually take me in hand and teach me, I might learn!" The remark was meant to be a slap at Bill, but I was aware that it came out like a demand for private lessons.

He sat back in his chair and sipped his tea. Slowly, he said, "I might have some time."

I panicked. Blood rushed to my cheeks and my pulse raced. A scene with the two of us alone in the kitchen splashed across my mind and I realized just how attracted to him I was. A vision of me reaching up to kiss him played in my head, swiftly followed by one of him pushing me away. I was mortified! Of course he wouldn't be kissing me. As if! I worked for him. I was American.

Plus, my hairdresser said he wasn't on the market.

"Well, I would certainly value your input," I said crisply, sitting up in my chair.

"I hope you don't mind my sayin', but you're a bit of an odd duck."

"Of course I mind you saying it."

"You misunderstand me, I mean it in a good way." Maybe that's what he said, but I felt under a spotlight. I got that hollow feeling in my belly, like when sexy Nate back at the HPC office called me "Pal" while sliding his hand around Padma's delicate waist. Wasn't I always the ugly duckling in a pond full of swans? Jordan sure brought the point home when he drooled all over our lithe cocktail waitress instead of paying attention to me on our date. I didn't need another handsome guy with tons of status to blatantly point out that I'm an also-ran and always would be.

"How can there be a good way?"

He sat up straight. "I meant that you're different." And here we were again…off on a bad foot. I should have known the ease wouldn't last.

"Different always means weird. Different is the sister's funny best friend." I sensed I should let it lie, but being insulted by Tom O'Grady shamed me. The shame was channeling itself into brattiness.

"I like funny," he said irritably. "I also like different. More's the pity for you if you don't. Anyway, I've just seen the time. If you'll excuse me, I have to get back." He threw a few notes and coins down on the table. As he reached the door, he turned back. Relief coursed through my veins. I wanted him to come back and have another cup of tea. He wavered for a second and I held my breath, waiting. Finally he said, "If you come back after dark, mind yourself on the main road." With that, he turned and walked out of the shop, the door easing to a close behind him.

Dear Mags, it's confirmed. I'm my own worst enemy. Why is it that when something is going smoothly, I have a compulsion to blow it apart? : See Assistant Job/HPC. I had Tom O'Grady right where I wanted him then I mouthed off and drove him away. Here's the idiotic thing — I imagined he was flirting with me. Stupid, I know. Now that Des opened up Pandora's Box (pun intended) I guess my subconscious is sniffing around to see what's available. OK, we agree. No more checking out Tom O'Grady's backside or wondering what it would be like to feel the stubble on his jaw. I think the next night out at the worker's pub, I'll just grab one of the myriad undergardeners/ bellmen/grooms/busboys who're anyone's for a pint and a glass of whiskey, and get it out of my system. There. No more Tom.

I can't believe I'm even wasting my time dwelling on Tom and his oh-so-obvious rock star hair and his come-to-bed eyes. What am I, every dizzy girl in town? No ma'am. I see beyond all that. My ex-partner, Noah, wore orthopedic shoes and a lavender Member's only jacket, and he insisted that we call each other "partners." (That still makes me shudder a little), but he did have a Ph.D. in physics. See? I saw beyond. And no one could ever accuse my first real boyfriend, Josh, of being good looking, am I right?

I can't believe I'm wasting time on all this trivial B.S. when I have actual good news. Here it comes! I figured out what this book is!!!

All this time I've been struggling, trying figure out how my book could compete with every high-end cookbook on the bookstores' gift tables, slick with haute cuisine food shots and intricate five-step/three-page recipes and the answer was right here: Don't compete. Simple.

Simple is the whole key. Instead of precise measurements weighed to the gram, I'll encourage 'Chef O'Grady,' (smug bastard) to suggest 'a handful of this,' or 'as much of this as you like,' offering a guide that's more like a recipe your friend's grandmother would have scribbled down for you on the way out the door.

When he talked to me about food just now, he spoke with such passion and delight. I just need to get him to talk so I can capture it. I can use it to write glorious essays about local food. The poetry is already there, in his language, in the way he paints the picture of what he loves.

I can fill in the blanks from experience. I'll weave the smell of Ireland's chimney smoke and the sound of its boat's horns into the headnotes. And of course, there should be photos. How could there not be with the landscape here and the atmospheric aspects of Mrs. O'Grady's kitchen? But here's where it's different — there should be also hand-drawn images of huge loaves of bread, and long, rustic farm tables covered with root vegetables, maybe a pot of chicken soup on the fire. Home.

"Hiya," a man said. I looked up from my journal, and standing there was an attractive 20-something guy with a charming smile and a nice, solid body. "I noticed you're alone. There's a pub not far from here, if you'd like to get a drink with me."

I looked past him out the window. The sun was setting behind the castle way up on the hill. He seemed nice enough, but I just didn't have the taste for it.

"Thank you so much for asking, but I have to get home." I smiled.

"Maybe another time, then." he said. He was gone as quick as he'd shown up. I opened my notebook and scrawled down one last thought:

Listen, Maggie, it's getting late and I need to head back to the Castle before dark so I don't get myself lost. I'll write again soon. Love, Shayla

P.S. I totally changed my hair. And guess what? A random stranger asked me out! I think I might love it. I owe you a selfie. xx

With the sun mostly down, there was a slight chill in the air. The cool air danced on my now-exposed neck. I turned up my collar against it. I retraced the steps I'd taken earlier alongside Tom. The foreign sounds all around kept me on high alert. A housecat screeched; I heard the distant sound of a horse galloping. A car horn beeped its high funny beep, and I realized I was walking on the wrong side of the road for safety. Once I was inside the walls of the estate, I felt safer but the twilight and the coolness heightened the fact that I was alone. Tired now, I dragged my feet the length of the driveway. Without Tom to argue with, the walk back was twice as long.

Chapter Fourteen

A promise is a debt.

I stopped at two cups of tea this morning. I was starting a week of "jobs rotation," meaning the goal was to expose me to everything on the grounds, and I was nervous enough without being wired on caffeine. I didn't relish the idea. My comfort in the restaurant was increasing but Mary explained that everyone doing work experience was required to do this, regardless of his concentration or specialty. "It's a benefit, really," she explained when I begged her to keep me put. "And Sheila," she said, emphasizing my fake name, "People would notice if I gave you special treatment. We don't want to be found out, do we, so?"

It was hard to believe another week had gone by without Tom telling me why hadn't fired me on the spot, the very first day. Since then, I'd learned a fair amount despite Bill's swim-or-die attitude. Brigid helped, and I always had one eye on Tom, watching the way he kneaded dough for the pie-crusts or the way he plated a simple stew with a sprinkling of fresh herbs on the top. On breaks, I jotted down notes and made simple sketches so I'd remember it all. The book was taking shape. As often as possible, I eased the stained and spotted recipes out of their plastic holders and into my pockets. More than once, Bill had dressed us all down for being careless, citing the extra work he had to do to replace all the missing ones. Lined up with the others, I gazed at him with a look of innocence. I couldn't get caught; I'd had to deliver Oscar-winning performances. Butter would not have melted in my mouth.

The book was coming along. I'd pinned down chapter headings and was narrowing down themes for essays. Once I presented it to him, there was no way he could say no. And thank God for that, my funds were dwindling and my student loans and credit card bills weren't going to pay themselves.

When I thought about Hank, there was a sickening dread in my bones. I hadn't spoken to him since I got here. It's not like we chatted daily when I was home in New York, but the amount of time that had passed was stacking up. He'd left a couple of messages asking how I was, which was unusual. I was generally the one who reached out. I hadn't told him I'd been fired from HPC.

I made it a point to stay off my phone since the international calls cost a mint. I did shoot out the occasional email, but to use the wifi I had to head to the lobby in the castle. Most nights, I was too tired. Also, I tried to keep away from snooty Catherine, the receptionist, as much as possible. I was up very early this morning to prepare for my unfamiliar day and I'd ducked her in the workers' canteen. She was dressed impeccably and clearly headed for the front desk. Clean and safe. That's the kind of life girls like that got handed on a silver platter. And where was I scheduled for work today? The chicken coop.

I wrestled with the lock on the gate. Here's a tip if you don't already know it: chickens are loud! By the time I gained entrance inside the fence, sweat drenched my body from the combination of the exertion and the tension of the chickens' insistent squawks. There was straw on the ground and birds milling around everywhere. There were white ones, black ones, large ones, small ones, spotted ones, and one poor hen hopping on one leg. They made me nervous. I kept my eye peeled for the rooster, who woke me up every day. I'd never laid eyes on him, but I had a picture in my mind and it wasn't pretty.

"Hello?" I called through the open door. Mrs. O'Grady rushed out past me, sending the birds scattering in terror, screaming louder than they had before, and slammed the gate shut.

"Dear, you mustn't leave that open. The hens'll escape." She looked me up and down with a skeptical eye. "I'm afraid that jumper is far too pretty to ruin out here in the yards. Oh, and your shoes. They won't do at all." I was wearing a pair of beige canvas espadrilles. Aside from my gym sneakers — which no women wear on the street — this was about as casual as it got in New York. "They'll be stained as soon as you step in your first cow pat." *My first cow pat? How many would there be?*

"Come along," she said, leading me out of the gate and closing it tightly behind us. "We'll find you a field jacket and some Wellies in the barn."

In short order, I was back at the hen house in a too-large canvas coat with the sleeves rolled up, clomping along with a green pair of rubber boots on my feet. I had to admit, it was pretty fun to step right in mud puddles rather than avoiding them.

"Now then, the chore list is on the wall, you may as well get down to it." She grabbed a bucket and scattered feed. Chickens everywhere scrambled, clucked, and pecked. I rushed inside the hen house, trying not to look like I was running. The chickens inside seemed to be napping. Much better.

"Right," I thought, "I'll just get down to it." I read the list:

1. Mend holes in walls. Hmm. I didn't know where to find a hammer, or even if that's what one would use to do the job. When Maggie moved to the city, her father had given her a dusty-pink "Do-It-Herself" tool kit that looked like an oversized cosmetic bag, but was filled with screwdrivers, nails, and pliers. The only time we ever took it out of the bottom of the closet was the night we rolled in drunk from the office party and couldn't find a corkscrew.

After an hour, we opened the bottle with a hand-drill. This seemed substantially more complicated. OK, on to the next thing.

2. Give the hens vitamins 1X/day. Syringes on shelf. I looked at the various chickens sitting around in their boxes. Their beaks looked sharp. If I tried to pry their mouths open, would they bite me? Surely one day without vitamins wouldn't kill them. Didn't *Prevention* magazine say vitamins were a scam anyway? I was pretty sure it did. Anyway, the fair-skinned holistic doctor who wore the turban down at Gramercy Apothecary told me that Vitamins D and B would increase my breast tissue (which I thought was pretty rude considering I was in there for an earache). Chickens wouldn't want big breasts. They'd be more likely to get eaten. Moving on…

3. Gather eggs 3X/day. Use wire baskets by door. I could do that! Eagerly, I picked up a basket and peeked into the straw for eggs. I didn't see any. Maybe someone had already done this?

Mrs. O'Grady came back into the henhouse, and set her feed bucket on a high shelf. She looked at my empty basket. "Are you collecting the eggs?"

"Yes!" I said, trying to look busy. I'd come too far to get sent home now. Joy! I saw an egg sitting in an unoccupied box. I picked it up, and put in it my basket. "There."

Mrs. O'Grady stood there, waiting. Finally she said, "And are you going to collect the rest?" I looked around and didn't see any more eggs. "The rest are under the hens, dear," she said helpfully.

"Yes, of course," I laughed it off. "That's because they came out of the bottoms of the chickens. Right." I approached a spotted hen and she turned her head to one side, giving me the fish eye. "I'll just check now." Mrs. O'Grady waited. Gingerly, I reached toward the tail of the hen. Maybe the egg was at the back. As I reached, the hen hit out with a lightning-fast peck. I screamed like a little girl and pulled my smarting hand to my mouth.

"Daisy!" Mrs. O'Grady scolded the bird. "Don't let her bully you, Sheila. You just pick up the hen carefully and hold the wings to the side, like so." She authoritatively scooped up the chagrined chicken and took the egg. "Then, you just set her down safely in her spot, no harm done." I stood frozen to my spot. I was saved when one of the maintenance men walked through the door, holding a huge pickle bucket containing nails, screws, and other tools.

"Came to patch up those coupla holes, but I can do it later if you're busy, Mrs. O'Grady."

"Not at all, Jimmy. I'll have one of the boys collect eggs when you're through here. We're just off to get Sheila settled in minding the horses. She signaled for me to follow and I did.

"Mrs. O'Grady? Sorry about that. I'm sure I'll get the hang of it soon."

"Don't worry, there's plenty to be done elsewhere."

The stables were a gentle walk away, and I enjoyed the rising sun of the April morning on my face. Horses sounded good to me. I'd read *Black Beauty* and *Misty of Chincoteague*. I could do that. Shielding my eyes, I could see all of the activity. Guests were being fitted with helmets and matched with horses, grooms were brushing down the shining animals, and two children were being trotted around in a circle, in a fenced-in circular course. It really was beautiful.

"Do you ride, yourself?" Mrs. O'Grady asked me.

"Sure, who doesn't?" I mean, I'd been taken around Central Park in a carriage the night of my senior prom, and my grandparents had set me on the back of a pony or two when I was a kid when we'd gone apple-picking upstate.

"Mornin' fellas! This is Sheila. She's on the work experience rota and here to lend a hand," Mrs. O'Grady called. As we drew closer to the action I grew more and more nervous. Some of the horses were way bigger than I'd imagined from this perspective.

"Hiya, Sheila," one of the men said offhandedly. He was leading a gleaming chestnut horse over to us. The animal's shoulder was as tall as my face, and its muscles flicked and rippled under its skin. Its hooves thudded heavily on the well-packed dirt, belying the fact that it weighed a ton and could easily crush me.

Don't ever get behind a horse, a voice echoed in my head. I had no memory of where I'd heard that, but I vaguely recalled a tale of someone doing just that and having his skull kicked at the soft part of his temple. Maybe.

Behind me, the thundering of hooves closed in. I whipped around in terror to see a black horse with flaring nostrils bearing down on us. I squealed. Realizing I'd turned my back on the first horse I jumped back and forth, trying to position myself away from any beast's hind legs. The black horse slowed to a stop about a foot from my face. It whinnied and blew a hot blast of air from between its lips, spraying me. I squealed again.

"Keep your voice down," the man on the ground chided me. "You'll spook 'em." I clamped my mouth shut. The rider dismounted and held the reins out for me to take. "Go grab a sweat scraper and a rubber curry and take care of Demon, here." *Sweat scraper? Rubber what?*

"On second thought, we'll save the stables for another day. Sorry lads. We'll leave you to it."

Without a word, I followed Mrs. O'Grady. She wasn't smiling anymore. Was she going to march me to Mary and tell her to have security escort me off the estate? As we passed one of the central fountains, Danny the gardener popped out from behind a bush, holding a giant pair of hedge trimmers.

"Mornin' Danny," Mrs. O'Grady said. "Those box woods are looking fine. I love the smell of 'em." She looked at Danny, then looked at me. "I don't suppose…"

I shook my head, then hung it in shame. What was the point in pretending I could garden? They'd probably sit me up on a backhoe and tell me to devise an irrigation system. "You wouldn't be headed to the church, would you?" Danny asked.

A light bulb went off for Mrs. O'Grady. "That's a grand idea!"

"Could I trouble you to take over a few armfuls of flowers? One of the boys set some aside for the grottoes and altar decorations. They're just here in the glasshouse…"

After a long, silent walk, Mrs. O'Grady and I ducked out of the sunlight and into the dark, cool stone church, arms laden with giant bouquets of cut stems. I wondered what she had in mind for me. She laid her blooms on a long, wide wooden table at the back and I followed suit. She dipped her fingertips in a marble font of water and deftly dipped to the floor on one knee, crossing herself. She moved to a kneeling bench and bowed her head in prayer. I felt awkward. I didn't want to do anything disrespectful. The little Dutch Reformed church to which my grandparents belonged was a simple wooden affair. This felt more like a museum to me.

At the front of the church was a carved, wooden life-sized crucifix. The altar, set up three stone steps from the floor, was covered in a white silk cloth, embroidered with green and gold thread. Everywhere I looked, there were friezes and Celtic crosses and statues of every type of wood and stone you could imagine. The simplicity of the exterior of the stone building didn't begin to hint at the splendor within its walls. The pews looked to be carved from cherry, and though the floor in the entrance and back of the church were slate and stone, the areas under the pews and toward the front were gleaming oak.

A priest came out of one of the several doors along the back side, near a glimmering bank of votive candles. He nodded to me solemnly and headed in my direction.

"Would you like to make confession?" He wrung his hands as he stood there.

My mind raced. If they knew, they knew. Mentally I calculated whether I had enough material to finish the book. For a second I wondered about priest-client confidentiality. If I told him I wasn't Sheila Doyle, did he have to keep it to himself?

"My child?" he probed. "Ah, Maeve," he said, looking over my shoulder. I exhaled in relief. "Are you here to make confession?"

"I'll do that on Saturday, before Mass," she said. "We're here to clean. Father, I'd like you to know Sheila Doyle. Sheila, Father Walsh."

"Hello Sheila. Are you a Catholic?"

"No," I admitted. I hated to be a disappointment.

"No worries. All are welcome, any time. Ladies," he said nodding and hurrying to the back, and out one of the many doors there.

"I'll just get you set up. Broom closet's that way. There's a mop and floor wax. After the floor, you can polish the brass and clean the pews with oil soap. You'll find a chamois on the shelf."

Oh man.

Mrs. O'Grady busied herself with unwrapping flowers from the brown paper they were bound in. Nervous, I went to the supply closet and looked at the bottle and cans of cleaning agents. How was I supposed to say I'd never even held a string mop in my hands? We only ever used a Swiffer. I chose a roll of paper towels and a bottle of electric-blue spray cleaner. Exuding confidence, I sprayed a bit on the very back pew and swiped a paper towel back and forth.

"Sheila! No." Mrs. O'Grady shouted.

I froze. As she marched toward me, I took her in. The solid Irish woman in her sensible wool cardigan and work boots would scorn me if I told her I didn't know how to do housework; that two able-bodied young women like Maggie and I availed ourselves of a cleaner every two weeks. She must think I'm useless. The lower part of my gut felt hollow. There was nothing to anchor my breath. She's right to think that. The closer the capable woman got, the more numb my fingertips felt. I was useless at my job. Again. Matty proved that to Lizbeth in short order. Brenda had no use for me as a writer. She only threw me a bone to get in Hank's good graces. And Hank, what Hank really wanted was a son who'd drink scotch with him, and chase women, and write about it, Hemingway-style for manly publications. And as a friend, I was utterly and completely useless. I made a mental note to tell Maggie to pick someone else as maid of honor. She deserved someone who knew how to do things, practical things.

Mrs. O'Grady closed in on me. I turned my back on her, and sprayed polish on the back of the pew until it pooled and trickled down onto the seat.

"Stop. You'll ruin the wood! Honestly girl, did your mother teach you nothing?"

"Obviously not!" I answered, exasperated. "There wasn't enough time."

That did it. I started crying full tilt, with no warm-up or warning. It made me feel even worse about myself. Women like Mrs. O'Grady had faced centuries of wars, famines, and other hardship. You didn't see Irish women collapsing into heaps and weeping. They faced their troubles and got on with it.

I was surprised when she folded me into her arms and pulled my head onto her strong shoulder. "Oh, my darling girl," she said, swaying slowly back and forth. "I didn't know. Ah, bless." She held me even when I tried to pull away, cooing vowels into my ear and murmuring "shh."

I cried because I missed my mother. I cried because I had no relationship with my father. I cried because Brenda didn't value me or my writing. I cried because Maggie got a book deal and I didn't. I cried because I didn't know how to wax a floor. I cried because Tom O'Grady didn't know who the real me was.

Mrs. O'Grady eased me onto the bench of a pew and sat with her arm around my shoulders as my sobbing faded to hiccups, and my hiccups faded to heavy breathing. Eventually, I was cleansed. No more tears came. We sat together in silence, with me gathered in to her breast, enveloped in the stillness and beauty of the church.

Finally, she spoke. "I think we've done enough work for one day. Let's skive off to mine and have a pot of tea."

Dear Maggie,

I know I could be writing this to you via email so that you'd actually get to read it this century, but I can't bring myself to type. The sound of the clacking keys reminds me of HPC, and of Brenda. Everything I do here is done at half-speed, and that seems to be working for me. My thoughts can't keep up with my fingers when I type these days. It feels more right to pull a pen across sheets of paper. I'm relaxing in Mrs. O'Grady's backyard, letting the sun warm my bones. That's right, I said relaxing. You'd hardly recognize me. To be fair, I am writing in my journal but that's pleasure, not business. The pleasure is bittersweet as I'm thinking about my mother today. I never said this before, but she would have loved you, Mags. She'd have picked us up on 43rd Street in her Volvo wagon, driven us up to Rhinebeck and listened to your spunky stories the whole weekend through. She'd have sat you on the comfy sofa, poured you a glass of the burgundy she loved, and just listened. My mom knew how to relax, and she knew how to listen. She loved my stories, Maggie. Maybe that's why I became a writer.

I spent the morning telling Mrs. O'Grady all about my mom. Talking about her hurt a little, I won't lie. This time, though, I saw the possibility of joy replacing the former darkness that threatened to diminish me. The grief used to make me small. Today, there was an unclenching inside me. Now I can have my mother here with me without…without what? Without fear, maybe. Mrs. O'Grady says my mother was always here, watching over me. I don't quite believe it the way she does. I can't picture guardian angels. But maybe in some way my mom is just beside me. Before, thinking about her pulled me into the past or the future; I was untethered to the earth. Today, I feel like a grown woman. Maybe Brenda was right not to consider my book. Maybe it wasn't finished because I wasn't an adult yet.

It's weird to say this Mags, but I don't really care about that book anymore.

More later… Love Shay xx

Fragrant steam bathed my face as I stood at Mrs. O'Grady's funny little stove stirring the pot of soup I'd spent the afternoon making. The morning had been whiled away in conversation over her tidy little kitchen table. She'd coaxed the story of my mother's diagnosis, illness, and death out of me using a combination of sensitivity and matter-of-factness born refined by her own suffering. After all the years of skirting the issue so as not to upset Hank, or the aunts who advised him about my upbringing, the lock on my heart had been picked. It was like taking off a corset, and putting on a flowing silk nightgown. I was floating.

Mrs. O'Grady, with her typical dry Irish humor, had asked me at one point, "If you can't milk cows, tend hens, groom horses, or clean a house, what can you do?" and we'd laughed until a different kind of tears streamed down my cheeks. I told her I could write, and that I was very, very good at it. And I told her I could make chicken soup.

"That's one thing my mother taught me to do," I said fondly.

"Then make me a pot of soup, why don't you? I've nothing for my tea this evening, so." She ducked up to the castle at the kitchen to fetch parsley, carrots, dill, and the rest of the ingredients, and left me drinking tea in her sunny garden, scratching Nap the collie behind the ears and throwing him the odd stick or two to fetch.

"Oh, look, Mrs. O'Grady," I called up the stairs. I gave the soup a final stir and put the lid on the pot. "Here comes His Lordship!" This was perfect. He'd been so kind at tea, sharing about his wife, listening about my mother. I longed to be surrounded by people around whom I could be myself.

I could see him out the kitchen window, walking the side path that led to the O'Grady cottage. The waning sun was behind him. He was dressed in riding clothes and walked with a thick walking stick.

"Mrs. O'Grady?" I called up again. She didn't answer.

I walked out the front door. Nap was standing on the table under the window, dancing and whining. I shared Nap's enthusiasm. When I opened the gate, he jumped down and shot out toward the Earl. He leaped up and banked his front paws off the old man's chest, doing a backflip.

"Nap!" I hollered. "Be careful!"

"Not to worry," he said, "It's a trick we perfected when he was a pup. We'll join the circus yet, won't we laddie?" He bent down and gave the dog a scratch. "You're looking well, Sheila. I didn't expect you here."

"Mrs. O'Grady should be down in just a second. Why don't you come in and wait? I could make tea." It wasn't my place to host, but I didn't think Mrs. O'Grady would mind. I didn't want to go back to my cell; I needed connection.

"I've just come to say hello to Nap, here. He hasn't been to see me in a few days. I wanted to make sure he was staying out of trouble."

"You've walked all this way, don't you want to rest for a few minutes before you head back?" I urged. He didn't answer, focusing on patting Nap instead. I'd never seen him look uncomfortable before but I could tell he was at a loss for words. Mrs. O'Grady came to the front door.

"Hello, Your Lordship," she called. *Lordship? That's weird, when I call him Tony.*

"Maeve," he said, seeming to savor the sound of the word. "Lovely to see you." Nap ran in circles around the man. We all stood there for a while, saying nothing, until I remembered I had soup on the stove.

"I was just telling Tony he should come in and sit down for a minute before he heads back." I really wanted company. The thought of going to the worker's pub didn't appeal. I was too raw for all the flirting and banter.

"I made soup, Tony. It would be rude to refuse a bowl, wouldn't it?" I urged.

Mrs. O'Grady's face drained of its color.

"Yes, soup," she said. "Won't you come through?"

"I, well, should probably be getting back to the…thingy."

"Please?"

"If you insist," he said. We all went in and I took Tony's walking stick, which I noticed was an elaborately carved trio of snakes topped off with a crown, and got him settled at the table. Nap was standing on the table outside the window, nose pressed to the glass.

"Your Lordship, would you care for a brandy?" Mrs. O'Grady asked.

"That would go down a treat," he replied, sitting tall in his chair.

In the kitchen, Mrs. O'Grady carefully placed three crystal glasses on a tray. "Jesus, Mary and Holy Saint Joseph," she said. "Company in the lounge, and me in an old housedress." She poured, emptying a bottle.

"It's just Tony." I washed my hands with the chunky bar of sage soap in the wooden dish at the sink. "Do you usually get dressed up when he comes over?"

"He's never been here."

"You have got to be kidding," I said, drying my hands on the dishtowel. How long had she lived here? Forty years? More? "Not even when his wife was alive?"

"Lady Helen was brought up to stand on manners and tradition. It goes without saying she was highborn. It just wasn't done."

"Because of her title?"

"Yes, that and more. If you haven't lived it, you might not understand. And it was a different time. There was no internet. People didn't have telly. Things were done a certain way, and that's that."

"But after she died?"

A flush ran up from the neckline of her cotton dress and landed in her cheeks. "An unmarried man and a widow having tea. This isn't America, you know."

She liked him. *Liked him* liked him. I was ashamed that I didn't think of it before. Just because she had gray in her hair didn't mean she was dead inside.

"Right, now that you've explained it, I see," I said. "But I'm here, right? So even Father Walsh couldn't complain. Go in, sit.

Keep him company. I'll bring this."

On the way out, she glanced at herself in a mirror whose glass was nearly obscured by all the prayer cards tucked under the wood, and cleared her throat.

"Sheila's bringing the drinks," I heard her say in a voice two octaves above her own. "Won't be a moment."

I opened the liquor cabinet from which she'd gotten the brandy and checked inside. I wished Hank could have found someone like Maeve O'Grady. I suppose he could have, but he'd chosen a series of gold diggers, dimwits, star fuckers, and floozies instead. Around my thirteenth birthday, I asked if he thought about remarrying. "Your mother was the only one," was his answer and we never discussed it again.

I heard laughter coming from the other room and Mrs. O'Grady's voice returned to the lilting alto that had soothed me in the church. The soup could wait until dinnertime.

There was another half bottle of brandy in the cabinet, plus some whiskey and a full bottle of claret. I put it all on the tray and carried it through.

Chapter Fifteen

"Morning, ladies!"

A little shiver ran through me as I crossed the threshold of the hen house. The May sun was so warm, I'd shed my field jacket almost as soon as I'd put it on. Now in the cool dampness, I could use the long sleeves.

I grabbed a wire basket and began filling it with eggs. After many run-throughs with Mrs. O'Grady, I was finally capable of a firm hand with the birds. A leaf-green inchworm was making its way across the chore sheet. I paused my work for a few minutes to watch it make its way across the wide expanse of the page, measure by measure. A cool breeze blew through the shed. My arms erupted in goose bumps and my nipples stiffened.

"Hello there," Tom said, ducking through the doorway, taking care not to hit his head. The low, chocolate timbre of his voice resonated in my chest, sending a signal to my brain to make my nipples even more taut. I noticed him looking. He flicked his eyes upward to my face. "I was after my mam."

"I'm on my own today," I said, picking up the basket of eggs to show off my accomplishments.

"Been awhile since I've seen you. How're you keeping?"

"I'm getting strong, that's for sure." I made a muscle with my bicep. My arm shot down immediately, once I realized I was showcasing my chest. "I just meant that working the rotation has been really physical. I like it, especially the horses. Other than Demon, obviously. Your mom's been really kind to me."

"She said you've been at hers quite a bit." He read the chores list. It was the same one that had been hanging there since I came.

"Yeah, Tony and I have been watching TV with her in the evenings. I'm loving Irish television. It's such a mixed bag of highbrow BBC and stuff that looks like someone filmed with their iPhone in a church basement. Tony loves spending evenings at your mom's. He seems so much more energetic now than when I got here."

"About that…I'm concerned that…" He stopped. "It's like this. Widows and widowers, well…that isn't really on. Not here in Ireland. You wouldn't understand."

"No, I get it," I lied. "Let me tell her you're worried." I didn't want Tom getting in the middle of Mrs. O'Grady and the Earl. I'd laid such excellent groundwork. Every night that I'd been free, I'd finagled a dinner plan with lots of glasses at cocktail hour. A routine was being established, and I think the Earl was growing to like it. I changed the subject. "After this, I need to go to my room and pick up some dishtowels we wrapped some food in the first time I ate with her. I finally did laundry and I've been meaning to get them back."

"No need," he said. "I'll walk you to yours and pick up the towels, then go tell her myself."

"I need to get these eggs to the kitchen." I really didn't want him to get to his mom before I did. Hosting the Earl suited her. She laughed all the time and looked ten years younger.

"I'll send one of the boys for them. Ready?"

I had no choice but to walk him back to the dorms. We fell into step, side-by-side. I didn't like having my hand forced. Despite the sunshine and soft air, I was edgy.

"So now you're not embarrassed to walk with me?"

"What are you on about?"

"When we walked to town. You were embarrassed."

"I never was. It was to protect you." He stopped and steered me around a pile of horse manure. "Sometimes photographers follow me. I wouldn't want them to get the wrong idea and splash lies all over the rags about how we're a couple."

"Thanks for protecting me." I felt like something had been taken away from me.

We walked the rest of the way without saying much. Tom seemed relaxed. He waved to some guests on a trail ride. He stopped to watch a rabbit chewing on a grape hyacinth. I didn't share his ease.

At the dorms, I expected him to wait at the entrance but he followed me in and down the hall. Brigid, wrapped in a towel and carrying her bath caddy, offered us a cautious greeting. When we got to my room, I went in to get the towels and was shocked when he pressed in behind me. He spied the sketch of me from the market and moved in to examine it. "Lovely," he said.

Panicked, I scanned the room. I rushed to my desk and pushed the photos and fact sheets from my file on Tom, along with my handwritten notes for the book into a pile. I threw my pajamas on top. My passport was lying out, but it was closed. There was a pile of recipes at the foot of my bed. These, he saw. I managed to flip them upside down and sit on top of them before he could examine them closely.

"Studying recipes?" he asked, looking around the room. His eyes landed on my tres expensive black satin bra with the hot-pink piping (a gift from Maggie) hanging on the back of the door. There was no point rushing to hide it, what was done was done. I kept my seat, trying to look like the kind of girl who doesn't care if men examine her lingerie.

"You know, I like to learn." I steadied my breathing. "Whatever." I leaned back on my elbows, trying to look relaxed. Realizing I was lying on my bed, I sprung to a sitting position and crossed my legs.

He nodded. "Anyhow, I think it's time you came back to the kitchen. I'll let Mary know later."

Oh, finally. I'd honestly been enjoying learning skills such as differentiating weeds from plants and pulling them, and milking the goats and rolling logs of their cheese in ash to preserve it. But I needed to get back into the kitchen. I'd been writing up the recipes I could get my hands on, and converting the measurements to United States standards as best as I could, but I needed to gather more, watch more, and ask more questions.

"Would you like that?" he asked, going back to my portrait, and leaning in close. "Being back in the kitchen?"

I watched him examining the likeness of me. He looked from the portrait to my eyes, studying me. "Yes, I'd like that."

He walked over to the door and pushed it closed. "Sheila," he said, walking toward me. My breath caught in my throat. I was aware that I hadn't made my bed. The pillows were akimbo and the sheets were rumpled. He sat down next to me. I turned my body to face his. Our shoulders nearly touched.

"Sheila, there's something I've been meaning to ask you. It goes back to the first day we met, if I'm honest. I had this idea, you see, but I wasn't sure you'd agree."

I could smell him, the heat under his hair. I caught a faint whiff of tangy apple under the clean smell of sweat. I inhaled. It was too loud.

"What?" I asked, to cover.

"Here's the thing," he struggled. "All right, here it is."

Without thinking, I tilted my face upward. My mouth was so dry. I felt my lips part.

"I need you to go out to dinner with me."

"Dinner?"

"There's more to it. It's a business arrangement, see?"

"Oh." I rose to my feet. I hoped he hadn't noticed how my body had been straining toward him. I grabbed my bathrobe off the pile of pillows on the bed and hung it over my bra. I could see that he noticed. He glanced at my chest and then looked away.

"But if you agree, it'll require bending the truth a wee bit."

I crossed my arms and kept my face placid. "Go on."

"This American distributor, he's considering backing a scheme for Castle Stone's range of natural and organic foods. The ace in the hole that my partners and I have in mind is rapeseed oil. You see, it's healthy and easy to produce, and could give a lot of struggling Irish farmers a leg up. The rest of the world just doesn't know it yet. Together with that, I've ideas about jams and pickles, and the like. Ingredients grown the right way, and processed without chemicals." His eyes shone as he went on to describe his plan. The main focus would be local. His idea was to produce locally and distribute locally. But he needed a wider sprawl to make it worth it for the number of farmers he had in his collective to make a financial go of it. Many of these farmers, he said, had been considering selling the land to manufacturers and real estate moguls.

"What if they win?" he asked. "Will this still be The Emerald Isle in a century?"

Family farms were having trouble competing, he explained. The plan was to keep production small, however, and even with success to avoid growing to the point where the business would abandon sustainable practices. The farmers and other workers would be shareholders, and a portion of the profits would be donated to endeavors that re-invested in the land and small farms such as reforestation and offering micro-loans to farmers who wanted to switch over to certified organic methods.

He impressed me. His enthusiasm caught me off guard and I found it sexy. My mouth got drier and drier as I realized my eyes were locked on his.

"Sounds like you're quite the businessman."

"Ah, never. The partners and I have come up with a scheme. Those with better skills than I will handle the money and management part. My role is to keep my eye on the flavors, and the quality of the foods we produce. If food can't be fresh, I like to keep it as close to its original form as possible. For instance, I've a blackberry jam recipe that's nothing but blackberries. Picked at the right season and canned right away, they wouldn't need sugar or preservatives. Just blackberries." He was smiling wide now, leaning back on one elbow across my narrow bed. I couldn't help smiling back.

"You should call it that. Just Blackberries. Boom. Sold to every Seattle foodie and L.A. mom of a private school toddler."

"That's the kind of talk I'll need from you at this dinner, if you can stomach doing this for me. The fella in charge is a real London bastard, pardon my French. He's the eyes and ears of the American in charge. He swans around in his Armani suits talking about the bottom line." He shook his head. His eyes were clouded and seemed three shades darker than usual.

"I can hardly stomach him. One of the sticking points is that he doesn't like the Irish. Thinks we're second-class. On top of it, this joker is a wannabe American, always going on about 'straight talk,' and 'no bullshit,' like he's some kind of cowboy. He's pure Oxbridge and his international banker dad pulled strings to get him across the pond and into Harvard Law. By the way he goes on, you'd think he ran with gangsters in Chicago rather than singing with the Glee Club in dear old Boston. I'd hate to see what he made of the Irish over there."

"When is it?"

"It's not far off. The meeting's to take place in Dublin. Ridiculous. We've a world-class restaurant right here. He said, and I quote, 'I've only one evening to devote to this. I don't have time to head out to the sticks.'" He sat forward, elbows on his knees. He punched one fist into the other hand.

"I'm not sure what I'll wear." My mind was racing, scouring over the handful of items I'd brought in my carry-on bag. I hadn't needed to buy anything to supplement, except for the kitchen clogs. What I wore around the estate were mostly hand-me-downs. Mrs. O'Grady had given me the field jacket and boots, I adopted a pair of overalls I found in the gardening shed, and Mary had donated a few pairs of cords and jeans from "the time before I sat on my arse in this office all day."

"I've known about it for ages. I should have said something earlier, it's just...never mind. I just didn't. This is gonna sound strange, but I've a friend in London. She did the wardrobe for this television show I was on at one time." He checked in, taking my temperature.

"Yeah, I heard about that," I offered vaguely.

"Right," he said after waiting a few beats. "Would you be willing to ring her, tell her about your sizes and whatnot? She can send you out a selection of dresses. I've seen her do that for girls who were going to red carpet awards shows, and whatnot. I'll stand the cost on my credit card and return the ones you don't keep." I thought about what a nice dress from London would cost.

"The thing is, I'm not getting paid for working here. I'm not sure I could afford a dress."

"Oh, no. I'll pay for what you end up wearing. Shoes as well. Whatever you need. It would be a big favor to me. Please?" He leaned forward, eyebrows up. His full lips were pressed together tight.

I would have done it just for the shoes, and the dress, and the trip to Dublin. If I were honest with myself, I would have done it just to have dinner with Tom, alone. But I knew an opportunity when it knocked. "I'll do your favor if you do mine."

He stood up and crossed the few steps needed to look down into my eyes. He stood there, breathing the same air as me, mouth slightly opened. "What's that, then?"

"Give me a private teach me to cook a gourmet meal, soup to nuts, like we talked about."

His bright eyes twinkled. "That I can do."

He left without taking his mother's towels.

Chapter Sixteen

Put silk on a goat, and it is still a goat.

Several days later, Mrs. O'Grady set a cup of tea in front of me without my asking. "The girls miss you," she said, laughing.

"I doubt that," I said, taking a large gulp. I was up early. I wanted to deliver her towels bright and early before my big day ahead. I didn't want to arrive frantic and rushed, the way I always did in New York. When I showed up places, Maggie used to always ask, "What happened? Was somebody chasing you?" "I think those hens prefer your gentle touch to my World Wrestling Federation moves."

"Not at all, you're getting to be quite the farm wife," she said with more than a smidgen of pride. "Father Walsh swore he could see himself in the pews on Sunday. Here, get a few of these inside you." She set down a plate of oaty bar cookies, studded with nuts and dates. "My special flapjacks. Tom could eat a whole tray, right out of the oven."

"Yum, could I get the recipe?"

"I don't see why not," she said, pulling a notecard out of her elderly metal recipe box. "How're you enjoying being back in the kitchen?"

"It's great, but with the weather so nice, I'd almost say I'd rather pull weeds."

"It's the warmest spring on record, surely since I was a girl. If this keeps up, we'll all need bathing suits and suntan lotion on the estate this summer." She laughed a throaty laugh at the thought. "Ahh! My life." Nap jumped up on the table by the window, and turned in circles on the small surface like a circus elephant. He barked like mad. I spied Tony in the distance, over Nap's head.

"That dog has a sixth sense where Tony is concerned," I said.

"Is that His Lordship coming?" Mrs. O'Grady stacked dirty plates in the sink and took off the apron she had tied on. "I didn't expect him. I'm not sure I've anything to make sandwiches. He likes ham and cress in his, you know. What's the time? Oh, it's far too early for brandy, not close to 5 o'clock. Or is it too early? He always takes a brandy or two when he comes." She rushed leaned over me, brushing crumbs from the table. I could hear Nap whining. There was a knock at the door.

"Come in, Your Lordship, what a surprise," Mrs. O'Grady said, a delighted smile gracing her lips.

"I hope you don't mind my intruding without an invitation. It's just that I noticed our Sheila heading this way, and I wanted to ask her a question: Sheila, is the capital of New York Albany or is it New York City." He stood in the doorway, walking stick in hand.

"It's Albany."

"Yes, yes, I thought that might be the case. Well then! Very good." Mrs. O'Grady continued to smile.

"Tony, why don't you come sit down? I mean, I'm sure Mrs. O'Grady wouldn't mind, isn't that right Mrs. O'Grady?"

"Mind? Why would I mind? Do come in, Lord Wexford," she took his walking stick and the light jacket he had on. "But Sheila, haven't we come too far for you to be calling me Mrs. O'Grady? It makes me feel a hundred years old. Won't you call me Maeve?"

"And why not?" The Earl asked. "If we're not standing on formality, I wish you'd go ahead and call me Tony, Maeve. Sheila has since the moment we met. If the suits of armor in the castle come to life and start to haunt us, you can blame her and her

American ways." He took a seat, looking very satisfied with the whole arrangement.

"All right then. Would you care for a cup of tea and some flapjacks, Tony? And perhaps a little taste of brandy?" She set a crystal glass on the table, then pulled it back. "If it's not too early for you, of course?"

"I've precious few years left on this mortal coil. Where's the sense in following rules?" he asked, signaling for her to set the glass down. Maeve filled it, and held the bottle up to me, questioning? I shook my head no, so she took a seat and filled her own.

"Ah, I do wish you could stay, Sheila. We've had a grand time together this past month or so. Sharp as a tack, this one. She learns anything I care to teach her. Through her, I can almost imagine having my own daughter."

The word daughter choked me up. I couldn't do more than smile.

"Tell Tom I requested you in an official capacity as the Right Honorable Anthony Stone, Earl of Wexford."

I stuffed the last delicious bite of the rich goody into my mouth, and washed it down with what was left in my cup. "I'm sorry to eat and run, but I don't want to be late for the Right Honorable Thomas, Lord of the Kitchen. As an American, his temper intimidates me more than your bloodline." He raised his glass to me in a toast, and howled with laughter.

Maeve glanced at the clock. "Surely you're not starting a shift at this odd hour?"

"No, but I do have to run an errand for Chef. In town. At the greenmarket." The flapjacks roiled in my stomach. I couldn't admit where I was really heading. Or maybe I could, but I just didn't want to share it. For now, I wanted to keep it as my own for some reason. I hated lying. No matter how much I lied, the guilt never rolled off my back. I wiped my mouth and folded my napkin. "Thank you for the tea," I said, standing up.

Maeve shot to her feet with me. "But do you have to go right this minute?" I checked my watch and nodded. Tony reached behind himself to the umbrella stand and grappled for his walking stick.

"Don't let me drag you away," I said. "Keep your seat. Enjoy your drink."

Maeve twisted her hands and looked imploringly at me.

"Oh, I get it." I moved toward the door, feeling the pull of time ticking. "Don't you think that's just kind of silly?" Tony chased a crumb around the table with his forefinger. Maeve pursed her lips. "I do. If you leave here, Tony, where are you going to go? Up to your rooms to watch an afternoon movie by yourself? Or into the lobby, in hopes of talking to someone who might be interesting? If you stay here, you know you have someone interesting to talk to."

"Sheila, it's about appearances…" Maeve said. She pursed her lips and sighed through her nose.

"People are going to pick today to start thinking badly of you? Maeve, there's not a person on this estate who doesn't think the world of you. And Tony," I laughed, "I'm sure you've heard everything anyone says about you by now."

"It's out of my deep respect for Maeve that I wouldn't want to cause her any unhappiness," Tony said.

"Then don't," I said, my hand on the doorknob. "Make her happy by staying. You both like each other's company. Enjoy it." I walked out the door and shut it behind me. If I didn't get to the self-catering cottage village in ten minutes, I'd be late. I didn't want to give Tom an excuse to criticize me. He'd gone to a lot of trouble to pull off this plan. I shrugged off my cardigan, warm from half-jogging during the fine morning. The sun had already burned all the dew off the grass, and there wasn't a cloud in the sky. I loved it. It was like the heat was pumping my blood.

When I crossed the little footbridge to the self-catering cottages "village," I glanced behind me to Maeve's cottage. Nap was still standing on the table, looking in the window. Good. Tony had stayed put. I looked to my left and right to see if anyone I knew was around. There weren't many people in the area. Guest occupancy was light this week. The few people milling around were strangers. I checked the number on the door and slipped my key into the lock.

From the outside, the cottages looked nice but not spectacular. The modern buildings, added when Tom took over, were simple wooden affairs with slate roofs, situated around a green with benches and a fountain. Inside, it was a different story altogether. A stunning chandelier hung in the foyer. Glancing around at the splendor, I realized I should leave my wellies at the door. I stepped out of them and hung my cardigan on a peg. The huge, open-plan kitchen featured a central island, a restaurant-quality range, and a large area with sofas and a window seat, and a working fireplace. Everything from the crown molding to the cabinetry was modern and tasteful, but hinted at the feel of the rest of the estate.

The sitting room's fireplace was as tall as I was, with a magnificent brick hearth. A brilliant designer had divided the spacious room into three conversation areas. My favorite was a grouping of chocolate-brown leather sofas, and two overstuffed easy chairs. I could imagine the cozy parties one could have during a family reunion weekend in that room. *Not that I have enough family for a reunion*, I thought with a little stabbing twang.

I wafted up the stairs and looked behind all the doors. Five bedrooms, a bathroom and two utility closets. I sneaked into the en suite bathroom of the largest bedroom and used the facilities. It was so pristine, I didn't want to throw my soap or its wrapper in the trash. I slid it into my pocket. On my way out, I avoided the window. No one was supposed to know I was here. I opened all the drawers and closets, the way I do when I first get to a hotel room. In the very last drawer I opened, there was a strip of condoms. I slammed it shut.

The next biggest bedroom was mostly done in shades of white, down to the carpet, which felt squishy and luxurious under my stocking feet. The king-sized brass bed was so tall, it had steps on either side to help you ascend. I couldn't resist. I climbed up, and lay down. The mattress would have been delicious under any circumstances, but after the grim bed in my cell, the luxury was almost more than I could bear. I rolled over onto my stomach and sprawled out like a starfish. I closed my eyes.

I heard the gentle, constant hum of a riding lawn mower and the occasional birdcall. The longer I lay there, the more I unclenched. I heard a cow lowing in the distance and it reminded me of the photo of Tom I'd seen long ago in New York. It was probably taken on a May Day like this one, all warm, clear, and bright. That photographer had known what he was doing. The sun warming Tom's caramel- and platinum-hued hair and glinting off the pale, vibrant blue of his eyes showed him to his best advantage. So did the jeans and tight Henley the stylist had no doubt chosen for him.

Drifting off, I imagined how firm the muscles of his upper arms would feel under the rough-hewn cotton of his shirt. What would it be like to sneak up on him from behind and put my hands on his broad, strong shoulders? Squirming, I wiggled myself a little deeper into the plush duvet.

"Sheila!"

Jumping up, I smoothed my clothes and tried to look ready to start my lesson. I smiled at Tom, inviting him to see the humor in the situation. His face remained placid. Like a sea anemone, I stretched out every tentacle to take his temperature. There was not a playful cell in his body. This was going to be a long day.

"I'll just wash my hands and I'll meet you in the kitchen," I told him. "If that's OK with you," I amended.

He gave a terse nod and headed down the stairs.

I tied on the apron he'd brought me and unpacked the groceries from the bags he'd carried in. His cell phone rang several times, but he ignored it. He set out various cutting boards and arranged bowls filled with flour and beaten egg and vinegar with oil. I didn't dare interrupt his flow, and he didn't bother explaining what he was doing. Finally, he got me started peeling and thinly slicing vegetables for a salad. He explained and demonstrated how to hold the knife, and emphasized the importance of uniformity without using a single superfluous word. Several times, he made me set aside my mistakes. He'd feed them to the goats, he said.

I stood chopping and mincing, increasingly uncomfortable in the silent atmosphere. Finally, he spoke.

"I'm just after calling into my mother's house." He let that hang in the air.

"I was there this morning," I told him, unable to bear the tension of the quiet.

Using a wooden hammer, he beat a chicken breast flat. "I'm aware."

We continued to work in silence. The cold shoulder began to piss me off. I carefully washed an array of delicate lettuces, while he roasted red peppers over the flames on the burners, holding them with tongs. At some point, the doorbell rang. I moved to answer it and he simply held up his hand, signaling me not to. From time to time, he explained what he was doing. Occasionally, he had me mimic his work, and corrected me until I copied his techniques perfectly. The pressure of trying to guess what was up his bum was making me pissy.

"Do you mind telling me why we're here?" I asked. There had been a huge shroud of secrecy about meeting him here and strict instructions about not telling anyone where I was headed.

"We're here because I promised you a cooking lesson. I'm a man of my word."

"But why here?"

He shrugged and turned his back to me, continuing to work.

"You could have just cancelled."

"We struck a bargain." He poured a bottle of rum into a flat dish and laid a row of ladyfingers in to soak.

"Well, if it's so awful for you to be here with me, I can let you out of it. I can just leave now."

"May as well learn to tolerate each other. We'll be spending the evening in Dublin together soon enough. Now, will you set that aside and lay the table for two? The linens and china are in that box, there."

Tolerate! How did I fall from friendly company to impossible to bear? I lay down my knife and, one by one, slammed pieces of silverware on to the table.

"Sheila, is that where your knife should be?"

For a flash second, I thought of where I'd like my knife to be. Containing my fury, I washed it and slammed it safely back into place with the other sharp knives while he oversaw. He was treating me like a baby. *Listen, Farm Boy*, I wanted to say, *you may be an accomplished chef but I grew up in the capitol of the world. Mess with me at your own peril.*

I felt him watching me. He was cool as a spring pond.

"Don't get cross with me so. There's a way to do things. An order. When you use a sharp knife, you don't leave it lying about. When you cut radishes, you don't do some bits in chunks and some bits in paper-thin slices." He lined up every knife neatly with points all facing in the same direction. "And here in Ireland, people don't swan around calling people 'Babe,' and 'Honey,' and Tony." Using long tongs, he lay a breaded chicken breast into a pan of hot oil and it sizzled angrily.

I tossed the pile of napkins I was holding aside. "When," I spat, parking my hands on my hips, "have you ever heard me call someone 'Babe' or 'Honey'? Don't show your ignorance by lumping all Americans into one pile."

"Ah, well, maybe not, but your liberal use of Tony is surely sweeping the land."

I shook my head. I could feel that I was making a nasty face at him, but I didn't care enough to stop. "You're mad because I've been hanging out with your mother and the Earl? For your information, they've been having a wonderful time and it's been nothing but innocent." I eyeballed him. He was squirming, so I added, "So far."

He tore off strips of brown paper and lined the countertop near the stove with them, whipping them around like sails in a storm.

"I'm not mad, for your information. Mad means mentally ill. The condition you must be suffering to want to muddle up the lives of two innocent people in their golden years. No, Sheila, the word you're searching for is angry, and you'd be correct." He lifted the chicken out of the pan and put it on the brown paper to drain. "I'm angry that you've come in here like an American with no regard to manners or decorum and encouraged my mother to disrupt her life and behave like a school girl. It's fortunate that I ran into Father Walsh on the way. I sent him over to 'Maeve's' to look in on the situation." His triumphant expression confirmed that he felt he'd won a point in whatever game the two of us were playing. "Imagine what people at the church would say about her on a Sunday," he muttered. "She's a proper Irish widow, not one of the Housewives of Beverly Hills." He took a metal bowl from the freezer and fitted it into a mixer. He poured in a pint of cream, and set it to whip. The roar of it filled my head.

Furious, I continued to set the table. What a spoiled brat to want to snatch his mother's flirtation away from her. Just because he had chosen to live the life of a monk, didn't mean Maeve had to suffer without romance and perhaps some twilight cuddling. If I didn't need notes from today for the book, I would have stormed out. But if I had, he'd probably have called me a lazy American on top of everything else. No way would I prove the jackass right. I set my face in stone and carried on working like a perfect servant. But I had an ace up my sleeve. I felt my face twist into a self-congratulatory smile, and I didn't care if he saw it. If he didn't watch his step, he'd be going solo to his dinner in Dublin.

While he was spooning superfine sugar and a teaspoon of pure vanilla extract into the whipping cream, his phone rang again and he checked the number. Switching off the mixer, he answered it. "Howya, Andrew. You got my message, did you? OK, go on and tell me." I set taper candles in crystal holders, pretending not to listen. "Good stuff! Yeah, tell me more." With the phone pinned between his cheek and shoulder, Tom deftly cracked half a dozen eggs, separating the eggs from the yolks. He poured the yolks into a saucepan, whisking them together with sugar and milk. I peered into the pan. The thin custard mixture began forming fat, languorous bubbles.

"Anyhow, did you want to take me up on it? Romantic dinner for two, set to go with the key under the mat. Nice surprise for the little missus, if you can get your Mam to take the baby. And the place is yours for the night. You can leave tomorrow at check-out time." He walked into the hallway. I strained to hear his side of the conversation.

"Something came up with the girl I was bringing." He laughed softly.

Girl he was bringing? So, not such a monk after all, huh, Tom O'Grady? Hot shame rose in my belly. I was the kitchen assistant on duty to make a seductive dinner for one of the faceless girls he bedded here, but didn't dare to name in public. No wonder he didn't want me telling anyone where I was going. It's his secret love nest. I pictured Catherine from the front desk, decked out in a silk negligee, rolling around on the sumptuous bed upstairs, calling Tom "Chef." I pushed the image out of my head.

Tom laughed again. "No, it's nothing like that. What do you take me for? Married men have the wildest imaginations. Just didn't work out the way I'd planned, that's all." He chuckled like a lad. "Well, if we're all set then…oh yeah, I never said. You and the missus will dine on a tangle of lettuces with our farm's goat's cheese, bacon-wrapped roasted peppers, breaded lemon chicken with garlic and rosemary over spinach linguine, and tiramisu to finish. I've got a couple of nice bottles for you, too, mate…Too true. She doesn't know what she's missing, but I hope you'll enjoy it in her place. Nah, you owe me nothing. Right, see you, then." I heard his footsteps, so I scrambled to open the wine, reasoning that it had to breathe.

Emboldened by my irritation, I took a stab at information gathering. "By the way, why did I have to keep my being here with you such a secret?"

Smooth as caramel he replied, "My time off is never truly time off. If people know where to find me, they find me." He pulled a carton from the refrigerator and scooped something thick and creamy into the custard.

"What's that?"

"Mascarpone cheese. People say Italian is the best, but I have an artisanal cheese-maker I source it from right here in Ireland. Our cows know what they're doing." He grabbed a clean spoon and dug into the soft cheese. "Try it."

He held out the spoon and waited. I moved my mouth toward it to bite, but got embarrassed. I gently pulled the spoon from his hand and slid it into my mouth. It tasted fresh and creamy, with just the faintest hints of sweetness and tang. "Mmm. That is really good." I lay the spoon in the sink and asked, "But what if there were an emergency?"

"If Bill rang and left an urgent message, I'd follow up. And Mam knows where to find me." He looked at me seriously. "Keep this to yourself, please. This is one place on the grounds where no one comes looking for me."

Like when you're plying the women from town with your fancy food and wooing them onto the pillow-soft mattress upstairs? My mind did a shuffle of all the workers at Castle Stone, the waitresses and shop girls in the village and, of course, Tabitha. Could she have been the one who stood him up? I hated the idea of it. The girl who did my hair swore he behaved like a confirmed bachelor. But he still had one foot in the world where people sent formal gowns upon request and had a fleet of drivers. He could be James Bond for all I knew. I guess he kept his manly behavior under wraps, here in this secret lair. There, done. The table looked gorgeous. I stood back to survey my handiwork and slumped against the wall. I was very tired.

"I've brewed espresso for the tiramisu. Do you fancy a cup?" It was the first human thing he had said to me all day.

"Yes, please, but could you turn it into a cappuccino?" I sat down.

"All right." He busied himself making coffees. "But I've another job for you. See those ladyfingers I baked yesterday? Split them in half, lengthwise, and use them to line the bottom of that serving dish. Set the leftovers to the side."

"Who's going to eat this lovely feast?" I asked, sitting in the charming floral-patterned window seat, even though I'd just eavesdropped like Mata Hari. I chose a serrated knife and began splitting the fragrant cakes. The tip fell off of my first torpedo-shaped delicacy. When Tom looked away, I popped it in my mouth. The sweetness of Tom's creation melted onto my tongue. I savored it, holding it in my mouth for as long as possible before swallowing.

"An old schoolmate of mine and his wife. They were sweethearts from age 16. Andrew got a scholarship to study in England, so they were apart for years. To Maisy's credit, she waited for him. She's a good old-fashioned girl. Always wanted to be a mum. After they married, they hoped for a child right away, but it didn't go according to plan. It was hard on Andrew."

"The ladyfingers are finished."

"Good. Now, see that chunk of dark chocolate? Use that microplane grater and shave it into that Pyrex bowl there, and set it aside. But first, here. Drink that." He quickly whisked together the leftover espresso with some rum and poured it over the layer of cake. He soaked the remaining cakes with the rest of the liquor.

He set my coffee before me. It was like sipping hope and happiness. I closed my eyes to enjoy the full impact of the aroma and flavor. "There's a dash of cinnamon in there, I hope you don't mind." I shook my head no. "Anyway, so, after a lot of heartache, my friends got the child they'd longed for. Healthy, chubby, full of giggles."

"Boy or girl?" I asked. I wanted to stay with this conversation, not to go back to our roles as teacher and student. I shaved the aromatic chocolate as we chatted. It was pleasant.

"Boy. He's my godson. Name of Thomas, after me." His face

bloomed into an expression of pride.

"What does a godfather have to do?" I asked.

"You know, promise to guide his spiritual growth, raise him if his parents pass, buy him gifts on his birthday and confirmation, and the like. He's no trouble at all. His mother's wonderful, and he favors her." He sipped his coffee. "Will you measure out a level teaspoon of that Dutch cocoa there and set it aside for me?" He asked. It was a soft request; the first time he'd asked instead of commanding.

I let myself imagine what raising a baby in a small village like Ballykelty must be like. Did this Maisy have chickens? I knew how to keep chickens, now. Did she carry firewood? Cook meals? Buy food at the farmer's market? I shook my head to clear away the daydreams. *Really, Shayla,* I said to myself, *no Irish working man would have you, given your checkered past, so what's the point in picturing yourself in the role?* An unwelcome scene of myself in a pinstriped suit with a baby on my hip, running for a cab, chased in hot pursuit by a uniformed nanny with a diaper bag played in my head. There was no dad in my montage. Maybe that's because I can't picture Hank ever having had a baby. I didn't have a single memory of him taking care of me when I was little. Or maybe it's because I can't picture a man wanting me enough to make a baby with me.

"Sheila?"

"What?" I looked at the spoonful of cocoa in my hand.

"I asked if you wanted a family of your own." I shifted my eyes to Tom's face. I hadn't quite surfaced from my daymare. "Ah, never mind, just making conversation." He took our cups to the stove, and topped them up. "It's certainly none of my business."

"No, it's alright," I said, dumping the chocolatey powder into the dish. "I guess…" I realized I didn't have an elevator answer prepared. "I guess I don't know."

"Fair enough, some women aren't meant to marry and have children, I suppose. A career can be just as important."

He saw me as a worker, not a wife and mother. The thought drained my energy. I was more exhausted than I'd been all day. Oh well, fair enough. If I got what I wanted, I'd likely turn out like Hank, flying from job to job and keeping company where I could find it.

"Talking about mothers, though. I've a favor to ask."

"Go on."

He began assembling the dessert. He spread the creamy cheese and custard mixture atop the ladyfingers in the dish. He smoothed on the vanilla cream, sprinkled on the cocoa, and did the same again, adding another layer. He scattered the shaved, dark chocolate in an artful pattern. "Here, will you slide this into the fridge?"

"Is that the favor?"

"No." He took his time before talking on. "I wonder if you might leave some space between yourself and my mother. Just while this all blows over with His Lordship, you see." He checked to see if I was with him. I felt like I'd been slapped. Concentrating on my poker face, I nodded encouragement. "Since my Da passed, my mother's kept herself content with the land here, and of course, the church. She's a routine. All this with Tony might just serve to confuse her. There's something about you that's…confusing. Ah, shite. That came out the wrong way. You're a nice girl. In fact," he looked me in the eye, "I'd say you're a very nice girl. It's just that you're different. If I can't make heads nor tails of you," he laughed, and twiddled his espresso cup around on its tiny saucer, "what chance does Mam have? She's better off carrying on the way she has been."

I put my cup down. "I see what you're saying." I nodded agreeably. "I'm a bad influence."

"Hold on, now, that's not what I meant. At least, that's too strong a phrase. It's just that you're very different to what she's used to. She's led a fairly sheltered life. Are you following me?"

"Yes," I said, my voice sounding hollow in my ears. "I hear what you're saying. You want me to stay away from Maeve."

He looked relieved. "You're ace." He smiled. "Listen, why don't you leave the clearing up to me? I promised you a cooking lesson, not a housekeeping lesson." He hummed a pleasant tune in his toffee-rich voice as he carried the cups to the sink. A letdown registered in my body. He was happy this was over with. He'd fulfilled his duty and protected his mother from my vicious ways.

"Great!" I said, straining my lips into a smile. "I was hoping to go hang out in the back of Uncle Jack's anyway. A couple of the boys have promised to buy me drinks."

"Like who?" He asked, rinsing the cups at the sink. He didn't turn around.

"Oh, you know," I lied. "Different ones."

"You mean like George from the stables?"

"Maybe. I'm just going to go use the ladies' before I head out."

"Help yourself."

I climbed the stairs and headed to the same bathroom I'd used before. I took the soap out of my pocket and washed my hands with it. This time, I threw the paper in the wastebasket and set the soap in the dish. I didn't care if Tom's parade of women found the place in pristine condition or not.

In the hallway downstairs, I stepped into my wellies. Tom had dimmed all the lights and lit a fire in the sitting room. There was soft music playing in the background. The scene could not have been more romantic. He clearly knew what he was doing. I peeked around the corner as he lit a pillar candle on the coffee table. The soft light shone on his face, illuminating his dark golden hair like the corona of an angel from a painting in an Italian cathedral. He looked perfect. He wanted things to be perfect. He was that kind of man.

But I wasn't that kind of girl.

I slipped out the door and pushed it shut quietly.

Back in my cell, I stripped down to my camisole and tap pants. It was far warmer than I would have imagined. I didn't think I could face the jolly drinking crowd at the worker's pub. Pulling out my journal, I settled on the bed.

Dear Maggie, I think my time at Castle Stone is coming to a close. There's no point in my playing Irish farm hand anymore. I've got more than half the recipes I need. I'll bet if I ask Mary and Brigid for help, they can help me get the rest, fast. I might be done here.

Up until now, I've just kind of been coasting and taking things as they came. Everything was working out fine. Today, I feel itchy. And oh! I have to call Hank and explain where the hell I am. I left two vague messages on his voicemail. Who knows if he sees Brenda or not? She might have spilled the beans. If I don't lock this deal down, Hank's going to think I'm an idiot. The way I feel tonight, I'd say he wouldn't be wrong. Did you say those sisters are in our place until the end of summer? I'll bet you can't wait for summer to kick in. One of the American guests here told me winter's marching right into spring in New York. Still, I think I'd rather suffer the cold chill of a wet Manhattan night than Tom O'Grady's brush-off.

I wasn't going to go into it, but he made me feel like a pile of crap tonight. He promised me this cooking lesson, see? And I kind of thought… Ugh, I can't write these words down and look at them. OK, here goes. You are my best friend. I kind of thought that he was looking for a chance to be alone with me. I'm so embarrassed. He was in my room the other night (don't get excited) and I convinced myself that he thought about kissing me. God, I'm an idiot. I was seeing what I wanted to see, because our little lesson couldn't have been a chillier transaction. And the worst part is this: the whole thing was a dinner for this couple that are wildly in love, who have this miracle baby, and are rolling in marital bliss. And Tom really respects the woman. I got the sense that he liked that she was pure, or whatever. But then, THEN! I overheard him talking and I think the whole thing was originally a set-up for him to wine/dine/slam-bam-thank-you-ma'am some tramp who stood him up. He told me to clam up about his little love nest, too. All I can say is that I hope he changes his own sheets and doesn't make the poor housekeepers do it!

As if that's not bad enough, he basically told me to break up with his mother! Apparently, I'm a bad influence and she's a senile old lady who can't protect herself from me or the filthy ways of The Right Honorable Anthony Stone, Earl of Wexford. As if Tony would do a thing to harm a hair on her head. You'd think Tom would want his mother to find love again. To hell with Irish traditions, or the Catholic Widow's Handbook, or whatever. I just know Tony likes her, in that way. I know I've watched a few too many Emma Thompson movies, but don't the quiet ones deserve love, too? God I hope so. I'm sorry, Mags, I know this is so stupid, but I want someone to light a fire and lay a table for me. Hank would tell me I'm thinking like a girl, and life isn't a movie, but I'd bet money on Tony and Maeve (if I had any!). I don't know what else to say. I'm just going to do as many shifts in the kitchen as I can and get this stinking book done so I can leave as soon as possible.

Hmm. That's weird. Seeing the word "leave" written on the page is making me feel kind of sad. I don't know…maybe after I go home and get the book done, I'll come back. Not HERE of course, but to Ireland. I feel like I've read about vacations where you can live and work on a farm. Is that crazy? Probably. I'm pretty sleepy, I'll write again tomorrow when I can make more sense. Love, Shay xx

Clank. I raised my head and looked around sleepily. The sun had set and the only light in the room was coming from the cracked door of my little water closet. *Kunk.* Something was smashing into the window and wall outside my room. I leaped up and fled into the bathroom, closing the door behind me. *Thunk, tinkle, tinkle!* Oh dear lord, someone broke my window. Should I scream? Oprah and Ellen and all those other daytime talk-show hosts always said blow a whistle or scream. I don't have a whistle! I took my toothbrush and banged it frantically against the tap, watching the door for help. It barely made a noise. I tried to scream, but my throat was closed.

"Shayla!" a man screamed in a whispery voice. "Shayla, it's

me, Des."

I cracked the bathroom door, listening hard.

"Shayla," he outright screamed. I ran to the window and opened it. Squinting, I made out Des's figure in the shrubs around the side of the building.

"Shut up!" I hissed. "Stay there. I'll be right out." I pulled my bathrobe off the hook on the door, and wrapped it around myself as I ran down the women's hall toward the entrance. He was there before I was and he pushed in.

"Shayla, I'm so glad to see you." He pulled me to him and growled in the back of his throat. "Oh, Shayla," he said. "Shayla."

"Would you *shut up*?" He smelled like a beermat the day after a party. "Let go of me."

"Shayla, don't treat me that way. You'll break my heart," he wailed.

I wriggled away from him and shoved him down the hallway. "Get in there," I said, when we got to my door. I pushed him into my desk chair with a hard landing. "And stop calling me Shayla. I'm Sheila here, get it?"

"You're in a strop! Feisty, I like this side of you," he said, standing up and swaying toward me. He caught me around the shoulders, and knocked me off my center of gravity. We fell onto the bed, and cracked my brow bone on the hard, metal frame.

"Fucking fuck!" I whispered.

"You are filthy, I love it" Des said, trying to kiss me. He was too drunk to realize he'd hurt me. With my hand to my eye, I slid out from under his weight and found my feet.

"What in the hell are you doing here? You're drunk."

"Ossified, I'll admit it. But I missed you, Shayla. I thought maybe you'd have a pint with me, talk about old times." He struggled to pronounce each word.

"Let me guess. Ashleigh sent you packing because she found out you're a cheating dog?"

"Ah, Shayla, let's not talk about her when we've so much catching up to do." He grabbed for the belt of my bathrobe and pulled it like a ripcord.

"Sheila?" A man's voice. There was a knocking at my door. "All right in there?"

"Who's Sheila?" Des demanded.

"Shut up!" I mouthed at Des. I rushed to the door, and opened it. Tom O'Grady stared openmouthed. My robe was flapping open, and hanging off of one shoulder. Beneath my thin white camisole my nipples stood at full attention and below I had on short, ruffled tap pants, cut up to my crotch. Another gift from Maggie, who, you have to hand it to her, knows a thing or two about this stuff. I wrapped myself up and held my robe closed with my hand. Tom strained his neck to look into the room behind me. Shit. Given Des's philosophy on cheating, you'd think he'd be smart enough to hide in the bathroom.

"Aren't you going to introduce me to your friend, Shay…?" Des began but I cut him off, screaming, "Seamus!" I laughed like a carnival clown. "No, Des, this isn't Seamus, this is my boss." I grabbed the tie to my robe from Des's hands and firmly tied it around my waist. "Please be QUIET while I step out into the hall with…my boss." I wedged my body through the door, backing Tom up as I went. Safely outside, I closed it, holding onto the doorknob lest Des get any big ideas about joining us.

"What can I do for you?"

"I brought you your cardigan. Here," he said, holding it out to me. "I thought about leaving it with one of the others, but I saw that your window was broken. Thought you might need checking on." He frowned. "What happened to your eye?"

"Oh, just…walked into the door." The minute I said it, I wanted to take it back. Between that and the broken window, he'd think Des had hit me. "I'm fine, really."

"Shayla?" I heard Des call.

"Who's Shayla?" Tom asked. His fists were clenched and he was looking past me, as if he could see through the door. I had to get him out of there. Des was drunk enough to spill the beans about who I was and why I was there.

"No one, he has a weird accent, that's all. His mom's Irish, but his dad is from…uh…Iceland."

"Did he break the window?"

"No! No, that was a finch." He looked skeptical. "Or a larch, lark! Some bird, some Irish bird, flew right into it. Crazy! I'll tell maintenance in the morning. So, thanks for the sweater and for all the fun today. I'd love to do it again." I was trying to wrap things up because I could feel the doorknob twisting in my hand. Des was trying to come out and join us.

"After the Irish goodbye you gave me, I thought maybe I'd upset you."

"Irish goodbye?"

"You did a runner." He rubbed his stubbled jaw. "I must've upset you."

"What?" I was keenly aware of Des fiddling with the doorknob. He'd obviously locked himself in and it was a matter of time before he got out. "Nothing you say could upset me." I was holding the knob firm. "I mean, what difference does it make? Like me, don't like me, I'm just the kitchen help."

His face went dark. "Right. Guess I was overthinking it. Didn't want to offend."

"Not possible!" At this point, Des and I were actively wrestling with the door.

"Good to hear," Tom said, heading for the exit door. "What I say should hold no store with you outside of the kitchen. You're a big girl, after all."

Des's arm popped out the crack in the door and snaked around my belly. Tom winced.

"Enjoy your evening," he said, letting the door slam behind him.

Chapter Seventeen

If you don't know the way, walk slowly.

I stretched out my aching neck and bent over as Des wound down his car window. Sleeping on a thin blanket on the hard floor of my cell hadn't been a picnic. I was as sore as I was sleepy.

"Sorry about being an arsehole, Shayla." A few birds twittered in the early morning breeze. It was still early enough to be cool out. I pulled my sweater tighter around my shoulders. Des had insisted that I didn't need to walk him out, but I wasn't doing it to be cordial. I wanted to make sure he drove off the grounds and away from Castle Stone. As welcome as the night we'd had together in Wexford had been at the time, it had served its purpose. Temptation hadn't turned my head one bit. Of course, knowing what I do now, I would never betray Ashleigh. But there was more to it than that. There was no denying that I had a craving for sex. It was spring. There wasn't a creature in Ireland, including me, that didn't feel the buzz in the air. Des just wasn't on the menu. It was like wanting spicy tomato pizza and being offered a dish of vanilla ice cream. Ice cream's good, but it won't do the trick.

"Water under the bridge. Are you sure you're sober enough to drive?" He looked worse for the wear. As much as I didn't want him here ratting me out, I wanted him to be safe.

"Fine. Slept it off last night. I'll stop on the way out of the village for a strong cuppa to set me straight." He reached out and looped his arm around my neck. He pulled me in for a kiss. I turned my head in the nick of time and got a wet one on the cheek.

"Good*bye*, Des." I stood up, massaging my cramping neck. Two spots down in the car park, Tom was lifting a wooden crate of carrots from his boot. I caught his eye, but he looked away. Balancing the crate on his knee, he slammed the boot shut and strode off toward the kitchen. After waving Des off, I stood in the dewy chill for a minute or two, giving Tom a head start.

I took a shortcut through the field on my way to the chicken coop, grateful that Mary had switched my duties from the kitchen to the yards. Behind me, I heard a horse trotting, then slowing to a walk. I turned to see Tony in the seat.

"Sheila," he called. "Good morning." He steered Pansy, one of the gentler horses, toward me. I reached up to stroke her velvety nose. "Won't you join me for breakfast? I've been up since before dawn and I don't know what to do with myself."

"Sorry, Tony, I'm on my way to do chores."

"Damndest thing, I've been falling asleep in front of the telly in my room after dinner." He looked out across the horizon. "After such early bedtimes, I'm up with the sparrow."

"Why not join the guests in the drawing room? Weren't there dance lessons last night in the ballroom?"

He shrugged. "I've no taste for strangers." We both turned our heads as a black and white streak appeared out of the periphery and made its way toward us. Stopping on a dime, Nap circled the Earl, the horse and me, panting eagerly.

"Shoo! Go home where you belong, you daft canine."

Nap sat down, still as a statue, with his eye on Tony.

"I mean what I say. Go on!" Nap didn't move a muscle. "Why must I be expected to behave properly when no soul nor beast around me does the same? If not breakfast, Sheila, how about dinner tonight?"

"I wish I could. I'm heading to Dublin after lunch for a business thing."

"Ah, are you looking for a job? Have you made a connection
from your work experience?"

I bit my lip. "No, it's not like that. It's actually Castle Stone
business."

"Tom didn't mention anything to me."

I realized I'd put my foot in it. Backpedaling, I said, "When I
say business, I don't really mean business. More pleasure. Tom
and I are going to see a little of the city," I riffed, "have a bite to
eat. It's nothing. We'll be back in the morning."

"You're stopping there overnight? With Tom?"

"In separate rooms."

"Of course," he said. "Tom wouldn't stand for the appearance
of impropriety, would he? If you'll excuse us, Pansy has a date
with a bag of oats. Enjoy your day." He guided his horse back to
the path and Nap followed along at a distance, dropping to the
ground and freezing every time Tony looked back.

Later, with my wire baskets filled with eggs, I started out toward
the kitchen. I looked up and saw Maeve O'Grady headed in my
direction, with Mary at her side. We exchanged greetings and
talked about the weather, as you do every day in Ireland. After a
chat regarding the health and temperament of a few of the favorite
hens, I excused myself.

"I'm headed up to the castle," Mary said, "let me carry them
eggs for you. No sense wasting a trip."

"Great, I'll just see if they need anything at the stables," I said,
eager to part ways with Maeve before Tom came out and spanked
me for talking to her.

"Nonsense," Maeve said. "We're at full capacity up at the castle.
An army of guests are doing lessons and trail rides this morning.
There's not a horse in the barn. Come with me and have a bite
to eat and a cup of tea."

"I really should go pack," I replied.

"Pack? You're not leaving us, are you?" Her brow wrinkled. "I've not kept track. Is your time finished?"

"No, I'm just heading into Dublin, that's all."

"Tonight? Funny, Tom's going to Dublin tonight. Come along, walk with me. I'm spitting cotton, as His Lordship says. Well, used to say." She pursed her lips and took my elbow. Before I could change course, I fell into step with her, walking toward her cottage. She sighed.

"I really shouldn't."

"You'll not deny me a bit of company and a chin wag, will you? I've gotten so I don't like a quiet house, lately."

"Well, maybe for just a minute." I looked around. Surely, Tom had duties in the kitchen this morning. "I would like to copy down those couple of recipes we talked about." As much as I didn't want to stir the pot with Tom, I needed to finish this book. The sooner I did, the sooner I didn't have to squirm under Tom O'Grady's scrutiny, pompous ass that he was.

Maeve sat me down at the table and brought in a tray with a pot of tea and some tiny mince pies on it.

"Of course it's the wrong season for mince, but I opened a large jar from a batch I put up last winter only last week when Tony... Lord Wexford mentioned his partiality toward it." She laughed nervously. "I made such a great batch, they're nearly running out my ears."

I took a bite out of one. A wanton moan escaped from my throat. That pie was hands-down the most delicious thing I'd ever put in my mouth, bar none.

"Oh, God, what is this?"

"It's mince. I make mine with real beef suet, and of course figs and almonds, and the usual. I've warmed these and opened the lid. That's Castle Stone's own Cashel blue cheese melted in there. Nothing like it in the world," she said, utterly confident in its excellence. Maybe you could carry a few up to His Lordship." Before I could answer, four pastries were wrapped in brown paper.

"Hmm, maybe. Would you mind if I got your recipe file? I should probably get back."

"Wait until you see," she said like the cat who swallowed the canary. She pulled a laptop out of one of the drawers in the dresser near the sofa. "Lord Wexford brought this to me and gave me my first lessons. Imagine the sight of it! Maeve O'Grady on the computer. It seems just yesterday that we got electricity in this cottage."

"Does Tom know you have this?"

"Phhtt! Tom hardly drops in. You only saw him here lately because he's been sniffing around, asking questions about you."

A hummingbird erupted in my ribcage. "Questions like, 'Is she an awful, immoral bad influence? And 'Does she carry a gun?'"

"Not at all! Questions like, 'Did she say she has a fella back in the States,' and 'Does she ever talk about me when she pops round?' He was being a right Nosy Parker about the Earl to boot. 'What did he eat? How late did he stay? What did you watch on telly?' I told him, 'Stop in more often yourself if you want to know my comings and goings.' Honestly, there's not a reason in the world why he can't. I suspect he's a," she dropped her voice low, "'workaholic.' I heard that daytime presenter talking about it one day. She said people who don't want to face their troubles head on bury themselves in work. I've wondered if I should mention it to Father Walsh." She fired up the computer and stabbed at the keys with her two index fingers.

"Troubles?" I prodded. Hank would be proud of me. No one could accuse me of being polite. The tiny notebook and pen I kept tucked in my pocket stood at the ready. I shoved the remaining half of my mince pie into my mouth. Oh, man, was that sublime. But I had come to do a job. Treats would have to wait.

She continued to tap the keys with great vigor. "Oh, you know, the business in London with that Tabitha. I knew she wasn't worth a penny the day I met her. She bit the head right off the girl clipping the microphone to her dress. Poor lass of about 18 years of age, just trying to do her best. I didn't mention it to Tom, but I kept my eye on Miss Tabitha after that. One face in public and another behind the scenes."

Oof. I felt as if I'd been punched in the solar plexus. I'd be sick if Maeve talked that way about me. In fairness, she had every right to. I really wanted to leave. I didn't like the idea of Tom catching me here after my promise to stay away. Worse yet, I liked that Maeve liked me. I didn't want to abuse her trust.

"Here's a photo of Tom on the set of the show with her. She turned the computer screen around so I could see it. Back then, Tom wore his hair a bit longer and his face lacked fullness and weight. He looked trim and sleek in a well-cut suit, over a crisp French blue shirt open at the collar. I preferred him now. He struck me as more solid and substantial.

"You see the paint she has on her face? That's not just for telly. She walked out of the house every day like that, even here on the grounds." Maeve clicked through some other photos in the album. I didn't really take them in; my mind was focused on Tabitha being here, in my territory. Eating in The Grange Hall, riding the horses, sitting down to tea with Maeve. Where had she slept?

"What did Tom see in her, do you think?"

"That's easy enough. He saw in her what she wanted him to see."

"What do you mean?"

"Let's just say that our Tom was always a good lad. Star pupil in the village school, altar boy, helped around here trying to fill his Da's shoes and doing a fine job I might add." Her eyes took on a watery shine. "Sometimes I think he should have tested the waters and sown some oats instead of devoting himself so much to me."

I felt a swell of humility. Who was I to think I knew what was best for Maeve O'Grady? Maybe Tom was right to protect his mother. The Irish had ancient roots, traditional ways of doing things. Perhaps I was like those scientists who trudged into an unspoiled terrain, infecting the peaceful inhabitants with my culture's ways. After all, I was a stranger here.

"In hospitality college and the fancy cookery schools, he hardly had time for girls." She shook her head, eyes focused miles away. "I had a bit of money. I'd have gladly given it to him to keep him from working so hard. It was a point of pride to him, it was, to keep his scholarships and earn his way. I see the damage it did him. As they say, 'All work and no play makes Tom a dull boy.' Poor lamb." She snapped her eyes onto mine and said brightly, "But he succeeded."

Her face warmed to a smile. "You have to hand it to him, he reached every goal he set for himself. He opened his restaurant with a loan from the Earl, and the next thing you know, the telly station showed up, sniffing around looking to snap him up and slot him into the show they'd thought up.

Those city wheelers and dealers had it all planned out. On the strength of his restaurant, they created the whole thing, and stuck a contract in front of his face. I believe he accepted in order to pay Lord Wexford back more quickly. Generous man," she said, her eyes shining, "he said from the start the money was a gift, not a loan. From the first day on set, it seems Tom was thrown into Tabitha's arms. Sometimes I wonder if the producers and the agents and the whatnots in London didn't have a hand in it so they could ring the papers themselves."

She pointed to a photo on the screen. "Here's a picture of the house they bought in London." Tom, in khakis and a slouchy weekend sweater stood on the stairs of a Georgian beauty with a bright-red door, arm slung proudly around a tricked-out Tabitha.

I recalled Tom saying he didn't like city life. "How long did they live there?"

"Not a single day. Tom wanted to make it official after the wedding." She poured us each more tea. "They never got that far."

"Why?" I realized this breached the bounds of polite conversation.

"We'll print these recipes, won't we, if you'll show me how." Changing the subject and pretending I hadn't spoken was an Irish tactic I'd seen before. A useful one, at that. I wish I could get used

to the discomfort and use it myself. Unfortunately, I had a case
of Clinical Compulsive Disclosure. I'd made up the condition in
my head to explain why I always answered questions when asked
point-blank. 'How much is your rent?' or 'Why aren't you married
yet, Shayla?'

Maeve stood up and flipped the switch of a small printer
that hadn't been there the last time I'd visited. I excused myself
to the bathroom and wrote down everything I could remember
while she printed out some of the recipes that she'd painstakingly
typed into files over the last few days. This had shaped up into
a productive morning. There wasn't a great deal more I needed
for Tom's cookbook.

Before I headed down the stairs, I tiptoed into Tom's room for a
sneaky peek. Scanning his boyhood lair, I took in the trophies, the
piggy bank, posters of old bands, some well-worn children's books.
My eye landed on a photo I hadn't looked at last time. It was of
Tom and his parents. His father stood in the back, wearing a suit
and tie, and a formal overcoat. A striking young Maeve, with the
same gorgeous bones under youthful skin, stood in front of her
husband. Even with her Sunday hat on, she didn't reach his chin.
In the very front, with his parents' hands on his shoulders stood
a seven- or eight-year-old Tom. His face was so open, his body so
easy, as if nothing bad had ever happened and nothing bad ever
would. A feeling of urgency came over me, my muscles leaping to
attention. I yearned to protect that boy, that boy who didn't exist.

"Sheila?" Maeve called.

"Coming!" I tiptoed back to the top of the stairs, and then
hurried down.

"Oh, there you are, pet. Will you let me pack some pies for
yourself?"

"Yes. Yes, please."

I tried to smash in among the tall potted plants surrounding the
main entrance to the hotel. I pushed my rolling suitcase as far in

among the boxwoods as possible without risking the ire of Danny the gardener. I reckoned this was a go-to meeting point for regulars on the Castle Stone estate, but Tom hadn't really thought through the part about being inconspicuous. Every minute seemed like an hour as I wondered who would pass by next. If Mary saw me hovering around, she'd surely ask what I was up to.

Brigid had carefully applied my makeup so that it would look like I was wearing next to none. The stylist who had sent the dresses had thoughtfully thrown in samples and testers from every high-end line available at Saks and Bergdorf's. We started with a color-correcting primer, which was a good thing. My skin was growing pinker each day from working outdoors in the unusually strong Irish sun. As spring was bleeding into summer, everyone was remarking on the banner weather. Brigid found a shade of foundation that matched my skin to a tee and powdered it to set. She had a surprisingly steady hand, so the liner she used blended in with my lashes, serving only to make me look alive and awake.

"You really know what you're doing, don't you, Bridge?" I wondered why she didn't doll up herself more often. She could snag that Kieran at the bar, no problem.

"And why wouldn't I? You think girls like me don't know fashion?"

"What do you mean girls like you?"

"Hold still! Stop talking." A few flicks of brownish mascara, and a matte pinkish-nude lipstick, and I was the picture of dew and youth.

Where was Tom? I glanced at my watch and saw that he was nearly 10 minutes late. *Oh well, he can wait for me, then,* I thought. I ducked into the lobby to use the restroom one last time before the trip. On my way out, I tried to blend in with a large party of guests in order to slip out the front door unnoticed. Duck-walking with my hand shielding my face failed to fool eagle-eyed Catherine.

"Sheila! Do you have a quick moment?"

Busted, I made my way to the desk, full of foreboding.

"I'm just after speaking to your father." My heart sunk. "We had the nicest chat. He's quite a charmer."

"Oh," I said, trying to seem disinterested. "What did he have to say?" If he'd spilled the beans about who I was and why I was there, it was over.

"Well, first of all," she said, giggling, "He demanded to know who had kidnapped his little girl and held her hostage on a shamrock farm."

Fear hummed in my cells. "Did he ask for me by name?"

"No, it was lucky we don't have anyone from the States in at present. Clever me, I reckoned at once that it had to be you." She beamed, looking pleased with herself. I saw Tom through the glass panes in the massive oak front door. He was talking to a delivery man. He didn't see me.

"Yes, clever you," I agreed. "Did the two of you chat about my job?" Had Maggie told Hank what I was up to?

"He asked me what Castle Stone is, so I explained. He said it sounded charming and that I'd better get used to the quiet now, as you'd be letting the world know about it once you got home. He said you'd write a book about your vacation!" Her laughter tinkled. "Have you sent him photos of yourself in an apron and a hairnet?"

"Did he leave his name?" I wondered if she'd recognize my famous father's moniker. If so, she'd surely blab to the rest of the staff.

"He said he was your father! I assumed you know his name. He was being cheeky, and said I was to call him Hank."

"Sounds like Hank."

"He only asked that you ring him. Here's another message, by the way. Honestly, we do have guest duties here at the front. We're not a message service." She slid it across the desk huffily. "I thought surely you'd get a mobile phone by this point."

This subject made me uncomfortable. The truth of the matter was that I should have. For ages, I'd complained that I couldn't figure out how to get signed up. Then I used the excuse that I was saving money. The truth of the matter is that I just didn't want one.

There's just something about the pace here that makes me want to stay out of reach. I've hardly logged on to the wifi the whole time I've been here. Back in New York, I never sat down at work or walked through the door at home without checking my email, Twitter, Facebook, Instagram, and Pinterest. I always felt like I would miss something if I weren't constantly connected.

Here, if I'm working in the kitchen, anything urgent is handled on the spot, in person. No assignment for the next day exists. You start fresh. I love that when lunch finishes for the day, it's finished forever. Very Zen. Very 'In the moment.' If someone wants to tell me something, they walk to the dorm block, or look for me in the back of Uncle Jack's. If they don't find me, they tell me later.

I glanced out the front. Tom stood staring straight back at me, raising his eyebrows. In a rookie move, I checked Catherine to see if she'd noticed. My guilty look put her on high alert.

"OK, then. Thanks for the messages." I made my way to the back door, trying to be nonchalant.

"Sheila!" Tom called in through the open door. Catherine's eagle eye was glued to me.

"Could you tell Chef O'Grady I need a word?" She asked, eyes narrowing.

"Of course," I said. I shuffled to the door as quickly as I could, and whispered, "Meet me at your car," to Tom. "Go."

It took him a second, but he caught on. I indicated that Catherine was watching through the window. He made a big show out of shaking my hand, then left, whistling. I checked to make sure Catherine's wasn't looking, and went for my case. It was gone. I pressed my nose to the glass. One of the young bellmen had wheeled it across the lobby and was handing it across the desk to Catherine.

"It's unclaimed. The handbook says to treat all unclaimed luggage as a potential risk," he said gravely. To my horror, Catherine was unzipping my bag.

"That's mine! I called, picking up the pace. "I'll take that."

Resting on the very top was a very high-end slip, embossed with diamante sparkles sent to me by the stylist. For all the world, it looked like a negligee. She held it to the side and continued to dig. "My bag!" I called. "You can put that down."

Under the slip, I'd packed the folder I'd stolen from Brenda's office. She'd opened the flap before I lunged the upper part of my body across the desk and slammed the whole case shut on her hands.

"Ow!" she said, leaping backwards. I ran around the desk and grabbed my slip. I stuffed it into the case and shut the whole thing without zipping it. Stumbling across the lobby's floor, I clipped more than one strolling guest. I wrestled with the front door and got myself outside, panting and sweating. It was a good thing I'd worn yoga pants and a t-shirt for travel; I'd hate to be doing this in my dress. I squatted down behind the boxwoods, far from the prying eyes of Catherine and organized myself. Fleeing to the employees' car park like a guest skipping out on the bill, I spotted Tom's car and wedged myself in the front seat, suitcase and all.

"Sheila, what the…"

"Just drive!" I crouched down, not even bothering to fasten my belt. I'd have Tom stop the car at the gates. Finally able to breathe, I sat up a little straighter. With the main part of the castle behind us, I dared look over my shoulder. Standing outside at the entrance was Catherine. Judging by the look on her face, she'd clocked us.

Chapter Eighteen

Even a small thorn causes festering.

Anyone who ever tells you that you can live through a couple of hours of anything is a liar. I don't know if it's possible to die of discomfort, but I'd say I was in critical condition following our drive to Dublin.

There was promise at the beginning. He'd snaked along at 10 kilometers per hour on the main drive, preaching about safety first. I'd joked that he drove like an elderly lady on her way to church, and I thought I'd caught a shadow of a smile. I must have been mistaken. With the focus and precision of a solder, he pulled to a stop on the shoulder before the gate, marched around to the left side, and commandeered my case. He deposited it in the boot, got back in the driver's side, then pulled my belt across me and fitted it into the buckle like I was a child.

"I'm responsible for you," was all he said in the way of explanation.

As we drove along the gorgeous back roads of the Irish countryside, I breathed in the beauty. There was a swelling in my chest caused by the expansive space. It threw me off balance. I regretted agreeing to come. I wanted to be back in Castle Stone. It was contained, easy to navigate. I felt safe inside the gates of the manor.

Driving along with Tom under the endless blue sky, my body felt like it was falling and floating at the same time. We drove in silence, but the silence was charged. In some people's company, silence is companionable and an affirmation that nothing need be said. The pressure of what was unspoken between us made my head hurt.

"I saw you leaving my mother's house this morning."

There it was.

I turned in my seat to face him. "She insisted that I come. What was I going to do? Blow her off? I have a rule: be polite to senior citizens, especially ones who were there when you needed them."

He didn't glance at me. "We had an agreement." He gripped the steering wheel tightly.

"No, we didn't have an agreement. You gave me an order."

"I asked for a favor."

"You ask an awful lot of favors for someone who isn't even my friend."

He kept driving, eyes forward.

I sat there smug, relishing the feeling that my being right made him uncomfortable. During my freshman year of high school, my English teacher had pronounced "Yeats" as Yeets instead of "Yates." The second it was out of her mouth, my hand flew up to correct her. Proud that I knew something so esoteric, I expected a compliment but was met only with a tight-lipped, low-volume acknowledgement. When I complained to my nerd-table friends, Lulu Chin fixed me with a wise stare and said, "Of course you're right. But would you rather be right or liked?"

The rest of the drive, I took awkward stabs at fixing the situation. I tried to crack a joke, but didn't even earn a smile. The few times I commented on the scenery, I got grunts and nods, the most baseline offerings one could get away with and not be accused of ignoring another person.

"Who are your favorite fiction writers?" I asked, cutting a wide swathe of possibility for discussion in the stagnant air.

"I don't read novels."

That shut me down. I considered apologizing. I wished I'd never brought up the fact that I was doing him a favor. I sensed bringing the subject up again would make the bad feelings worse. Pride in an Irish man was something to be respected. I'd just pointed out my upper-hand status by virtue of my heading to the Gresham Hotel with Tom to try helping him win something he truly cared about.

The excitement of seeing the city of Dublin temporarily cheered me. I have to admit, I felt a little rejected when Tom pulled up in front of the main entrance of the hotel on O'Connell Street, and dropped me off.

"They have your name at the desk," he told me from the wound-down window. He didn't even get out to unload my case. "The room's been charged to me. All you have to do is sign in. I'll ring you once I'm settled. We're meeting Burton at 8 sharp in Toddy's Brasserie downstairs." He pulled away while I was still standing on the pavement.

Inside the deluxe lobby, I approached the polished wooden reception desk. "Hello, I'm Shayla…" I dropped off. I had no idea under what name Tom had booked me. Panicking, I recalled something about hotels requiring passports of foreign guests. This could go sideways, quick. "I'm here with Tom O'Grady," I began again, putting the ball in the court of the young woman behind the desk.

"Lovely, and welcome to the Gresham. If you'll give me a moment, I'll just check." I watched her type, starting to sweat a little. If I was going to have to check in as Shayla de Winter to match the name on my passport, I wanted to get this sorted before Tom parked the car.

"Are you an Irish citizen?"

I shook my head no.

"Passport please." I handed it over. She looked at it, typed something into the computer and handed it back, folded closed.

She smiled. Well, big money certainly bought discretion. If she noticed my name didn't match the one Tom had given her, she didn't let on.

"You're in Mr. O'Grady's suite," she said, sliding a room key toward me.

My heart flipped. Had Tom assumed I'd sleep with him? A short film of a bare-chested Tom O'Grady reclining against luxe bed pillows with a room service tray of champagne and oysters across his lap played in my brain. Cut to me in a shimmery satin teddy. Dissolve! The only pajamas I'd packed were my Sarah Lawrence College t-shirt and a pair of running shorts.

"He booked into two Bijou Singles, but when I realized it was Chef O'Grady," she said with a pretty blush, "of course I upgraded him to a two-bedroom suite. You'll be staying in the Elizabeth Taylor suite. It features a private balcony. After all, it's Tom O'Grady, isn't it?" Her eyes sparkled. "Oh, look. Good afternoon, Mr. O'Grady," she called, waving. I whipped around to see Tom coming in the front entrance.

"Thanks a lot." I snatched the key and took off, hoping to duck the lobby before she asked any questions about who I was.

"Miss!" she called. I froze, but didn't turn around. If she said my real name, I could just start running and keep on till I hit the street. I crouched, as if at the starting line of a race.

"The elevator you need is in the other direction!"

Turning on my heel, I saw that it was open. Bursting into a sprint, I made it in before the doors closed. I slumped against the wall, panting. The sensation of whooshing upward was pleasant. I hadn't been in an elevator since the day I'd landed at Shannon Airport. In New York, there was rarely a day when I didn't ride in an elevator. In Ireland, the act was an event.

I gasped as I pushed into the suite. There was a formal sitting room boasting sweeping gold drapes, richly upholstered sofas and chairs, and a fireplace. I knew Tom had to be at my back, so I ran into the first bedroom I spied and shut the door behind me.

I felt a twinge of guilt as I saw my ginormous four-poster bed kitted out in gold-and-red striped linens, complete with curtains. There was a little writing desk, an area where I could make tea or coffee, and joy of joys, slippers and a bathrobe. Only on Hank's coattails did I stay in rooms like this, and the occurrence of that had grown increasingly rare since I'd graduated college. In my usual digs, facial soaps and body lotions were one in the same, and the menu didn't include conditioner. I slipped off my traveling clothes and shimmied into my plush robe, taking note of my iron, hairdryer, and the dizzying array of gels, mouthwashes, and lotions, all scented with rarefied herbs and flowers.

I set the little hot drinks machine up and started myself a cup of tea.

I heard the door to the suite open and pulled my robe closed tightly around myself. I heard Tom walk through to his room and the click of the door to his bedroom. *Of course, Shayla,* I told myself. *He's going to rest and change. What did you think? He'd barge into your room like Fabio and throw you to the king-sized bed, uninvited?*

Breathing out, shoulders slumping, I checked the clock. Hours and hours until the dinner with the distributors. I ran a bath instead of taking a shower, because, well, that's what you do in Ireland. I noticed myself picking up little habits like this. In the back of Uncle Jack's, Mary and Brigid had weaned me off of the vodka and soda and onto cider or brandy, because that's what they ordered for themselves. I could hear the change in my language as well. After the tenth time of calling the back of a car "the trunk" and getting called out, it's human nature to start calling it a boot. I vowed to myself not to continue the practice at home like so many junior-year-abroad assholes back from Prague and a tour of Europe who claimed they couldn't bear ice in their water and walked around calling everyone wankers and promising to ring them up. But for now, it was nice to have chocolate with my afternoon tea and to eat beans for breakfast.

I took my time dressing. While I didn't miss having to put on a day's armor in the form of dark nail polish on squovally filed fingernails, and a pair of boots that could simultaneously get you a table at Per Se and kick a pervert on the subway, it had been a while since I'd taken care with my appearance. I spread out the samples of cosmetics sent with my dress and surveyed my treasure. Tom's friend had even thought to include little samplers of scent from various designers. I took my time sniffing each one before deciding on a green apple and grass fragrance. For one thing, the Irish spring was here in full force. People had gone so far as to comment that it may as well be summer. For another, it reminded me of the way Tom smelled, only more like a distant memory than the real thing.

I applied my makeup the new, modern way I'd been taught, starting with moisturizer and eye cream. I moved onto undereye concealer, color-correcting primer, and a light foundation. It was like Sephora had exploded in front of me. I took extreme care with every step and added touches like bronzer and highlighter. Even though I knew Tom preferred a fresh-faced look, I went for a smoky eye. I could just picture Mr. Burton, the opponent we'd be up against. I imagined he liked his women hard.

My garment bag contained three dresses. I'd narrowed it down from eight, but didn't want to wind up feeling awkward here in Dublin with no back-up plan. There was a simple black sheath, utterly timeless and with clean lines. I also brought a sleeveless pale-pink 1950's-style dress with a tight bodice and flared skirt because I imagined that it would be Tom's favorite out of the bunch. Silly, I know. In the end, I chose a deep red 1940's number with undertones that made my eyes pop like follow spots. With its long, tight sleeves and a plunging neckline formed from twisted fabric that drew attention to the décolletage, my neck looked like a swan's. *Well, Shayla, you get what you pay for.* Breaking the 100 mark, price tag-wise, was big news for me. I could only assume this one broke the 1000 mark.

In deference to the show-stopping color of the dress, to which

I was not at all accustomed, I wiped off my bright lipstick and relined and filled in with nude tones. Emboldening my eyeliner was the final touch. I looked modern and bold, but not costumed. Tom's contact had included the perfect shoes. They were muted gold, with a very high heel. Shaped like a bootie, they were more like a sandal with cutouts and straps. Elegant and light, but not delicate.

Dressed and ready, I considered diving onto the sumptuous bed for a lie-down, but didn't want to risk looking like a pile of wrinkled laundry at dinner. Just as I was about to brew myself another cup of tea, there was a knock at my bedroom door.

I opened it and had to catch my breath. There stood Tom O'Grady in a navy suit with a subtle stripe that fit him like a glove. He wore a white shirt and a solid, pale-blue tie that matched his eyes exactly. His wavy hair was brushed back from his face, styled but not fussy.

"Wow," he said, scanning me from the toes up.

"Wow yourself, Mr. London."

"If I'm Mr. London, then you're Miss Manhattan." He gave me a slow smile. "Our costumes for the fancy-dress party. No one would guess we're simple country folk."

I forced a laugh.

"Listen, I had some drinks sent up. Seeing as you're here on my behalf, I'd like to make sure you're comfortable. I hope something's to your liking." He waved his arm toward the coffee table to indicate a huge silver bucket filled with ice and bottles of beer and some Cokes, another smaller bucket with a bottle of white wine on ice, and a bottle of red standing by some assorted glasses and a plate of cheese. "Of course, if you'd rather have sparkling water, or tea…"

"No, I could use a glass of wine. White, please." I could just see myself spilling the red down the front of myself before dinner.

"I might stick with something soft."

"Really? You're going to make me drink alone?"

He hesitated. "I haven't been on the drink for quite some time."

"Oh, if you don't drink, don't let me pressure you."

"That's not it. I do drink. After…well, after I came back from London, drinking became less of a pleasure and more of an escape for me. Once I saw it, I laid off." He leaned back and smiled at me. His eyes crinkled up merrily at the corners. "There's a difference to drinking to forget and drinking to enjoy. Right now, I'd say I'm enjoying myself more than I thought I might."

"Is that a compliment or an insult?" I sat down on the sofa and he poured me a glass of wine.

"Take me as you see me is my best advice," he said cracking open a beer and offering a crooked grin. I loved the way his canine teeth were just the slightest bit prominent. It suggested wolfishness; something just slightly wild.

I had the impulse to recline and smile back, but I reminded myself that this was a business arrangement. As such, I plunged right into banishing a few elephants from the room. Taking an unladylike slug of my wine, I got right down to it.

"I know you're mad at me about your mother. Let's talk about it."

"Ah, Jaysus," he said, raking his hand through the waves of his hair. "I was just beginning to relax." He took a drink of his beer straight from the bottle. I approved. I prefer men who drink from the bottle. "You Americans. Always wanting to talk."

"You're mad at me. We should hash it out."

"Who said I was angry? And if I were angry, who's to say it's about my mother?"

"Well, are you angry about your mother?"

"Yes."

"What else is there to be angry about?"

"Nothing. I've let it all go." He helped himself to a slice of cheese. "Moving on."

"No really. What else is there to be angry about? If it's about me salting those strawberries instead of sugaring them, I've already groveled to you and Bill."

"Forgotten."

"Did I break an egg on the way to the kitchen from the henhouse? You see, Brigid started chasing me and singing Yankee Doodle, so the basket…"

"Not at all." He took another swig of his beer. His face was smiling, but his eyes weren't joining in the fun. He was mad.

"Is it about Tony? Lord Wexford?" I sipped my wine to give him time to answer.

"As I said, I don't approve of you meddling in the affairs of my family, but no." His eyes softened for a moment, and he laughed lightly. "As if I could control how he behaves with you. He is an entity unto himself. He's a good man," Tom proclaimed, clinking his bottle to my glass.

A shadow formed in the back of my brain, telling me he was mad about Des. I blushed at the egotism. But still…wasn't there some fire to his exit? I tried to recall how he'd seemed in the car park.

"All right?" Tom asked, still smiling.

I chose my words carefully. "Are you angry that I was…unavailable to speak to you the night you came to my dorm?"

His face closed up. "No. Why should I be?"

Damn. I'd stepped right in it. "You shouldn't, of course. Right." I felt like I'd passed him a note in class saying, "Do you like me? Check yes or no" and he'd checked no. Idiot me!

"If you want to break the rules and bring strange men into the women's dorms, I'd think you'd want to sleep with a real man instead of a pimple-faced boy who can't hold his drink, but to each her own."

"Wait a minute, he's not a boy!" Indignation rose in my chest.

I couldn't read the placid expression on his face. "As I said, it's not my business if you want to sleep with lads."

"He was drunk. He showed up at my window!"

"Ah, so he is the one who broke it. A boy and a hooligan."

"He was having trouble with his girlfriend!"

"Ah, sure, and you were the port in the storm."

"I put him to bed…"

"I've no doubt of it."

"I put him to bed and told him to sleep it off. Why do you care?" My breaths were coming double-time and Tom's gaze landed on my heaving chest, lingering.

"I don't care. I told you that at the start," he said, topping up my glass. "Looks like you could use another drink."

"You know, *Tom*," I began. He raised an eyebrow and treated me to an amused smile. "I wouldn't be so quick to judge if I were you."

"Is that right?"

"Yes, that's right."

He stared at the floor for a minute, then looked at me hard. "For your information, I don't bring liquored-up party girls around Castle Stone just to kiss them goodbye in the car park and send them on their way the next morning like some people I know do."

"Oh, puh-leeze. What about the tart you cooked that dinner for?"

He set his beer down. I was hoping he'd open another. With all of the high emotion, I'd downed two and a half glasses in short order. I reached for some cheese and a large cracker to soak up some of the alcohol.

"What tart? Come to that, what dinner?"

I didn't like the feeling that bubbled up in my chest. "You know. The dinner we cooked together." I couldn't help myself. I reached for my wine. I'd hardly had two drinks in a row since I'd been in Ireland. But Tom threw me so off-kilter. "For that girl."

His eyes searched mine over the rim of my glass. I saw the memory kick in for him. "Ah, that girl. Right. Turns out it was bad idea from the start. I got the sense I couldn't trust her."

"That's what you get for picking the wrong ones. Maybe you shouldn't always go for the pretty, exotic ones." I sounded like a preachy priss, but I didn't care. I felt small. I hated feeling like one of the ones who never got picked first, but I knew that's what I was.

"Maybe I shouldn't. You might be right, Sheila, you might be right." He stared at me with a strange look on his face. He didn't speak. I took a few sips of my wine as an excuse for something to do with my hands.

"I mean," I blathered in a fit of discomfort, "there was Tabitha, after all." Her name sent a scalding poker through my gut. I suppose it's because I hate fakey girls like that who trade on their looks and their charm. That stuck in my craw back in New York, and I certainly didn't want to be compared with that type on this side of the pond. I was glad to leave my old private high school classmates and strivers from the HPC office behind. They always won for the wrong reasons.

"From what I hear, she couldn't be trusted." I willed myself to shut up, but I just couldn't. I knew I was picking at a wound, but couldn't stop myself.

"You are right," he said, standing up. "Tabitha could not be trusted. Anyway I think I've had enough to drink. I prefer to keep my wits about me. We've 20 minutes before we need to be downstairs. I'm just going to go freshen up. If you'll excuse me, I'll meet you at the lift."

"Tom, wait."

"I want to thank you again. I know this is a big favor to ask. Trust me, I'll find a way to repay you." He walked into his bedroom and closed the door behind himself.

I slumped over on the sofa, and drained my wine glass. In the dark tunnels of my heart, the secret of what I was looking for when I goaded Tom beyond his comfort zone lay curled in a ball. I wanted to be picked. I wanted Tom to say, "You're better than my self-catering cottage slut, you're better than Tabitha, you're better than Catherine at the front desk and any other woman I've ever met." And because I couldn't leave well enough alone, here I sat with my answer. Not only was I not better than all those women, he couldn't even force himself to have a drink alone with me.

I took a deep breath and wobbled in to brush my teeth and reapply my lipstick. Maybe Tom's important contact, Mr. Burton, would have a different opinion.

Chapter Nineteen

If you lie down with dogs, you'll rise with fleas.

Dinner started with a round of cocktails. On the spot, I panic-ordered my old standby, vodka and soda with a lemon. Tom ordered a screwdriver, otherwise known as vodka and orange juice. Or so it seemed. I wasn't the daughter of a journalist for nothing. I'd seen him pop over to the bar for a private word with the barmen. I put two and two together and surmised that he'd put in a standing request with the barman to hold the booze, but serve the mixer in a cocktail glass with the appropriate garnish. That was a trick I'd learned from a friend at Sarah Lawrence who worked as a stripper to pay her way through grad school. I wished I'd thought have my booze held tonight. On top of the nervous drinking I'd done up in the suite, I was tipsier than I wanted to be. On the plus side, the liquid courage fueled my sweeping assertions about all things organic and sustainable. Anyone would believe that I farmed right alongside Tom's rapeseed oil producers.

The waiter had cleared out starters and just opened a second bottle of wine for our table when Mr. Burton (call me Chris) leaned over and put his hand on my knee.

"Isn't she a gem, Percy?" he demanded of his junior colleague. It was no surprise to anyone that Percy agreed.

"I realize this is inappropriate, Miss Doyle, but I shoot from the hip. Are the two of you an item?" He pointed from me to Tom to me to Tom, with a sly grin on his face.

Before I could answer, Tom jumped in. "Sheila works for Castle Stone and our subsidiary brands. She's Chief Cultural Liaison and Marketing Director for North America."

"I love that!" I enthused to Tom. Catching myself, I turned to Chris Burton and amended, "He's correct. I am...those things."

"Good. I'll need a friendly contact in order to do business with Castle Stone. It's no secret that Tom and I don't always see eye to eye, right Tom? I'll need a liaison."

"Sheila's a bright and capable woman, but business is where our relationship ends," Tom said. I felt my smile evaporate. "We're strictly colleagues." He looked me in the eye. "Romance with a co-worker is a game for fools."

"In that case," Chris said, topping up my wine glass, "I'm tempted to shut this deal down before it leaves the ground." Percy laughed a little too loudly. "You haven't told me, Sheila, where do you hail from?"

"New York."

"Ah, yes, the Big Apple. You may not know this Percy, but when I was at Harvard, I took the train down there for dirty weekends on more than one occasion. Percy's only ever been to Cleveland, right Perse?" Percy shrugged an apology. "Whereabouts in New York."

"Well, I grew up on the Upper West Side but after college I moved to Hell's Kitchen."

"Upper West Side." He nodded knowledgeably. "Posh. What business was your father in?"

"He's a journalist and a novelist."

"Sounds glamorous."

"Eh, eating dinner four nights a week at Elaine's and getting dragged to Michael's to hear jazz when you just want to get your homework done gets old fast."

"Is your father anyone I've heard of?"

"Yes, Sheila, anyone we've heard of?" Tom asked. I panicked. What had I said? Between the liquor and the role-playing I'd clean forgotten that I wasn't Shayla de Winter trying to best some hotshot asshole at his own game. I took a deep breath and tried to remember who I was supposed to be in this hall of mirrors.

I smiled what I hoped was a mysterious, seductive smile. "Let's just say yes, but I'm not going to tell you who he is." The more I drank, the sassier I got, and this masochist was eating it up with his dessert spoon.

"I'll get it out of you. I have my ways. Say, let's order another bottle. Percy, when you see a waiter…"

"Chris," Percy said, "We've only this evening and we haven't heard much from Tom regarding global appeal and plans for consumer education."

"Quite right," Tom replied. "Admittedly our research team is small, but we've data to show that home-spun Irish products hold huge appeal for Irish-Americans ranging from your ex-pats to third- and fourth-generation folk. We've pinned down major markets such as Chicago and Philadelphia, and of course Queens in New York with high concentrations of Irish-identified shoppers."

"Ah, Queens," Chris said, putting his hand over mine on the table. "I spent a wild night in Astoria I'll have to tell you about some other time."

"And in my reports to Percy here," Tom cut in, "we demonstrated that keeping an Irish slant will drive sales through both nostalgia and the desire to be 'in the know' around Irish exports. For example, we wouldn't change the name of rapeseed oil even though Canada has branded it as Canola oil and there's familiarity with the term."

"People can be trained to view bottled rapeseed oil as a regional specialty, with small-batch, artisanal cache, the way the world sees Italy's wines," I piped in. I found myself wishing we'd done more prep work for this meeting. The few facts I had at my fingertips would only stretch so far.

"Same with fraughans or wild bilberries," Tom went on. "Rather than call the jam blueberry, we maintain Ireland's unique signature."

"Sheila, as an American, do you find it difficult to deal with the Irish guardedness? After all the time I spent in the States, I've come to prefer people who just tell it like it is." He winked at me.

"I'll tell you how it is, Mr. Burton…" Tom began.

"It's a sound idea, Chris," Percy cut in. "Thanks for sharing those facts, Tom. In fact, I hope I'm not speaking out of turn," he glanced nervously at Chris, who had just used his own knife and fork to sample the rack of lamb from my plate, "when I say that our company is keenly interested and would like to discuss signing a letter of intent."

"Mmm, God, that's delicious!" Chris said, leaning back in his chair with his eyes closed. He smacked the table with his open palm. "It's official."

Tom sat up in his chair, looking expectant.

"Sheila ordered best!" Chris pronounced.

Tom slumped backward, his brow knit and his full lips pressed into a tight line. "How about a bottle of port to go with our pudding?"

As the plates were cleared and dessert orders taken, I tried to signal to Tom that I had this covered. He wouldn't look at me. Instead, he kept hammering on about dry business details. I had Chris in the palm of my hand. Tom needed to stand down. By the time coffee arrived, we were practically shouting over one another in an attempt to steer the conversation. For every one of my "Chris, you might as well be American, you know so much about it" there were two "Blah blah business blah's" from Tom.

Finally, Chris overrode us. "Right then, everyone. I've heard everything I need to hear in order to make a decision." He stood up, making no attempt to reach for the bill. Percy shot to his feet, brushing crumbs off of his lapel. "Night then, Tom." He extended a hand to Tom, who stood up to shake it. Clapping Percy on the shoulder, Chris said, "Lobby at 8:30 sharp, right mate?" Percy looked momentarily confused, then gathered his wits.

"8:30 it is, Chris. Goodnight." He shook Tom's hand, then mine and walked out of Toddy's.

"Thanks for your time tonight, Chris," Tom said, taking a few steps toward the door. He turned back and looked at me. "Coming, Sheila?"

"Actually," Chris broke in, "Sheila promised me a nightcap."

"Did she?" Tom glowered. "I never heard her say that."

"Sure she did, mate. You were ordering coffee. She promised to reminisce about New York with me. Isn't that so, Sheila?"

I raised my eyebrows at Tom, indicating that he should go on and that I would take one for the team and fill him in later. Perhaps that was too much information to convey with one gesture. He shook his head at me and shot me a look that could only be characterized as judgmental. Turning his back on us, he strode out of the restaurant.

The next half hour at the bar found me engaged in an athletic dance of slapping hands away from my rear and ducking out from under arms draped across my shoulders in such a way as not to express my lack of interest with full-on indignation. Chris ordered me a vodka and soda and told the barman to make it a double. I looked around for a houseplant into which I could dump it but found none. I limited myself to tiny sips, but I was fighting a constant barrage of "drink ups" from Chris.

"How about we head to my room for a nightcap?"

"We're drinking our nightcap."

"Fair enough. Then how about coming up to look over that letter of intent? I could meet Tom at 8 a.m. and we could have the whole deal sorted before the start of the business day."

I bit my lip. Going to his room posed a risk. He'd had a lot to drink and I doubted Chris was often told "no" about anything. Under different circumstances, I could argue with myself that it might be an adventure or at the very least, a romp. He was good-looking enough. And I'll bet opening with the fact that he was a lawyer garnered him the attention of interns and admin assistants at his firm. He could hold his own during flirtatious banter, and I usually enjoyed competing in that arena.

"You!" I said to stall. "You should finish that drink. Waste not, want not." He laughed a throaty laugh and held his glass up in a toast.

It surprised me to realize that playing games with Chris held no appeal for me. Here I was in a historic, romantic city in a luxury hotel. I wanted someone to peel this expensive dress off of me, and to lay me back in high-thread-count sheets. While it's true that I was never promiscuous, it's also true that I love a good story. The story of getting ravaged at The Gresham would be a good one to tell at book club when I'm 60.

"All done," Chris said, holding up his empty glass to prove it. "Don't good boys deserve rewards?" He put his hand on my bare knee and I put mine on top to discourage his from creeping up my thigh.

Was the answer that I'd gotten my need for pure release out of my system with Des? There was more to it, though. Usually having lots of sex makes one want lots of sex. I did want lots of sex. I just wanted it with Tom.

I shot to my feet, flicking Chris's hand off of me as I stood. My heart was racing. Chris smiled and stood up, too, thinking it was a signal that we were bound for his room. It wasn't. I was in full fight-or-flight response mode. I wanted Tom O'Grady. Now that the floodgates had been flung opened, I couldn't stop the barrage of related thoughts. I wanted to go up to the suite, barge into his bedroom and climb on top of him. I wanted to pull him into my luxury shower and soap up every inch of his muscular body. I wanted to make him moan so loud that the guests in the room below us would have to ring the front desk and complain. I had to get rid of Chris Burton without blowing this deal.

"Wait! Chris! Before we go, let's each do a shot."

"I like your thinking," he said. "Like my college days back in Boston. Barman, two shots of Jägermeister."

"No! Let's make it vodka. You know what they say, 'Never mix, never worry.'"

"Vodka it is."

We picked up our glasses and toasted. Using the fine art of misdirection, I made a big show of looking excited, and then turned my body slightly so Chris wouldn't see me throw the alcohol past my cheek and onto my shoulder and the floor. The barman, who was polishing a glass, scowled at me and shook his head. I hated ruining my dress, but at least vodka did less collateral damage than Jäger.

"Off we go," I said, taking Chris by the arm. "Let's go to yours and have a drink from the mini-bar." I steered him into the elevator. "Which floor?" He pushed the button for the floor our suite was on. When we stepped off, I glanced down the hall in the direction of my room. I couldn't be sure, but I could almost swear I saw Tom's face in the shadows, then the door closing.

I got Chris inside, lay my bag on the dining table, and parked him firmly in one of the chairs. I didn't want him heading for the bed.

"What's your poison?" I asked, swinging open the door to the mini-fridge.

"Whatever the lady's having," he shrugged out of his jacket, and loosened his tie.

I glugged an airplane-sized bottle of vodka into a glass for him, and some still water into another for me. I set them on the table, and he pulled me into his lap, burying his head in my neck. As I struggled to pull myself up to standing, Chris used his palms to survey all of my most private parts. It galled me that I was feeling turned on, but I kept my eye on the prize.

"You know what I'd like to see?" I flirted.

"I'm hoping the answer to that is 'your clothes in a pile at the foot of the bed,'" Chris answered.

I had to hand it to him. That was smooth. *Focus, Shayla.*

"Silly!" I laughed. "While we relax and have our drinks, I'd like to see that letter of intent."

"Fine," he said grinning. "But you'll have to get it yourself."

"Great. Where is it?"

He lay back in his chair, and spread his legs wider. "In my pocket."

I spied a leather briefcase on the chair. "Is it in here?"

"Could be," he said, "But my you'll need a pen. Guess where my pen is."

"Clever, Chris," I said, bending over the chair and rooting through his case. Success. I found it in the first folder I opened. By the time I turned around, Chris was sitting on the chair wearing nothing but his boxers. Oh dear God above, he was fit.

"Did you hear me say where my pen is?" he inquired. With a will of their own, my eyes landed on his crotch. There was little doubt about his feelings toward me. "God, you're so hot, Sheila. Come and have a seat." On one crazy level, it was tempting. If ever the perfect storm for a one-night stand existed, it was here and now. Good-looking guy I'll never see again, anonymous hotel room, lots of liquor.

"You know, I'm just going to pop to the ladies' room," I said, putting the letter in front of him. "While I'm in there, sign this so we can get all this pesky business out of the way." Without looking back, I ducked into the bathroom and closed the door behind me.

I looked in the mirror and whispered to myself, "You big dumb idiot. Wanting Tom O'Grady is very, very dangerous. You are on this tiny island to get his information so you can go home, write this book. Score this and the big-time's right around the corner. Ray Diablo and real New York deals."

As I ran cold water on a washcloth, I noticed a feeling of dread in my belly. I didn't want to go back to New York. The thought of sitting in Brenda Sackler's office getting yelled at held no sway for me. I'd miss my hens. I dabbed the smears of makeup off my face, then lay the cloth across my forehead to cool my feverish thoughts.

"Stop it, Shayla," I whispered, looking into my own green eyes. "Go out there and ride Chris Burton if you need to get something out of your system, but leave Tom O'Grady out of it." I ran water on a clean cloth and scrubbed at the vodka on my dress. "Tom O'Grady's just a grouchy, egotistical anachronism anyway." I took a deep breath, willed my face to fall into a relaxed, seductive smile and opened the door.

"Oh, there you are, Shayla," Chris said. I stopped in my tracks. He was holding my passport in his hand. There were two freshly poured drinks on the table. "I didn't mean to snoop; I opened your bag looking for a pen. As you can see," he waved a hand over his near-naked body, "I don't have one on me."

"It's a long story," I started.

"No need to explain. I'm a bit of a true-crime buff, myself. I never miss an issue of *Vanity Fair*. The fact that you're Hank de Winter's daughter makes me want you all the more." He drained his glass of vodka and stood up. I saw that he'd signed the letter. He advanced toward me and took hold of my body in a ballroom dance-style hold, pelvis-to-pelvis, with the flat of his hand on the small of my back. "What your farmer friend doesn't know won't hurt him. Just answer me one question, Tokyo Rose. Do you really work for Castle Stone? Because if you don't, that's a deal breaker."

I crossed my fingers way down below my rear. "Yes, I do work for Castle Stone." I did. Kind of. Just not as a Cultural Blah Blah or a Blah Blah of Marketing.

"Right, then, Shayla, seems we're good to go." He waltzed me toward the bed. When I saw where this was heading, I maneuvered my body so that I wouldn't be pinned under him when we landed. He wasn't prepared for my trying to lead, and his heel caught on the carpet. We went down hard. Right before his head hit the corner of the bedside table, I cradled it in my hand, protecting it slightly from the sharp corner. I saw stars and yelled every permutation of the swear "fuck" that I knew in rapid-fire succession.

Despite my rescue effort, his skull still caught the side of the table and he was out like a light. Panicked, I rolled his head onto the pillows and put my hand on his chest to check for breathing. His skin was warm and his smooth chest was, indeed, rising and falling. His lips were slightly parted and he looked serene, not in danger. After one last look at his long, lean body, I wrapped what I could of the bedspread around him. I gathered the signed letter, my pen, and my passport, and shoved them into my bag. Carrying my high-heels, I crept into the hall, leaving the door on the latch. I knocked on the room next to Chris's, praying that it belonged to his business associate Percy. Thankfully, Chris's bleary-eyed sidekick, dressed in a matching cotton pajama set did, indeed, answer the door.

"Percy, sorry to bother you. Chris had a bit too much to drink and he hit his head." Percy looked at my naked feet and my disheveled dress. "He seems alright, but could you be a friend and watch for signs of a concussion? Great!" I said, not waiting for an answer. "Door's open. Goodnight," I said scurrying back to my door and fishing in my bag for the key.

"They don't pay me enough…" I heard Percy grumbling from behind me in the hallway as I opened the door to the suite I shared with Tom and slipped inside. It was pitch black. I had imagined Tom might be up waiting for me. I felt my way across the furniture and glanced into my room. The digital clock read 3:22. Easing my way through the darkness, I turned on the bedside lamp. It threw just enough light out into the common area to light my way to Tom's door, in his corner of the suite. I wanted to show him the letter. Proof that I was on his side. It was my "get out of jail free" card – evidence that I'd only gone back to Chris's room for the good of Castle Stone, and to champion the Irish farmers. I wanted Tom to love me for it. I tiptoed up to knock and then I saw the sign hanging on his doorknob.

Do Not Disturb.

Chapter Twenty

Truth stands when everything else falls.

"It's been nearly an hour." I'd be the worst prisoner of war, ever. Tom blanking me from the driver's seat had turned me into a coiled spring. I tried looking at the scenery, meditating, counting backwards from 100, singing through The Sound of Music in my head. Nothing worked. I had to know what he was thinking. "At least tell me you're happy that the deal's done."

"I am."

Oh, the sweet relief of interaction. "Don't you want to say thank you?" I teased.

"I'll do you one better. I'll find a way to pay back the debt."

That stung. I didn't want him to pay me back. I wanted us to be friends, people who did things for each other. "I did it because I wanted to."

"Nevertheless."

We rode in silence. There was a trailer in front of us, and a horse stared at me.

"Are you at least impressed?"

"Aye, you did things I never could."

I let that sit there. I took a sip from the diet soda I'd picked up at a newsagent before we got on the road. I didn't normally drink soda, but I was kind of hungover. Finally, I couldn't stand it. "Like what?"

"You're an excellent liar."

That was it. "You asked me to lie!"

"I asked you to play a part. The only fib I suggested was that you say you worked for Castle Stone. And there you sat, banging on about your life in Manhattan and how much you had in common with your man Chris."

"He's not my man."

"Oh, isn't he?" Tom thundered. "Whose man was he at three o'clock yesterday morning, then?"

"If you think I slept with him, you're wrong. I didn't."

"Just like you didn't sleep with the lad who broke your window. Save your breath. I've heard it before. Now I know how easily lies roll off your tongue. Well done, you." His face was hard as a rock. He breathed in and out through his nose, nostrils flaring.

I felt a little scared. Not like he'd hurt me or anything, but like he'd cut me off. I chose my words carefully. "I did not sleep with Des at Castle Stone." It was a half-truth. I couldn't summon the bravery to tell the whole story. Tom could put me on a plane tomorrow, end of story. I wasn't ready for that.

He drove on. I pretended to drink from my empty can, just for something to do with my hands. The horse still stared at me, sideways, out of one huge eye. I put the can down.

"I'm not a liar, Tom."

He let that hang there in the air. He took his eyes off of the road for a moment and looked me full in the face. "Did you lie to Mary?"

Oh my God and Jesus. Has Tom known why I'm here all along?

"What do you mean?" Hank always told me that diarrhea of the mouth never helped anyone. Shut up and let the other person talk, he said. That's how you get the story.

"You want me to spell it out?" he asked, tersely.

I didn't really, but there was no choice. "Yes."

"Do you like girls?"

The tension drained out of my body like water through an open dam. "No, I like boys."

"Oh, that's grand," he said. "'Course I've no judgment, I didn't mean it like that. But why in heaven's name, then, would you lead Mary on? It's just cruel."

"Mary's a lesbian?"

"Too right, and she seems to have a little crush on you."

I felt awful. Thinking back on it, I noticed the small things. The smiles she gave me and the fact she had always given me the best jobs. And she always offered to walk me back to the dorms from the main building. I felt so bad! This is why I've never been a liar. Someone always gets hurt. It's my number-one rule. Lies always snowball. Starting with the ones in Brenda's office back in March, mine certainly have.

"It's complicated," I told Tom.

"The truth is the truth. There's nothing complicated about it." I watched the horse trailer pull off the M11 (check this), and felt more alone than I had in ages.

"I'll talk to Mary."

"Good."

I had the rest of the trip to think in silence. I felt sick about Mary. I couldn't count the times I'd been on the other end of that equation. Even if I hadn't misled her on purpose, my tunnel vision had prevented me from seeing the forest for the trees. Looking out the window at the beautiful countryside dotted with sheep and colored with wildflowers, I noticed that I didn't feel joy. I just felt scared. Where had all the lying and jockeying for position as a writer gotten me? All of my New York ambition and desperation to please Hank had turned me into someone I never wanted to be. Someone like Matty, like Lizbeth, like Brenda. I felt like there wasn't a floor underneath me. Lost, I turned my head to the side so Tom couldn't see the tears racing down my cheeks. Mom knew me, but she was gone. Maggie knows me, but she's far away. The thought of driving away friends, of driving away Tom, sent cold water through my veins. I was twelve years old, running down the hallway of the hospital wailing; the day mom slipped away.

When we got back to Castle Stone, I said polite goodbyes to Tom in the parking lot and made my way back to the dorms alone. I didn't want to get into a conversation with him. I had thinking to do. As much as I didn't want to be by myself, my instinct told me to batten down the hatches. I didn't trust my judgment. Being out in the world seemed dangerous. I was a hermit crab who had left the safety of one shell without the protection of the next. I silently thanked God I had the day off tomorrow. I stayed off the paths, dragging my case across the field in order to avoid people. Looking both ways, I sneaked in the main entrance and quietly crept down the hallway. I finally breathed out when I closed the door behind me.

Dear Mags,

You have no idea how much I wish I was with you in our old apartment, sitting on our IKEA loveseat and drinking coffee. I feel a world away from you (which I guess I am). It's not just the distance, though, it's the change. I had a fantasy of hopping on a plane tonight and heading home for a hug. Tonight, I'm staying in my room. I keep a stash of bottled water and juice and some random snacks in here, so that's my dinner.

Remember when I told you on the phone that I was going to Dublin to help Tom with a business deal? Well, even though it shames me to write these words, it was a disaster. I wanted to be the hero. For once, I wanted to be the star of the show, the one whose name everyone remembered in a good way. I wanted Tom to like me for it. Really, I wanted Tom to love me for it. Really really? I just wanted Tom to love me. Oh, God, Mags. I'm in love with Tom.

Shit.

Love Shay xx

Chapter Twenty-One

Burning embers are easily kindled.

The grass was still dewy at 6:30 a.m. when I made my way to the back door of the kitchen. I needed to speak with Tom. I'd hardly slept and my brain spun from a lethal combination of fogginess and buzzing. It was now or never and I planned to tell the truth, whatever the consequences.

I threw open the screen door and scanned the room for Tom. Brigid stood arranging scones on a tray, dish dogs were carrying clean plates to the dining room, and Bill assembled quiches.

"Where's Chef?"

"Not here and you're late," Bill snapped. He turned his sautéed spinach out into several waiting crusts.

"I'm not on this morning."

"Then get out of here, you're in the way."

"He's gone to his mam's," Brigid told me. "By the way, Mary wants to see you in the office."

"Thanks, Bridge." I shoved the information about Mary to the back of my mind. One thing at a time. I followed the path to Maeve's cottage part of the way, but kept running into early-rising guests out for brisk walks and gardeners trudging along with buckets, wagons, and spades preparing to start their day's work. I cut across the grass and let myself in the gate. Nap was standing on the little table by the window, tap-dancing and whining.

"Sheila, dear," Maeve greeted me as she swung open the door. "I was beginning to think I'd never lay eyes on you again." I saw Tom over her shoulder, sitting at the table.

"I've been…uh…busy, Maeve. It's nothing personal, I promise."

"Well, get yourself in here and sit down with a cup of tea."

"No, thanks. I came to have a word with Tom."

"I won't hear it. Come through, I've a batch of mince pies, warm from the oven."

I sat at the table. Tom sipped his tea without even a glance in my direction. Maeve set a cup and a plate with two pastries in front of me.

"Maeve!" I heard a man call from upstairs. "Could I trouble you for a glass of water?"

I looked at Tom. His face was thunderous. "Tony?" I asked.

He nodded and looked away. Maeve rushed through with a glass in her hand and called, "Don't you dare get up! I'm on my way."

"Your matchmaking worked," Tom said to me coolly. "The day we left for Dublin, His Lordship stopped here. I suppose he heard I'd gone on a journey and seized the opportunity to swoop in on my innocent mother. While he was here, he claimed to have a pain in his heart. McGeever, the physician from the village called in, and insisted that he be put to bed. I can't see why it had to be my bed in this cottage given that he owns Castle Stone and all the land it sits on, but here we are."

A laugh bubbled up from my depths and burst out from behind my lips. The more I tried to hold it in, the throatier and chestier it became. Aware that I was infuriating Tom, I strove to contain it but that only served to make the barks and snorts louder. Soon, tears were streaming down my face.

Tom stood up. "You're beyond belief! You think it's funny that an innocent elder is being taken advantage of? That she'll have her heart broken and be left to feel like a fool?" he shouted.

"Shh!" That stopped me laughing. I didn't want Maeve to hear, or she would feel like a fool. "Will you at least step outside if you're going to yell stupid jackass stuff?" I whispered.

"It's the truth," he hissed. "But yes, let's step outside. He indicated the door and I walked through.

"Mother!" he called. "I'm just showing Sheila out. I'll be back in two shakes." He closed the door behind himself. Nap jumped down from the table and started circling the two of us, herding us and pushing us closer together, barking the whole time.

"Nap! Go," Tom shouted. "You," he said to me, "follow me." He marched across the grass at a pace twice as fast as mine. I burst into a sprint to keep up. I was winded by the time we reached the catering cottages. He pulled a set of keys from the pocket of his hound's-tooth chef's trousers, opened the door to the unit in which he'd given me a cooking lesson and pushed me inside. He shut the door behind himself, and started in.

"This isn't working out. I'm going to have to ask Mary to terminate your stint in the work experience program."

I couldn't speak. All I could hear was static. I realized Tom was upset but I did not see this coming. "You can't do that," I faltered. "What about Chris Burton and the plan for the Castle Stone line of products?"

"Fucking *Chris*." Tom ripped the snaps open on his chef's coat. It was boiling hot in the cottage. He stormed from window to window in the kitchen, opening each while wrestling with the shades. I guess he didn't want anyone to see us. "It's for the best. You should never get into bed with someone you don't trust, and I don't trust him as far as I can throw him."

"Speaking of trust…"

"Yes, speaking of trust," he said, eyes flashing. "I thought I told you to stay away from my mother. Now look what's happened."

"I did stay away from Maeve, even though it broke my heart." I sat in one of the chairs at the dining table.

"Don't be so dramatic. Next you'll be telling me that she's like a mother to you." That stung like a slap. Tears popped to my eyes.

"She is."

"I don't know what your game is, but I can tell there's something you're hiding from me."

Swiping my eyes with the back of my hand, I said, "There is no game where your mother is concerned. Laugh in my face if you want to," I could hear my heart, and each breath caught on the jagged beats. I was so afraid he would laugh, "But your mother means something to me. I feel close to her. I want her to be happy." I was blazing hot. The shades were blocking the breeze and the air stood still. I peeled off my cardigan and threw it on the table.

"Then why set her up to get hurt?" He smacked the countertop with his open palm, hard.

I was angry now. "I'm not setting her up. Just because you picked the wrong girl and got your heart smashed, and wound up unable to connect with anyone on a real level doesn't mean it's the same with Maeve. She had her heart broken. She loved your father and he died." Tom winced. "And they're not my stories to tell, but ask your mother about life before she married. She was a good girl, she had passion in her heart. Your father wasn't her only love. Do you think the only choices are to be celibate or to have nameless, faceless sex with a string of nobodies?"

"Don't you tell me that my mother has been…?"

"No, idiot. You!"

He narrowed his eyes and shook his head in confusion. "For your information, there hasn't been anyone since Tabitha."

"Bullshit!" I yelled before my brain could catch up with my mouth. Off-balance, I couldn't suss out whether that could be true or not. My intellect told me no, but my heart soared with hope. "What about the slut you made me cook dinner for when you were pretending to give me a cooking lesson."

"I'm not the liar round here. That dinner was for you, stupid." He was sweating around his temples. He ripped off his chef's jacket. Underneath, he wore a blindingly white, ribbed cotton undershirt, the kind New Yorkers called "wife beaters." He ran both hands through his damp, curling hair, pushing it out of his eyes. "I wanted to do something nice. And you ruined things before they even got started."

"You are so Irish!" I shouted. "I didn't ruin anything. I knew you were mad at me that day, I knew it. And you just brooded around here with storms in your eyes, talking sharply and not telling me what the problem was."

"There was no point. We didn't see eye to eye about my mam. End of. What's the point of talking about it?"

"Talking is the point of talking about it. Like today. I went looking for you so I could talk to you. You're right. I haven't been honest. I wanted to tell you something."

"You slept with that fucker Burton. I knew it." His hands tensed, and he stalked in a circle. This time, he banged his fist on the countertop.

"No, I swear I didn't. I couldn't. I mean, I could have, obviously, he had his pants off and everything?"

"Which kind of pants?" Tom thundered. "American or Irish?"

"Trousers! But it doesn't matter. That's what I tracked you down to tell you. And it's about a zillion times easier to tell you now that you've fired me." I leaped to my feet and flew across the room to where he was standing. "I couldn't sleep with Chris because I like you. There! Fire me again why don't you?" I jabbed him in the chest with my index finger.

"I said I'd tell you the truth, so there's the truth. I wanted to sleep with you that night, so I'm the big fucking idiot, because you wouldn't have me. There. Done. Truth. I've wanted your mother to get together with Tony all along. They make a darling couple, and they deserve a second chance at romance, and I wanted to be the one to make it happen. Ha! Truth! And like every other lovesick girl in Ballykelty, I have feelings for you. Truth, truth, truth." My head was on fire. I threw myself back down into my chair, panting.

He stood in the middle of the kitchen floor, fists still balled.

"I'd have had you."

My eyes locked on to his and my hands began shaking. My brain clicked on with complete lucidity, like it had been jolted with electricity. I had utter clarity, as if someone had washed my brain with rubbing alcohol, yet my body was confused. The words "fight or flight" flashed like a stock ticker through my mind. Was he going to attack me or was he going to run. I could hear his breathing. I could hear mine.

"And I'll have you now," he said quietly, his words full of intention. "If you'll have me."

I couldn't move. My brain told my body what to do, but it wouldn't do it. Finally, after a lifetime, I felt my head bob up and down on my neck. Yes, I nodded.

Tom's eyes didn't leave mine. He took three purposeful steps toward me, then his lips were on my lips. His skin was so hot, and it augmented my own heat. Fuel on a fire. He kissed me hard, showing me how much he meant it, but his lips were soft and lush. My nuclear-powered brain perceived every nuance of every flick of his tongue, every note of his scent, every scratch of the hint of his beard on my cheek. My arms rose up of their own volition and I took hold of the muscles of his shoulders and pulled myself up to standing. The bare skin of his broad shoulders was slick with sweat. He grabbed me by the waist and pulled my body flat against his, never ending the kiss. His hardness pressed against my belly. I opened my mouth wider to receive more of his tongue. His hands dropped to my bottom and pressed my hips close. I heard myself moan.

Standing up straight to his full height, his lips left mine, and he looked me in the eye. "Alright?"

"No," I answered honestly. "I'm not going to be alright until you're inside me." I took his hand and went before him up the stairs. I couldn't stand to look at him. I was terrified the spell would be broken; that if he got a good look at me, he might come to his senses. I didn't care if I was staying or leaving, or if he hated me or loved me. I just knew that I'd die then and there if he refused to make love to me. I steered him into the first bedroom I'd tested out back on the day of our cooking lesson. The other bed was nicer, but I remembered the condoms in the drawer. *'Dear God, please let them still be there.'* I prayed, perhaps inappropriately.

The minute we reached the bed, my time of being in charge ended. Tom spun me around and lay me backwards before I could think. With a combination of his strong arms and a belly-melting pelvic thrust, he pushed me up so my head rested on the pillows. If the kitchen was hot, the upstairs was scorching. As he kneeled between my legs and pushed up my shirt to kiss his way up my stomach, sweat dripped from his damp hair onto my slippery skin. Still, I willed him not to get up to open the window. If he broke contact, even for a second, I'd surely go into hysteria. I could feel a scream rising up in me at the thought of it. Instead, he pulled my shirt over my head. My nipples stood like bullets underneath the lace of my bra cups. "Please," I begged. I wanted to say, "Put your lips there," but he was already undoing the button on my pants, sliding them down and off. I spread my legs to welcome him back on top of me. I'd sent shame packing. I needed Tom. Truth.

Kneeling at attention in the vee of my legs, Tom peeled his undershirt over his head. I watched like it was a show, unapologetically fixated. His shoulders were muscled and broad, and his biceps were solid and defined without that cartoonish look of a body builder. He'd come by his physique through the hard work of the farm and the kitchen. Lifting, hauling, beating. I could not take my eyes off of him, and my own hand wandered to where my panties were dampening. He wanted honesty. Here I was, exposed. I honestly wanted him more than I wanted to breathe. I propped myself up on an elbow and unhooked my bra. Tom took the straps and pulled it off as I slipped my arms free. Feeling his eyes on my naked breasts inflamed me. I lifted my hips off of the bed, signaling for him to take off my underwear. He answered my call and I lay naked before him.

It was at this point he slowed down. He'd stripped down to his boxer briefs, but stopped there. He slid up the bed, laying his body against the length of mine. I strained to make more contact with him but the only places he touched were my cheeks, my neck, my hair. He kissed me till I was drugged. The yearning to have him inside me was a distant, dream-like ache as I drowsed beneath his lips, his tongue, his taste.

"I've waited for this," he whispered between long, deep kisses. "So long."

His mouth was my mouth. I was sure he was breathing for me.

"Do you want me?" he asked, then plunged me back beneath the surface with more kissing.

"Yes."

"Then tell me."

"Tom, I want you. Nothing else matters."

Keeping me suspended with his kisses, in a world between here and there, he managed to strip himself naked, and find the condom I had fished from the drawer without breaking the delicious contact of our lips and skin. He ran his hands all over me. His toes sought my toes; the hair on his legs tickled my legs. My eyes stayed closed. Every cell in my body hummed.

I heard the foil of the condom rip, and felt Tom position his weight on top of me. His skin was searing hot and I pulled him toward me, my arms circled around his waist.

"Please," I whispered. "Now."

I opened my eyes. His blue eyes were fixed on mine, deadly serious. There was a flash of fear there, but then he kissed me. He entered me hard, with no teasing. Groaning, he took me, there's no other way to say it. Claimed me. Let me know that I was wanted. All I ever wanted was for someone to want me this way. All I ever wanted was this kind of precise attention, whole and encompassing.

I breathed in Tom's hot breath through parted lips. Moaning and crying out, and rolled on the waves of our bodies' motion. I didn't bother to be coy. This was the truth. I tilted my hips and used my hands to pull Tom into me. I ground against the delicious bone above his hardness, pushing myself toward pleasure, letting him see my hunger.

I came first and I did it raw and real. I cried out, I panted like an animal. I moved him where I needed him to be and held him there tightly. I kept going until every twitch and thrust of my body stopped on its own. I kept going until my muscles shook with fatigue.

"Good girl," Tom growled, his eyes locked on mine. "Gorgeous."

We had almost ceased rolling together, but slowly, slowly, he picked the pace up again. Chin on my shoulder, mouth by my ear, Tom uttered noises of appreciation. He hummed low and sustained moans, punctuated by catches of his breath. "Oh, God, so sexy," he grunted. He lured me back to his heights with his thrusts, and his unedited lust. Before I knew it, I was bucking with a desperation to quench my need. We fell into a rhythm. It heightened, growing wilder and wilder. He stopped breathing. His body rocked, but he fell silent. Then the dam burst. His animal cry against my ear ramped me up, and I held stock-still, receiving his pulses, listening to him come.

I felt it when he finished. His breathing went back to heavy and steady, and he slipped himself out of me. He clamped his lips over mine and reached for my aching sex. Using his broad fingertips, he expertly worked to help me find relief while using his full, sexy lips to tease and pull my stiff nipples. I came again in minutes, groaning loudly, ending in a scream that faded to a laugh. I laughed and laughed, feeling all the tension and worry evaporate from my muscles. He stretched out on top of me and kissed me, and began to laugh, lips against mine. The shaking of my naked belly against his, made him start to chuckle, and soon we were both roaring and crying. Every time our laughter died down, one of us would start again. I don't know how long it went on, but it felt like hours. At the end, we were well and truly spent.

We fell asleep on top of the covers, arms and legs entwined.

"'Morning," Tom whispered in my ear, his voice ragged and husky. I awoke with alarm bells in my chest, with the sensation of being late for something. Tom pulled me in close and kissed my forehead. I breathed out.

"Is it?" Shadows danced in the room. I squinted at the blinds, trying to gauge where the sun was or wasn't.

He checked his watch. "No, it's just after lunch time."

"I guess you should be getting back to the kitchen."

"I suppose I should," he said, looking down at me. My heart swooped into a free fall. I shouldn't have expected more than a one-off, but it still stung.

Tom propped himself up on his elbow and looked down at me seriously. "But I'll skive off if you'll stay here with me."

I wrapped my arms around his neck and reached up to kiss him. He rolled over, pulling me on top of him. Our hands and mouths were everywhere, taking possession without the urgency of the early morning. We spent the next hour or so slowly touching, tasting, learning the curves and angles of one another.

Finally, languid and sedated, Tom said, "I could drink water for Ireland. Will you excuse me?" He pulled on his boxer briefs and headed down the stairs. I wrapped the sheet around myself and took advantage of the break to use the bathroom, rinse my mouth, and splash water on my face. One advantage to not wearing makeup is that you don't wind up with post-coital raccoon eyes, but to be honest, had I known I'd wind up in bed with Tom I'd have at least slapped on some concealer and mascara. I smiled at my own blotchy, beard-burned face in the mirror. On the plus side, if my bare face and unstyled hair could provoke Tom to take me with such desire, maybe I'd never need to break the bank at MAC again.

I turned on the hot water and stepped into the shower. Face to the spray, I felt a pair of arms encircle my waist, pressing a bar of soap to my skin. Before long, the bar of soap wound up melting in the drain, as Tom used his hands to wrest yet another climax out of me. He used his farm-boy strength to hold me upright as my knees buckled. "That was lovely, Sheila," he declared, mouth against my ear. "Now dry yourself off. There's a bottle of water for you on the vanity."

I stepped out, leaving him to it. I drained the bottle of water in one go. I doubted I had a drop of water left in my body. Tom had done a round of the house, opening the windows, and I breathed in deeply, welcoming the fresh air. I pulled on my bra, t-shirt and underpants, and left it at that. The doorbell rang. I froze.

"Don't answer that!" Tom called over the running water. I sat down on the edge of the bed, nervous, like Goldilocks about to be caught in the bears' house. Tom walked out with a thick, white towel wrapped around his waist, drying his darkened blonde curls.

"I called in sick." He smiled at me. "I've not taken a sick day since I came to Castle Stone and opened The Grange Hall." I opened my mouth to protest. "Shh, you're worth it. I'd have just said I won't be in, I'm the boss after all," he flashed me a wicked grin. "But it was easier this way. Now no one will come looking for me."

"Who's downstairs?" I whispered.

"I called catering services. Told them there was royalty in from England, and they weren't to breathe a word as the Duke and Duchess wanted their privacy." He winked. "Are you hungry?"

"I could eat," I smiled. My stomach growled in the most un-lady-like way imaginable, and Tom stifled a laugh. He pushed me down onto the bed and kissed me sweetly on the mouth. "If you can't think of anything better to do."

"Oh, I can, but I have to keep my strength up. You can't expect a man to do this kind of work without sustenance."

"Work?" I bit his lip.

"Ouch! Yes, it's work. But as the old Irish blessing begins, 'May you always have work for your hands to do…'" He slid his hand under my shirt. "Amen."

That made me giggle. We kissed and laughed for a minute or

two, then I looked him in the eye. "How did you know there were condoms in the bedside table?"

After a pause, he said, "I put them there."

I braced myself. I knew this was too good to be true.

"For Catherine?"

"Who? What, the girl at the front desk. Never! Where did you get that idea?" From her, I thought. She'd surely love it. "For Tabitha, then?"

"No, not for Tabitha." A dark cloud rolled over his face. He laughed a mirthless laugh. "No."

"Are you dating lots of girls, then?" I heard glasses clinking, and the oven door slamming shut downstairs. How many girls had received the Duke and Duchess treatment in this cottage?

"Hang on, let me do the maths. Carry the one…divided by three…Let's see, I'm dating exactly…zero girls." He stood up and pulled on his underpants, then sat down on the bed next to me. I sat up and looked him in the eye. "Tell me the truth. Who are the condoms for?"

I could see him deciding something. His eyes were on my face, but they darted back and forth, processing something. "Are we telling the truth, Sheila?" His calling me Sheila sent a pang of regret through me. How much truth could I tell him? I nodded.

"I put the condoms there for you. Are you angry?" I was not. I was elated. "Before the night I planned to cook a meal for you. But you have to understand something. I'm not some animal. And I didn't imagine you'd fall right into bed with me, honestly. I just refuse to leave something like that to chance." He stared at the wall behind me, his breath coming fast. "I'll never do that again."

I sat still, like a rabbit before a dog. I gleaned that this was a bigger story than 'Tom behaves sensibly.' I looked down at my own hand and steadied my breathing.

"You see," he said, "Tabitha left me, shortly before we were to be married." I knew this. I waited. "We'd bought a house in London, and everything. A large house, four bedrooms." He stopped talking.

"Four bedrooms?" I prompted.

"Four bedrooms, near good schools. She told me she wanted children, early on. Turns out, she didn't."

"So, she admitted that and called off the wedding?"

"Hardly," he snorted. "She wouldn't have. She'd have married me, lying to me all the way up the aisle. It's worse than that. She was pregnant." The angry expression on his face frightened me. "She took care of it." He shook his head. I noticed his hand was gripping his thigh, hard.

"She told you she had an abortion?"

"No, she didn't even have the decency to tell me the truth after the fact. Her PA from the show took her to do it. Some bastard from one of the London rags offered the girl a sack of money for the story and she caved. The producers were on it in a heartbeat, and they killed the story but then I knew. We had it out on the street in front of the house. The producers couldn't kill that story. It was all "Famous Chef and TV personality Tom O'Grady's temper is as hot as his food," and "Domestic violence on the menu for TV's top power couple," and other lies."

"But you didn't hit her, right?" Tom gave me a withering look. "I mean of course you didn't hit her, so it wasn't the truth."

"Since when does truth matter in London, or on television, or in the papers?" Tom stood up, and began pacing the room. "Then she was off on a plane to America with some man I'd never met. She said he was a friend, but for all I know he'd been her lover all along. I'll never know the truth, and I'm beyond caring now. But that came at a cost." He sighed hard and massaged one of his shoulders, stretching his neck. "So, that's why I had the condoms. I hope you understand."

I nodded.

"Now tell me the truth, Sheila. Did you give it to Burton?"

"No!"

His eyes searched mine. "OK, did you sleep with that boy in the dorms?"

"Des? No." I watched Tom watching me. "I mean yes, I did."
I reached my hand out. Tom looked at it. "But not then. Please,
come sit down." He sat on the bed without touching me.

"I slept with Des the first night I was in Ireland. And I'm glad
I did." Tom winced. "Because before that, I hadn't had sex for a
very long time. If I hadn't had that fling, I might not have been
brave enough to make love with you this morning."

He leaned in and kissed me softly on the lips. "Thanks for being
honest." He put his arms around me. "The condoms," he began,
stroking my hair, looking over my shoulder. "That was a big deal
for me. I haven't been to bed with a woman since Tabitha."

I stayed in our embrace, saying nothing. It had been a very
long time. I felt honored.

Finally, Tom broke the silence. "Right. I don't know about you,
babe, but I could eat a horse." He waggled his eyebrows and leered
comically. It was clear he'd had enough heavy talk for the moment.
"You've unleashed a mighty hunger in me." He pinned me to the
bed and I pretended to struggle.

"No, Your Lordship! I'm spent. 'Tis only right to feed a lady
before another round in the royal chamber. I demand jellied eels
and beef in aspic!"

He stood up and pulled me to my feet. "Works out then. That's
what I've ordered." He shrugged into one of the bathrobes from
the closet and held another out to me. "Care to dress for dinner?"

As I sat at the table in luxury accommodations, drinking excellent cold, white wine and dining on pasta with fresh scallops, clams,
and mussels, I gazed across the table at Tom. Gorgeous, sexy, manly
Tom, who by a miracle from heaven seemed to want me as much
as I wanted him. Our dining-table conversation twinkled with
trivial topics and time melted away as we laughed and chatted.
We found out that we had nearly everything in common, the way
you do when you're first dating. You like pizza? I like pizza! We
agreed on deal breakers: Elvis Costello? Love! Horror movies? No
thanks. Traveling to Tokyo? Meh. Traveling to Vienna? Yes, please.

When did you lose your virginity? Both late bloomers: 18.

After we ate, we took our wine into the lounge and curled up on the plush sofa. It was still warm, so we didn't light a fire, but Tom did light a few of the votive and taper candles scattered around the various tables. I heard his phone vibrate and felt disappointed when he pulled it out and checked it. I didn't want to let him go.

"That's just my mother. Hope you don't mind if I take it?" I gestured for him to go ahead and he stepped into the kitchen.

"I'm fine, Mam. Just a head cold. Nah, if I need anything I'll have the kitchen bring it." I strained to hear. I heard him open the fridge and the sound of bottles clinking. Yay! If he was opening a second bottle, it meant we were staying. "Ah, yes, Sheila. As a matter of fact, I sent her to Swords, uh, Screen, on the train. She's going to talk to a farmer there for me, and um, pick up some cheese." I heard a cork pop. Hooray! "I'll let Mary know. She should be back on the grounds tomorrow, maybe. Maybe the day after. He was short of breath? Ring the doctor, Mam! Oh, he's called in already?" Tom walked into the room and set the bottle down on the table. "Well, that's certainly a relief. Thank God. No, I'm not cross anymore that he's there." Tom smiled at me and topped up my wine. "I'm glad he's not alone."

Chapter Twenty-Two

Instinct is stronger than upbringing.

After two solid days of non-stop sex punctuated only by the delivery of gourmet meals and the occasional luxury shower, a twelve-hour shift in the kitchen really took it out of me. Harder still than the labor and the standing on my feet, though, was pretending not to be intimate with Tom. He didn't go out of his way to make it easier on me, either. As I stood at a metal counter beating dozens of eggs with a whisk, Tom reached above me to grab a flour-sifter from a high shelf. No one paid the slightest bit of attention as he pressed his pelvis against my back during the stretch. My body remembered the position and sprang to attention, involuntarily pushing back against him. I had to cough in order to stifle a moan.

"Sheila, come here" he ordered at one point. "Take a taste of this and tell me if it's too salty." With my back turned to the rest of the staff, no one could see that Tom slid his finger, along with the spoonful of soup, into my mouth. By lunchtime, I didn't think I could make it through the day without spread-eagling myself on the kitchen island and begging him to take me right there, on its floured surface.

My reprieve came in the form of Mary's request for me to fill in at the hostess stand in The Grange Hall. "I know you've not been trained but you work in pairs. Mairead is the head waitress; she knows the seating charts and what have you. You're in capable hands with that girl. We just need another body to greet the guests and direct them to the toilets. You'll need to dress smart, like. Take your cue off the others. D'ya mind?"

I didn't mind a bit. It saved me the torture of being near Tom without laying my hands on him. "Mary," I said, closing the door to the office and peeping around the cubicles to see if we were alone. "Could I have a private word?"

"Ah, sure, have a seat," Mary said, taking her own chair. I sat across from her.

"Mary, I have to get something off my chest."

"Go on."

"You and Brigid are really the only ones here I trust. You set me up with my paperwork and didn't breathe a word of who I was. And I'd have been put out on the curb my first day if Brigid hadn't helped me in the kitchen. And for no good reason. Just because you're kind."

"Ah, well, you're easy to be kind to. Always making me laugh. And you're good people. I can always tell."

"I don't have many friends here, Mary. I appreciate all you've done for me."

"There's Mrs. O'Grady."

"That's true, but I can't tell her this. Anyway, you've kept my biggest secret, from the minute I got here. I feel I can trust you." I knew I was taking a gamble. Mary had been good to me. I didn't want to see her hurt or embarrassed. "I'm going to tell you something that I hope you won't tell anyone else." She didn't say a word. Very Irish of her, not to tip her hand, I thought. "I'm having a secret affair with Tom O'Grady." There. That defined the type I liked and identified an individual. And I'd shown respect about sharing sensitive information. I watched her carefully.

"I am gobsmacked," she said simply. I waited.

"I just had to tell someone," I explained. "It's exhausting to keep secrets. So I picked you. Hope that's OK."

She looked straight at me. "And why not? That's what chums are for." She smiled. "I'll do you one better and tell you my secret."

'*Oh, God. Please don't let it be that she has a crush on me,*' I prayed. I remembered what it felt like when Tom rejected me. I didn't want the shoe to be on the other foot.

"I like girls."

"Oh. Really?" I replied, with as little emotion as possible.

"One in particular."

"I don't want disappoint, Mary but…"

"Does she already have a girlfriend?" Mary looked worried. "It's only that she's been sending me signals. She made me a quilt for my bed, then asked me if I needed help putting it on there."

My face nearly cracked with a huge smile. I giggled with relief. "No, uh, I was just going to say that I didn't want to disappoint you with what I was wearing tonight. I only have a few skirts and dresses."

"Just do me a favor, will you? Let's keep this between us. Ashleigh's been trying to throw me together with her cousin. Insisted we all go for pints at the pub down in Ballykelty. I don't want to hurt Ashleigh's feelings, but her cousin has as much personality as a wet rag. Science fiction novels and the great battles of Ireland were the only topics on offer with that one. Mental! I'm really not one for historical reenactment. Apart from that, even," she looked at my shyly. "I like Brigid. Don't breathe a word about that, either!"

"My lips are sealed."

She came around the desk and gave me a hug. "It's funny, Sheila. Ashleigh told me you like girls."

"Did she?" I kept my expression blank.

Mary put on a brave face. "Never believed it, myself. Hope hearing that doesn't offend."

"I'm not offended at all. If I did like girls, though, I'd be fighting off Ashleigh's boring cousin for a chance with you. I'd even don historical reenactment gear to do it." It was true. Mary was kind and capable, and funny.

"Ah, get on with yourself," she said, opening the door and pushing me out. "I already give you the best shifts, and I'm lying to my own government so's you can work here like an undercover spy. Flirting with me will get you nowhere."

That night, I stood at the hostess stand freshly washed and groomed, and wearing a respectable face of makeup. Brigid had spied me in the hallway of the dorm wearing the red dress from the meeting with Chris Burton, and had shooed me into her room.

"You can't dress better than the guests!" she told me. "Where did you get a frock like that? Must've cost thousands! We're about the same size, take what you like from my wardrobe. When I came here, my mother insisted I bring a trunk filled with dresses 'suitable for church.' Even if I went to church, I defy her to show me a priest who requires a new outfit at every mass. She'd have me dress like a spinster schoolteacher, if she had her way. The ones she sent are at the back. Pick from the front."

"Brigid, these are stunning! You must spend every cent of your wages on clothes!"

She looked pleased. "Not at all. You see, I went to art college. It's just I couldn't get a job after doing anything in the fine arts or design field. I have eight brothers and sisters, so I've been cooking since I could stand on a stool without tipping a pot down my front. With the recession, I was lucky to get my job here."

"But these are amazing. I rifled through 40s and 50s-style dresses that had been reworked to include modern touches. Some featured appliques, some spangles, and some had ironed-on graphic words and phrases.

"These could hang in a gallery, Bridge."

"Aw, go on. But lookit, I also quilt. When you have eleven people in a household to feed and clothe, you have to make do with what's there."

She waved her hand toward the quilted wall hangings and bed coverings on the other side of the small room. The textiles showed solid craft skills, but the 21st century spin set them apart.

"These would go for a fortune in boutique stores in Manhattan."

"I'll admit," she blushed, "I've a man selling them for me on Stephen's Green, in Dublin. I don't want to get my hopes up, but a woman from New York was grilling him about my pieces, asking where they came from like, and who the artist was."

"Well, I can see why. You should move to a big city where you could be in an artist's community."

Her face closed. "Nah, I'm happy where I am. At the moment, I'm in no hurry to go."

"Do you have a special friend around here?" I asked innocently.

She grabbed two or three dresses from hangers in an obvious move to change the subject. "Let's get you kitted out."

Gauging from everyone's muted compliments, I gathered Brigid's china-blue sundress with the ruffled petticoat, topped with a vintage flowered cotton cardigan, fell under the category of "appropriate." Mairead turned out to be nice, and in addition to kindly teaching me the ropes of dealing with reservations and assigning tables, she cracked jokes in between customers.

"Shayla?" a big voice suddenly boomed from behind me. "Is that you, dear? Look at the sight of you! Of course it is," he said, wrapping me in a huge bear hug. "You remember old Brian Lynch from the airplane, don't you? Sure, it's been ages."

"Who's Shayla?" Mairead whispered.

"Shayla," he started.

"Sheila," I explained to Mairead.

"I'm here on a little GlobeCo business. It's only a shame the wife couldn't join me. Don't go reporting me to GlobeCo, mind. I pay all her expenses when she travels with me. I'm known for keeping meticulous records, me. My colleagues call me Mr. Spreadsheet, don't they? The Mrs. sprained her ankle playing golf, thought it best she should stay home. Ah, well, she'll have the girls to keep her company."

"Golf! Now that is quite a sport," I said, hoping to steer the conversation away from me.

"Mairead, let me just seat our guest," I said, picking up two menus and trotting ahead to a table as far from the hostess stand as possible. It turned out to be the one with the nicest view of the grounds, the outside dining area lit up with torches for the evening. "Mary instructed me to seat you at our VIP table." That wasn't true, but Brian had been so nice to me on the plane, and what was the point of having a service job if you couldn't use your powers for good once in a while.

"The Mary who gave me a tour of the grounds?" he asked. I nodded.

"Sturdy lass, that Mary," Brian said. I handed him a menu, and stepped to the side while one of the busboys filled his water glass. "You know, Shayla, I might have remembered you'd be here chasing after your man Tom O'Grady." I faked a coughing fit to drown Brian out. The busser gave me a look as he moved on to the next table.

"Just a reminder," I bellowed, "the offerings at The Grange Hall include locally sourced ingredients whenever possible, and we cook with the freshest, most organic vegetables. Our meats, eggs, dairy, and seafood include the best nature provides. Chef Tom O'Grady develops and executes the recipes for our dishes with the help of a blue-ribbon staff. We hope you'll enjoy your meal, and let us know if there's anything we can do to enhance your experience." I'd taken the kernel of the welcome speech Mairead gave customers and made it my own.

"Lovely, lovely," Brian responded.

"I'll leave you to your dinner. Oh, and Mary asked me to send over a bottle of champagne. It should be here shortly." I'd pay for that myself. I walked back to the hostess stand hoping I could afford it.

The rest of the night went swimmingly. Mairead handled the seating charts and timing of the reservations, and sent me to greet, sweet-talk and smooth ruffled feathers. I met a couple from Amsterdam on a 25th anniversary tour of Europe, a jockey from Lexington, Kentucky, who'd ridden in all three races of the Triple Crown, and a pair of Irish-American schoolteachers from Sheboygan, Wisconsin, who had saved their whole lives to make a pilgrimage to the motherland. I surprised myself at how much I enjoyed interacting with the guests. I loved the hens and horses, but at a certain point, conversation with them fell short.

After my shift, I was so energized that I couldn't wind down. Instead of heading back to my dorm, I paid a rare visit to the back room of Uncle Jack's for a drink.

Kieran, a strapping lad who sometimes worked in the kitchen doing prep or dishes, acted as barman. "Would you look at the high-fashion model who's graced us here tonight, fellas? I'd swear that I know this girl, but the one I'm thinking of only wears men's clothes and usually has enough dirt on her face to grow a crop of potatoes in."

"Hilarious, Kieran." I headed for a table.

"I'm just funnin' with you. Sit here at the bar and tell me the craic. You look gorgeous tonight. Good on you."

I broke my rule and climbed up on the barstool.

"Can I have a glass of water, please?" I was parched. I had worked hard. I'd probably talked more in the last six hours than I had in a month. Most of the time, being on the estate was an exercise in Zen. In the city, I constantly interacted with people. There was hardly a moment without small talk. Here, I spent swathes of time gardening, cleaning the church and tending animals. And while it's true that the Irish are truly raconteurs, they aren't afraid of silence.

He set down a pint glass of water and I drained it in one go.

"Here," Kieran said, setting a glass of whiskey in front of me, "this one's with me. You're doin' my head in drinking nothing but water at my bar."

"Make that two, willya, Kieran?" Tom's voice boomed out from behind me. He still wore his head wrap and chef's whites. I checked my watch. Dinner service had ended.

"My pleasure. Good to see you in here, Chef. It's been a while."

"I'm not really a brown-liquor kind of girl," I whispered to Tom.

"Nonsense, what whiskey and butter won't cure, there's no cure for," Tom declared, raising his glass.

"Slàinte!" cried the people in the bar, toasting to the old adage.

"And don't bother telling me what kind of girl you are," Tom whispered, lips grazing my ear, "because I happen to know." Without taking his eyes off mine, he drained his glass. Game, I took a big slug of my own. It tasted like the air smelled on a cool, Irish night. "Why don't you finish your drink? I've Castle Stone business to discuss with you. Over in the tower. It's a private matter."

Kieran pretended to polish glasses, but I could see his ears perking up.

"There you are, Sheila," called Brigid, pushing through the door. "I've spent half the night looking for Mary, so I could drag her in for a pint. No sign of her, so you'll have to do. Come into the snug and have a drink with me." Tom turned around on his stool. "Erm, that is, unless you're still on duty. Alright, Chef?" Her wheels turned, trying to work the scene out.

"Maybe I'll catch you back here in a while, Bridge." Tom got up from his stool and headed for the door. There's a scheduling issue Chef needs to go over with me." I slid down and scooted out the door before anyone else had a chance to ask questions.

Out in the warm, June air, I burst out laughing. My heart thrilled, like I'd stolen something. "Isn't it pretty out tonight?"

"Aw, sure lookit. That's not the only pretty thing 'round here, so." Tom pulled me into the shadow of a huge oak tree and stifled my laughter with a deep kiss. "Mmm…you taste delicious."

"Thank you."

"Don't get too big for your britches, it's the whiskey."

I swatted him as punishment and he sprinted to get away from me. With all I had, I ran after him, and dove at his legs. We tumbled to the grass, and he rolled on top of me, pinning my hands to the ground.

"Stop," I begged, gasping for breath and giggling. "This isn't my dress!"

"Then we should get it off of you, right away," he said, tugging the skirt upward.

"Tom!" I shrieked, "No!"

Chuckling, he stood up, and held out a hand to help me to my feet. Walking along the path, Catherine appeared from the shadows.

"Chef? Alright, then? It's only I heard shouting." Her cold gaze passed over me.

"Right as rain, thanks for asking," Tom said without stopping. "Home safe, Catherine." I burst into a jog to keep up with him, leaving Catherine standing with her painted mouth hanging open.

"Tom," I whispered as soon as I figured we were out of earshot. "I think she was on to us."

"So be it," he said, as we approached the back door to the castle. He pulled a skeleton key from his trouser pocket that I thought must surely be a joke. "After all that business with Tabitha, I learned the key to happiness is to please myself."

He turned the ancient key in the lock and pushed open the heavy, wooden door. I didn't ask where we were going, but I hoped it was his bedroom. He led me down a dank corridor, its stone walls covered in a combination of giant oil portraits and faded tapestries, which I could only assume were older than anything I'd ever laid a finger on. We headed up a narrow staircase. At the top, Tom opened what appeared to be a closet door and shoved me inside. It was pitch black and hung full of dank and musty garments. My claustrophobia kicked in just as Tom flung open a door leading to an oddly shaped room, half-bathed in moonlight. He strode ahead of me and flicked on a lamp.

"The Triangle Room," he announced. "Otherwise known as

home."

The first thing I noticed were the shelves and shelves of books. I browsed the spines. There were biographies of Napoleon Bonaparte, Abraham Lincoln and Simone de Beauvoir. He had Dante's *Divine Comedy*. The volumes of poetry included works by Emily Dickinson, Walt Whitman, Charles Baudelaire. "You told me on the drive to Dublin that you don't read."

"I said I don't read fiction."

"Well, I see *Ulysses* right here, and *The Complete Works of Shakespeare*."

He grinned wickedly. "Maybe I stretched the truth. Only for effect, mind you."

"You're full of surprises, Chef O'Grady."

Someone had valiantly fitted the strange angles of the walls and ceilings with elaborately carved crown molding, and the fireplace boasted a magnificent marble mantle. Still, there was no denying that the effect of the narrowing of the room to a sharp point lent the effect of a fun house. Deep-burgundy linens that matched the quilted and carved headboard adorned the bed. You couldn't help but call the room opulent. "It's gorgeous."

"'Tis, but back in the day, they called it 'The Insult Room.' If you were invited here to a function, and these were your assigned sleeping quarters, you'd have done well to check your copy book for blots." Tom picked up the phone and called down for ice, a bottle of whiskey and 'some snacks.' I couldn't wait to see what would be sent up. After my long stint in the dorm with warm UHT boxes of milk and the odd packet of crackers, I had to admit I welcomed the service Tom commanded.

"Come here and kiss me." Obediently, I tilted my head up to meet Tom's lips. "I haven't tasted whiskey since, well, for a while."

"You mean since Tabitha?" I decided to call a spade a spade. I looked forward to when all secrets would be stripped away. I took his hand and led him to the bed.

"Yeah, that's what I mean. After I found out about the baby

and all, I was only too happy to come back here. People made me out to be a hero for helping Tony, but I wanted a change. As I said, drink became my companion for a time there." I knit my brows. "Don't worry, though. As I said, there's a world of difference between drinking to celebrate and drinking to forget. I didn't miss it when I was teetotal. Now, I view it like I would sweets. Makes life nicer, but I could do without it." We sat quietly, Tom twisting the rings on my right hand. A small emerald-cut diamond in a white-gold setting, flanked by a thin, plain band. My mom's wedding set.

"Her real name wasn't Tabitha. It was Susan. She changed it to sound more glamorous when she started getting breaks in show business. I only found out when we were at the bank to sign papers for the house."

I felt sick. "I need to tell you the truth, Tom." After we'd made love the first time, I vowed I'd put my skates on and finish the book fast. Then, I could drop the whole thing in his lap to accept or reject. Keeping secrets cost me too much. "My mother is from Rhinebeck, upstate. I'm from New York City."

He let go of my hand. "So then, all that talk with Burton wasn't a pack of lies?"

I shook my head.

"So you told him the truth. Why'd you lie to me?"

"I thought you wouldn't like me otherwise." I gulped air in through shallow breaths. If this went well, I'd do my best to tell the truth about everything. Just as soon as I could.

He cupped my face in his strong palm. "I like you plenty." He pressed his lips to mine and kissed me gently. "Now tell me the truth about something. Do you like me?"

I looked into his clear blue eyes. I trembled. "Truth?"

"Truth."

I considered letting my mouth form the words. *I love you*, I imagined saying. I couldn't speak. He took my face in both of his hands and looked at me hard. I flinched, fearing a lecture on how girls never leave well enough alone, or how having sex didn't make us a couple. I'd heard it all before, from a variety of men.

"I like you, too."

"That works out well, then," he whispered instead, grazing his stubbled cheek against mine. A feeling of well-being overcame me, and warmth pumped through my blood. Peaceful didn't describe my state, though. Yearning made me edgy. Every cell in my body was on high alert and each of my five senses functioned at full tilt. Despite the niggling fear at the top of my spine, I felt alive.

When room service knocked, I didn't want to part lips with Tom for fear of breaking the spell. He rose to open the door and I moved to hide in the closet.

"Leave it," Tom said. "I'm not bothered if people know."

I sat down on the edge of the bed and watched my boyfriend arrange our midnight feast. When the boy left, Tom handed me a tumbler of whiskey and ice. Everything felt warm; the smoky, woody liquor, the early summer air, Tom's breath and skin. I'd been cold for so long. He laid me back in his big soft bed and slowly and gently stripped me bare. I welcomed the weight of him. Later, as he moved inside me, he breathed, "I love you, I love you." It was so nice to be warm.

I woke up with a start, wondering where I was. 5:40, the clock read. Tom lay on his side, his bare back rising and falling with his sleeping breath. I wrapped the sheet around myself and eased out of bed to pour myself a glass of water. As I drank, I gazed out the window in the pointy corner of the room. It was dusky out, with only the slightest hint that the sun would be rising soon. A couple walked arm in arm along the main path, one of the pair leaning on a cane. Only when they stopped beneath one of the gaslights did I make out that it was Tony and Maeve.

Quietly, I pulled my journal from my bag. I sat at the room's antique desk and flicked on the little lamp. I held very still to see if Tom would continue sleeping. His breaths were deep and steady.

Dear Maggie,

I'm in love. And it's not just me, he likes me, too. At least he told me that. I wish I could call you right now. I can't even email you because I'm in his room. Tom's room. Isn't Tom the sexiest, most beautiful name you've ever heard in your life?

Mags, what if I scrapped this book? You could tell Brenda I'm not doing it, and I could just stay. Then I'd never have to tell Tom why I came here in the first place. I could just let him go on believing that I came here to learn food safety and animal husbandry. Would that work?

You've always given it to me straight, Mags, from telling me I was a crap actor when I was taking those improv classes to telling me to watch my back because Lizbeth didn't like me (you were right) to telling me that sitting around waiting for Hank's approval was keeping me infantilized (sorry we got in that big fight about that one. I'm so glad I didn't move out in the end). I wish you were here in person. You'd see it all clearly.

In my dreams, you'd say, "He's perfect, Shay. This is why you've never had a deep relationship. You had to wait for Tom." Then, you'd tell me, "Your mom would have approved."

I put down my pen. Tears swam in my eyes and I couldn't see to write. I pictured Hank walking me down the aisle, Tom waiting at the end, expectant and smiling. I scanned the room for Mom, but she wasn't there. Of course she wasn't there. But Maeve was. In my fantasy, she wore a periwinkle and lavender flower-print dress and a hat adorned with tasteful feathers. Tony stood at her side. She smiled at me, waving, encouraging me to move forward, to keep walking. I felt my lips curl into a smile, and I let out a laugh. Clamping my lips together, I checked to see if I had awakened Tom. He stirred, but settled down.

In my dreams, you'd say, "Shayla Sheridan, that is the hottest piece of tail I've ever seen you with, so don't let him get away." Seriously,

Mags, if you could see this man's body, you would get down on your knees and thank God for the miracle. You know those ridges of muscle some men get right around their hip bones when they're young, athletic, and fit? That!

OK, sorry to cut this short but the sun's coming up soon and I have a hot naked man here in bed. Sorry to be rude, but what's a best friend for if not to understand? I swear I'll try to call you soon. I've pretty much stopped trying to make my cell phone work, but now I might be able to borrow my boyfriend's! (Just to be clear: I have a boyfriend!)

More soon… Love Shay xx

I crawled back in to bed, turned Tom on his back and straddled him. For half a second I worried he'd wake up and tell me to find my socks and move on. Could someone so handsome, famous, talented, and self-assured really want someone like me? I had to wheedle to get a book deal, and it wasn't even solid. I'd gotten fired from my job, and they'd only ever hired me in the first place because of Hank's name. I looked down into Tom's beautiful face. My heart pounded. Deep down, I knew I wasn't lovable. On some level I thought it was my fault that my mother had died. If I were enough, maybe I could have convinced her to stay here on earth. My own father didn't cherish me. I needed to get out of here.

Without opening his eyes, Tom grabbed my wrist and pulled me down on top of him. "Where do you think you're off to? Lay down here, you. Now I have you, I'm not letting you go."

Chapter Twenty-Three

You've got to do your own growing, no matter how tall your father was.

The week had flown by since the first time I saw Tom's room. I buzzed from lack of sleep. He and I were both back to work, only mine had largely shifted from the kitchen to front of house in The Grange Hall. I didn't want to cash in on favors, but I asked Mary if she wouldn't mind moving me. She did it cheerfully. It appeared my playing cupid had paid off, so she didn't even bother asking me why. I was happy not to have to confess that the first day back in the kitchen after all the sex I'd been having with Tom, I'd cut myself, bled into a pot of potatoes and ruined a large batch of scones because I couldn't count cups of flour.

Guests commented to the maître d' about me. She's so sunny and cheerful, they said. We love her American accent. She solved every problem we had cheerfully and made us feel like a guest in her home.

People from HPC would not have recognized me. It made me uncomfortable to think of how sour I'd been working at that office. I was really happy. I wanted everyone else to be happy, too. For once, I didn't take it personally when this lady didn't want to sit in a draft, or that gentleman needed more ice in his drink. It didn't mean that those people felt they deserved more than everyone else. They just wanted what they wanted. Since I had what I wanted, it cost me nothing to help others get theirs.

Coming off the lunch shift, I made my way to the front desk. I really had to call Maggie.

"Sheila!" Tony called out. He sat reading a magazine, wearing his dressing gown, as ever. "Come over here and keep an old man company." Catherine kept a keen eye on us as she typed, phone pinned against her shoulder. Damn. I had hoped she wouldn't be on today.

"Why are you in the lobby all alone?" I asked.

"I got bored in my room. There are only so many hours one can nap, and there's nothing worth watching on telly."

"Where's Maeve?"

"She mentioned that Tom was calling in for a visit. I thought it might make things easier for her if I left them to it."

"Let me talk to him."

"Tom's stubborn as a mule. You're likely to get your head bitten off. Or worse yet, sacked."

"I don't think that will happen. Excuse me, Tony, I have to make a phone call."

"Carry on, my dear," he said, pulling himself to his feet and reaching for his cane. "I'm off to find a cup of tea and something sweet to have with it. I fancy a mince pie," he continued to talk as he walked away from me, "It's been donkey's years since I've had a ready supply of mince pies about. I own a bloody castle, one might think if the lord of the manor fancies a mince pie, he might be able to procure one, but if I can't go to Maeve's..." he trailed off.

"Catherine, I need to make a phone call."

She screwed her face into a look of extreme concentration. "Hmm, officially it's against policy to dial overseas unless the call is of a business nature. Unless your call is local?"

"No, I need to call the States. Come on, Catherine, everyone does it. I'll keep it short."

"I suppose if someone asked, we could claim it was an emergency. We could say you had to call your doctor to get some lotion for that extreme dryness on your face." She scanned my complexion and tut-tutted.

"Can I just go back into the office and dial?"

"Ooh, sorry. No can do. That's a privacy violation. You aren't authorized. Guests' confidential files aren't for the public eye." She pushed the desk phone toward me.

"Fine." I dialed Maggie at work. Creepy Matty picked up her phone, so I disguised my voice, throwing a little bit of an Irish accent onto it. Catherine perked up. I could tell she was listening for all she was worth.

"Maggie, there's some Ukrainian woman on the phone for you." Matty didn't bother pushing down the hold button.

"Hello, Maggie Doyle."

"Mags!" I cried, keeping one eye on Catherine. She was at the far end of the desk, organizing a drawer. "It's Sheila."

"Is it now, Sheila? What have you done with my best friend Shayla?"

"I swallowed her whole," I said, laughing. "I have so much to tell you. For one, I'm nearly done with…the thingy."

"Do you mean the book? Are you serious? Never mind the proposal, you just finished the actual book?"

"Almost. I've been into Ballykelty a bunch of times to meet with the artist. You should see the hand drawings. How could any editor not love them? I'm still doing conversions. When you do these measurements, you can't just go grams to cups, you know. They weigh most ingredients, but depending on what it is…say butter versus sugar, you have to reason it out. It's complicated. But that's not the hardest part. What's tripped me up was the tone. I needed to know who Tom O'Grady really is." I turned my back, and cupped my hand over the phone, "and Mags, now I know inside and out."

"You dirty bird! Anything for the story, is that what Hank

taught you? Oh, by the way, why haven't you called him? He's called my cell a bunch of times, and left a message here. I can't keep putting him off."

I got a sinking feeling. "I know. I will. I just don't know what to tell him, you know? I mean, what if I want to stay here?"

"What do you mean, stay there? Don't you need to come back here and meet with Brenda about the book? How else are you going to lock down Ray Diablo?"

"Mags, what if I didn't finish it? What if I dropped it?"

"The book?"

"Yeah." There was silence down the phone. "Mags?"

"Think about it, Shay. If you drop this book, you'll burn your last bridge. You'll kill your career."

"It's just, if I drop it now, I feel like I can untangle this mess more easily. I've had to tell so many lies. And it might make Tom mad, you know, when he finds out why I really came here."

Maggie sighed. "I don't know what to tell you. You're more worried about making some guy mad than you are about your writing career? Are you going to marry him and become a house-wife?" Maggie may have Eric and a plan for four kids, but that plan included a nanny. Maggie's ambition wouldn't be swept under the rug.

"Nobody's talking about getting married," I said. Catherine pulled a feather duster from the drawer and made her way toward my corner of the counter.

"Just be careful, Shay. You may think you're in love, but giving up your life in the city, your career, all the groundwork you've laid. What if he's not worth it?"

"He's worth it. Plus, I don't know, I just got tired of fighting for my little square of the sidewalk. I like going to work in the morning knowing that at bedtime the day's problems won't follow me to the next day. It's just easier here."

"That's because the post office doubles as the vacuum repair shop and they roll the sidewalks up at dusk. It's great to be there on a vacation, but think hard, Shay. If you lose all your contacts in New York, you may find yourself crawling back and starting from the ground up someday."

"I hear what you're saying," I told her. I knew she didn't understand. Hank wouldn't either. I'd have to make this decision on my own. "Tell Hank I'll call him, OK?"

"I will, and listen Shay, you can have it all, you know. The man, the career, the Manhattan apartment. You don't have to settle."

"I have to go, Mags. I love you."

"I love you more. Call me soon and let me know what your plan is."

"Bye."

I heard Catherine giggle and turned around to see her checking in none other than Chris Burton at the desk. I froze like a deer in headlights. He spotted me before I could skulk out the back way.

"As I live and breathe!"

"You know Sheila, Mr. Burton?" Catherine cooed.

"I'd say we 'know' each other, wouldn't you, Shayla? Sorry I never called. Things got mad at the office, I'm sure you understand."

Was this clown blowing me off? Indignity rose up in my chest. Last time I checked, I'd left him untouched and unwanted, half-naked on a hotel bed.

"I understand perfectly, Mr. Burton." *Keep your cool, Shayla. The only thing that matters is getting Tom the distribution contract.* "Chef O'Grady didn't tell me you were due in for a meeting." Catherine was watching us talk like she was a spectator at Wimbledon.

"I'm not here to meet with old Tom O'Grady. I've business to discuss with a chap from GlobeCo. I'm only here for one night. I'm afraid it'll have to be a quickie," he said, waggling his eyebrows.

"Do you mean Brian Lynch?" I asked.

Chris knit his brows. "You're not in bed with Lynch, are you? It's only that I'm viewing my business with him and my business with Castle Stone as two distinct entities."

"All's fair in love and war," I said, in what I hoped was an enigmatic way. After all, I was supposed to be the Chief Cultural Liaison and Marketing Director for North America. I felt like I should know something about what's going on. Meanwhile, it was in my best interest to distance myself from Catherine. Chris had already called me Shayla once.

"I'd ask you to dinner, but I'm having it with your man Brian Lynch. Maybe a nightcap after? If you're free?"

"I'll have to check my book and get back to you." At this point, I'd wriggled from behind the desk and was halfway across the lobby floor.

"How can I get in touch with you?" he asked.

"I'll find you," I said, slipping out the side exit.

I headed straight for my dorm room. I changed from my hostessing outfit into a t-shirt and yoga pants and sat down at my desk. I put my head down and dug into the book. I wasn't sure what I'd do with it once it was finished, but I had to do something to move myself forward.

I got to work incorporating all of the notes I'd hastily scribbled standing at Maeve's side the times I'd watched her cook. I forced myself to work through the math and investigate recipe after recipe for comparisons and hints regarding conversions. I wrote headnote after headnote explaining to an American audience what Demerara sugar and treacle and dulse are, and what one can use in their places if they cannot be found. If I could manage to get through the scientific parts, all the chemistry and facts, I'd get a reward. I could tweak all of the essays about the land, the ingredients, the traditions. I finally felt confident that I could write in the voice of someone who felt passion for Ireland and Ireland's food. I could write in Tom's voice.

Hours later, addlebrained and bleary-eyed, I abandoned my desk and went looking for Tom. I stayed off the paths. It was the dinner hour and smartly dressed guests were taking evening strolls, enjoying the balmy summer night before heading to the dining room. I peeked in the back door of the kitchen, cupping my eyes so I could see through the screen. There was Tom, hair pulled back off of his angular, stubbled face with a headwrap, lifting a giant roasting pan from one of the ovens. He'd be on through dinner and probably well into the night. My body ached to think we hadn't planned to spend the night together. I didn't really feel like hitting Uncle Jack's for a drink. I needed to be away from my work for a while.

I took off walking toward Maeve's. When I neared her cottage, I noticed that Nap wasn't outside. I opened the gate and approached the house. Maeve dozed on the sofa, an open book at her side, and Nap curled at her feet. She must have been lonely to bring the dog in. It was ridiculous that Tony wasn't there to keep her company. I headed back in the direction of the dorms.

"Hello there, Shayla," came a voice out of the darkness, stopping me in my tracks. Chris Burton sat on the bench near the main entrance to the door. "You said you'd find me." He stood up. "Here I am."

"Oh, hey, Chris. Is your dinner over already?"

"It is. I thought we could have our meeting now. Or over dessert." He put his arms around me and put his hand up my t-shirt.

"Hey," I pushed him away.

"Oh, come on, Shayla. It's nothing I haven't seen before."

"Actually, it is. You were drunk before, Chris. Nothing happened." I made a quick decision not to try to get in the dorm. If no one was home, it would be dangerous to be alone in there. I walked onto the path and began power-walking toward the castle. "Why don't we go get a drink?"

"I'd rather be alone, Shayla," he said, catching up to me. "I've quite a nice room. We can have a bottle sent to us. Pick up where we left off."

"Chris, if you make this awkward, you won't be able to carry on conducting business with Castle Stone."

"Fuck Castle Stone's business. It's small potatoes. I've bigger fish to fry. I think I've just pulled off quite a pretty little deal with GlobeCo. Castle Stone's business isn't a patch on it. I've half a mind to stop wasting my time with that smug Tom O'Grady." Chris tripped over his own foot and nearly went down. Drunk, obviously.

"Listen Chris, there's no reason to throw the baby out with the bath water. We both know it's a smart business model to have small deals alongside your big deals." I knew nothing of the sort, I just didn't want him to drop Tom and all the farmers who depended on this. "The food venture with Castle Stone is a sound one. And Tom O'Grady's not that bad. I can talk to him and remind him that you're in charge."

"That's right, Shayla, I'm the boss." He grabbed me and kissed me hard. I pulled away. "I think the two of us can work to salvage this deal." He pushed me up against the trunk of one of the huge trees just off the path. Panicked, I realized we were out of the light. He had his arms wrapped around me and held my wrists behind my back.

"Chris, let me go."

"Not unless you agree to come to my room." He kissed my neck. I tried to wriggle away and he bit down.

"Stop it! I swear, I'll scream."

He kicked my knees out from under me, and before I knew it, I was lying in the cool grass with him on top of me. "Feisty, aren't you?" I saw an older couple walking up the path, headed to the Mews Cottages. Chris saw me see them and put his hand over my mouth. "Don't cause trouble, Shayla. Just be quiet now." He was kneeling on top of me and it hurt. I watched the couple fade out of sight. I figured I could salvage this.

"OK, let's go to your room. That's a good idea." I tried to get up.

"Do you really mean that, Shayla, or are you playing games with me?"

I relaxed my body. If I could convince him I was being honest,

I'd have a chance to get up and get to where people were.

"Of course I mean it." I forced a light laugh. "You caught me. I was playing games. It's hotter that way, right?"

"You are a filthy thing, aren't you?" he gave me a rough, sloppy kiss. I went with it, doing my best to act like I was into it. I broke away as soon as I could without giving it away.

"Yes, now let's go to your room."

"We will, but now you've got me all wound up. How about a little relief here and now. He kneeled on my elbows and fumbled with his button and fly. A wave of fear rolled up in me. He was serious.

A saw a distant figure on the path. "Help!" I screamed. "Help me."

Chris tried to pull his trousers down with one hand, while covering my mouth with the other. I bit his hand.

"Ouch, he screamed loudly. "You bitch." The bite threw him off balance. His elbow came down on my chest and it hurt.

"Help me, you there! Help me!" I yelled. I tried to shove my thumbs in his eye sockets, like my Women's Self-Defense Class coach had demonstrated. He grabbed my wrists and dug into the flesh.

"I'm having a heart attack! Call 9-1-1!" Of course I wasn't having a heart attack, but my coach said to scream this phrase. People are more likely to get involved with a health emergency than an attack. But did they have 9-1-1 in Ireland? Chris tried to cover my mouth with one of his hands, while keeping both of my wrists in the vice-like grip of his other.

"I mean call 9-1-9 or whatever!" I shouted through his fingers. "Call an ambulance, I'm dying!" I tried to bite his palm, but couldn't sink my teeth in. Instead, I spat in it.

"That's disgusting," he hissed, pulling his hand away. "Here comes someone. Shut your gob or I'll shut it for you. The man on the path was jogging toward us. Chris wrestled his zipper back up. "You'll be sorry for this."

"All right, there? Can I help?" It was Brian Lynch. Chris scrambled to his feet. I tried to get up, but I had twisted my ankle in the fall. "What on earth is going on here?"

"Brian! Mate!" Chris cried, trying to appear normal. Brian held out his hand to me. I grabbed it and he pulled me to my feet. I could stand, if I didn't put much weight on my bad foot. "Just a bit of fun. You know, being naughty outdoors."

Brian looked at me, trying to get a handle on the situation. "Shayla, are you alright?"

I hesitated. I didn't want to blow the deal for Tom.

"She's alright. It was her idea, actually," Chris said, barking out a laugh. "She's just embarrassed. You know, that you caught her like this."

"No, in fact I'm not all right, Brian." I took in a sharp breath, and felt the bruised place where Chris had elbowed me. "He just attacked me."

Brian stepped forward and balled up his fists. "Step over onto the path, Shayla. Burton, you stay where you are."

"I'll stay where I am, but don't let her fool you. She's a tease. She started this, then wanted to save face when you came along and saw what kind of a girl she is."

"Shut your mouth, Burton. Shayla, do you want me to call the guard?"

"The police?" Chris asked incredulously. "And say what? That Shayla here is a nasty little tease?"

"Shut up, Burton, or I'll be calling an ambulance."

"It's OK now, Brian. Don't call anyone. He's not worth it."

"You wouldn't know, would you?" He shot me a look. "Fair enough, then. We all agree it's been a misunderstanding. Let's just go our separate ways." Brian put his arm around my shoulders and steered me back toward the castle. "I'll see you at breakfast then, Brian." He leaned in as he passed me and hissed, "Dyke."

"What did you say?" Brian asked.

"Nothing Bri, it's just between me and the girl."

"I'll have you know I think of this girl as one of my daughters. And furthermore, one of my favorite workers at this establishment is a lesbian, so I'll thank you not to speak so hatefully." I was stunned. I didn't know that Brian realized Mary liked girls. He seemed so conservative, but so much for judging a book by its cover. "You won't be seeing me at breakfast. In fact, pack your things and leave here tonight." He stopped on the path. "The deal's off. My partners will understand completely. They've daughters of their own."

"No, Brian! Let's discuss this, man to man…"

"If you haven't checked out in one hour, I will call the guard. My eyes are getting old and it's dark out. Who knows what facts I'll remember?"

"Fine! Who wants to do business with an aging Irish albatross, anyway?" Chris stormed off down the path, yelling over his shoulder. "You're washed up, old man. Call me when you've joined this century. Keep doing business with your rolodexes and your handshakes, and your verbal agreements. You've done me a favor." We watched the back of his head as he barreled away down the path.

Brian put both of his hands on my shoulders. "Tell me the truth, love. Are you alright? I'll call a doctor or the guards and it won't be a speck of bother."

"I'm fine, Brian, it's just that I cost Tom a deal. And, oh gosh, I've cost you a deal, too." I buried my face in my hands.

"You've done nothing of the sort. That bastard Burton, pardon my French, showed his true colors and we're well rid of him. Tom O'Grady seems a good man. I'm sure he'll agree that it's better this way. Now, where can I walk you?"

We headed back to the dorms and Brian didn't leave until I was safe behind my own door and he'd patrolled the hallways.

"If you feel the slightest bit of worry, call for help. No good man would ever blame you for a false alarm. The only call you'll ever regret is the one you don't make, I tell my girls."

"Thank you, Brian."

"Not at all, pet."

I sat down on the edge of the bed and closed my eyes. I remembered being about 16. Hank had hosted a small party for one of his book launches at our apartment. It was a Tuesday night; he never took my school schedule into consideration. An editor of his, a man I'd always liked, remarked on what a lovely young woman I had become, so like my mother. "I guess it won't be long before you're walking her down the aisle, eh, Hank."

"Nonsense," Hank had replied. "If she chooses to marry, she'll walk herself down the aisle. She's her own woman. She doesn't need me to give her away."

I imagined such a discussion would never take place in Brian Lynch's household.

My body urged me to go find Tom, but my brain told me to sit down and work on the book. I had to make something work. Now that I'd blown the food deal, I wanted to salvage something. If I did a good job, this book could help put Castle Stone on the map. If the brand became known, offers to create products could pour in. My gut clenched. I knew how tenuous launching the right book at the right time could be. Still, I had hope. DIY movements still roared on back in the States, and I felt they'd never died among the practical people of Ireland. Tom's sincerity around home gardening, respecting the earth, and working hard to sustain oneself had to shine through. If I could pull this off, he'd approve. He'd forgive me.

I dug in and wrote like my life depended on it.

Chapter Twenty-Four

It is not a secret if it is known by three people.

I awoke the next morning to Mary rapping on my door, and calling "Sheila, Sheila, open up."

I jumped out of bed and flung the door open. "Oh, Mary, am I on in the kitchen? I thought I was free today. Give me two seconds and I'll be dressed and ready to go."

"Not at all," she said. "I've been sent to tell you that Chef wants you to pack a bag and report to the employee car park." My mind whisked me to a variety of dark places. Tom had found out who I was and was sending me home. He had used me for sex and now wanted me out of his sight. Chris Burton had told him that I lied about my identity and had single-handedly blown the deal. Father Walsh found out I was a birth-control-using, pre-marital-sex-having agnostic and had called the Vatican for a decree to remove me.

"Why?" I asked with a dry mouth.

"I wasn't told. I just work here, you know," she said with a wink. She strode toward the exit door.

"Mary! You know everything. What's going on?" She continued walking without turning around and disappeared out the door.

Quickly, I brushed my teeth and ran a comb through my hair.

Making sure I had clean underwear, I stuffed random clothes and toiletries into my bag, trying to consider what I'd need on a plane if I were driven straight to the airport. I pulled out the red pashmina I'd stolen from Brenda's office all that time ago. Its color was so harsh compared with the various pastel and white things I'd bought or inherited as hand-me-downs. I didn't pack it. I couldn't see myself wearing it ever again. My guilt pinched. At some point I should give it back to Monica. What would they do with the stuff I didn't bring? Would Mary be dispatched to ship it?

I rushed to the car park, thinking, *Whatever this is, I might as well get it over with.* I scanned the lot, not knowing who or what to look for. Finally, Tom appeared dressed in dark-wash jeans, a fitted black v-neck t-shirt, and aviator sunglasses, his wavy hair going wild in the warm morning breeze. It made me nervous that he wasn't smiling.

"Go ahead and get in the car." He stashed my luggage in the back and climbed in the driver's side.

"Right then, a little birdie told me you have a birthday coming up."

"June 22nd," I answered. Same as my mom's. She'd always said I was the best birthday present she'd ever gotten. In a few short years I'd be the age she was when she died. Maybe that's why I'd pushed my birthday to the recesses of my mind. I didn't feel like an adult. I hadn't yet pulled anything off to prove myself. I wracked my brain to suss out today's date. I didn't even know what day of the week it was. I marked time here assignment by assignment.

"I'm not fired?"

"Fired? You're not paid, how can I sack you?" He smiled. "Today is Thursday, your birthday is Saturday. I'm taking you on a mini-break."

"What's that?"

"A holiday, but a short one."

"A long weekend?"

"A dirty weekend, more like," he said, leaning over to kiss me, planting his palm at the base of my belly.

"What about work?"

"Fasten your belt," he said. I did and he eased the car onto the main road. "I had Mary cover your shifts, and I simply told the kitchen they'd have to handle it without me. Do you know how long it's been since I've taken off two days together? I don't either. I honestly cannot remember."

"What did you tell your mother?" I wasn't sure who knew what or who was allowed to.

"You mean what did I tell my mother at 6:30 this morning when I was summoned to hers for breakfast with Father Walsh? Old people and priests don't need a lot of sleep, do they? Here's what my mother and Father Walsh told me, so. They told me I should stand aside and let two Catholic people enjoy each other's wholesome company. Father Walsh said something about matrimony and welcoming any children God intended, something about Sarah and Abraham and you never know what can happen. Mam got embarrassed and glossed over that portion of the conversation He banged on about the rights of two Catholic people being allowed to spend time together without the community thinking impure thoughts and the balm of friendship. I couldn't help thinking that was about himself and Danny. They do enjoy gardening together, and their opera records. In the end, Mam told me that you're a sensible girl, and that I should take a leaf from your book."

"Well, you should." I looked around the village. Ballykelty was drenched in sunshine. The cobbled street was tidy and clean. Residents and shopkeepers alike had filled window boxes and wooden barrels with brightly colored flowers, and villagers in their shirtsleeves bustled busily, tending to their morning chores.

"Should I? Tell me what you know, Sheila. We've a long drive ahead of us. I'll listen."

"Here's something I know: I don't like surprises."

"Too bad. I'm full of 'em. You'll have to adjust. Next."

"I know sitting on bar stools isn't any fun."

"So you'll sit on my lap. No complaints from me about that. Anything else?"

"I know how to avoid dangling participles."

"I'll have to trust you on that one."

"I know where to get cheap ethnic food in New York City."

"I know how to cook anything you could ever want to eat, and I won't charge you for it."

"That sounds even better." I took his hand. He looked so sexy and in control at the wheel. Watching his thighs rise and flex as he worked the pedals of the car was turning me on. So was the brightness of the sun and the vivid jewel-green of the fields we passed. It was probably my imagination, but I swore I could feel the warmth of my blood in my veins. I felt alive.

"Here's something, I know your mother and Tony might like each other."

"Might they? Are you an expert on such matters? Did you know I liked you, from the first moment I laid eyes on you?"

"No." I wanted to tell him that I'd liked him from the moment I laid eyes on him, from the first moment I'd heard his voice. But then, I'd have to tell the whole truth. "I didn't know that."

"I did." He glanced sideways and caught my eye. "Do you know how much I like you now?"

I hesitated. "I want to know it."

"But you don't?"

It was complicated. How could I explain how lonely I'd been, for so long? After Mom died, I saw my grandparents less and less. Hank was always busy, always traveling. Before long, they were gone. No one stuck around to love me. If I told him that, he might look for reasons why.

"I know I'm happy right now. Can I have one of those bottles of water?" I wanted to talk about something else.

"Help yourself."

"By the way, where are we going?"

"It's a surprise."

I lay back against the seat and closed my eyes. I wasn't in control. I opened one eye and took a look at capable, strong, beautiful Tom. I stopped trying to be.

When we pulled in to the Cobbler's Hill Country House Hotel, I startled Tom by screaming, "Oh, look. Deer!" A whole family stood at the edge of the woods, nibbling on fresh, green shoots.

"Here we are, in the 'land of heart's desire,' according to one W.B. Yeats, who lived not far from here."

The Georgian main house featured antique furniture with modern comforts, and the lady who checked us in lived locally. She didn't draw a single breath during her speech outlining the local history. She offered us tea and scones in the drawing room, but Tom was clever enough to ask if we could have it sent up as we needed to freshen up from the trip.

We were settled into the School Room, replete with flocked wallpaper, Chinese rugs and a spectacular view of the river running through the property. Our bathroom boasted a roll-top tub with brass fixtures.

"Ooh, that's the first thing I want to do," I told Tom.

"I'll do you one better. Slip your shoes back on and follow me."

After a short drive, we wound up near the sea's edge. Tom pulled into the car park of an Edwardian bath house promising "Organic health and beauty, from the sea to you."

Tom confirmed our reservation at the desk. We were led to a sort of a wet room featuring a bathtub, something that looked like a cedar coffin with a hole for your head, and a shower. We spent the next hour lolling naked in the hot, salty water tinted the color of tea from the iodine given off by long ropes of fresh, slimy seaweed, and enclosing ourselves in the steam cabinet to open our pores and perspire out toxins. In between, Tom pushed me under the freezing cold sea-water shower, where I shrieked and danced and protested as he held me tightly around the waist to keep me in my place.

Neither of us had a condom. I wanted Tom inside me so badly. The sensations of oil and fragrance and temperature along with the slickness of our naked bodies tortured me. I knew both Tom and I were safe; we'd done the practical unromantic work of going over our sexual histories. Reckless with passion, I begged him. In that moment, I was willing to take chances. If my future were decided for me, I could stop worrying about what to do next. Tom held strong and we made do with pleasing one another in more creative ways. I felt like a teenager and Tom proved to be as nimble and renewable as one.

I could barely dress when it was over. My muscles wobbled as I staggered to the lobby and drank what must have been a gallon of cool water.

"What next?" I asked Tom. He was starting out across the car park.

"Quick, let's get to the car," he said, gathering our things, and pulling me by the elbow.

"What's the matter?"

He unlocked the passenger side and pushed me in. He grabbed his sunglasses from the visor, clapped them on, stepped on the gas. "Damn," he swore. "I thought all this was over."

"What?"

"Photographers. My face on the cover of cheap, glossy magazines."

Tom pulled in to the hotel, and barely said a word as we walked back to the room. His mood scared me. I hovered around the coffee and tea service, not sure what to do next.

"I was thinking we'd go for a drink at a pub I like down by the sea, but now I don't really feel like it. I thought coming all the way up to Sligo would take care of it. I'm sorry, Sheila."

"Sorry for what?"

He sighed. "They've left me alone for some time now. There wasn't much to write about with me sticking close by the estate. I hadn't anything to do with women since you know, Tabitha. There was the odd photo of me standing next to some girl in Ballykelty saying we were to be married or I'd broken her heart, or what have you. I didn't mean for you to have to cope with this."

"Is it that big a deal? So what, they print an unflattering picture of me, saying Tom O'Grady's standards have fallen?" I laughed.

He shot me a stern look. "Don't talk like that. It isn't true," he kicked off his loafers and sat on the edge of the huge, king-sized bed. "What I'm sorry about is that those sleazy reporters will start digging into your past and printing God knows what. Could be that you failed your college exams or that you were arrested for shoplifting. 'Course it doesn't even have to be true." He slapped his hands on his knees. "If I find out someone at the Castle sold this story, mark my words, heads will roll." His expression was hard.

"Let's just have a drink here." I really needed one now. "Wine OK?" I asked, eyebrows raised. He nodded. I called room service and had them send a bottle of Sauvignon Blanc and some sand- wiches. I figured gentle was the name of the game. Whiskey on an empty stomach seemed the wrong choice for Tom at the moment.

I excused myself to the bathroom and took a long look in the mirror. The end of the road was nearing fast. How soon would it be before someone outed me as Shayla de Winter and Tom put two and two together? I pushed the thought of it out of my mind and changed into one of the robes that were hanging on the back of the door. We had now. We had this weekend. I didn't want to think ahead to anything else. For once, things just had to go right for me.

I opened the door and made a beeline for Tom, who was lying on the bed, propped on his elbow, drinking a glass of wine. I took it from his hand and set it on the bedside locker.

"I'm sorry the trip went arseways on us. I wish my ridiculous notoriety, if you can call it that, hadn't spoiled the fun for you."

"Let's just stay in all weekend, can we Tom? Can we pretend there's nothing outside these four walls, and just be with each other?"

"I can think of nothing I want more, Sheila. Beautiful Sheila."

I covered his mouth in kisses to stop him from calling me by the wrong name.

Chapter Twenty-Five

Speak of the devil, and he will appear.

The day we got back, Tom dug straight into work. Separating from him had been difficult after our intense long weekend. He'd barely been off the property since he'd come back to help Tony. People weren't used to managing without him. I had the morning off. On my way to stash my luggage back in my dorm room, I ran into Brigid going in the main entrance.

"Jaysus, it's quare warm today." She took the bandana she had tied around her neck and used it to tie up her hair. "Anyone would think this is the Bahamas and not Ireland. A word to the wise: You'll want to watch your back around Catherine."

"Why?" I motioned for her to follow me.

"She's found out about you and Chef and she doesn't like it."

My heart sunk. "How did you know?"

"Come on, Sheila. I worked right alongside the two of yous. I'm surprised you didn't shag right there in the scone dough. I told Mary from the start that what Ashleigh said about you couldn't be true. And it's fairly hard to miss the fact that you disappeared together for days."

"Does everyone know?" I unlocked my door and waved Brigid inside.

"Not at the moment, but I'd say they might soon. Go talk to Mary. She's got her finger on the pulse. If there's something to be sorted out, she'll sort it." Brigid smiled a wicked smile. "She's just back herself. She was away looking after her gran, and I went to a quilting convention in Cork at the weekend. Now we're both back, I'm going to drag her over to Jack's for a round or ten. Things were too quiet here without her."

"Are you headed to Jack's to put your moves on Kieran?"

She laughed. "Close, but no banana, as they say. But maybe tonight will be my lucky one, anyway. Wait until you hear it, Mary's looking into whether she can take me on as a full-time paid worker." She blushed. "Don't spread that around, though. Wouldn't want Mary to get in trouble for doing me special favors.

"Aw, that's brilliant, Bridge." I took off my jacket and hung it on a peg. "I'm glad you're going to get what you want."

"Mary's a good friend." She smiled. "Mary's grand, she is. Now get yourself over there and find out what's what."

The second I poked my head through the door, Mary was up on her feet to shut the door behind me. She told me to sit down, then handed me an envelope.

"Remember when that Chris Burton left in the night?" she asked. I nodded. "He left this note for Chef. Thanks be to God, it got stuck in one of the pigeonholes up by the front desk. Far be it from me to snoop into other people's private correspondence, but in my defense, the envelope wasn't sealed. You and Chef were gone by the time I knew what I had in my hands. Go ahead, take a look at it."

I slid the paper out of the envelope. It was a letter telling Tom that their business relationship was over, no surprise there, and that it was my fault for being unprofessional. I scanned down the page. He went on to say that Tom should know that I'm not who I say I am and that he advises Tom to contact the authorities as I may be traveling under false papers.

"Right," Mary said. "We could have handled this had Catherine not stuck her pointy little, turned-up nose into it. She'll never admit to reading Chef's post, but I know she did. I saw her take it out of her pocket and stuff it back into the pigeonhole, and ever since, she's looked like the cat who ate the canary. If she's asked me once, she's asked me a dozen times when Chef would be back on the grounds."

"Mary, there was a photographer following us around up in Sligo. You don't think Catherine...?"

"Well, if she did and we can prove it, she'll be sacked quicker than you can say Jack Robinson. Chef hates the paparazzi worse than poison. For now, let's deal with the facts. Chef's in the kitchen for a twelve-hour shift today, and she's on the desk from now till midnight, so you're likely fine until tomorrow. You're due at the hostess stand for dinner service tonight. Unfortunately, I won't be here. My home parish priest is retiring and I'm expected at his leaving do at 6 o'clock. How do you want to play this?"

There was no choice. "I'll have to tell him the truth." I'd gather up what I had of the book tonight and get it ready to show it to Tom. "Mary, can you fix the schedule so Tom's free in the morning?"

"Ah, sure, I'll do that." I stood up and headed to the door. "Don't look so worried, pet. It'll all work out, so. He loves you."

"He never said that."

"'When the apple is ripe, it will fall,' my gran always said. Good luck to you."

Standing at the hostess' stand that evening, I felt a million times better. I'd gone straight back to my room and organized the book. I arranged the drawings, inserted dummies and descriptions of how I envisioned each photograph, and reread and tweaked my essays. I threw out any recipes that I deemed leprechaun twee or modern foodie. I even wrote out an explanation of why I lied, and how being in Ireland and watching Tom had changed my thinking. This, I stuck in my journal. I'd only hand that over to

Tom if my words failed me.

The cheer of the expectant diners took my mind off my troubles. Before I knew it, I'd lost myself in the familiar rhythm of seating guests and chatting with my colleagues. Through the glass picture window, I saw Nap running back and forth, a black and white streak. Sure enough, not far behind Lord Wexford followed. He no longer had his cane. They headed in the direction of Maeve's cottage. I crossed my fingers and said a silent prayer that all was well in their corner of the world.

I seated a group of ladies from Philadelphia who were travelling around Ireland on an ancestry tour, each tracing her roots. Also in that night was a couple from Scotland whose brogue was so thick I had to ask three times what their name was. My favorite clients of the evening were a young couple from Screen who'd gotten married two days before. They had spent their honeymoon night in the hotel in Enniscorthy, where their wedding took place, but as a special treat, their myriad brothers and sisters had pitched in and given them two nights at Castle Stone. The young pair seemed nervous, as though they had never dined in so lavish a restaurant. I bent over backwards to make them feel at home and asked the waiter to comp them desserts, on me.

Eventually, there was a lull. Mairead and I stood gossiping and laughing when Catherine approached.

"What brings you into the restaurant tonight, Catherine?" Mairead asked, wary. Catherine wasn't what was known as a girls' girl. Everyone knew she was a stickler for rules, and fun-loving Mairead knew to watch her back.

"I wanted to let Shayla know that she has a visitor at the desk in the lobby. Mairead, can you spare Shayla for a few moments?"

"I can spare her, but would'ja stop saying her name that way? Geez," Mairead replied. I felt sick. I wanted to think that it was the young couple I'd bought desserts for, but I had a dark feeling it could be Chris Burton. Or worse. What if it were people from immigration. Was it possible I'd broken some Irish law by interning under the wrong name?

A man with a full head of gray hair stood at the reception desk, his back turned to me. Catherine called out, "Mr. de Winter? Here's your daughter, Shayla," with a glint in her eye and a smile on her face.

"Hank? What on earth are you doing here?

"Shayla, I could ask you the same thing. I've tried to reach you on and off for months. Do you know I had to hear you were fired from Haversmith, Peebles, and Chin from Brenda Sackler? I'd been leaving you messages on your old work number, and no one bothered to tell me you didn't work there anymore."

Catherine didn't even bother to hide the fact that she was taking in every word.

"So you came to track me down?"

"Hell no. I was the keynote speaker at a writer's conference in Dublin last night. The only way I had to get hold of you was by leaving a message at the desk for you here. From what I understand, you've been MIA for the last four or five days. Do you know the trouble I went to getting myself out to these godforsaken sticks? I had to wrestle out of your friend Maggie where you are. She didn't tell me how off the grid this place was. Didn't anyone tell you I was coming tonight?"

"No," I said, glaring at Catherine, "they didn't. Come on, let's step outside so we can talk."

I led him out the front and around the side of the main building. We stood on one of the smaller paths, under a gas light.

"All right, Shayla, just tell me what you need and I'll fix it. One phone call to HPC and you'll have your job back. Or do you want me to talk to Brenda? After the weekend we had on Martha's Vineyard, I'm sure she'll give me whatever I ask for. Wouldn't be the first time, heh heh."

"I don't need anything. I came here to get a book written, and I'm just about done. Once I turn it in, Brenda won't have any reason to doubt me."

"You mean that cookbook? Shayla, when are you finally going to let me walk you in to George at Atlas Talent? I've told you a hundred times, as a favor to me he'll tailor-make a project for you. A real book. Not a Dumbass Guide and not a cookbook."

"My cookbook is a real book."

"To housewives and suburban soccer moms. Maybe that's what you're cut out for. Who am I to say?" He looked around. "I'm flying out tomorrow night. Let me get you a ticket and bail you out of this mess. Don't you miss New York?"

"A real bagel and some lox would taste good," I admitted. There was no point in explaining to Hank that Ballykelty offered its own delights. To him, if it existed off the island of Manhattan, it wasn't worth hearing about.

"At any rate, it must have been easy to get the material you needed out of these rubes. Do you have what you need to write this pamphlet?"

"It pretty much was." I wanted Hank to see that I'd done a good job, that I was going to wind up on my feet.

"Did you use all the tricks I taught you? Did you make them trust you?"

"Aye, she did," Tom said, stepping out of the darkness by the castle wall. "Catherine told me you wanted to see me, Shayla?" His face betrayed no emotion. "And you must be Hank de Winter? You might be shocked to hear that I've read your books. You see, I'm naught more than a simple country rube."

"Tom, I was going to explain in the morning."

"You're no better than those filthy paparazzi who follow me around snapping pics and selling my story." His mouth twisted into a mean line. "What's your angle, Shayla? An intimate tell-all? Who bought it? Hello? The Sun?"

"Hank, there's a bar attached to the restaurant. Go have a drink, and I'll meet you there later."

"Don't have to ask me twice," he said, heading toward the castle's main entrance.

"Tom you have to listen."

"I don't have to do anything." He pulled off his headwrap and unbuttoned his chef's coat at the throat, and strode off in the direction of the back castle entrance to his room. I ran after him, barely able to keep up. I grabbed at the back of his coat. He shrugged me off angrily and stopped in his tracks.

"Tom, I didn't sell an article. I'm writing your cookbook. Brenda Sackler's my agent."

He stared at me coldly. "You're not writing my cookbook. I'll see to that." A look of understanding came over his face. "Oh, I see it now. God, how could I have been so blind? You're the girl who rang me. The girl I almost said yes to." He shook his head like he was trying to shake the memory out of it. "You've been lying to me for that long?" His eyes beamed disgust. "Who are you?"

"I'm me, Tom!" I said in a ragged voice.

"Who? Sheila?" he said, in a voice dripping with scorn. I grabbed for his hand, desperate to hold it, but he just pulled away.

"I know you'll love this book." I pleaded. "It's you, inside-out and backwards. I wrote it for *you*." Panic rose in my throat. I could see I wasn't reaching him. "Tom? It's the kind of book I know you've always wanted."

His eyes went cold. "You don't know what I want. You don't know me at all. You and Brenda Sackler and the whole lot of you can go stuff yourselves."

"Can I just show you the book?" I pleaded. "I did it for you!"

"Shut up!" he roared. "You did it for yourself, and I was a fool to trust you. Lesson learned. Again."

He looked up at the sky, mouth a thin line, and scrunched his eyes shut. "Jesus Christ," he swore under his breath. He opened his eyes again and looked straight at me. "Leave this property."

He turned away from me and started walking. "I never want to see you again. End of." He kept on walking into the darkness until he reached his entrance. I watched the back of his dark-blonde head disappear. Without warning, my mouth filled with vomit.

I ran to the bushes at the castle wall and heaved until there was nothing left inside me.

Chapter Twenty-Six

A bird in the hand is worth two in the bush.

The elevator doors opened onto the floor for Global-Lion literary, and I made my way to reception. "Shayla Sheridan here to see Brenda Sackler. I don't have an appointment."

"Please take a seat."

I was only too happy to. After three days back, I still felt foggy and exhausted from jet lag. Or maybe it was a hangover from my break-up with Tom. I pushed the thought aside. This was going to be hard enough to get through, without my crying on top of it. As usual, it was freezing in the building. I wished I had a giant extra-hot misto from the Starbucks in the lobby, but girls who'd just humiliated themselves by borrowing five grand off their dads didn't deserve to blow that much on a coffee. At least I had a job, sort of. A pair of snowbirds – old people who summered in the Northeast but spent the cold winters in Florida – in Hank's building needed someone to housesit. It worked out nicely for me. Not only did I now not have to live with Maggie and Eric, or God forbid Hank, I'd get a small stipend for bringing in the mail and doing light cleaning.

I pulled my old Adirondack jacket out of my plastic carrier bag and slipped it on. I knew it looked sad and unfashionable, but couldn't be bothered to care. Underneath it was Monica's pashmina, poised to be reunited with its coat rack.

"Brenda said she can fit you in. You can go back."

I pushed through the glass doors and walked the familiar expanse of industrial carpet to Brenda's desk. She was on the phone and she held up a finger to indicate that I shouldn't speak. I sat in Monica's chair.

"No," Brenda said into the phone. "No, absolutely not." I could tell that Brenda was paying no attention to me whatsoever, so I started rifling through my bag, trying to get to her pashmina. Trying not to make noise, I pulled out a brown-sack lunch. I couldn't afford to get caught on the streets of New York hungry. I set that on the corner of Monica's desk, along with two library books, a bottle of water, and my journal. My formerly dazzling journal had endured a rough journey. Covered in dirt, coffee spills, and tiny rips it was now conjoined with a second kitten-printed volume I'd been forced to pick up in the newsagent's in Ballykelty. Eyeballing Brenda, I visualized pulling out the pashmina and slapping it up on the coat rack. The time wasn't right. I pulled it back under the chair with the heel of my shoe.

"I can't go any lower than that. At this point, you are insulting me and my client. No. I said no."

I had to pee. I tried to catch Brenda's attention, just to mime that I was going. She refused to look at me. She must have thought I was going to complain about waiting. I didn't mind a bit. I was in no hurry to tell her I'd failed on the book deal.

It took forever to get the key from reception, walk down the endless hall to the ladies' and then to wait because there was a huge gaggle of interns gathered around one of their sobbing own. The poor girl had forgotten to messenger a contract. Whether she'd be fired remained unclear. I did not miss days like that at HPC. I managed to press myself into an empty stall, do my thing, and wash up without getting involved.

A few minutes later I slipped myself back into the chair next to Brenda's desk. She didn't look at me. For once, she didn't have the phone glued to her ear. She had my journal in her hand.

"Oh, hey, Brenda. Give me those." I swiped for the journals. She dodged me.

"The Irish cookbook's been pushed back, by the way. Pub date was meant to be June, a year from now. Now it's St. Patrick's Day, the following calendar year." Brenda barked out a laugh. "They think it's their idea. Want to know how I got so rich? I'm a genius, that's how."

"Brenda, I came here to tell you that Tom O'Grady will never sign off. There's not going to be a book." I reached out to take my journal from her hand, and once again she pulled it out of my reach. "I failed."

"You don't know what you're talking about," she said, flipping pages. She pulled out my handwritten letter explaining to Tom. "I've been down this road before."

"You told me before I left not to count on this book deal going through!"

"Made you hungry, didn't it?"

"I'm telling you that Tom O'Grady will never let this book happen."

"Did you write it?"

"Mostly."

"Send me what you've got and forget about it. Meanwhile, you want a book deal? I want this book."

"That's not a book, it's my journal." I tried to snatch it, and Brenda literally stood up to avoid me.

"I still haven't figured out where you were going with *How to Be an Adult in the City* nonsense you trotted in here last winter, but this is fresh. You are the opposite of cool. You're the anti-Carrie Bradshaw."

"Thanks a lot." I pulled my Adirondack jacket a little more tightly around myself.

"Could you whip this into a book? Fast?"

"I guess I could, but I don't want to."

"Sure you do. I'm assuming you took lots of pictures. You with goats, people on picnics, etcetera. It could be something like, *The City Girl and the Irish Chef,* but better? Do it anonymously if you have to. Call him the Farmer and call yourself the Student, or whatever. I happen to know Vera over at Piccadilly Publications is dying for non-fiction that reads like a novel. I also happen to know Pam Dowling had a young woman's memoir fall through, and now she has a hole in her schedule. Hold on to your hat, Shayla. If we sell this as digital-first, this could all happen faster than you can imagine."

"I never said I'd do it."

"You should. This is good writing, kid."

"Really?" I didn't think there was much left in me that was good.

"Really. Reads like a dream."

I let that sit there for a second. Brenda saw a chance for the kill and swooped in. "Are you a real writer, or not?"

When I didn't answer, she pushed on. "I think I can sell the hell out of this. Now, unless you want to write *The Dumbass Guide to Shingling Your Roof,* I suggest go home and get to work on this."

The conversation was over. I stood to leave and stepped on my plastic bag. I picked it up, pulled out the pashmina, and handed it to Brenda. "Here's Monica's shawl."

"Why do you have it?"

"I stole it."

"Huh. That's rich. I can't figure you out, Shayla. What kind of a girl are you?" she asked.

"That is a good question."

Chapter Twenty-Seven

It's better to be sorry and stay, than to be sorry and go away.

I awoke that night at 2 a.m. I hadn't slept more than four consecutive hours since the plane landed in Newark and Hank's car had chauffeured us into the city. I was starting to think something was wrong with me. Matty must have said a dozen times that he thought I should be on Ativan or Klonopin. Maybe he was right. Even when I managed to fall into a blank, black sleep, I awoke with my pulse racing and my heart skipping beats. Tom O'Grady had cast me out. I'd never see him again. It was the same feeling as when mom had died.

Maggie had left me about five messages. I kept meaning to call her back, I never found the time. I should have called her by now. Between writing my proposal and changing my old blog over to the new one, I barely raised my eyes from the computer. Also, I found it hard to talk to her right now. I found it hard to talk to anyone in the city right now. No one understood that the rattle of the subway added to my anxiety about my failure. I couldn't explain that the huge crowds of people overwhelmed me because I inadvertently scanned all the faces for Tom's. I wanted to talk about the weather. I wanted to hear what people were cooking for dinner. No one I knew in the city cooked.

My very rough draft of Tom's book was off my desk. Out of sight, out of mind. I'd sent it to Brenda almost the minute I had walked into Fred and Irma's apartment after the meeting. Handing it over felt like ridding myself of a problem. It was in Brenda's hands now; I didn't have to feel bad about it or dwell on it. If I could forget about it, maybe I could forget that last look on Tom's face when he said he never wanted to see me again.

Working on my memoir — if that's what we were calling it — on the other hand, soothed me. I could tell the truth. No one had to know who I was. I still wouldn't have my name on the cover of a book, but I could tell my story. In my story I was the girl Tom O'Grady had chosen. In my story I was Sheila from Castle Stone. I had become a ghost writer for my real self.

If I didn't need groceries, I would never have gotten out of my chair. My mind and spirit were still in Ireland, even if my body sat in the sprawling kitchen of a pre-war apartment on the Upper West Side.

The only time I could breathe properly was when I flipped through all the photos I'd taken in Ireland. Pictures of Tony in his dressing gown, posing like he was sitting for a portrait. The girls at the hostess stand, all dolled up for the night. The first blossoms on the trees, the animals and their sweet faces.

I had photos of most of the dishes for which I'd gathered recipes. I'd taken pictures for the proposal, and so I could eventually show them to the photographer as mock-ups. They weren't good enough for a hard-cover cookbook, but they were certainly good enough for a blog. I lost myself in posting images of mince pies, and *Barm Brack* and spiced beef, and writing rhapsodic love letters to their flavors and textures.

The corner by the kitchen table became my nerve center. I taped up the sketch of my hair after it had been cut and colored in Ballykelty. I taped up brochures I'd picked up at the tourist's office with maps of the counties printed in shades of green ink. I taped up pressed flowers I'd taken from weddings at the church, and menus from the restaurants. I sat there drinking cups of tea, content to be surrounded by my souvenirs.

I took license with the blog. Brenda planted a seed by saying my words read like fiction. In a way, this story was my fairytale. It was my truth, and if I didn't stick cleanly to the facts, well, hey. Wasn't that the way of the Irish storyteller?

I didn't know how I would end it, but then again, I'd never been in control. The whole thing had started against my will. As reporter, scribe, and poet, I strove to simply put words on pages without editing myself.

In Love with an Irish Farmer
American City Girl meets Irish Country Man

My home page featured a photo of me, dressed in the wellies and coveralls Maeve had given me, obscuring my face by holding up one of the hens. My introduction reads:

Hi, I'm Sheila. That's me and a Bluebell hen on a certain farm in Ireland. I hope you enjoy my diary. It's essentially bits and bobs about replacing my former identity as a downtrodden, harassed, New York City office worker with a new one: A pseudo-Irish country girl who gardens, tends animals, cooks, and actually draws deep breaths. Being in love makes everything better.

As I lined up post after post, to be launched once daily, I always included images. I'd taken so many photos of things like the giant locks and skeleton keys from the castle, and the sweet faces of the horses and donkeys, and the church doorway. I had stacks of hand-drawn pictures of the Irish coastline, the village of Ballykelty, stone fences, and wooden wagons courtesy of my artist friend. If there was to be no book, why not use them for my blog?

For over three weeks, I poured my heart into blog posts and whipping my journal into readable shape. I saw no one, other than the doormen and the counter people at Trader Joe's, where I got my groceries, and at the pet store. I avoided Hank, even though he was in the same building. He asked me down for a drink a few times, but I declined. I wanted to be alone with Castle Stone.

To be fair, I wasn't entirely alone. My blog began to pick up traction and followers started interacting. It started simple, with reactions like, "Gorgeous photo of homemade Irish cheeses," and my saying a simple thank you. I never told my loyal readers that I was back in New York. I'd have to eventually, I knew. I liked the idea of still being in Ireland.

Lots of Irish-identified Americans and ex-pats followed and posted their two cents about the way things were done on their grandparents' farms. My biggest group of followers became single girls, though. "Why don't you marry him?" they asked me. "Because he didn't ask," I'd tell them. This spurred essay after essay about what real love is and how not to lose it.

Readers asked me to give tips on how not to screw up a good thing once they'd found it. Girls began posting pictures of their men who had gotten away. I added a separate section for that: Lost Loves. I encouraged girls to tell the stories in 300 words or less. They asked me to rate my daily pain on a scale of 1 to 10. I added a bar graph. One follower called me "her favorite loser," and the moniker stuck. This grew into an agony aunt Q&A page entitled "Dear Loser." Other bloggers began blogging about me and linking to my blog.

All the while, I'd carefully gone over my journal, line by line and turned it into a piece of epistolary literary non-fiction, and written a forty-page proposal to pitch it. I finally handed the proposal over to Brenda, who'd called me twice daily since our meeting to tell me to hurry up. I relaxed into the blissful feeling that it was out of my hands. But with that done, I couldn't ignore the question: what next? I had to admit, I'd been using the blog to distract myself from the fact that the five grand Hank had lent me wouldn't last forever. Sick to my toes, at Maggie's urging, I updated my office resume. Eventually, I'd send it out to the usual suspects in publishing. Eventually.

"You have to get back on the horse sometime," she told me. I didn't know what I would hate worse: getting job interviews or not getting them.

I was already in my pajamas when I heard a knock on the door. I looked at the clock. It was nearly 10 p.m. It was strange to have someone knock directly on my door. People in New York called to tell you they were coming. They didn't drop by. I missed that about Castle Stone. There, if you wanted to talk to someone, you walked around the grounds until you found them. In this building, anyone from outside had to buzz for permission to come up. Figuring it must be the super about the leaky sink, I twisted the knob.

"Outta the way," Maggie said, pushing through. "You don't even get a chance to pretend you're not here." She barged through to the kitchen and deposited a large pizza box onto the table. Opening the fridge door, she shoved in two bottles of white wine.

"Where's the corkscrew?" I pointed to the drawer. She opened the bottle and flung open cabinet doors until she found wineglasses and plates, poured us each a drink and sat down.

"So, you wanna know what I think?" She pulled a gooey slice off of the pie, plated it and scooted it across the table toward me.

I took a huge bite of the spinach and garlic pizza. It was my favorite and Maggie knew it. She was buttering me up. I nodded.

"I think you should just admit who you are. Put your name on all of this."

I choked on my slice and glugged down half a glass of wine to stop my coughing. "Don't be an idiot, Mags. For one thing, I don't really want the whole world knowing I'm a big fat loser."

"You're not a loser. Do you think you're the first girl to get her heart broken?"

"It's not just that. People will know I lied about everything."

"Yeah, they'll know you're a human being. You made a choice, you regret it…next!"

"That's easy for you to say, Mags. You have a book deal, a trophy boyfriend, you always look like a million bucks. No one is judging you."

"You're wrong, there. I never lie about where I came from. People judge me all the time. How did that low-rent mick from Jersey bag that hot, rich dude? Who does she think she is, wearing Chanel? It's what makes me interesting."

"But the thing is…you don't have far to fall, you see? It's different with me."

"Because Hank's famous? You're the one who said you want to be out from under that shadow. Here's a chance to have your own story: the good, the bad, and the ugly. Give people a chance to love you for it. Or give them a chance to hate you. That could happen, too."

"That sounds enticing."

"Better than having people ignore you." She bit into her slice. Her words cut me to the quick. No one from Castle Stone had contacted me since I left.

"Anyway, I flat-out can't. It would out Tom."

"Out Tom as what? The object of your desire? So what? He's a player in your story. It's no reflection on him."

"I just have a gut feeling that he wouldn't like it."

"Then maybe he shouldn't have sent you packing in such a harsh way."

"I'm not looking for revenge."

"That's not what I'm saying. All I'm saying is that he's not in charge of the way the world sees you. Your life, your story." Maggie put our plates in the sink and slid the pizza box into the fridge.

"Let's just drop it." I gathered our glasses and the wine bottle, and moved them to the coffee table. I turned on the TV to discourage Maggie from lecturing me further. We snuggled our feet under a shared afghan and settled in to watch *The Late Night Show*. We chatted through the opening monologue but focused in once Miranda Swanson came on for an interview. She was on to push her latest rom-com movie. She'd done so many BBC costume dramas and Merchant Ivory films using a posh, British accent that it sounded odd to my ears when she spoke in her native Irish lilt.

"So we know you've been busy with the film," Dave said to Miranda Swanson, "what about your love life?"

"You know, Dave, that is a good question. What *about* my love life?" Miranda asked, pulling a face. "I'm not dating anyone at the mo…"

"Not since you're big break up with…"

"Stop! Do not mention he who must not be named. It's funny, while I've been in this, shall we say, *fallow* period, I've been loving this blog called *In Love with an Irish Farmer*. Honestly, Dave, I've been wondering if I shouldn't just give this up and start growing my own beetroot and raising chickens."

I could see Maggie's lips moving. I watched her jump up off the couch and point at the TV screen, but all I could hear was my own blood roaring through my ears like the ocean.

"Tell me more about that," I read Dave's lips saying.

I popped back in to reality just in time to hear Miranda say "crazy, quirky girl who's down on her luck with love, but who may be on to something. I wouldn't mind feeling a bit of grass beneath my feet after the hard work of shooting that last film. And if there were a sexy farmer willing to set a roast dinner in front of me on any given Sunday, so much the better."

"You heard it here first, folks," Dave said. "Run, don't walk to your local cinema to catch *The Engagement Watch* starring the lovely Miranda Swanson. Could be your last chance as she transitions from top Hollywood film actress to Irish chicken plucker."

Maggie flicked off the set and screamed. She climbed up onto the sofa and started jumping up and down. My phone rang. I looked at the number. Brenda.

"Hello?"

"Who's got their finger on the pulse? Me, that's who. Be in my office tomorrow morning at 10."

Chapter Twenty-Eight

A story without an author is not worth listening to.

"Have a seat, Shayla."

The mention my blog had been given in the New York Times styles section had secured me Brenda's full attention. I knew they worked fast over at the famed Gray Lady, but I had no idea it was this fast. Apparently, yearning for life and love outside of the concrete jungle was the new black. According to Brenda, my memoir could go to auction, meaning multiple publishing houses could get into a bidding war. I just had to agree to name myself.

"It's a no-brainer, really, Shayla. If you go by Sheridan, you can tie in the couple of articles you did way back when for The Observer. If you go by de Winter, well, you know what kind of clout that brings. What's the point of being anonymous?"

Way deep in my gut niggled a memory. Tom's voice railing against people who'd used him and exploited him. He hated the reporters, he hated the paparazzi, and it was crystal clear that he hated me for tricking him into helping me write the cook book. He considered me a slick, New York City opportunist. The kind one could never trust. That would never change. I could explain and apologize till the cows came home, and he'd still hate me. I'd made my bed and now I'd have to lie in it. I was a city girl now.

"Brenda," the intercom buzzed on the desk. "Ray Diablo is here to see you."

"Son of a bitch! Shayla, with all the excitement from the TV shout-out and the Times article, I double-booked. Just let me get rid of him."

"I hope you're not talking about me," Ray said, grabbing Brenda's tweed-clad shoulders in his giant hands for a neck massage. I could tell by her expression that she hated it.

"Of course not, Ray, don't be an ass! We're talking about Shayla's dad. Can't do a business lunch and a spa day at the same time, now, can we?" She flashed him a pinched expression that she probably thought read as a smile.

He rolled a chair over from another desk and sat down. "Shayla? I feel like I ought to know you."

"Last time we met, my hair was blonde. And long. And stringy. You know me from here."

"That's right, I do. You said you'd call me and you never did." He treated me to a slow smile.

"I left the country."

"Not to get away from me?" he flirted. "Don't believe everything you read. Aren't you a writer? Hey Brenda, that's what I'm here about. It's been two weeks since I cut that other clown loose. If we're going to get this thing done and turned in, we need to get on it. I'm starting a barbecue tour of food trucks across America soon, and I won't have time for all this book shit." He glanced at me. "Pardon my French."

"Ray, you're the talent. Don't worry about steering the ship. I'm on it."

"What about her?" he asked, jabbing a thumb in my direction. "She looks like someone I can work with. Can I get her cheap?" He flashed me a grin.

Brenda sat up in her chair. "You know, that's not the worst idea I've heard today. I'm not saying it's a deal but what's the harm in a couple of getting-to-know-each-other dinners, somewhere hot and high-profile? Just say the word and I'll get you a table wherever you like. I have two or three up-and-comer clients with restaurants that'll be in The Times by next week. I could get you in now. *And call a few reporters I know from* The Post," she muttered under her breath.

"That's settled, then. I need me a co-writer. And we've gotta eat, don't we?" He pulled his card out of the back of his jeans pocket and handed it to me. "Call me, and tell me when and where. See you tonight." We both watched Ray push through the glass double-doors and disappear down the hall.

"Lookit," Brenda said. "How long are you back in New York, and I've got you set up with a blog that made the New York Times, a soon-to-be very nice book deal, and now a replacement boyfriend? Who's your fairy godmother?"

"Boyfriend? I thought we were talking about me co-writing his book?"

"Eh, that we'll see about. Although," she tapped her head, "If we slid you in to that slot, it might be that much easier to sell you to Tom O'Grady."

"I don't want you to sell me to Tom O'Grady! Just…just leave him out of all this."

"All right, for now. We'll cross that bridge when we come to it. For now, just make sure to be seen with Ray. A lot."

"Brenda, I'm having a business dinner with him to pitch myself as his co-writer."

"Fine," she said, standing up to signal that the meeting was over. "Just make sure you do it somewhere with lots of cameras."

Maggie zipped me into the tight sheath dress. "There," she declared. "You look perfect. But please try not to spill anything on it. I may have bought it at Housing Works, but it is an Alexander McQueen."

I looked at myself in the full-length mirror on the back of her closet door. "I don't know, Mags. It's kind of…black."

"And? What were you looking for? Pink? It would be much

better if we could have booked you in for a half-head of high-lights, but you look fine." I shot her a look. "Better than fine. It's a black dress, in a classic line. You'll fit in. Once I get your makeup done, Ray Diablo will want to eat you alive." She pushed me into a chair in front of her new vanity with the light bulbs encircling the mirror, and gently pulled my hair back into a cloth headband.

"I'm going to talk about co-writing. It's ridiculous, really. I could just email him a set of proposals and manuscripts."

Maggie laughed. "Do you think Ray Diablo is going to read them? Shay, do you think he's even read his own books? He's the kind of guy who has people for everything. He has a stylist who created that signature look with the jeans and custom-designed bowling shirts. He has business people planning and running Austin Heat. Do you think he could have opened a restaurant and kept it alive? He's very, very cute but he doesn't strike me as the brightest bulb on the tree. I heard he's not even a chef. Mark my words, they gave him that cooking show on the strength of his good ol' boy charm and his pretty face. I dare you to ask him where he went to culinary school."

"You'd think if he needed a writer..."

"You'd think, but then you'd be wrong. Like I said, he has people for that. Your job tonight is to get in there and tell him whatever it is he wants to hear in order to become one of his people. Now pucker."

I held still while Maggie did my lips. Six months ago, I would have killed for this chance. Now it just seemed like so much work. I heard my phone ping on the desk. An email. I signaled to Maggie to let me pick it up. It could be Ray canceling. I crossed my fingers that it was.

It was from Brigid! My heart started pounding. I hadn't heard from anyone at Castle Stone since I'd left. "Give me a sec, Mags. I'm just going to use the bathroom."

I went in and closed the door behind myself. I didn't want to share this.

Hiya Sheila

I'm sorry I haven't gotten in touch before now. It sounds silly to say, but I just got caught up in the routine, you know? Seems like life here on the estate takes place in a bubble. You've been on my mind. The kitchen isn't a patch on what it was when you were here alongside me. There's not a bit of craic in there. Without you messing everything up, Bill has no one to be cross with, ha ha. Just kidding. You really were getting better at cooking toward the end.

So, Mary told me the whole story about how you're a famous New York writer and you were going undercover to do a story on Chef. I googled your Da. How'd ya stand living in the dorm after growing up in such a palace (Google Earth)?

Same old, same old here, except maybe Chef. He's back to being his old way. He's short-tempered and he never jokes around. I spoke with his mam after church last Sunday. She said it's not right for such a young man to behave like an old man. She was off to give Sunday lunch to Lord Wexford, so we didn't speak for long.

You must be grand now, back in the big city. Just do us a favor, don't forget Mary and me when you're eating a bowl of gold up in that high-rise apartment of yours!

Brigid xx

When I came out, Maggie waved me back into my chair. "No, no!" she said, dabbing at the corners of my eyes with a tissue. "Don't destroy my work. Keep those eyes dry. Anyway, what I was saying was, get in there and tell Ray Diablo you're the right one for the job. Don't let him argue with you. Imagine it, between the blog and the book…what are they going to call it? I'm in Love with an Irish Farmer?"

"No, not that."

"Anyway, between your two projects and one of Ray's books under your belt, you may never have to work as an editorial assistant ever again. My agent's pitching the synopsis for my next novel. If I sell 'Unwritten works 2 and 3," and a film option, I'll be tap-dancing topless on my desk the next day to the tune of "Take this job and shove it!"

"Maggie, I don't want to sound ungrateful, I really don't, but what's the point in doing Ray's book? Or my book, really?"

She put her hand on her hip and stared right into my eyes. "What's the point? The point is that you've worked your whole life to be a real writer, and you're steps away from it becoming a reality. What else is there?"

"You're right." I conceded.

She nodded and smiled a satisfied smile.

"There's really nothing else, now, I guess. Now let's get me ready." I closed my eyes and let her paint the rest of my face on.

"Sorry I'm late," I told Ray as the waiter pulled out my chair. I had no real excuse, so I didn't offer one. I'd hung around at Maggie and Eric's drinking wine until she literally walked me downstairs and put me in a cab to Yong Sook Korean Bar-B-Q.

"No worries," Ray drawled easily. He took a pull from his longneck beer bottle. "You want a drink?"

"White wine."

Ray ordered my drink. "After I left Brenda's, I went back to the office and told my assistant about you. Not ten minutes later, Brenda called and gave me the exclusive scoop. Looks like you're poised to be a household name. My PA did her magic on the computer, and sat me down in front of your blog. Sounds like you've had your heart broken, little lady."

"Yeah, I'd rather not talk about that. Why don't we order?"

"Already taken care of." That annoyed me. How did he know what I wanted to eat?

"My PA explained to me that if your book takes off the way your blog has, we could leverage the cross-marketing." I could tell he was concentrating hard to pull off this speech. "It seems young women are a demographic my brand of raisin' hell and inch-thick steaks have failed to pull in. She put a call in to the head of marketing at Ray Diablo, Inc., who said I should definitely make this a go."

My wine came and I took a long drink. I forced a smile. This was going exactly the way it was supposed to. I felt nothing.

"But don't get excited yet. I told him that this wasn't about the money, it was about the chemistry. If I don't feel it, it doesn't happen. Know what I mean?"

"I do, Ray. I really do."

A throng of waiters appeared and arranged pots, dishes, plates and bowls on our table. I got a whiff of something so foul that it brought me to my feet. "Wow, I think something's really wrong here," I said, hands cupped over my mouth and nose. "Do you want me to call someone?"

Ray laughed. "Naw, that's just the hongeo. It smells strong, but if you breathe in and out through your mouth, you'll be able to get it down."

"Is it *food*?" I considered myself to be fairly worldly, but this was pushing it.

"It's fermented skate. Skate's a weird fish. It doesn't pee like other sea creatures. It just passes the uric acid through its skin. Once they ferment it, that acid smells exactly like ammonia."

"And you want to eat it because…?"

He laughed. "That's the beauty of being who I am. I can go wherever I want and do whatever I want. I never get bored. My show took me on location in Korea and while I was there, I ate all this stuff. Now I'm in New York City, and all I have to do is snap my fingers and I can get it again." He picked up his metal chopsticks and began heaping what appeared to be chicken feet onto his plate.

"What's that?" I asked, pointing to a glutinous brown dish topped with finely chopped vegetables.

"Acorn jelly."

"I thought I read somewhere that acorns are poisonous to humans."

"They are. Unless you cook them, grind them into a powder, and cook them again using precisely the correct method. Try it."

"No thanks, I'll just stick to the wine."

"Where's your sense of adventure? I'm supposed to be the backwater hick from Texas. Weren't all you New York babies given sushi and champagne in your cribs?"

"I've lost my taste for it. I've become more of a meat and potatoes girl." With the extra glass of wine on my empty stomach, I felt dizzy. Or maybe it was more than that. I couldn't catch a deep breath, and I felt like the floor was dropping out from underneath me. It dawned on me that I was having a panic attack. I looked around wildly for a paper bag to breathe into. "Ray, I hate to do this, but I'm not feeling well. Would you mind terribly if I just took a rain check?"

He stood up immediately. "No, of course not. I'm sorry you don't feel good. Let me take you home."

"No! Please. You stay here and enjoy…all this. I'll be fine." The floor was modulating in waves under my feet. I just wanted out of there.

"I'm going to put you in a cab. There's no arguing about that," Ray took me by the arm and let the waiters know he'd be back.

Ray gave the driver a twenty-dollar bill and told him to make sure I got inside the lobby of my building. "You don't have to do that, Ray." I just wanted to be alone. I didn't want Ray looking at me.

"That's how I operate," he explained. "The sooner you surrender to Ray, the better off you'll be." He knocked the passenger-side window, and the cab took off. "You look like you could use a little babying."

As I watched the buildings speed by on my way uptown, I thought about Maeve. If she were here, she'd insist that I eat broth and bread, tuck me into my bed, and turn the lights down.

But Maeve would never be here. And I will never be there again. *Time to move on, Shayla,* I coached myself. Tomorrow would be a new day.

Chapter Twenty-Nine

It's more difficult to maintain honor than to become prosperous.

I handed Hank his scotch, and sat down on the couch.

"Glad you could finally make the elevator ride down to have a drink with your old dad. It's been over a month since you've been back. When you're the flavor of the day, I guess you have to make hay while the sun shines or lose your chance. No time for the likes of me."

"It's not like that, Hank. Mostly, I've been trying to work."

"You're either working or you're not working. I've been working for 30 years straight. There is no try, only do. Writer's block is a myth. When there's something to be written, you put your head down and you write it." His face softened and he took a long look at me. "So, how does it feel to finally have a book deal of your own?"

"It's not 'finally.' I've had book deals before," I defended.

"I mean a real one."

I shifted uncomfortably and took a sip of my wine. The deal was done. Brenda had sold my book. She had me re-envision it as a confessional/memoir/how-to book and had advised me to write in tips and tricks for farm life. I had essays on burying eggs to keep them fresh, how to prevent botulism when canning vegetables from your garden, and of course, how to approach a horse without getting your head kicked in. The title had been decided: *The City Girl's Guide to Irish Farm Life*. The thought of Tom ever seeing it filled me with dread so I just didn't think about it. At least the title didn't mention my being in love with an Irish farmer. I must have been out of my mind when I let Maggie convince me that outing myself was the solution.

"Brenda told me she's trying to get you booked onto the national morning shows."

"Yeah," I admitted. "She is."

"You don't sound too excited about it."

"No, I am. It's great. Really. It's just that it's not really me, you know. Ever since the blog took off, I've been doing a print interview a day. Photographers have been coming by and making me pose with, like, fountain pens and maps of Ireland. You know how it is."

"I do. That's all good publicity. It's what you wanted."

"It is, but I just want to take a break sometimes, you know? It's a lot, and it's all happened super-fast."

"That's fame, Shayla. It's not yours to control. It belongs to other people."

"I guess."

"That's the mark of success."

I thought about that for a second. Maggie would probably agree. But Mom had been a success, to my mind. Maeve, too. And no one knew Mary's name from Adam, but she earned her own money and she could do things with her hands. "Maybe," I said.

"Hooking up with that Ray Diablo seems to be working for you. I saw that picture of you guys eating blintzes together in Time Out."

"Yeah, that was embarrassing. We went down to that Kosher dairy place on the lower east side because I thought we'd have some privacy. Instead, I ended up with a picture of me with cherry jelly all over my face in a magazine."

"No press is bad press."

"I don't know about that. I'm trying to keep our meetings to the office but Ray can be very, uh, persuasive. He's used to getting his way. Every time I meet him at his restaurant, or take a walk in the park with him, someone's snapping a photo."

"That's what you want. Like they say, it's just as easy to fall in love with a rich and famous man as a poor one."

I blushed. "We're work colleagues. He asked me to go to the James Beard awards."

"If I were you, I'd tip off some reporters. Call the story in yourself."

"That's weird."

"That's how things are done in this town." Hank took a long drink of his scotch. "I never wanted this for you, you know."

"What?"

"All this. The perpetual self-promotion. The need to constantly be better than the last thing that got you noticed. It's a hard life."

"Well, you manage."

"I'm kind of a bastard, hadn't you heard?" he smiled and raised his eyebrows. "It was hard on your mother." I looked away and sat very still. I couldn't recall the last time Hank had mentioned Mom. "She didn't like any of this. She liked my writing, at first. The early stuff that I wrote before I had deadlines to meet and editors to please. She'd have been much happier if we'd never gotten married, I think."

"That's not true! She loved you!"

"She did, in a way. In the beginning. Before it changed me. And she had to put up with me to get you. You're what made her happy. You and being up there in Rhinebeck." Hank's eyes glistened. "I think about all the trips up there I cancelled. 'I can't go this summer, I have a book tour,' or 'We need to do Christmas in the city because I can't miss networking at all the holiday parties from the newspapers and publishing houses.'" He rattled the ice in his glass. "If she hadn't gotten sick, I think she would have left me."

"Don't say that."

"Doesn't matter now. You can't fix the past, can you?" He stood up and walked toward the kitchen. "Do you want a sandwich? I have that good rye bread from Zabar's and some pastrami."

I put my wineglass in the sink. "Nah, I'm not very hungry." I watched Hank pull the deli meat and mustard out of the refrigerator. I stared at his broad back, noticing that his shoulders were starting to slope. He looked shorter than he used to. I thought about giving him a hug. Instead, I patted him briskly on the back.

He turned around and smiled. "Let me know when you get booked on *The Late Night Show*. I'll tune in."

I felt less and less like that was going to happen, but I just smiled back and said, "You'll be the first to know."

Chapter Thirty

God is good, but never dance in a small boat.

"Hey, waiter. Another bottle of beer, and keep them coming. I don't ever want to see an empty in front of me. And whatever the lady's having."

I made a face at the waiter, to try to apologize for Ray's gruff behavior. "Just a club soda with lemon for me, please," I whispered.

"What? Club soda? Not on my watch. Throw some vodka in that, will ya?" I shook my head at the waiter. I hadn't been drinking for a while. I couldn't tell if it was all the drinking I had done since I'd been back in the city that made me so dizzy and out of sorts, or if I was developing some kind of anxiety disorder. I made a vow to quit drinking for a month, and if I didn't feel better, I'd see a psychiatrist. I couldn't go on like this. The waiter gave me a non-committal sniff and moved on. God alone knew what he'd bring me. Ray owned a restaurant. You'd think he'd have heard tales of waiters spitting in food. Oh well, I was in his hands tonight.

"Just think, Shayla, if *Real Man's Barbecue* wins best overall cookbook here tonight, you'll have your work cut out for you. He put his hand on my knee. He'd been doing that more and more lately. "Do you have it in you to write a James Beard award-winning book for ol' Ray?"

"I don't have anything inside me right now, Ray." I said, moving his hand back to his own knee. "Probably best to keep it that way."

"You are a hoot, you know that?" He gave a big belly laugh and squeezed my knee again.

I surveyed the room and saw lots of usual suspects from the lifestyle sector of the publishing world. Across the room, Brenda was in her element. She shared a table with her client who'd recently won first place on the reality cooking show *Prime Cut*, and a couple of editors from fancy houses that did coffee table books.

Ray started chatting to a heavily made-up young woman at the table next to ours, talking across the aisle. She appeared to be the date of an older, bearded man who examined the contents of the breadbasket as if they were meant to be offensive. I introduced myself to a few of the other people seated near us. One was a nervous, skinny woman up for an award for her cookbook *Vegan Every Other Week*. She just kept twisting her napkin and sipping her water. Her agent was there, talking to her in soothing tones. The editors and their assistants who rounded out our table seemed more interested in gossiping with one another than in making friends.

Various presenters came and went from the podium, all making too-long speeches that were meant to be clever but generally falling short of target. Awards were handed out as appetizers were served. Agent of the Year (not Brenda, and she looked pissed), Best Food Memoir (*My Life with Matzoh*), Best Diet Book (*Never, Ever Eat That!*), and Best Health and Fitness Cookbook (*Greens, It's What's for Dinner*) were all announced and awarded.

My drink came, loaded with a double-shot of booze. I pushed it aside and picked up the program of tonight's events. I glanced at Ray, who was still chatting to the woman across the aisle, to the annoyance of every waiter trying to serve his or her section. For a second, I considered slipping out the back way. It would be such a relief not to be there. The room thundered with the undercurrent of constant conversation. The stale, hot air hung low. I couldn't get a deep breath. *"Just get to the entrée, Shayla. Then you can make your excuses."*

I scanned down the list of awards nominees and lifetime achievement recipients. Tom O'Grady for *The Elite Kitchen*. His first and only book, he hated it. It was the book that soured him on writing cookbooks. Fucking Brenda — she knew it was up for an award but she didn't tell me because she knew I'd bail. Just reading his name dried my mouth up. I picked up my drink and drained it in one go. I had to concentrate on sitting up straight in my chair.

The appetizers were delivered. "A trio of foams," the waiter announced. "You have duck, salmon, and beef liver." I stared at the spongy sputum on my plate. It didn't appear to be food. My stomach lurched.

"Another drink, please, waiter." The server had the gall to sneer at me and shake his head no. I helped myself to Ray's fresh beer and took a long pull.

As I watched the nervous woman next to me scoop the mess up onto her water crackers, I had the feeling I was in a funhouse. I rose halfway to my feet. From the podium, I heard, "The winner of this year's Best Gourmet Cookbook is…Tom O'Grady." I slammed back down into my chair and kept my eyes glued to the stage. My breathing slowed nearly to a halt as I watched a man in a suit take the microphone from the woman in the long gown and cover it with his hand. A third man, this one in a tux, climbed onto the stage and a general shuffling of the plaque and certificate ensued.

"Ladies and gentleman," tux-man said into the microphone, "Chef Tom O'Grady planned to be with us tonight, but has experienced some unforeseen difficulty. As many of you know, Tom is an old pal of mine from our days in London." I squinted my eyes. Who was this guy? "I'll just say a few words on Tom's behalf. First, I know Tom would like to thank each and every one of you. Nothing is closer to Tom's heart than fine food, presented gorgeously, to those with refined palettes who can fully appreciate its magnificence. His reclusiveness now only serves to make us want his white-glove service all the more. Some say it's harder to get a seat in one of Tom O'Grady's restaurants than it is to get a camel through the eye of a needle. Har, har!"

I stood up on my feet and made my way up the aisle.

"Hey, where you going?" Ray asked, but he was already in my rearview mirror.

I climbed the three stairs to the stage, while the man in the tuxedo prattled on about visual excellence. I tapped him on the back. He gave me a small smile and kept on talking. I noticed that the low-grade din in the room had hushed. That was good. That helped my headache. I put my hand on the microphone and pulled it toward my face.

"This is all wrong," I said, as the man pulled the mic back. I could see Brenda standing by her chair, waving as if luring a plane into the hangar.

"As I was saying," tuxedo man went on, "Tom O'Grady's motto is that the mark of a top-caliber chef is one who combines architectural elegance with the exquisite ingredients one can only find at the far reaches…"

"Tom hates this book!" I said shoving my face against the man's chest to give me access to the mic. I grabbed it with both hands, but he wouldn't let go. Without thinking it through, I licked his hand. He promptly pulled it away, giving me sole proprietorship of the microphone. "He'd be embarrassed to receive this award. He hates pretension, he hates exclusivity, he hates fussiness for the sake of fussiness — note to you, caterers. That foam thing was beyond!"

I was dizzy from adrenaline and anxiety, and from mixing vodka and beer. I knew I should stop talking, but I couldn't. "Tom O'Grady's food speaks for itself. It's simple. He doesn't gild the lily."

A blonde young woman in a cocktail dress ascended the stage, yelling "Thank you, thank you for your speech," and smiling tightly. I saw that she intended to take the mic from me, so I launched into my final remarks. "If Tom O'Grady were here right now, he'd be appalled. He'd tell his agent that she's a sneak and a liar." I looked down to see Ray at my feet, urging me down off of the stage. "No, Ray. Leave me alone! You and your smoke and mirrors. You represent the worst of this world, with fake dates for the cameras, and your pre-planned package of a life. For the record," I shouted to the crowd, "we are not an item." The young woman now had her arm around my waist and was kicking at the left heel of my shoe, trying to push me to the ground. "Tom and I... however... well, I blew it. I acted like all of you, a money-grubbing, success-hungry liar. Of course he didn't want any part of that."

The blonde was wily. She pressed me downward by the shoulders as she kicked me in the back of the knees. From a kneeling position, I managed, "I love Tom O'Grady! There, I said it. But I don't deserve to stand in his shadows! And neither do you bitches..."

The last thing I remember before I blacked out is grabbing the blonde's shoe, and her crashing down on top of me, and Ray yelling my name from the far distance. I'm pretty sure my head hit the stage, hard.

I still held the mic in my hands.

Chapter Thirty-One

There's a cup for every saucer.

"Look who's awake," Maggie said, as I shielded my eyes against the light. Do you want coffee?"

"Too harsh. Can I have some tea? Thanks for staying, Mags. Like I said, you really didn't have to."

"Don't be ridiculous. When Hank called me to meet you guys at the emergency room, it was pretty clear he didn't know how to be a nursemaid."

"I'm saying I can take care of myself."

"You have a concussion, Maggie. Someone had to keep an eye on you."

"I'm going to have to take care of myself eventually. Might as well start now. It's pretty obvious I'll be found dead in my kitchen someday, being eaten by my own cats."

Maggie poured hot water into a cup. "It's pretty obvious you aren't going to wind up as Mrs. Ray Diablo, that's for sure."

I winced. "Forget marriage. I got myself fired from the co-writing gig." I eased myself into one of Irma and Fred's kitchen chairs. "The whole thing was pretty bad, wasn't it?"

"Hank said when Brenda called him to come and get you, she told him she wouldn't dump you because your blog is still hot and

341

your book stands to make money but that you're batshit crazy so don't expect any new deals out of her."

"I think I'm done, Maggie."

She put a cup of tea and a slice of buttered toast on the table in front of me. "Oh, it'll blow over. Hank can sweet-talk her." She sat down and sipped her coffee. "And that clip of you trashing the publishing industry-slash-declaring your love for Tom O'Grady can't circulate the internet forever."

"No! You've got to be kidding me."

"What did you expect, Shay? Everyone in the room had a cell phone camera. And you kind of can't ignore the fact that the whole event's recorded by professional videographers."

"Do you think Tom will see it?" I whispered. I tried to comfort myself with the fact that he didn't believe in having personal accounts on social media. After all the mess with Tabitha, he'd become a recluse in the virtual world.

"There's a chance he won't see it on YouTube," Maggie soothed. "But he's fairly likely to see it when they send him his award plaque and a copy of the video. On the plus side, all the lovelorn girls on your blog are bound to love your stunt. Humiliating yourself publicly for love. It's pretty genius. You could spin this to your advantage."

"It wasn't a stunt. I'm done, Maggie."

"Don't jump the gun. We can figure a way out of this."

"No, I mean *I'm* done. I don't want this anymore."

Maggie put her coffee down. "Then what do you want?"

"I know what I don't want. I don't want to write." Maggie's mouth fell open, and she was about to speak, but I cut her off. "I mean I don't want to write what the world wants to hear. If that means no one wants to read my words, fine. I'm not Hank."

"Maybe Eric could get you a desk job at his firm. He got another promotion, you know. Just until you figure out what's next."

"Maybe," I answered, knowing I'd never, ever do that. "For now, let's just hang out together for the morning."

"Let's," Maggie said, getting up to put on the kettle. "It'll be like old times."

I let Maggie make me another cup of tea. As we sat on Fred and Irma's unfamiliar furniture, talking about Eric's huge salary bump and how it would enable the engaged couple to buy a bigger apartment before the wedding, I knew that it would never be like old times again. I studied the lines and planes of my best friend's face, and listened to the honking cabs outside, and the sounds of the carriage horses hooves on the pavement. I didn't know yet where I belonged, but I knew it wasn't here.

It's a well-known New York fact that all of the therapists and psychiatrists leave the city for the month of August. On the one hand, who can blame them? It's the sane thing to do when steam is rising from the blacktop and the violent crime statistics are skyrocketing. You have to leave the city if you want to catch a deep breath. On the other hand, leaving all of the crazy people here to rub sweaty shoulders in the sweltering subway without anyone to listen to their tales of woe or soothe their rampant anxiety seems pretty irresponsible to me.

I might have snapped myself as I dragged cartload after cartload of my stuff from the old apartment I had shared with Maggie down the stairs and over to the Salvation Army. The girls who lived there now wanted to keep the big furniture. I just had to get rid of my personal effects. I'd spent the morning packing sparkling three-inch heels and shiny metallic purses into bags. Tight leather miniskirt? Donate. Metrocard pouch? Donate. Neon faux fur vest? Donate. I could start a museum of mismatched trendy items that shared no common thread. In front of me lay a graveyard of items documenting the years I'd tried so hard to fit in. In the words of Gwyneth Paltrow, I "consciously uncoupled" from the objects, and my former desperation to be picked for the inside of the velvet rope. I felt light with relief.

Starving and dehydrated, I treated myself to a smoothie before

I ducked down into the sweltering inferno of the subway to head back to my temporary home. The drink cost the better part of ten bucks. Like most things in the city, it was a ridiculous extravagance. I had a momentary panic about how I'd ever pay Hank back the money I owed him. After my internship, I'd get a job, I told myself. And when you live and work on a farm upstate, there's not much opportunity to throw away wads of cash on upscale health drinks and coffees. It would all work out. It had to. It was my one and only plan.

Hair still wet from the shower, I flung open the windows at Fred and Irma's. It only served to let in more hot, humid air. Someone knocked on the apartment door. Pulling a tank top over my head, I cautiously went to the door and yelled, "Who is it?"

"It's Mary and Brigid, from Castle Stone," came the cheery reply. "We buzzed and buzzed, but there was no answer. I hope you don't mind that the doorman let us up."

I scrambled to open the multiple locks and the chain to let them in.

"Surprise!" Mary said, giving me a big hug. She wore a canvas hat with a string that made her look like an explorer from the Australian outback, and a fanny pack around her waist that sat right below her belly. In stark contrast, Brigid had on a pair of black cat's-eye sunglasses, an A-line mini dress printed with a large pattern of tropical fruits and a pair of Israeli clogs. It occurred to me that I'd never seen Brigid wearing anything but chef's whites or jeans and wellies, despite the treasures in her closet. Her developed sense of style caught me off guard. It suited her. I waved them into the apartment, sat them on the sofa, and gave them ice-water.

"Sorry we didn't call to tell you we were coming, but Maeve made us swear on the graves of our ancestors that we wouldn't. She said you'd refuse to see us."

I thought about it. Mary was right.

"It wasn't easy finding out how to get in touch with you. I pressed Timmy to go to his sister Ashleigh and ask Des to get in touch with his cousin Maggie. She's the one who gave us your address. By the way, Ashleigh and Des finally tied the knot. It was touch and go there for a while. They had a big row about Des cheating on her with some nasty slag." I squirmed in my chair, hoping the slag in question wasn't me. "After that, he became a model citizen. Guess you don't know what you have until you're likely to lose it."

"Yeah," I agreed. "That's the truth. Why are you two here?"

Mary smiled. "You see, Brigid here is being headhunted to be the curator of the quilt collection at the Folk Art and Craft Museum here in New York. And I came to see for myself what living in the big city might be like. So far, I'm finding it tolerable."

"Are you serious? What about your job?"

"Ah, I can find a job anywhere there's a hospitality industry. There's a hotel every other block here. Barring that, I saw some horses in Central Park. Where there's horses, there's stables."

"But wouldn't you miss Ireland? Wouldn't you miss the country?"

She took Brigid's hand. "Not as much as I'd miss Brigid."

A lump formed in my throat at the naked expression of affection.

"Oh, here," Mary said, "Before we forget. We've something for you. Brigid," she said. Brigid rooted in her hand-sewn shoulder bag and produced a large, creamy eggshell-colored envelope. "Open it."

I could tell it was a wedding invitation. Theirs? No, they weren't excited enough. "The marriage of Mrs. Maeve O'Grady and Lord Anthony Stone, Earl of Wexford." The relief I felt at not seeing Tom's name as groom flooded through my limbs.

"Oh, that's wonderful," I said. "Perfect."

"Maeve sent me to get your promise that you'd come."

There was no way on earth I could sit in a church with Tom O'Grady during a wedding. I was sure the pain would actually kill me. Luckily, I wouldn't have to.

"I'd love to be there, but I can't afford it."

"Lord Wexford insists on paying."

"I can't take his money."

"He told me you'd say that. That's why I got together with your friend Maggie and booked you onto a flight." Mary produced some print-outs and lay them before me. "Once you're in Ireland, you're a guest of Castle Stone, so that's sorted. His Lordship's putting you in a real room, no dorm for you this time. And here's an envelope of cash for incidentals." She put it on the coffee table.

"Listen, even if I wanted to go, I can't. I start an internship at a farm upstate in ten days. It's all set."

"Not a problem," Mary said. "Flight's tomorrow, and the wedding's the next day."

"Sorry, I can't just up and leave."

"Maggie said that you could," Mary said firmly. "She told us you've no job, no appointments, and could give us no reason not to go. She basically told us you don't have a life."

"It's good to have a best friend, isn't it?"

"In this case, I'd say so. She told us she'd personally put you in a car to the airport."

I was starting to get angry. "Why do all of you think you get to decide what I do?"

Brigid glanced at Mary. "Maggie said you've been miserable, and that maybe this would sort you out once and for all. Your Maggie is nothing if not American. She said perhaps if you faced your problem head on, you'd come away with closure."

"And you see, Sheila, Chef's been a holy terror ever since you left. Maeve thinks having it out with you might set him straight. Closure may not have made its way to Ireland yet, but we were all taught in church that leaving things unsaid ruins the soul. She told me that after she read your cookbook…"

"How did she read my cookbook?"

"Your Maggie sent her a copy and begged her to show it to Chef."

I felt faint. "And did he see it?"

"That I don't know," Mary said. "I do know she sat him down

in front of your blog, though."

"My blog? How does she even know about that?"

"Maeve's gotten to be quite the computer whiz. You should see her Pinterest boards. Anyhow," she said, standing up, "we've an appointment with an estate agent this afternoon. "Can you picture it, Sheila? Us an old married couple living in a New York high-rise apartment?" Mary threw her arm over Brigid's shoulders.

"All I can say is grab happiness where you can find it."

Chapter Thirty-Two

What the heart knows today, the head will understand tomorrow.

I was very glad it was after eleven at night when the cab pulled up at reception. The air was warm and a sweet breeze blew. It was so quiet, I could hear the leaves rustling in the trees. Inside, seeing a new girl working the desk filled me with relief. When I asked, she informed me that Catherine was no longer employed at Castle Stone.

She gave me the key to The Pink Room. Mary had told me that I'd be given a proper room, but I never dreamed I'd be assigned to one of the best guest rooms, right in the castle. I sneaked up, looking both ways. I knew I'd see Tom eventually, but a public place surrounded by people sounded a lot better to me than alone on a secluded stairwell. I didn't like to feel hated, even if I knew I deserved it. Now, he'd hate me more because his mother was marrying Tony.

There was a bottle of wine waiting for me in my room, but I didn't have a taste for it. There was an envelope laying on the tray next to it that read, "Sheila." I opened it and read:

Our Dear Sheila,

Exhausted from the trip, I set the letter aside and slipped on my nightgown. I was too tired to even take a bath. I felt happy. I couldn't wait to see Maeve. Losing her had been the most painful part of being banished from Castle Stone. It was strange that she hadn't been in touch. But then again, neither had I. She must have felt as awkward about my lying to Tom as I did. I was surprised, frankly, that she'd cared enough to include me. Maybe it was something Irish that I didn't understand, like you owe a debt to the matchmaker.

As my head hit the pillow, I thought about how strange it was to reassure an invited guest that she was welcome at the party. I fell asleep hard and dreamed that I gave birth to a baby goat.

The invitation said that the ceremony was set for 11 in the morning, with a wedding breakfast to follow in a marquee on the lawn adjacent. Dressed in a Grecian blue and white toile sundress, with a pale-blue cotton pashmina I had purchased, not stolen, I walked the path from the castle to the church. I felt my outfit was appropriately respectful and festive, and that it would garner me not the first ounce of unwanted attention. Laying low was the order of the day for me. On my feet, I wore a pair of white, low-heeled sandals. Gone were my days of letting Maggie costume me. For one, I couldn't afford her suggestions anymore. And more importantly, I had learned to hold my own comfort at a premium. On my way there, I ran into Brigid on the path.

"Sheila," she cried, running at me and flinging herself into my arms. She was dressed for the kitchens.

"Aren't you going to the wedding?"

"Some of us had to work it and I drew a short straw. Look at the sight of you! You look perfect for a summer wedding." She glanced at her watch. "We'll have to have a proper catch-up later. I'm nearly late and I don't want to hear that gobshite Bill laying into me this morning."

"I've missed you, Brigid. I have to tell you everything. I'm going to work on a goat farm in upstate New York."

"Why on earth would you go to someone else's goat farm? We've plenty of goats here."

"Maybe because I was invited never to come here again?"

"Well, that can't be true, can it? Look, here you're standing."

"Brigid! I'm talking about Tom."

"Do us all a favor and make up with him, willya?" She started to jog down the path to the castle. "When the two of you were having it off, life in the kitchen was a hell of a lot lighter. See ya!" she said, and broke into a full run.

I expected to see more wedding guests assembling outside the church. As I approached the ancient stone building, I heard the lilting notes of organ music float out the heavy, wooden doorway. I peered in. It took a moment for my eyes to adjust from seeing in the bright morning sun, to seeing in the dusky darkness. There was no sign of Tom. I breathed out. About 40 people sat scattered in the ribbon-bedecked pews. Simple but gorgeous arrangements of flowers and greenery festooned the altar. I wondered if there was a bride's side and a groom's side. I slipped into one of the pews near the middle. I didn't want to draw attention to myself by being too far forward or too far back.

I watched people arrive in twos and threes. Most genuflected at the pews before entering, and most knelt on the low, leather-covered kneelers before taking their seats. I wondered what they were praying about. Did they want something, or were they simply giving thanks? Apart from poetic speeches around the

Thanksgiving table, and the rote nighttime prayer my mother said with me when I was little, I'd never been taught to pray.

A phrase popped into my head. *"God, please show me the way."* I heard the plea in my own voice. A thrill took over my blood, like I'd just committed magic. Rather than a sensation or waiting for something to happen, though, I felt a sensation of relaxation. I slumped back on the bench, listened to the music, and looked at the elaborate stone carving on the pillars and the grotto around the altar.

Then he was there. Tom, dressed in an impeccable seersucker suit, with a French-blue shirt, and thin black tie. His hair was longer, and had more gold and platinum streaks than I remembered, but then again, it was August. He'd no doubt been walking the grounds in this summer's glorious and surprising Irish sun. I pictured him digging in the gardens and riding one of the horses. He genuflected and slid into a pew in the front, next to a petite redhead, with smooth hair and a pink linen dress. Before lowering himself to the kneeler, he gave her a quick kiss.

The ceremony itself was part of a Catholic mass. I'd never been to one. I watched altar boys dressed like junior versions of priests march up the aisle to assist. Father Walsh presided. His singing voice surprised me. It was like being at the opera. Danny sat in the front, moving his lips along to the words, closing his eyes in rapture. There were other priests there, swinging smoking vessels filled with fragrant incense and dipping gold ornaments into buckets of holy water and sprinkling the congregation. When Maeve entered, my heart lifted. She wore a silk suit and it was periwinkle, just as I'd envisioned it.

At the end of the ceremony, I waited for the couple's kiss, but none came. I wondered if that was Catholic tradition, or simply another modesty on the part of the bride. I wasn't sure what to do next. I watched the crowd for cues. Everyone stood as the priest and his entourage filed out, then one by one, they made their way to the aisles, genuflected again to the altar, and exited. I kept my seat, waiting to leave the empty church. When Tom turned around to make his way to the back, he clocked me. For a second, he began walking toward me and his eyes lit up. I swallowed hard. It was like a bird with a broken wing was trying to flap and peck its way out of my chest. As fast as he had lit up, he then shut down. He looked away from me, face closed off. He put his hand on the small of the redhead's back and steered her out with the rest of the crowd.

I gave him some lead time before rising from my pew. I peeked outside the door, terrified that there would be a reception line, with Tom standing in it, alongside his girlfriend. It was just Father Walsh, Tony, and Maeve. When I shook Father Walsh's hand, it dripped with sweat. I discreetly wiped it off on the skirt of my dress.

"No matter how many holy unions I have the privilege of overseeing, I never quite get used to the feeling of stage fright. It's a good thing I quit competitive Irish dancing to enter the priesthood. I don't know how long I'd have lasted."

"Well, it was beautiful, Father."

"And so are you," Tony said, gathering me into a hug. "You're a sight for sore eyes, my dear." He held me at arm's length and looked at me, then leaned in and whispered into my ear. "Maeve has missed you. And she's not the only one." He then literally put my hands into Maeve's. I had dreaded this moment. Surely, she must have forgiven me if she'd invited me to the wedding. On the other hand, I'd lied to her. Afraid to look down into her eyes for fear of seeing disappointment, I closed my own and waited for her to speak. She didn't say a thing she just clasped one hand and walked me away from the light crowd to the shade of a big oak a little farther out into the churchyard. She kept silent until I couldn't take it anymore.

"Maeve, I'm sorry I didn't tell you the truth. I'm not a liar. All signs point to the fact that I am, but that's really not who I am."

"I know that, dear girl, or we wouldn't be standing here. Don't tell Father Walsh I said this, but sometimes the end justifies the means where love comes into play. Remember Tony's heart scare? The poor man needed constant care, so, and there was little choice but to move him into Tom's bedroom." She winked at me. "And if Tom's old bedroom wasn't the most comfortable for the patient, and he required a softer bed for convalescing, that must have been God's plan."

"Maeve!"

"And here we stand today, married under the watch of heaven. As I said, the end sometimes justifies the means. So, then. I've looked at your cookbook. Not bad."

I held my breath and waited to hear more.

"A few recipes need tweaking, I'd recommend putting in a few traditional ones you left out, and there's a fact or two that's wrong. But it feels like something Tom would write. If you want to do some real good in this world, convince him to publish it. It's a natural marketing tool for the Castle Stone range of foods and products."

My heart sank. "If they ever get backing. I ruined that deal for Tom."

"That's not the way Brian Lynch told the story to me. He's sorry that Burton fellow ever crossed your path, but he's grateful that you brought our business venture to GlobeCo's attention. Apparently, they were looking to expand into the natural and organic market. Brian Lynch came off as a hero for landing the Castle Stone account. It goes without saying that the farmers around here are tickled pink. And so's Tom."

My heart dared to open a crack.

"Mary told me you showed him my blog." I felt sick thinking about it.

"Aye, that I did. Sat him down in front of it, but he said he wouldn't read a word. From what I heard from the girls around the office, though, he sat at Mary's desk for over an hour doing just that."

"So, now he knows I love him." I felt raw.

"Don't you wager he knew that before?"

I felt crimson climb from the neckline of my dress, all the way up to my face.

"Don't you wager everyone knew that?" She laughed softly. "You're not the only Cupid on the estate. Why not go and tell him?"

"What difference would it make? He already read it online. And anyway, I'm too late. What am I supposed to do? Declare a dual with his perfect girlfriend?"

"I don't think my niece is the dueling type."

My chest lifted like a thousand helium balloons had been launched in my heart. I gave Maeve a hug, and my feet began carrying me to the marquee, where the guests had gathered. My eyes picked through the crowd, looking for Tom among the blossom-colored clothes of the attendees. Landing on a pair of broad shoulders clad in a neat, striped jacket, they drifted upward to find a loose, sunny mass of wavy hair. Tom!

Marching up to him, I tapped him on the shoulder. Smiling, he turned around, holding a delicate glass cup of frothy, pale-peach punch. For a split second, his eyes crinkled into the familiar smile that bathed my brain like a drug, lulling me into knowing that the world was safe, and all would be well. I felt a jolt of heat. I was sure I saw it in Tom as well. At least I hoped I did.

"Tom, may I have a word with you?" There wasn't much point in calling him Chef or Mr. O'Grady at this point. The cat was out of the bag.

"Certainly," he said to me. "If you'll excuse me," he said to the several people gathered around him in conversation. "Why don't you follow me?"

He began walking in the direction of the castle. He didn't look at me and he didn't say a word. His long strides sent him sailing across the grass as he deviated from the path. As had so often been the case, I wound up jogging to keep up.

"Tom," I tried, but he held up a hand to quiet me. I kept following.

Finally, we stopped at the back entrance to the castle. He unlocked and flung open the door, and went in, taking the stairs two at a time. Panting, I ran to keep at his heels. He led me through to his triangle-shaped room and closed the door behind us.

"Why?" he demanded in a loud, ragged voice. His face contorted in anguish. I wasn't sure if he might hit me, or harm himself, or burst into tears. I looked away from his face. It scared me. Now I wasn't sure this could be fixed.

My eyes looked past his, afraid to meet them. I spied something new above his desk. There, taped to the wall, was a line drawing of me. Clearly, it had been drawn by my friend down at the market in Ballykelty. But I hadn't commissioned it. With hope in my heart, I jumped off the ledge.

"Tom, I didn't mean to lie."

He started to yell, but it was my turn to hold up my hand for silence. "Yes, the lie at first was mercenary. I wanted what I wanted. But my lie would never have caused you harm. I knew I could be good for you."

He turned his back to me and looked out the window.

"Yes, I wanted the book for me, but here's the truth: I know I'm good. I knew that if I could convince you to let me make this book, you'd come out on top."

"You could have told me the truth at any time," he said, still looking away. "You made a fool of me."

"How did I make a fool of you? Oh, do you mean by plotting to get Tony and Maeve together? Look, I'm sorry about that…"

"No!" he roared, turning to face me. "By letting me fall in love with you." His eyes blazed and he panted in quick, shallow breaths. "I swore I'd never do it again after Tabitha." His fists balled up, and he paced a short line back and forth, never taking his eyes off my face.

"But I'm not Tabitha!"

"You lied like Tabitha."

"I didn't, Tom, I really didn't. Anything that mattered, I told the truth about. I told the truth about being in love with you."

He relaxed his hands. "I'm supposed to believe that?" He held his palms out to me. "You lied to me, Sheila." He scoffed. "I mean Shayla."

"What does it matter what my name is, Tom? You know who I am." I searched his eyes, but he gave nothing away. "Do you really think I'm a liar?"

"Bear in mind, I saw the tape from the James Beard Awards Dinner." I saw the slightest crinkle at the corner of his eyes. "You put on quite a show."

I took a step toward him. "I told the truth."

"Sure, you threw away your career telling the truth."

"I'd do it again." I raised my chin and looked him in the eye.

He crossed the floor until he stood in front of me. "What's the rest of the truth, Sheila?" It was warm in his room with the window closed. I could smell his musky sweat, overlaid with the grassy smell of his hair.

"The truth is, I'm an anxious mess."

"Go on," he said, inching closer to me.

"The truth is, I'm not cut out for the city. I'm moving to a goat farm."

"More," he said, advancing.

"I just want an easy life, even though that's supposed to be embarrassing for a 21st-century woman." I stepped so close to him that the tips of our shoes touched. "I want to be taken care of."

"And," he breathed, gripping my upper arms in his broad, flat hands.

"And," I was scared. I knew what I needed to say, but I couldn't bear being sent away again. I breathed in and jumped off the cliff. "And I love you."

"I know that," moving his hands down to my hips. "The whole feckin' world knows that you've gone and posted it on the bloody internet," he said, smiling in a wicked way. He looked up at the heavens, "What can I do with this girl? Everything she touches goes arseways. Go on then," he instructed. "Say even more."

I tilted my head back and looked up into his blinding-blue eyes, "I want you," I whispered.

He covered my bottom with the expanse of his hands and pulled me into him. "Mmm…" I moaned. Every memory of his skin rubbing against mine; the feel of him inside me sang in my body.

"A fool could see that from a hundred miles away," he whispered, voice husky, stubble brushing my ear. "Tell me more. What else?"

I could barely make enough noise to say it. "I want to marry you," I breathed. He spun me around and lay me on the bed. Immediately, he started clawing at his tie and unbuttoning his shirt, his hot mouth covering mine with deep slow kisses.

"You're mine now," he said in a low, growly voice, and stripped me naked. "And when we marry, it's my name you'll be taking. Shayla O'Grady."

"Yes to the O'Grady part. I want to be part of your clan. But I'm not who I was before. I'm Sheila now, and always will be. Will you have me as Sheila?"

"I'll have you alright, let me show you."

Over the next hour, slow and deliberate, and sweet, he showed me how much I belonged to him.

By the time we walked hand in hand across the lush green grass to the marquee, guests were halfway through the festive meal. A small band, consisting of a bouzouki, fiddle, banjo, tin whistle, accordion, and a hand-held drum played with a stick that I was later informed is called a bodhran played merrily off to the side. I noticed most musicians had a pint close at hand, despite the early hour. It clearly didn't do their playing a bit of harm. Father Walsh raised his eyebrows at our joined hands, swinging between our bodies as we rejoined the throng. At least I hope his reaction was to our hands and not the state of my bedhead.

"Where did the pair of you skive off to?" called Tony. "We've been having a whale of a time. We meant to put you to work serving the guests."

"Tony," I bantered back, "I know it's your wedding day, but should you be drinking, given your delicate heart?" I winked, and he burst into laughter.

"I thought the point of being married is that your wife minds your secrets," he replied. "I can see nothing's sacred among you women."

"Get yourselves a plate, you'll miss the buffet," said Maeve. She didn't have to tell me twice. I'd worked up a fierce appetite, and of course everything looked beautiful. It was, after all, a wedding at Castle Stone.

"You go ahead," Tom said, "I'll just have a word with my mother here."

I heaped my plate full of Irish bacon and sausages, coddled eggs, kippered fish and smoked salmon, and the prettiest strawberries I'd ever seen. Just as I was about to sit at a table with some of the older folks from town who belonged to the church, Maeve waved me to pull up a chair next to hers.

I watched Tom lean in to the band leader, and the music came to a close.

"Friends, I'd like to make a toast to the newlyweds. I'll be the first to admit that I'd scales on my eyes when I first became aware of their friendship. For the life of me, I couldn't imagine it working out. Had it not been for Sheila, it likely wouldn't have," he said, raising his glass in my direction. Now, two have become one and they'll enjoy the blessing of companionship and love for the rest of their days, which God willing, will be many. To Maeve and Tony."

The crowd erupted into cries of "hear, hear," and "to the blushing bride," and "may they have joy all their days," and glasses were refilled all around.

"Quiet, quiet please. I have another bit of news I planned to keep to myself, but my Mam insists I announce it now."

"I knew it! Maeve's expecting!" shouted an old codger from the back, who was decidedly in his cups.

"I'd hold your tongue, or her new husband might brain you."

Tony jumped to his feet and held up his fists in a mock-fighting stance. "Disparage my lady and you'll have to answer to St. Brigit of Kildare and James Joyce here."

"St. Brigit would never punch a man," Father Walsh exclaimed.

"I'd take my chances with them two," the old codger said standing up.

"Another toast! I'd like to make a toast to my fiancée, Shayla de Winter Sheridan Sheila Doyle soon to be O'Grady. Will you all join us back here in a week's time for our wedding?"

The crowd roared and everyone jumped to his or her feet, clapping and shouting. The band took off in rollicking, double-speed version of "Whiskey in the Jar". I could hardly breathe for being covered in kisses, and squeezes, and while I watched all of this happen around me, I felt my cheeks stretching into a smile I didn't know if my face could contain.

Someone pressed a glass of champagne into my hand. A week's time? What if Hank couldn't make it? I breathed in and out, knowing he either would or he wouldn't, and that if he didn't I would be OK with that. I'd love to have him at my celebration, but he could no longer let me down. I was a grown-up. I could rely on myself for happiness. *Plus*, I thought, as Maeve took my hand in hers and squeezed it, *I've found a family*. No one could ever replace Mom, but Maeve was a close second.

Tom pulled me onto the dance floor. Where would I get a dress in time? I took in the gorgeous wrinkled faces of the old folks and the fresh-scrubbed freckled and strawberries-and-cream complexions of the young, and realized that it didn't matter at all. The people of Ireland had seen thousands of brides over the centuries. Legends and poems talked of the brides' characters, not their dresses. It would all work out. And as for Maggie, she'd show up. There was no doubt in my mind.

As if on cue, the clouds above our heads parted and a blinding beam of sunlight illuminated the dance floor, firing up the tresses of the redheads bouncing around me, and warming my skin. I looked to the heavens and thought of my mother. For the first time since her death, I didn't feel emptiness and loss, I just felt joy. Had it not been for her love, I wouldn't be clapping and reeling with these good people, on this sacred land. I decided to believe that the part of her that lived in my heart had guided me to leave what I knew and find what I needed. Her strength was my strength. Twirling, I blew a kiss to the sky.

I jumped up and down with the group, filled with a wild abandon until my fiancé took me in his arms and kissed me. All motion stopped. I closed my eyes and breathed in his smell. He smelled of trod-upon grass, late-summer Discovery apples, and ancient, vital, metallic blood tinged with the fragrance of the sea. Joined together on the estate at Castle Stone, music and voices shouting in Irish brogue surrounding us, I already felt married. These were now my people. I was home.

Enjoyed *Summer at Castle Stone*? Then don't miss Lynn Marie Hulsman's hilarious debut *Christmas at Thornton Hall*.

Turn the page for an exclusive look at the first chapter.

Christmas at Thornton Hall

Chapter One

"Juliet, it's Phillipa from The Gastronome's Trust. Big stuff. I hope I'm not calling too early," she said, not sounding sorry at all.

I held the phone with one hand and stroked the still-warm, empty space next to me in the bed with my other, drinking in the sensation of being a grown-up.

I seriously cannot believe I'm me, I thought, suppressing a manic giggle. *I'm in my boyfriend's Mayfair apartment – which he owns! – answering a phone call from my agent who's about to offer me real money for my very much in demand culinary skills to put in my – wait for it! – savings account. A savings account which now has enough for me to go back to college and complete my sociology degree. Who would have thought it? Juliet Hill – back on track. Certified Grown-up. Even my mother would have to agree.* My mind was racing, even though my body hadn't quite caught up, yet.

I'm on the brink of a new beginning, I'm moving back to New York to complete the studies I'd dropped all those years ago. And I'm moving back with my successful boyfriend…successful and athletic, I thought, wincing as I stretched out my aching limbs. After recent work trips to the States, then New Zealand, Ben seemed determined to make up for lost time: he was like the cat that swallowed the canary. Absence had certainly made his body grow fonder, and his heart, too, I hoped. So maybe, if I'm honest with myself, my world hadn't been properly rocked last night… but then he'd practically just stepped off a plane, for heaven's sake, I couldn't expect nirvana. We'd have plenty of time this holiday season to get back on the same page in the old sex department.

Where is he, anyway? I peeled one eye open to check the clock on his night table. 6:55 a.m. My agent, Phillipa, certainly was getting the worm, as it were.

"Juliet," she said sharply. "Are you listening to me? I asked if I've awakened you."

"No, Pips, it's fine," I lied breezily, forcing myself to sound alert, "I've been up for ages." Phillipa Burton, owner of London's top agency dedicated to placing chefs in private households, expects everyone's full-on attention. I've always thought of her as one of those British school-mistressy types. She scares me a little, but I pretend she doesn't. I'm a favorite because I've always behaved like a soldier in her army.

"Darling," she said crisply, "I've just had a specific request come in for you to work over the Christmas holiday. I explained that you blacked those dates out with us, but the client insisted I ask, and here's the kicker…You'd need to be there tonight." She paused. "The housekeeper rang and said if I could send Juliet Hill, they'd pay a fee for the late notice, and a holiday bonus. The call came at six, and I'm sorry to say the offer's only good until eight o'clock this morning."

I let her talk, knowing I'd be turning the job down. I'd tell her about my plan to move back to New York with my soon-to-be fiancé and having to leave the business altogether once the holidays ended. No need to stir up emotions and spoil the joy right now. While she tried to sell me on the job, I let my mind wander to thoughts of caroling around the piano with Ben's cousins and uncles, mugs of warm mulled wine on the sofa, and smiling faces peeking over a crispy roast goose flanked by massive tureens of root vegetables. This Christmas was going to be special – a real family celebration. Impeccable Ben, in his well-cut suit, standing possessively with his arm around my shoulders, welcoming me into the fold, and for once in my life, I'd be wearing the right thing. Nothing too slutty, or cheap. And certainly no stains on my starched, white blouse. His family would murmur among themselves about what a perfect match I was for their Ben.

I was determined that all would go according to plan. When I'd phoned him last week to firm up this year's holiday plans, he'd been kind of quiet on the phone from his office in New Zealand – he's on location there for a film his firm is representing. I'd chalked his lukewarm mood up to exhaustion. Poor Ben, I'd thought. He's lost without a girl like me to loosen him up. After all, he is English. He can't help it if he's tightly wound.

He told me he had something important he wanted to talk about with me. Once he said that, I'd changed the subject, fast. I hadn't wanted him to spoil the big surprise, hoping he wouldn't discuss logistics until after the thrill of the engagement wore off. I couldn't help grinning and giving myself a little hug just thinking about it.

Anyway, back to the present. Focus on Phillipa. I would never act like a diva with my agent so I let her ramble. "Keep your head down, do excellent work and don't cause trouble," is a roadmap I try to stick to. Well, for the most part, if you don't mind turning a blind eye to the whole Paris debacle.

"Juliet!" Phillipa barked, snapping me out of my daydream again. "Did you catch that? I said eight a.m."

"Of course, sorry," I said, stifling a yawn. "Who requested me?" I asked, though I pretty much knew.

"So you're interested? Are you changing your mind?"

I wavered for half a second. Of all the food-forward, over-the-top, gourmet meals I'd created, I'd never once done a traditional Christmas feast at an English hall. My wheels started to spin, planning menus and visualizing the tabletop in full cinematic Technicolor. The chance to design a dinner that would simulta-neously hearken back to childhood roots so different from mine, while putting a surprising, modern spin on conventional favorites like sage and onion stuffing, roasted Brussels sprouts with chest-nuts, a flaming Christmas pudding, drew me in – quite against my will. My cells started tingling, just thinking about the chance to put my signature all over a meal that jaded guests thought they knew inside out and backwards. I bit my lip.

"I'm sorry, Pips," I said, honestly. "I want to, but I just can't." I was surprised to feel my eyes beginning to well.

"Well, if you change your mind, you know where to find me," she said crisply. "If I don't hear from you, I hope you have a happy Christmas and check in with me in January."

"I definitely, definitely will!" I said, pushing the "end" button on my iPhone with my left thumb. I looked at my naked ring finger. *And when I do call, you'll be stunned to hear that not only am I moving to New York, but I'm also engaged to be married.*

So, I'm a chef, but not a chef like you'd think. I'm a chef who makes my living cooking not in any restaurant where a regular person – or a rich, powerful or famous person, actually – could book a table, but behind the legendary "green baize doors" of some of the most posh private residences in the world. I've made it to an apex in my career. All the meals I cook now are invitation-only.

I eventually escaped upward from testosterone-fuelled kitchens in France, and the early days of the London restaurant scene, but not before honing my culinary skills, growing a T-bone-thick hide, and a tongue like a sushi knife. Nothing else has ever come as naturally to me, and I have to say, so far, it's given me a pretty good life. I've done more traveling than most people do in a lifetime, and I've stood in rooms with princes, war heroes and TV stars. And, indirectly, it led me to Ben. Handsome, funny, swaggering Ben in his well-cut suits.

In my wildest dreams I'd never thought I'd attract such a catch. He was the type of man who simultaneously made office interns swoon, while garnering nods of approval from mothers and gran-nies. Sexy, but respectable.

Rolling over onto Ben's pillow, I put my phone down on the night table, on top of his *Financial Times*.

"Ben? Good morning!" I called out, propping myself up on an elbow and craning my neck to look around the corner into the bathroom. "Are you making coffee?" I really had to pee. We must have had a bottle of wine each last night. I'd talked a little about how giving up The Gastronome's Trust – Phillipa's agency – made me sad, but he just told me again, firmly, that going back to The States and finally getting serious about my life was the sensible thing to do. Deep down, I knew I didn't have a leg to stand on in that department, after dropping out of college to chase a man to Paris – and look how that turned out.

So I let Ben have the last word, and wrap up the conversation. Anyway, he wasn't much in the mood for talking, if you follow me.

I got up off the bed, and pulled the sheet around myself, just to be safe, even though I was pretty sure now that he had already left the flat.

Where would he have gone at this hour? He didn't say anything about an early client. I walked to the bathroom using tiny geisha-like steps since the bottom of Ben's sheet was winding itself tighter and tighter around my ankles, practically hobbling me. Stupid, maybe, since Ben saw me naked on a semi-regular basis. Then again I've never been a flaunter or the parade-around-naked type, whereas my best friend Posy would happily drink tea and read the morning papers without a stitch on, all the while chattering about the weather. The combination of growing up with servants and living at girls' boarding schools had cured her of modesty.

Posy Wase-Bailey is my closest friend on earth and why I live in London now. You've no doubt seen her in the papers, attending this gala or that premiere. Owing to the fact that her dad is that charismatic airline owner – the one who took himself to outer space – she has spent her life in the limelight. It doesn't hurt a bit that she's a fearless trendsetter, often spotting the next "it" designer, and that she's always good for a controversial quote. We're like chalk and cheese in that way, but under the surface, where it matters, we're soul sisters separated at birth. I cannot imagine what my life would be like had she not spotted me crying into my coffee that day in Paris. I might have fled home to the States, or worse yet, begged Stephen for one more chance.

Anyway, back to the present! Memo to self, must not dwell on the past.

Normally, by this hour of the morning, I would have mainlined caffeine. Being an addict is a job hazard. In every kitchen where I've ever worked, there's been a top-shelf espresso machine and we staff pound coffees all day long. I had the briefest fantasy that Ben might bring me a cup, then sighed. I was the coffee bringer in this relationship.

I dropped my sheet and eased, undrugged, into the trickle of tepid water the English insist on calling a shower, beginning to suds my hair with the Jo Malone Lime, Basil and Mandarin shampoo sitting on the ledge, delighted to find that there was a matching bottle of conditioner. It smelled heavenly and his thoughtfulness warmed my heart. It more than made up for not bringing me a cappuccino. Normally, there was only a sad jug of Boots brand baby shampoo.

He never said so, but I could tell Ben wasn't wild about my keeping toiletries here. He's a neat freak, so I made it a point to carry out whatever I'd carried in, like my travel toothbrush and trial-sized toothpaste. I'd left my gold drop earrings on the sink once, and the next morning, after he left for work, I found them on the kitchen table in a creamy, business-sized envelope with my full mailing address on it. I smiled thinking about it. It's habits like uber-organization that got him a place as a solicitor at Thompson Loyal, his logical stepping-stone to his goal – being a real New York lawyer. What a mature quality. It would make my mother drool. Posy on the other hand once said she thought Ben was a bit OCD.

Did he leave for work? I thought to myself, rinsing the last of the conditioner out of my hair. Ben's usually like Pavlov's dogs when he hears shower water running, sprinting in and stripping along the way. He loved shower sex. Me, not so much. "Where's your sportsmanship?" he'd ask me, winking. "It's a challenge when I'm slippery." Usually, I was glad to give him what he wanted as, let's face it, most females of the species would kill to be with Ben. I could see it in super-hot girls' eyes when Ben and I were out for drinks or dinner. And I could practically hear them thinking, "He's a solid 9 and, she's, well…not."

Clean, I stepped out of the shower and grabbed a white Turkish towel off the towel warmer. English people are so weird about bathrooms. They aren't interested in ambient heat or water pressure, but they'd rather die than press a room-temperature towel to their bodies. I could forgive the quirks, though, since being converted to full-on Anglophile. I'd lived here long enough that England felt like home, and there was no denying that Ben being an Englishman was part of the turn-on.

It had been over a year since I'd met Ben at the London Aquarium benefit. I guess you could say we went from zero to sixty, fast. I think I called him my boyfriend the first day we woke up together. If I was honest, I'd have to admit it stung that he still hadn't introduced me to any of his family, except for one sister over a quick after-work drink.

Well, the tide was about to turn, and I had big plans to make it all turn out like in the movies. Maybe his mother would invite me to call her "Mum"? Could I say that without feeling like a poser? Or would it be "Mother Flannery"?

I was determined that this Christmas would be perfect, especially since the last one had been a major disappointment. He had invited me to his family's home, but at the eleventh hour, he'd called from the New York office. He made a thousand apologies and cancelled the whole holiday plan, explaining that he'd have to stay in the U.S. through New Year's, while I was stuck in London alone.

"I'm crushed, Darling," he had cooed transatlantically into the phone. "And so's my family. Dad especially. He said he wanted to get a good look at my girl to see if she fit in with the Flannery clan. Please try to understand."

I remember the squeezing feeling I'd gotten in my stomach. At the time, I'd sensed a whiff of Stephen. *Don't catastrophize, Juliet. Ben is not your old boyfriend.*

"You do wish you were here with me, don't you?"

"Don't be an idiot," Ben had replied impatiently. "Of course I want to be with you. It's just quite impossible at the moment. Be practical, Juliet."

It sounded like something my mother would say, and I was embarrassed. I was being selfish, wasn't I?

"Any man who wants to put a little money in the bank, maybe raise a family someday has to get ahead, right?" Ben asked. "It's torture to climb the ladder at Thompson Loyal, but those who can't stand the heat should get out of the kitchen. I am proving my worth. If my boss says jump, I have to ask how high? Being abroad at Christmastime is just one of the many small sacrifices I have to make while I'm junior."

I chose to ignore the fact that Ben had called me an idiot, and focus on how my heart sizzled at the word family. *Oh my god, does Ben want a baby? Wait! Do I want a baby? Would we have more than one? 28 isn't that young, after all and...*

"They call work *work* for a reason," he'd lectured on. "I have to be on location in the Big Apple because old Martin Loyal has us representing that film production studio in Soho – The New York Soho – and it's all hands on deck here. Contracts for directors and film stars, insurance riders for the special effects...you know, boring."

"I'm sorry you have to work," I had told him. At that point, I'd started feeling dumb. Who wouldn't rather be wined and dined and taken to bed than stuck in a boring law office discussing contracts and insurance? This was proof that he was good husband material.

Don't fight him on this one, Juliet. Support him, and soon, you'll

"Sorry, Ben. Of course you're right. Just making sure you don't have something cooking with The Statue of Liberty," I'd said, trying to laugh it off.

"You're the only absurdly tall woman who carries a torch that I'm giving it to," he'd flirted.

"What'll you do for the holiday? You won't be in some diner eating pressed turkey and instant mashed potatoes alone, will you?"

"Don't worry about me, one of my mates from the office here has claimed me. I'll be seen to…Look, I have to run. I miss you like mad and can't wait to get a handful of your…Yes, Bob? Right! I'm just hanging up! Bye, Jubes," he whispered, "Happy Christmas. I'll call when I can."

Today would be more about getting back to normal as a couple than about fantasy land, though. We had trip plans to solidify, details to discuss about scheduling. I was tired but running on twitchy excitement. *With Ben gone already, I could have slept late,* I thought, wrapping myself in his waffle robe ("It's a dressing gown, Jubes, I'm not a judge," Ben would have scolded me). I went into the kitchen, still harboring a tiny glimmer of hope that he might be sitting at the table going over briefs and sipping a cup of coffee.

No such luck. No Ben…and no coffee. My brain felt like lead. I didn't think I could make it to the *Pret* around the corner to buy one before getting dressed, so I grabbed a bag of ground espresso from the freezer. I twisted off the portafilter and saw that there was no filter basket inside. Urghh! I'd asked Ben a dozen times to tell his cleaner to leave the machine alone. First, she washed all the parts with soap, which ruined the taste of the lovely pure Kona coffee I kept here, and second, she never put it back together properly.

Irked and jonesing for my java, I held onto the kitchen counter with a tight grip, plotting out my next move. Go out for coffee, or look for the missing piece. *Just be methodical,* I told myself. *It can't have disappeared. Just look one place at a time, and you'll find it.*

I'll admit to feeling a bit smug as I worked from top left to bottom right, searching the cabinets. I was thinking how adult it was of me not to flip out just because I'd been awake for this long with no coffee. And wasn't I grown-up for not wishing that Ben's cleaner would be deported before her regular Wednesday shift so she could never touch this espresso machine, ever, as long as she was alive?

As I rifled through each cabinet and cupboard, I grew more and more frantic. Agitated, I moved on to the drawers. Rubber bands, twine, and scissors in this one. Potholders, tea towels, and sponges in that one. Soon I was ripping through the deep drawers all the way over by the table, where, realistically, no coffee filter would ever dwell. Still, I was on a mission.

A tiny, distant voice tried to tell me that I'd crossed a line. I had the vague sense that if Ben walked in, he wouldn't be amused at my ransacking his flat. But that didn't stop me. Another drawer. Place mats, table cloths, and candlesticks, but no filter. A cabinet. Photo albums, maps, and board games, but still no filter. Deep in my rational mind, I knew that the filter wouldn't be around the corner in the lounge, but my rational mind was deeply asleep and my coffee-addicted animal sense was propelling my body.

I flung open the double doors of the cabinet below the television set, and pulled out a stack of file boxes. That's when I saw the corner of the padded envelope sticking out of *The Economist,* on top of a pile of folders. My body beat my brain to the panic. Blood roared through my ears as I eased out the envelope and held it in my hand.

Amanda Selmont
39 East 79th Street
New York City, NY 10075

Amanda, the 5' 2", ice-blonde from Manhattan? The one who called the cocktail dress I'd worn to the company party "appropriate"?

I watched my hands tear it open like I was watching a movie of someone else's hands. I slid out a thick, creamy slice of stationery and watched a tasteful pair of platinum hoops fall to the floor. Amanda's earrings.

Is that who had *seen to him* last Christmas?

I flashed back to the cream-colored envelope that had once held the earrings I'd left overnight. The envelope that had my full mailing address on it. The one I'd been naïve enough to be charmed by. Ben wasn't a neat freak! He was a son-of-a-bitch liar who walked around behind me cleaning up any proof that I'd set foot in his bachelor pad.

Tucked inside the large envelope I now held was a thinner, smaller envelope. I pressed it between my fingers and thumb. Whatever was inside crackled against the paper. My heart was clawing at my ribcage, skittering and wild. I knew I didn't want to see what was in there, but my eyes couldn't convince my hands to stop tearing paper. To my horror, I reached in and pulled out the world's scratchiest lace thong, dotted with rhinestone studs. I held it up to find that one side of it was ripped, threads dangling.

That goddamn son of a—He'd lied about his flight! To my face! He'd gotten back a day early and holed up in his love cave with Amanda. Right here in London. Had that bitch been in his bed – the bed that I'd just crawled out of – the night before I was? Did he leave early this morning to meet her for a quickie before work?

Oh my God, did I just use her shampoo?

I had to get out of there…I was wearing nothing but silk underwear and a trench coat when I'd shown up last night (on Posy's advice), so I tore into Ben's bedroom and grabbed a pair of his gym pants, rolling them up at the waist, and his black Ralph Lauren cashmere turtleneck. I stepped into my high heels as I was running, leaving the door to the flat wide open in my wake. Dramatic maybe, but after what I'd been through with Stephen, there was no way I was going to be made a fool of again.

Out on the street, I pulled my coat tightly around myself and marched towards the tube station. The wind was bitterly cold, but the air was dry and its sting felt harsh on my face, like a slap. I welcomed it. It cut through my numbness.

I was a girl without a plan. Suddenly single, obviously there would be no wedding in my future. Without Ben to encourage and support me, would I be able to finish my studies and become a therapist? A small voice inside asked if I'd even want to. I felt as though I were filled with helium, hovering.

It was only 7:45 a.m. and the street was busy with commuters. Eyes brimming, I stopped dead in the middle of the sidewalk, where many a worker bee slammed into me or swore at me under his breath.

As far as I could see, I only had one option. I dug in my bag for my phone and stabbed in the number for The Gastronome's Trust.

"Pips, Juliet Hill here. I'll take that job. Where do I need to be and when?" Although I didn't really need to ask. There was only one client who I knew would play a card like a two-hour deadline – Jasper Roth.

"Oh, my dear, that *is* good news," she trilled. "Fab, just fab. You report late tonight, I'll text you the details. You'll be working at Thornton Hall."

Acknowledgments

I send out deep thanks to my editor Charlotte Ledger. She's as kind as she is shrewd. She teased out the best of what I had to offer, and polished it further from there. I'm very lucky to be in her care.

Thank you to Alexandra Allden for my beautiful cover. You're a real artist.

A well-deserved shout-out to the whole HarperImpulse team, including our leader Kimberley Young. You're all working at full tilt to make the imprint (and me!) a success. Katie Sadler and Richard Parfitt, you are appreciated.

To Carmel Harrington, I send out thanks as a friend and a writing colleague. I found a sister from another mister in you.

I wouldn't have had the courage to face the blank pages without the support and encouragement of my girlfriends. Heartfelt thanks to Kate Bushmann, Molly Sackler, Meirav Duffey, Anne Hulsman, Claude Louissaint, Laura Feldman, Zahava Tzur, and Marina Kubicek. And special thanks to my friend Dan Diggles.

The wonderful reviews, and support I get from my readers on

Facebook and Twitter has been invaluable. It means more than you know.

Best wishes and many thanks to all of my Irish friends and first readers, especially the wonderful people of Wexford including Maria Nolan, Margaret Bonass Madden, the members of the Esquires Book Club, and Roger Harrington. I appreciate being included.

Finally, thanks to my husband, Sam, and our kids for keeping the household going while I was off writing at The Center for Fiction, in Bryant Park, and between the Lions at the Main Library. You were brave soldiers when I gallivanted around Ireland doing research. You kept the household running, and cheered me on.

www.ingramcontent.com/pod-product-compliance
Lightning Source LLC
Chambersburg PA
CBHW010631100726
47900CB00011B/2781